TO DESIRE THE STARS

This multi-cultural sci-fi romance contains reference to
abusive relationships and non-consensual sexual situations.
The story is gender and non-binary inclusive.

TO DESIRE THE STARS

VENUS CAMPBELL

Book of Venus

To Ms. Taylor, the goddess of sci-fi romance. No other has captured the mixture of science fiction and romance like you. Thank you for combining the two genres perfectly! To Rowan for dealing with mom's obsession; to Michael for reading my obsession; lovingly to the Mudpuddle who tore every word apart, and to Sheryl, Theresa and Lori for seeing that my idea could become an epic love story.

And to Josh who convinced me Jarren
could exist. Thank you, my love.

CONTENTS

PROLOGUE

DARKNESS MEANT SAFETY, and there was little dark left. Hours became minutes, as Lynta's two moons inched down behind the Black Mountains. Within the Peddler's Forest, the sounds of night creatures lessened amid the cold silence of a lingering winter.

High Prince Jarren Graf stepped out through the airlock of his sub-light space jumper. His black military-issue pilot's boots fell heavy on the moist ground. Queen Celina stood at the clearing's edge, her dark-robed frame braced to bid him goodbye. Her mourning robes flipped crisply about her.

Jarren halted before her and grimaced. His previous life had evaporated in the wind. Chest tight, he noted fresh tears streaked his mother's face.

"I will return as soon as the Alliance has stabilized," Jarren said. His words echoed heavily. His mother nodded but didn't speak. Jarren's jaw tightened, but he resisted the urge to grip her hands. She did not need his pity.

Having Jarren flee their home planet wasn't the preferred next step. But when his father died without a presumption of rulership, Jarren's cousin, Milovar, had deposed him as king presumptive. All within the week. If Jarren remained, his assassination was all but ensured. The system of rulership by scent was millennia old. The system repelled Jarren even as he benefited from it…until now. And his mother had weighed every known variable; they'd agreed. Fleeing so he could regroup his off-world allies was the best option to manage the upheaval. Still, it grated on his morality to run. To delay the elimination of a caste system that kept so many subjugated was simply unacceptable even if it was necessary.

The pungent scent of hunters wafted close. Too close for comfort. Jarren reached out and pulled his mother's tired body close. He rested his chin on her head. The wind whipped her dark hair, long and gray streaked but otherwise like his own. His eyes caught the tinge of morning, on the horizon. Time was up.

Stepping back, Jarren closed his eyes to focus. He breathed deep, patterning his mother's scent, memorizing her new smell in his heightened Lyntan olfactory lobe. Her mixture of aromas would be his beacon home. The slowly dissipating essence of his dead father, the hint of heated chulaa cream, and the subtle-sweet presence of his mother's favorite flower, the red decypheny, imprinted on his memory. And more subtle; an "Of the Family" scent without high birth. The almost unique scent of one not high born but whose scent set them above others. A determined grin danced briefly across his face, and Jarren squeezed Celina's shoulders.

"I will follow your scent when I return. I'll find you no matter how Milovar tries to cover your presence. Remember, you are not a threat to his ascendancy. He certainly won't waste any energy on punishing you for my disappearance. Just…keep out of his way," Jarren said.

Pursing her lips and lifting her chin, his mother nodded. "There is much to do. Be safe. Stay under the radar, for Galactic's sake. I scent the bounty hunters Milovar commissioned to find you even now."

Jarren nodded. They both had caught the scent. He released her.

Celina looked away as a tear slid down her cheek and escaped into the dark. Jarren studied her face as determination thinned her lips. She reached within her heavy robes and pulled out a brown envelope. "Your papers: birth certificate, driver's license, social security card, and documentation of your schooling. All humans directly connected with your documents are inaccessible."

"I almost forgot." Jarren frowned, grasping the packet. "It's all I am now with my essence so diminished." He turned toward his ship. "Trust Princess Veena will do what is necessary. She knows Milovar's reign would mean the end of peace in our quadrant. She'll find Council Advisors who don't want war any more than you or I."

"Veena will organize the Inter-planetary Council Advisors who support you. And the people of Lynta *will* support your right to the throne against Milovar's claim. But the Guard won't fight for you until you reclaim the scepter. We can't end this system without that power." Celina's gaze penetrated him. "You must find a way to ensure our future."

"As you say, Mother. A way will be found. I just need time. Exile on Terra gives me that. My essence will be lost among the variant trees and animals, muted among Terra's people. No bounty hunter could trace me. I'll be a ghost to Milovar."

Celina frowned. "But—"

Jarren stopped her entreaty with a shake of his head. He tucked his packet under one arm and stepped back through the prime airlock and into his ship. If he wasn't gone in the next few minutes before the sun began rising, the Guard scouts would register his craft launching. Their high-powered spacers would take chase immediately, and no doubt they had been ordered to destroy his jumper.

"Jarren," his mother interrupted.

Without looking back, he paused.

"Be careful who you share scent with. Terrans are… innocent. Should Terra's smells not cover your presence completely, those around you will pay with their lives. Especially any humans. You know what Milovar would do if he thought…" Her voice faded.

Jarren nodded. He risked more than his life alone. Hers was necessary advice to heed. He wouldn't put another person in danger if he could help it.

His mother stepped away, her footfalls loud in the dangerous still of early morning.

He gazed out a last time, his eyes scanning the dense cobalt trees that circled the clearing. Celina was gone. With his fingers tapping the airlock keypad, Jarren stood, stalwart, as the door slid shut and the cabin pressurized. Just him now. Alone. Jarren exited the metal decon room and secondary airlock and trotted through to the small front cabin. His eyes glazed over the jumper's empty passenger seats and the blank vid screen right of the pilot deck. Walking forward to the cockpit door, he turned the knob and entered. At least the cockpit didn't feel vacuous.

Jarren curved his frame into the captain's chair and flipped three switches on the Pilot Panel Array. The familiar whisper of his craft's engine whirred around him. He swiveled to his right and grasped the metal navigation stick. Soon he'd be safely beyond the lightening horizon. He was overdue meeting Marcus at the rendezvous point.

The ship lifted with a twist of his wrist. Jarren looked down through his vidscreen at the retreating ground. Jaw tight, he peered ahead as Lynta's celadon sun rose ominously. *Creeds, no time.* Jarren tapped the green power button at the stick's tip. Up he shot, with quick efficiency, leagues above the coal tops of the distant mountains. He eased the stick forward. Moments remained to get out of the atmosphere.

A sudden warning tingle in his spine forced Jarren straight. The ship's com unit crackled; he perused his front viewer. The three burnished Elite Guard ships flanking him pushed a curse past his lips. He'd waited too long to leave. *Have to run.* Jarren tilted the stick and veered his ship away.

"Your Highness Prince Jarren, stand down," barked a male voice over his com unit. Jarren barely glanced at the gray box.

"Not yet ready to die," Jarren grumbled as he thought through the variables. Minor adjustments to his route. Just minor adjustments to be made. He hit the power button again and pulled the stick back. The ship plummeted into the receding shadow of the mountains behind him. Within the safety of the dark, he slowed to a hover then shot the space jumper forward with an experienced twist. Blue and brown treetops blurred by at the bottom of his screen. The maneuver was an old trick for shaking pursuing ships. Effective, unless they were seasoned pilots.

"Commander!" the voice barked through the com. "Ground your ship. Take no more evasive actions, or we shall be forced to shoot you down."

Jarren scanned the screen with singular efficiency. He couldn't get a front visual of his pursuers.

"Unit, split visual of front and rear, ascent and descent areas," Jarren bit out as he loosened his grip, and the ship hovered again. His head throbbed.

"Affirmative, Captain," his ship's unit replied. The front screen visual turned gray while Unit uploaded the zones around the ship.

Jarren's eyes darted over the screen. His hand grew slick on the stick, but he dared not pause to wipe the sweat from his palms. Likely only one route could get him out. He accelerated again. Finally he spied the Guard ships aft. They hovered at points A, B, and M.

Acceleration at four hundred regs. Gravitation minus two. Jarren's brow crinkled in concentration. *Variable, the variables.* He almost had the route calculated.

The Guard crafts' golden bellies glittered green in the dawning sunlight as his ship pulled ahead. Jarren wasn't sure if they'd lost visuals on him as he sped off into the disappearing shadows. He might have just been outdistancing them. But he wouldn't stop.

Again the com blared at him. "Last warning, Commander. Stand down, or we will be forced to fire!"

Equations banged within his head until only one remained, and then he had it—his new route. His heart hammered against his chest. Sweat moistened his face. Now or never.

"You need a target first, you Creeds." Jarren laughed. The odds of his success were favorable. Twisting, he reached over and hit three blinking green buttons. The beige side paneling beneath the lights lowered. His red slipdrive switch waited a hand's reach away.

"Unit, prepare for Light Slip." He didn't wait for the ship's computer to confirm. Jarren flipped the switch.

"Go."

CHAPTER 1

THE CRASHING DEMITASSES shouldn't have startled her. In a coffee shop packed with people, Melissa Reyes should not have blinked at the sound. Instead, she cringed instinctively. Breaking ceramic was out of routine, and routine was her bread and butter. Sure. That story always worked. Old memories were definitely not the reason she wanted to jump out of her own skin.

"Can I get a java to go, Sammy?" Lissa called out with a shaky wave as she navigated the maze of people. Her nose registered the rich, freshly brewed coffee, and she breathed in the calming aroma. Nothing bad here. Get back on routine.

She stopped mid-stride as a surge of bodies blocked her path.

Sammy nodded. "Sure thing, overachiever." They flipped their lazy brown hair off their forehead and turned to put in her regular order.

Lissa silently counted, tapping her tan pumps on the lacquer floor. Calm loosened her chest. She spied her order coming up as the "routine" took over.

She felt bad for Sammy. The overworked college student was twenty and selling four-dollar cups of coffee to help pay for college. Their efforts wouldn't make a dent. Lissa had worked in a little coffee shop in Kansas nine years ago for the same reason.

Ninety-seven, ninety-eight, ninety-nine, one hundred. Lissa nudged her way to the counter and threw down four crinkled singles then snagged her cup just as another customer nearly knocked it over. There wasn't any more crowded a place than Max's Coffee Shop in springtime in Baltimore. Her morning rote was firmly back in place.

Lissa saluted Sammy then navigated to the exit, her heels clicking solidly amid the muffled stomp of business loafers. She pushed the glass door open with one hand and her long beige coat flipped back as air rushed in through the entryway. Cup in hand, the breeze settling, she planted a foot in the doorframe.

"See you tomorrow, Lissa," Sam called at her back. Smiling distractedly, she waved without turning as she skirted out of someone's way.

A dark suit and tie brushed past her going in. Tall. The suit was tall. Professionally tailored, expensive material towered in front of her like the Romanesque pillars holding up one of those derelict plantation compounds near her grandmama's house in South Carolina—powerful, unyielding. Maybe that was why her cup slipped; she got pulled out of routine again. And for the first time in five years of ducking and dodging in and out of Max's, she didn't make the save.

The cup jostled out of her hand and toward the beautifully cut blue material. The world slowed, then paused, stretching out that moment.

"Spit and hellfire." Lissa's words slipped out as the cup fell. The cheap paper container crashed to the floor, splattering the last of its creamy insides onto a stiff pair of $1,500 A. Testoni shoes.

"Shit," she hissed. Silence blanketed the coffee shop.

Without looking at the suit, Lissa ran over to the condiment counter and grabbed gobs of napkins from the built-in dispenser. The door groaned softly closed. Cheeks burning, she looked anywhere but at her victim. No need to be slammed with an accusing stare.

"I am so sorry," she began as she knelt down and wiped at the stiff brown tips. Heart sinking, she saw the leather darken. It was no good.

Lissa struggled to her feet, gingerly dabbing at the coffee drops she spied sinking into his suit jacket. "I'll pay for that, I promise," she said hesitantly as she raised her gaze and forgot to inhale. And it was probably for the best that her mouth ceased functioning.

The man was…beautiful. He stood tall, with dark thick hair that curled right where his crisply pressed—she spotted the Armani cut now—shirt met his tanned neckline. She just knew powerful muscles rippled beneath that cloth. *Breathe!* With a lungful of fresh sweetness, her fantasies took off.

So he was tall and dark, but handsome wasn't the right word for him. Ruggedly dangerous was a better way of putting it: stubborn chin, sensuous lips, high cheekbones. Chris Hemsworth had nothing on this guy. And Melissa Reyes, executive assistant and powerhouse problem solver, had dumped her four-dollar cup of creamed-down coffee all over him. If there was an impression to be made, she surely must have made it.

Her hand slowed to a still at the lapel of his jacket. Exactly how would she afford to replace his fifteen-hundred-dollar shoes? She could barely pay her rent. Lissa tried to speak. She only exhaled.

Finally, Tall Dark looked into her eyes. His oddly hazel orbs, half shielded by thick black lashes, seemed to see into her soul. Lissa shivered.

"Don't worry about it." The soft words caressed her like a lover's kiss. Lissa shivered again.

"But—"

He leaned toward her as the scent of hot chocolate teased her nose. "Don't worry about it," he repeated.

Lissa might have been frozen. She could not have been more still if she had been stone. Tall Dark drew the soiled napkin from her hand and walked toward the counter. His gaze released her. Her body awakened and, dumbstruck, turned, pushed through the shop's door, and tramped out into the morning air. Her brain slowly revved up to its normal speed.

What time was it exactly? Melissa squinted up at the sun then glanced down at her classic Timex. 9:45 a.m. She would be late for the staff meeting, or she'd be unprepared.

Distractedly brushing at the splatters of coffee on her own brown skirt suit, Lissa shuffled. *Get it together, chica!* She breezed through the glass entrance into the office building where the Earth Microfinance Institute was housed. At the elevators, she stepped through the nearest set of closing mirror doors and pushed ten.

What. An. Idiot. What a ridiculous response to a man, she thought as she pictured, with relief, her small, immaculate, no-window cubicle with a "door." With luck, Mr. Bigsby's four-window office, adjoining hers, might still be dark.

At least she'd be in comfortable surroundings. Good or bad, work was like a second home, and she appreciated that routine. The heat of her embarrassment would cool as she checked her e-mail and shuffled papers. Besides, she still couldn't seem to formulate words yet. And her numb tongue obviously originated from embarrassing herself in her favorite morning hangout spot and not from brushing up against Mr. Tall Dark. It had to be the former, because she'd barely gotten a good look at the man.

Getting off the elevator, Lissa waved a distracted hello to Jean at the front desk. The older woman winked and saucily patted the neat auburn bun at the back of her head. Lissa hurried by. She couldn't field questions at the moment, and Jean read people as easily as she read a tabloid's feed. She'd know something was up.

Lissa made her way out of the bright reception area and down the two short halls to her office. Mr. Bigsby's office was still dark. Immersing herself in her morning ritual, Lissa exhaled. She removed her coat, hung it on the coat rack next to her door, flicked the light switch, and pulled out her chair.

The earlier coffee incident and her potent awareness of Tall Dark were pushed to the back of her mind. A perfectly stacked pile of papers in her wire in-box and the red message light on her phone hailed her attention. She exhaled. Stupid crashing coffee cups. And no coffee to show for all that drama either. Her gaze only lingered a moment on the hand that Tall Dark had touched. Time to work.

*   *   *   *   *

TEN MINUTES LATER, Lissa took off her reading glasses, let out a deep breath, and grabbed a pad and pen. She hadn't gotten nearly enough work completed before the staff meeting, but she'd wing it. Arriving late was not an option. Mr. Bigsby always began staff meetings on time.

Lissa made her way back to the reception area. Feeling more collected, she stopped to chat with Jean and laughed as the woman immediately began dispensing the latest office gossip. "Staff meeting, Jean," Lissa said, fixing her expression into an irritated scowl as she leaned away from the reception desk.

Mr. Bigsby ran a "tight ship," as he called the office. It was probably the mathematician in him. All things in neat order. Lissa epitomized orderliness. That was why she complemented him well.

Jean wiggled her eyebrows. "Yep. I can see that, honey. You need a map, too, or can you find the conference room on your own?"

Lissa shrugged and rolled her eyes. "Rude vixen. Do your job." She slapped her writing pad on Jean's desk with a wink.

Pivoting, she walked into the adjacent conference room and pulled out her regular seat near the front of the long conference table. Ten o'clock, staff meeting time. Lissa expectantly eyed the conference room doorway. Others entered and took seats around the table. It was five minutes before everyone was settled and another five minutes before Mr. Bigsby appeared with someone in tow. The meeting was starting late.

*   *   *   *   *

"MY ASSISTANT, MELISSA, is the one who keeps the office afloat. Everyone defers to her on administrative issues when I'm absent. And half of everyone defers to her when I'm here. They just won't admit it," Jim Bigsby rumbled low as he led Jarren into the conference room. "I defer to her as well. She'll get you set up and feeling right at home in no time."

Jarren observed Melissa with a troubled gaze. He'd been intoxicated by her scent from the moment she glided near him in the coffee store. His skin tingled as he continued to breathe in her fragrance. Her closeness made his body warm with anticipation. Of all that was holy, he could easily lose himself in her sweet earthy smell. He'd never been enveloped in its like before; a complex mixture of Egyptian musk and the tropical papaya, she smelled like the rarest of beautiful Lyntan flowers.

Jarren took another moment to breathe in her essence. His gaze strayed over her. Melissa sat relaxed and attentive in a swiveling black chair. Her long ebony hair cascaded down her back, flicking flirtatiously as she shifted in her seat. Her smooth skin radiated tanned warmth from days of play beneath a forgiving sun. Her full lips pouted with innocent sensuality. He couldn't see her eyes from where he stood, but Jarren remembered their sky-blue intensity. She had looked up at him, abashed, gently patting his chest with those ridiculously brittle napkins. Her eyes had flickered with self-assured intelligence and a well-hidden sense of humor. He was sure she had broken more than a few hearts with no more than a glance.

Creeds, but Jarren wanted to reach out and touch those silky-smooth tresses, bury himself in her scent, gently suckle her rouge lips. He could almost feel her hair's alluring softness as he imagined drawing the fanning locks close to his face and breathing in her scent. He wanted her. He wanted to combine his essence with hers and claim her. Need tightened his expression as he fought to control his Lyntan mating instincts.

The power of his desire was noteworthy. No possible mate's scent had ever affected him with such strength, but claiming a mate in his current situation was a troubling thought. He couldn't understand her scent's potency, but he knew one thing. His attraction to her might present a problem. The Lyntan urge to mate could distract him when he should be concentrating on claiming his rulership and finally eliminating the Lyntan caste system. Distractions would threaten the security of his world and the lives of those who supported his return to power. He would have to be extremely wary around Melissa Reyes, for both their sakes.

"Let me introduce you," Jim said as they advanced into the conference room. A tall portly man, he didn't seem wasteful with thoughts or words. Jarren respected the man's efficiency. This morning, Jarren was similarly inclined.

Jim took the chair at one end of the table, next to where Melissa sat conspicuously staring down at the notepad she held. Twenty people, aside from her, sat before him. Leaning toward Melissa, he spoke quietly. Immediately, she straightened and leaned in. Jarren didn't like it. His eyes narrowed. Exactly how involved was their relationship? Not that he had a right to ask. But not knowing irked him.

Finally she looked up, her cheeks red but her gaze resolute. Jarren's skin tingled again. She had strong character. She believed he would be angry about the coffee incident earlier, but even concerned, she refused to cower. Jarren didn't care about his shoes. Earth currencies were easily duplicated; he could easily buy another pair or have his ship's fabricator make another set. But Terrans were materialistic.

Jarren should have fumed at Melissa's klutziness. He hadn't, of course. But Melissa didn't know he placed more value on people than possessions. The perks of an advanced civilization, even one such as his. Given Terran material priorities, Jarren was more than impressed that she met his gaze with such solid determination.

"Have a seat, Jarren," Jim said as he gestured to the empty chair at his left. Jarren sat where bid, the chair briefly bending to support his lithe figure. He met Melissa's gaze and nodded. Jim swiveled to face her.

"Lissa, this is Dr. Jarren Graf. He has graciously accepted the director of microfinance options position we've been trying to fill for so long. He and I will be shut up in my office for about an hour after the staff meeting. It's not on my calendar, but reschedule around that time, okay?"

Melissa nodded. Egyptian musk caressed Jarren's nose. Jarren's body responded; his briefs grew snug. That would not do. He nodded in Melissa's direction once more, then angled away from her scent. "Ms. Reyes."

For a moment, she paused before responding and seemed thoughtful. "It's nice to meet you, Dr. Graf. Welcome." Her eyes flickered first to his newly changed suit, then toward the floor. She was thinking about the shoes.

Almost as if he'd read their parallel thoughts, Jim apologized. "We are late starting here. Dr. Graf had an unfortunate incident down at Max's this morning. You'll be getting a receipt from Burberry for a new suit."

Melissa's face reddened, but she nodded. Tight-lipped, she grasped the smooth side of the table. Her knuckles blanched as she pulled her chair under. And Jarren could do nothing in their current setting to ease her embarrassment.

Jim was oblivious to his assistant's discomfort. Promptly ignoring them both, he sat forward to address the rest of the staff.

"Good morning, everyone. I apologize for being late. Let's hear the weekly project reports, and then I'll introduce our new staff member."

Out of the corner of his eye, Jarren noticed Melissa's glance dart under the table, probably to check again on his ruined shoes. Her hair tumbled forward, temporarily hiding her face. Jarren inhaled, then let out a strained breath. Her smell haunted his thoughts. This had to stop. Think of someone else—the Terran in the coffee store who resembled his crewmate, Faheel. Or the muscular security guards at the building entrance. Anyone but her. Resolutely, he shifted his attention away from the stimulating intrigue that was Melissa Reyes.

CHAPTER *2*

PEERING THROUGH HER office doorway, Lissa bit her lip. Jim had been sequestered with the object of Lissa's anxiety for the better part of an hour. She should have interrupted Jim's discussion with Jarren—Dr. Graf—five minutes ago. That was her job. Apprehension made her hesitant. Instead, she stood in her doorway staring at the mahogany wood that separated her ears from the conversation Dr. Graf was having with her boss.

The spill was an accident. Surely he wouldn't make a huff about it—at least not now. It wouldn't surprise her if he did, though. She remembered the horrendous ink splatter incident with the visiting dignitary at her last job. Pivoting and going back to her desk, she plopped down into her chair and interlocked her fingers, distracted. Lissa planted her elbows on her armrests. Her eyes slid to the long thin Burberry Men's Clothier credit card receipt.

She'd tried not to look confused when Jim handed her the Visa receipt for Dr. Graf's new suit. She'd been sure that he had revealed her blunder in a less-than-complimentary way. She knew Dr. Graf recognized her. But Jim simply said, "List it under office expenses, Lissa," then promptly led Dr. Graf into Jim's office and closed the door. He'd made no mention of her personal responsibility for the incident. Nor had he cracked any succinct jokes about it. It bothered her that she wasn't sure what information Dr. Graf had divulged.

Not good. She could feel the crinkle of anxiety on her forehead; that same look had gripped her mother's face right before Lissa's father left and again when her cousin, Miguel, moved from Baltimore to restart his life.

Twisting her chair toward her door, Lissa steeled herself and got up. Jim needed to be on the elevator in two minutes. She walked the two steps up to Jim's door and raised her hand to knock. It took her one surprised moment to realize the door had swung open without her polite rap. Golden eyes peered down at her. Lissa caught her breath and resisted the urge to swallow.

Right. Melissa Luisa Reyes practically ran this office. She would not—after working five years for Jim Bigsby—cower from one incident. That train of thought made no sense. Such anxiousness at work was totally unlike her. Lissa looked around Jarren's tall figure, spying Jim sitting at his desk. "Jim, you need to be out of here now to make your 12:45 appointment. Also, don't forget your London trip itinerary. I put your tickets on your desk. You'll only have time to go home and pack before your evening flight."

Jim glanced up from his computer screen and nodded. "Yes. Cutting it close today. I'm walking out now, Lissa. Thanks." He swiveled, presenting her with the back of his chair. Lissa nodded. He would be up and moving in a moment.

Jarren Graf's powerful torso blocked her view as he shifted. His dominating physique, not to mention the waft of smooth sweetness that floated her way, diverted her attention. Funny how he attracted yet irritated her at the same time. Looking up, she nodded once out of politeness. He was still unbelievably attractive. She narrowed her eyes. He was also an enigma—a virile male enigma, but an enigma nevertheless. Lissa turned away, retrieved the printout of Jim's daily calendar from its usual spot on her desk, and headed toward the elevators. Jim's footsteps sounded right behind her. Jarren must have matched Jim's pace. She couldn't hear him, but she knew he was there.

She turned a corner, pushed the button for the elevator, and held out Jim's calendar. "Sir," she said as the elevator doors opened. Jim nodded and stepped through.

"Lissa, put Jarren in Peter Right's old office, and prep his computer. I need him ready to work by midday."

"Yes, sir."

The elevator doors tapped shut. Lissa looked up at Jarren. Now what would she do? Setting Jarren up in an office and getting his computer login keyed to him would take at least an hour. Was she stuck with him for that entire time? She barely lasted the length of the staff meeting without constantly glancing down at his shoes. Her face wasn't burning anymore, but her nerves teetered. He unbalanced her, and she didn't know why. Was it just bad luck that she was now lassoed to the most alluring man she'd ever met yet? She seemed compelled to act irrationally around him.

"Dr. Graf, if you will follow me," Lissa mumbled as she walked out of the reception area. Hopefully Jean was too preoccupied to pay them any mind. She waved a hand for him to trail her as she glided down another hall. Internally, she scowled. Her discomfort had humbled her. What had happened to the woman who ran the office with her eyes closed? She needed to regain some self-control. She'd be off-balance until she did.

Jarren moved silently behind her. The long hall seemed to stretch the space between them, but Lissa wouldn't look back. She didn't have to. She knew he watched her—she stopped before Peter Right's old door—but what was he thinking? That she was an untrustworthy person who wouldn't accept responsibility for destroying another person's property? Did he think she should be offering blustering "thanks" for his silence about the coffee incident? Her father, Ulises, used to say every mistake would be like three strikes against her. Perfection was her only protection. This morning hadn't been close to perfect. Lissa snorted. Maybe he was plotting some sort of blackmailing scheme. More likely he barely knew she existed. He certainly hadn't known who she was at Max's.

Jarren watched Ms. Reyes' skirt sway as her hair swept down her back. Beautiful. He could tell she was wary of him. Her mannerisms were so formal. She entered a dark office and flipped on the light before turning and pausing. She seemed…uncertain. Apparently, it was up to him to defuse the situation. Jarren thought back to his lessons on United States office protocol. Traditional. It was too bad he couldn't touch her as he would have an anxious courtier on Lynta. Touching was prohibited here. Touch was too closely associated with sex. Lyntans made that same association with smell.

Absently, Jarren rubbed his thumb across the skin covering the small Subduer next to his right carpal tunnel. The mechanism slowed Jarren's hormonal scent production and release. A dangerous thought entered his mind. His scent might calm her as it did his people. He quashed the idea as soon as it materialized. Releasing his scent would be thumbing his nose at fate.

Okay. Touch was not possible, and smell was plain stupid. Jarren cleared his throat and spoke.

"Ms. Reyes. I appreciate you setting me up." Jarren forced his voice to vibrate smooth neutrality. She nodded and walked around an oak desk where a computer screen and telephone had collected a layer of dust. She leaned over and pulled out power cords, shifting the mouse and keyboard on the desk.

Jarren paused beside a guest chair. He could sense her percolating anxiety. The no-touching protocol was really a problem. He could have diminished the tension in her spine immediately. Jarren sighed inwardly. Terran social restrictions truly presented challenges.

She turned to him, her expression doubtful. Jarren waited. Why hadn't she spoken yet? Certainly his behavior fell in line with the normal office power dynamic. He had maintained a balanced tone and respectful manner toward her. Jarren took a step forward. She took a step back. Her pouty lips parted as if she were about to speak. But she stopped, shook her head, and pulled out the task chair, pausing a moment.

That scent, her scent, pervaded the air around him again, and he clenched his hands at his side. Distant or not, her body called to his on the most basic level. He was Lyntan. Smell was the most powerful of their senses, overruling evolution in some circumstances, making them primitive, animalistic to some degree; he could barely think around her.

He wanted to blame Melissa but couldn't. Humans couldn't control releasing their essence as Lyntans did with implants and training. They weren't enslaved to scent like Lyntans and thus had no need for devices like Jarren's Subduer. At least that's what he understood of Terran human physiology from his training vids. Which left him now surrounded and almost drunk on her scent, his body aching to respond, his mind fighting for control over his natural instincts. He wanted to touch her, wanted to turn off his Subduer so she could breathe him in too—she and any sensory board keyed to his scent and monitoring Terra. Dangerous. Instead, he forced a tired smile, hoping he maintained a modicum of normalcy.

She sat, then turned on the computer. Her hair settled in long dark waves around her face. His groin tightened a fraction. "If you want to have a seat, Dr. Graf, I'll get your computer up and running, then set up your phone and voicemail. I'm usually more on top of things within the office than you've been witness to."

Well, she was speaking now, and by her tone, she wasn't pleased with him. Good. The better to help him keep his distance. Her last statement seemed particularly telling. Was she talking about his workspace or the cup of coffee she spilled on him earlier? Both, probably. Jarren waved away her invitation to sit. Instead he advanced to the edge of the desk and splayed a hand across its surface.

"I understand my arrival was not foretold. I—" Jarren began.

"Dr. Graf." She cocked her head at him, a resolved expression on her face. "I need to explain what happened this morning." Again, Jarren waited. "I am so embarrassed. This situation is very uncomfortable for me."

A male voice originating from the implanted communicator in his ear overpowered Melissa's determined lilt. Jarren didn't process her next words. His second-in-command Marcus Naas's urgent voice reverberated into his eardrum. "Jarren. I have an urgent report coming in from Nine Sector."

Nine Sector encompassed this solar system as well as the Trention—where the bounty hunters had been tailed to last. One quarter of his crew's families lived on planets circling the Trention sun. Easy targets for well-paid assassins. But many of his crew weren't Lyntan. Milovar wouldn't be stupid enough to enrage other Alliance members by killing their citizens. Not just to secure Jarren's return. At least not until Milovar was crowned king. The hunters might have tracked him, but there were too many variables to act. Jarren raised a hand at Melissa for quiet then cocked his head as he waited.

"Naso's ship reports hunters scanning this system's planets. Please respond." Jarren's ship, *Stardesire*, hovered above Earth's atmosphere. They were cloaked from Terran technology, but Alliance technology wouldn't be fooled, and Jarren still wasn't sure who'd been sent after him. Once more, too many unknown variables.

He couldn't concentrate. "Ms. Reyes," he said, interrupting the ongoing hum of her voice. "I have to ask you to leave.

I will complete any setup for my work area, if you will just provide me with the log-in information."

Melissa stared at him. "But—"

"Commander," his communication unit piped. Jarren gritted his teeth. He wasn't used to dividing his attention between speakers. Frustrated, he clipped out his request again.

"Please leave, Ms. Reyes."

Her hand stilled on the mouse. Pushing the chair back, she got up, her mouth a thin line.

Jarren moved aside as she walked around his desk and out the door. She averted her gaze, but not before he noticed a flash of determined anger. She would have to be dealt with later. Jarren shut the door and sat in the chair Melissa vacated. Pushing a button implanted under his earlobe, Jarren spoke.

"Go ahead, Marcus. I'm listening."

"The subspace transmission states: 'Hunters scanning planets in this and Jeyna systems. Location of resistance scout ship still safe. Recommend removing *Stardesire* to coordinates outside of this galaxy. *Stardesire*'s energy trail may have been detected. End transmission.' Orders, Commander?" Marcus returned.

Jarren thought a moment. Not the Alliance but mercenary hunters? It could be a mistake to move his ship away from the planet while the mercs were searching the vicinity. If they were close by chance, creating another energy signature would definitely give away Jarren's star-system location. On the other hand, if they happened upon Jarren's ship orbiting Earth, they would have specific planet coordinates. The hunters would attack Earth, locate Jarren, and kill all those near him.

He swiveled his chair to look out of his office's solitary window. Thousands of people milled around outside, navigating their day completely unaware. Their lives could be extinguished so easily.

"Move *Desire* away, Marcus, slowly. Light-slip her out of the system then shift up and scatter an energy trail in another direction. Protecting this planet is of the utmost importance."

"You'll be stranded. If our false trail doesn't reorient their search of the sector, you'll have no help."

"I know. I won't take any unnecessary risks, so I should be safe until you return. Sacrificing other people for the possibility of easy escape cuts against me. I took enough privileges exiling here. Besides, even if you remained, there's no guarantee that you could get me off-planet before they found and captured me."

Marcus guffawed. "Well, I understand your moral resolve, but I don't have to agree with it. Don't get me wrong. I have seen the merc hunters come in with their firearms blasting. But not unnecessarily. And your concern for these Terrans must be weighed against the possible outcome of your death and Milovar's unchallenged succession to the Lyntan line. Your life is worth more than any other's, because you can prevent intergalactic war."

"I couldn't prevent Milovar's coup even with sympathizers' help. You believe I can command intergalactic peace?" Jarren snorted with self-derision.

Shutting his eyes, he attempted to block out the feeling of having failed, of being an inadequate ruler, that crept up on him. He wouldn't even consider the variables preventing him from ascending the throne—some of which his father had put into place. The gods should have protected his ruler-ship. Apparently, Jarren had been too cocky, too sure of his right to rule. Now the idea that the gods found him lacking haunted his every decision. He sighed. "There are others in succession to the line. Veena could as easily stand in. Sinal simply needs her focused attention. Her claim is as valid as Milovar's."

"She might have been willing to marry you, Jarren, but she won't attempt to rule two empires on her own. Not even to upend the 'Family' system."

Jarren's mouth curved slightly at Marcus's comment. Veena was a strong woman. But Marcus was right. She wasn't crazy. It had been easier for her to rule her planet, Sinal, before Jarren's father's death. Then, she'd only been the betrothed to Lynta's Prime Heir. Now, Lynta was ruled by a madman whose solitary belief seemed to be that peace only existed under his dominance. Veena would not assert her right of succession against Milovar while ruling Sinal.

Jarren leaned back in his chair then spoke, thoughtful. "I understand your reasoning, but the answer is still no. I can defend myself easily. I know what is hunting me. These Terrans have no idea of the danger I put them in." Melissa's face flashed before his eyes a moment, and those basic instincts kicked in—to claim and protect. He absolutely would not endanger Melissa to avoid capture.

"Move off before the next solar cycle ends. Accelerate outside of this sector. Keep in transmittal contact with me through my jumper," Jarren continued. "I'm perfectly capable of disappearing when needed and certainly of fighting when necessary. I've got to go. Jarren out."

"Commander," Marcus affirmed before Jarren's communication device went silent. *Stardesire* would be light-years away by tomorrow. Jarren would be on his own until the bounty hunters departed or until he was forced to call for assistance off-planet.

Jarren stood and absently began hooking up his laptop. His thoughts turned bleak as an image of large metallic ships hovering over Earth's atmosphere, pinpointing his location, and firing appeared in his mind. Milovar brought death and destruction to any and all in his way. He'd relish the hunters reporting the humans they massacred while "protecting" the prince. Jarren could not let that happen.

CHAPTER 3

FIVE THIRTY. LISSA turned off her little desk lamp and got up to stretch. Pulling her coat off the rack and piling reading materials into her canvas bag, she headed out to reception. Lissa had been too tired to be productive. It took energy to seethe. Inattentive, she drifted into the reception area, glanced down at her watch, then reached into a coat pocket and pulled out her cell phone as she stopped in front of the elevator. Jim should be heading to the airport now. Distracted, Lissa turned up her phone volume as her anger grew. Jim had a habit of making last-minute phone calls.

And what would she tell Jim of Jarren Graf when he called? Would she tell him how rudely Dr. Graf dismissed her? Would she stutter explanations for why she had not personally assisted in setting up his office? Lissa glowered with embarrassment. She'd put Stacy, Mark's assistant, on call to assist Jarren with any other issues. If Jarren wanted Lissa's help, he would have to ask personally.

Still no elevator. She jammed her finger against the elevator button. She couldn't wait to get home. She would give Jasmine a hug and put a book in her hands, then slide into a hot bath, three things that would return order to Lissa's scattered day. Only one thing now stood between her and escape. She glared at the closed elevator doors.

A sudden whiff of warmed chocolate assaulted her senses. "Ms. Reyes. May I speak with you a moment?" Jarren. Lissa stiffened. She'd been two feet from freedom. Lissa flipped her hair back with a twist of her head then exaggerated a glance at her watch.

"I'm just on my way out, Dr. Graf. Might I have Stacy assist you? She's still here."

"Unfortunately not. Jim would like to speak with you. He rang my line directly. I told him I would find you. If you would take the call in my office." He turned without another word and headed back the way he'd come. With a ding, the elevator door opened. Lissa sighed then turned away from her exit to freedom.

"Yes, sir?" she said into the speaker of Jarren's phone minutes later.

"I'm on my way to the airport. While I'm away, you will assist Jarren with any administrative needs. Jarren, I'll call you from London."

Lissa cleared her throat conspicuously. "Shall I begin the process of recruiting Dr. Graf's program assistant?" She would not stay in this untenable situation any longer than necessary.

"That can wait until I return." A week and a half. Lissa glanced over at Jarren. His face was impassive. Lissa opened her mouth to speak.

Jim's clipped voice reverberated from the speaker. "Anything else?"

Mr. Bigsby had closed the debate, and Lissa had to pick her battles. She bit her lip, resigned. "No sir." The phone clicked as Jim hung up.

Lissa looked at Jarren as he pulled back his chair to sit. This guy was the web to her fly. Why hadn't he insisted on someone else supporting him? He obviously had not told Jim about Lissa's part in the coffee incident, but based on his blunt dismissal earlier, it seemed odd he hadn't asked for someone else to assist him.

"May I help you anymore, sir?" Lissa's voice flattened like a horn. A strong eyebrow rose at her tone, but Lissa met his stare. She was too tired and emotionally taut to care.

"No. I'm fine. I will see you tomorrow," he said as he looked down at papers on his desk. She was again abruptly dismissed.

Good enough. Lissa escaped. She exited the back of the building and walked out into the early evening. The alley's wind tunnel whispered against her. She pressed on to the sidewalk and up a half block to the bus stop. She checked her watch. 6:00 p.m. Ten more minutes before the next bus arrived. Adjusting her coat and shifting her bag of paperwork up her shoulder, she leaned against the bus signpost. At least she had a moment of internal peace against the loud grind of evening traffic.

Jarren Graf's face materialized in her mind. Peace deserted her.

*   *   *   *   *

JARREN KNEW THE moment Melissa stepped onto the elevator. The potent link to her fragrance abruptly diminished. All that remained were drafts of office air containing left-over particles of her sweetness. Jarren leaned his chair back, looked out the window, and stared at the slowly darkening sky. His brow crinkled in concentration. He couldn't figure out what had happened that so upset her, though he should be glad she kept her distance. He'd taken all the necessary steps to reaffirm her importance in the office. He'd fabricated a need for someone with Melissa's expertise so Jim would be inclined to assign Melissa to assist. He'd thought she would feel some renewed validation to offset his earlier rude dismissal. But she'd glanced at him with the most aggrieved expression when she'd been given Jim's directive. There had been no looks of relief, no release in the tension Jarren noted in her walk all day. Then she left.

Creeds! He did not understand Terrans. He did not understand non-olfactory communication. Jarren sat up in his chair. Why *had* she left so quickly? He'd thought he was the reason for her hasty departure. But maybe there were other factors influencing her behavior. Jarren got up and followed Melissa's scent. Curiosity motivated him, not desire, he told himself. In the dark crevices of his mind, his primal side laughed. Terran behavior wasn't curious. The curiosity was her scent. Her aroma was so riveting he could find it even a mile away. Outside the building, as he left the back alley, he spied her. She stood alone at a bus stop. If she was going to take the bus, he would need his car to follow. Jarren jogged back to the building, entered, got on the elevator, and pushed the button for the parking garage.

Five minutes later, he pulled onto the street and cruised around the block to slow down near where she'd stood. Melissa was already gone. He rolled his car driver's side window down and breathed in. Like tasting a juicy plum, her fragrance floated sweetly into his nose. Jarren shifted the gears of his BM-EV. The car's blue metallic paint reflected splotches of light from illuminating streetlamps as he accelerated.

Jarren drove on. Melissa's potent scent lured him like an olfactory drug. Within ten minutes, he came up behind the long blue bus and trailed it as it moved farther away from the business district and surrounding well-groomed neighborhoods. The bus slowed and then stopped for the hundredth time. Melissa stepped off, crossed a cobbled intersection, and walked down a street lined with rows of midsized brick townhouses.

Watching her, Jarren waited for the traffic to pass his parked position before whipping his car onto the one-way street. He couldn't see her anymore, but he knew she headed toward the end of the block. As he coasted along, he spied her standing on the steps of the last row house on his right. The front door opened, and Melissa bent low. A squeal of happiness erupted from the entryway. One little girl—all smiles, almond skin, and poofy pigtails—bounded into Melissa's arms. A child. A daughter?

Jarren swiftly tapped down the button of his passenger's side window a bit. Denial stabbed at his heart. He searched out the little girl's scent, a familiar but youthful sweetness, and confirmed his suspicion. Melissa had a daughter. A child meant a partnership. The girl's hormones placed her at age five Terran development. Jarren breathed deeper. The subtle smell of male covered them both, shocking him back in his seat. He didn't pause to invade Melissa's privacy further. Pressing his foot down on the gas pedal, he took off, his mind numb. Jealousy ate at his insides.

Melissa had a family: a partner and child who loved and supported her. Why he hadn't sensed her bonded status earlier baffled him. Maybe he hadn't wanted to know someone had proven worthy of her. Unusually somber, Jarren drove home, his hand gripping the steering wheel with forced control, his thoughts oddly empty. A constricting feeling of loss threatened to overtake him.

*   *   *   *   *

"CUANDO USTED TRABAJE inesperadamente tarde, Melissa, Jasmine se da cuenta," Lissa's mother said as Lissa stood with Jasmine in her arms.

"Si, Mama. I should have called when I knew I would be late."

"You should plan your work hours better. Make sure Jasmine knows when you'll get here," Brenda Reyes added, smoothly switching to English. She ran a hand through her graying dark hair, exasperated. "When you come home later than usual, she gets nervous. She's five. She doesn't understand the difficulties of having a job."

"Yes, Mama, I know. You've already said this." Lissa pursed her lips and squinted to keep her eyes from rolling. She leaned forward and planted a quick kiss on her mother's soft cheek. Ulises's voice echoed in her memories. *Your mother deserved my loyalty, Lissa. She worked herself into the ground supporting me while I was in school. That is real love. Not these office affairs you all have nowadays.* He'd been a crappy husband to Brenda, but she should have listened to her father. Wisdom sits with those facing death. Lissa's office romance aside, no one excelled at work like her. He would be proud of how far she'd come. She wished she could return the admiration, but penitence right before one passes does not dissolve the memories of absentee fathering and whispered arguments on nights Papa smelled like perfume.

Ignoring her mother's judgmental stare, Lissa spoke. "I'll talk to you tomorrow. I need to get Jasmine to bed." She bent low and put Jasmine down, then clasped her daughter's hand. Taking a step down from the porch, she waved to her mother and turned away.

"Wait, Mommy." Jasmine pulled back, and Lissa halted. "I want to see the Crux constellation." Her excited voice floated to Lissa's ears. She paused to study her daughter's matter-of-fact expression. Even on days like these, Jasmine's bright countenance brought a smile to Lissa's lips.

"You're going to have to wait until later, sweetie. You won't see much in this light."

Jasmine's head tilted up toward the darkening sky. "Okay, Mommy. But you have to promise to let me stay up. Abuela and I watched a special all about constellations. I want to see the stars like the science guys do. The 'special' said 'cause it's April, I could see the Crux and Virgo constellations 'specially. I want Uncle Mickey to see too. Did you know that constellations aren't even really pictures? *Really*, they're mimics."

Brenda laughed. "Mnemonics, little butterfly! Now, enough chatter. It's time you went home. Mommy's tired, and you must eat and bathe before you can go out and be a scientist later. There was a beautiful light in the sky a few nights ago. Something amazing happens every night."

Lissa threw her mother a thankful glance. The day had been hard. She was mentally wiped out.

"I promise, Jasmine. We'll all look at the stars tonight and see what we can see, okay?" Lissa's smile grew as Jasmine nodded and skipped down one step.

"Good." Lissa turned back to her mother. "Gracias, Mama. Hasta mañana. Tell Miguel I'll see him this weekend." Lissa held Jasmine's hand as they made their way down to the sidewalk.

"See you tomorrow, Melissa. Bye-bye, Butterfly," her mother called out. Lissa waved as they walked away.

CHAPTER 4

BIRDS CHIRPING BY the window woke Lissa from a fitful sleep. Light slowly filtered into her room. The sun glimmered between the lime-green blinds that kept out the bustle of the world. Lissa blinked as the sun rose, pushed back her comforter, and stretched. Half awake, she glanced up. Her alarm clock sat next to Jasmine's book on stars and solar systems and Lissa's James Webb Space Telescope photo album on her bedside table; the clock's numbers glowed red. She hadn't overslept, at least.

Lissa slipped her feet into warm red-plaid slippers and lumbered across the room, down the hall, and toward the bathroom. Slowing, she paused at Jasmine's partly open door. She could hear Jasmine shifting in bed. With a smile, Lissa patted the door then continued on her way. She needed to take a shower and wake herself up before her daughter realized she'd slept enough and started pleading for breakfast.

In the shower, minutes later, her thoughts turned to Jarren Graf. Barely up and she was already thinking about him. It boiled her blood. His mere memory raised her ire.

She leaned her head back into the steamy spray and washed the shampoo from her hair. There was something about him she could not put her finger on. Something odd that threw her off. He had been no ruder than any other executive she'd encountered. But she'd never been so embarrassed or infuriated by any of them.

His annoyingly riveting features danced into her mind. The smell of melted chocolate haunted her memory. Even now she could visualize his hazel eyes penetrating her, uncovering her deepest secrets. One would think it was the first time she'd bumped into a handsome man. Well, he was more than handsome. He was outwardly perfect. She couldn't ignore how her insides grew warm when he gazed at her. She might have been sixteen again. But feeling anything at all was the last thing she wanted. Whatever the cause of her discomfort, she would have to get a handle on it. She would be working for him for a while.

Lissa bent down and flipped off the water. "Get a grip! He may be a jerk, but you've dealt with his kind before," she lectured herself as tear-sized water droplets fell from her hair to her white-and-green-tiled floor. She remembered his eyes mentally caressing her locks from head to tip. He liked her hair, even if he could stand nothing else. If she hadn't known men so well, she would have questioned his attraction. But she knew. Well, today she'd wear her hair up. Stepping out of the shower, she snagged a towel off a hook.

Lissa dried off, muttering away. "A week and a half, and your life will return to normal." She refused to give him another thought.

*   *   *   *   *

JARREN SAT AT his desk staring at his closed office door. He wouldn't consider that his distracted behavior had anything to do with waiting for Melissa to make an appearance. He looked down at the papers in his hand and absorbed the words without paying attention to them. His senses strained for any steps in the halls beyond his door, or worse, that alluring essence of hers.

The office was silent. He'd come in at 7:00, far earlier than anyone else would arrive. He hadn't been able to sleep; thoughts of Melissa had plagued him incessantly. His interest in her should have waned, not increased. She was, after all, mated. It wasn't the first time he'd been attracted to someone unavailable. But usually his interest would diminish, not grow, with the knowledge that they'd been claimed by another.

He had waited for the normal slowing in his blood pressure. He'd waited for the tension gathering inside him since he'd met her to unravel. Plagued by her smell, he'd sat up all last night in bed. Bare from the waist up, his skin caressed by a torturous breeze, his thoughts had turned primitive, possessive.

Now he tossed his handbook on office etiquette to the floor in frustration. He couldn't remember a word he read. His thoughts kept returning to Melissa. The depth of his desire for her made no sense. He wanted to steal her away, separate her from her mate and woo her until she accepted him. Breaking a bonding was one of Lynta's harshly punished crimes. Last night, his crankiness was potent. Today, Jarren was no better.

Jarren stared at the door, frowning as he returned his handbook to a drawer. He hated waiting. Reaching over, he picked up the phone and dialed Melissa's extension. He would fabricate a reason for calling her by the time she answered.

"Hello. You've reached the voicemail of—" Voice recording. Scowling, Jarren hung up and glanced down at his watch. It was 8:45. Why wasn't she at work yet? Picking up the phone again, Jarren dialed Stacy's extension.

"Yes, Dr. Graf?"

"Where is Ms. Reyes?" Jarren asked.

"She usually doesn't come in until nine, Dr. Graf. May I help you with something in the meantime?" Stacy's normally chipper voice was unusually cautious. It didn't bode well when an executive was searching for his assistant. He spoke again, his tone a soothing burr.

"I'm accustomed to debriefing with my assistant in the mornings. You needn't concern yourself. I would appreciate it if you let Ms. Reyes know I want to meet with her once she settles in for the day."

"Yes, sir. I'll let her know."

Jarren thanked Stacy, hung up, and went back to staring at the door.

*　*　*　*　*

LISSA SHRUGGED OFF her bag and coat as she juggled her silver traveling coffee mug in one hand. Sitting down, she turned on her desk lamp and scooted her chair forward. Mug safe on the desk, she turned on her computer as her eyes shifted to the silver container. She had made her own brew today.

Lissa looked up at the knock on her door. Through the slatted opening, she saw Stacy peek in. "Hey. Come on in."

Stacy entered, her island skin complementing her crisp plum skirt and silk blouse. Lissa gestured to the chair beside her desk. "What's up?"

"Dr. Graf would like to speak with you when you're settled," Stacy said as she lowered herself into the seat. Lissa's hands shook a moment. Thankfully the coffee was safely out of harm's way. Subconsciously, she straightened her ankle-length navy-blue suit skirt.

Stacy cocked an eyebrow. "Something wrong?"

Lissa shook her head casually. Now was neither the time nor the place to divulge the coffee incident. Stacy's eyes narrowed. They'd been close friends too long for Lissa to hide her distress completely. "I didn't sleep well," she finally conceded.

Stacy's eyes twinkled. "Hmm. Okay. Lunch today. No excuses." She got up and ambled out without looking back.

Lissa sighed and stared, undecided, at her desk. She might as well find out what he needed. She grabbed a pen and blank pad and headed for his office.

Her mind remained oddly blank as she paced through the halls. At least she wasn't wound up like yesterday. She lifted her hand to knock just as his door opened. Seemed he liked to answer doors before knocking occurred.

Lowering her arm, she stared at him resolutely. "You wanted to see me, Dr. Graf?"

He stepped back and nodded. His towering frame was poured into another Armani suit. "Please come in."

Lissa walked past him, conscious of his closeness. Her heartbeat increased. She sat as the door clicked shut.

Lissa glanced around. The walls of his office remained bare. Lissa's office was littered with Jasmine's artwork, school pictures, and photos of her, Miguel, and Jasmine at the last company picnic. Dr. Graf had not bothered to bring in pictures of his family, no mugs his children had painted, if he had any. Not even a picture of his mom. There weren't any expensively framed doctoral diplomas prominently displayed. But at least the dust was gone. One clean cell, occupied. She forced down the feeling of being trapped in a cage with an angry, powerful beast. This was where she had worked the last six years. Her imagination had gotten out of control.

As Jarren claimed the seat across from her, Lissa took a deep breath and made a snap decision. If she was going to have to work with him, she needed to defuse the tension. "I would like to apologize, Dr. Graf."

One beautifully arched brow rose. "Okay," he responded with what she was beginning to recognize as his notable neutrality.

"I spilled coffee on you. Then I made very little effort to rectify the situation. I was in a hurry. I should have at least given you my contact information."

"Ms. Reyes, we are not cars. There wasn't a need to exchange information. I have already replaced the shoes, and as you know, Jim replaced the suit, although there really was no reason. I sent my soiled suit to the cleaners. Only my shirt was lost."

Lissa nodded. He wasn't angry with her. He wasn't planning some great blackmailing scheme for sexual favors. Lissa let out the breath she'd been mentally holding. "I appreciate that you harbor no ill feelings. I've treated you in a less than welcoming fashion since you arrived. I felt unresolved regarding the incident."

His expression remained neutral. "We've made amends. Good. Now, I have a few things I need you to do. Behind you are four boxes of materials. I need them organized and categorized. Also, if you could arrange meetings for me with the East Africa microfinance project supervisors, I would appreciate it. An hour for each should suffice. I would like to get to everyone by the end of next week. I have given you access to my online calendar. All of my appointments will be there. Just schedule around what's existing. Okay?"

His phone rang. Nodding for her to wait, he picked up. "Jarren Graf." An amiable silence surrounded Lissa as he listened intently.

"Yes. One moment." Jarren hit the speaker button and placed the handset back on its cradle.

"Jim, we can hear you. Go ahead."

"Lissa. I'm glad I caught you both. I just informed Jarren that he'll need to travel next week after I get back. In the meantime, go ahead and place the ad for his program assistant. You made the right suggestion earlier. We'll begin interviewing when Jarren returns."

"Yes, sir."

"Arrange Jarren's travel. He needs to go to the London office to meet with Andrej. Andrej's assistant will e-mail you the specifics."

Jarren leaned over the phone without looking at Lissa. "That's alright, Jim. I'll take care of my travel. There is no need to increase Ms. Reyes's workload."

Lissa cast him a querying look. He didn't want her arranging his travel? Well, she wouldn't give in to negative assumptions again. She spoke up. "I'll arrange his travel, Jim. It's no problem."

"Good. Settled. Anything for me while we're speaking? I'm off to Geneva in a few hours."

"I've got your itinerary at my desk, sir. I'll e-mail or call you if any issues arise before your departure."

"Jarren. Anything?"

"No. I will have the report you requested out to you before you get to Germany."

"Great," Jim replied. "I'll be in touch."

Jarren looked over at Lissa, his glance still unreadable. Surely he couldn't be angry that she'd been eager to help? As his assistant, pro tem, she should be arranging his travel. Pushing still-suspicious thoughts to the back of her mind, Lissa stood, turned, and picked up a white banker's box from the floor. It overflowed with a mess of papers and folders. Adjusting the burden in her arms, she walked to the door.

She'd just grasped the knob, readjusted the slowly slipping box in her arms, and pulled when she realized Jarren was next to her, his palm against the door, inches from her nose. Lissa stopped and followed the line of his arm up to his face. He stared back at her and leaned in slightly.

Lissa blinked. Jarren jerked back. Taking his hand away from the door, he gruffly spoke. "You have family, Ms. Reyes?"

She was a little taken aback, but she didn't hesitate to respond. "Yes. I have a daughter; she's five." She shifted the box in her straining arms and waited. Her discomfort was starting to sour her mood.

"You have other children? A husband?"

Lissa stilled. "Excuse me?"

He took a step back, his brows curling together. "I am inquiring about your family."

Suspicious irritation brewed within her, cornered as she was in his office. *So much for not making negative assumptions,* she thought. The last time she'd heard that question, three years ago, she'd had to make a mad dash from the man's office. Hiding in her own office and holding back tears of anger, she'd wiped spittle off her neck with a Kleenex. Absolutely not this time, Lissa thought as she drew herself up to her full five-foot-six-inch stature.

"I am not married. I have my daughter and a cousin. He has spina bifida." Lissa paused. This wasn't his business. She would not ignore his line of inquiry. "You should know, Dr. Graf, that I feel your questions are totally inappropriate. And although I answered these questions, I refuse to answer any other inquiries of a personal nature." Lissa ended with an angry hiss. Her face reddened as she struggled to keep her voice even while not dropping the file box. He didn't respond to her statement, but she didn't give him time to respond, anyway. She jostled the door open and walked out.

*　　*　　*　　*　　*

FRUSTRATED, JARREN WATCHED Lissa leave. He'd known his questions were generally unacceptable, but he hadn't been able to stop himself from asking. Her cousin. That was the male scent that blended so well with hers; he'd been unable to distinguish it. Apparently, she wasn't mated. Maybe, subconsciously, he'd known. That would explain why he'd been unable to stop thinking of her even though morality and biology dictated he should.

Jarren shook his head as he closed his door then sprawled back in his seat. His behavior didn't make sense. He wasn't the type to obsess about a potential mate. Something made Lissa different.

An old Lyntan folktale tickled his Lyntan olfactory recollections: the story of the first true life-mates of the royal Lyntan line. Closing his eyes, Jarren sifted through his younger memories.

In the small meadow-like clearing of Lynta's South Irelie palace atrium, surrounded by lush periwinkle and green leaves, eight-year-old Jarren had sat on the rounded edge of a tall granite fountain. His mother sat across from him, smiling, her long fuchsia dress swaying slowly in the breeze from the fans above. He peppered her with questions as they swirled their fingers through the fountain pool's water. The liquid tinkling off the elegant upstretched arms of Lynta's love goddess statue burbled in the afternoon air.

Jarren had breathed in the scent of the decypheny his mother had planted. "Tell me, Mama, how the royal Lyntan line began and about the goddess Janelle and the lost child," Jarren asked.

His mother reached out a wet hand and flicked water in his face. He laughed. "Please?"

She cocked her head and shrugged. "Alright. But why a child your age would want to hear such a flowery story again is beyond me."

"It isn't the story. I like the words. They sound like a riddle or something. Doesn't it?"

Celina shook her head. "It's a mystery. Maybe that's why it sounds like a riddle to you."

Jarren nodded. He pulled his short legs up under him, twisted to get comfortable, and then returned his fingers to the pool's cool current.

Unwavering, Celina began. "Millennia ago, a lonely goddess, Janelle, roamed Lynta's fertile lands. She was amazed by our golden hills of rolling crops and our abundance of good soil. Who, she wondered, took such great care of the land, making it plentiful? Then she saw a beautiful young woman moving steadily down a small dirt road. She was wrapped in thin golden cloth, her milky-white hair flowing out behind her.

"She glowed with health, yet a tall walking stick worked to hold her up. The goddess could see nothing wrong with the woman, no matter how hard she looked. It was as if an unseen burden weighed her down. The goddess took the form of a warm breeze and caressed the golden cloth. Her voice emanated from the trees in the distance and blossomed out of the wildflowers and thistles that grew near the road twisting through the countryside.

"'Gentle lady. Why do you lean so on your stick?' the goddess asked.

"The young woman looked about her, searching for the source of the voice, even as she answered. 'I once had a mate who walked beside me. So incapable were we of being apart, I became dependent on him to hold me up. One morning I awoke in the darkness of a small tent in a foreign land—a harsh desert land—with no memory of how I got there. My mate was gone.'"

The memory faded. Jarren blinked at his sparse office. He had no idea why that memory had surfaced. His computer bleeped, and he slowly straightened in his chair. Why would he think of that Lyntan origin story now? Lynta's first life-mates did not hold the answer to his new obsessive tendency. His mother often recounted the myth to explain the erratic behaviors of those given the gift of true life-mating, but Jarren wasn't behaving erratically. The implications of his reactions to Melissa, though, were disturbing. She was of unviable ancestry. Lynta's Council of Rule would have loved to see her line end.

* * * * *

LISSA'S WALL CLOCK chimed lunchtime. She got up from her desk and pulled her suit jacket off her chair just as Stacy stuck her head into the office. Stacy shoved her black wire-frame glasses back up her nose, and her short brown curls sprung childlike to the side. "You ready to go?"

Lissa nodded.

"Where to today? Italian?"

Lissa shook her head as they paced through the halls to the elevator. "I don't care. I just need a break. My eyes are crossing."

"I saw the files on your floor. I haven't seen your office this messy since Jim's last assistant left. What was that woman's name? Jim's last assistant?" With a ding, the elevator opened to swallow them up then release them into the first-floor lobby.

"Deeny. She seemed nice enough. But yeah, it was a mess when I got here."

"Where'd the files come from?"

Lissa tried not to hesitate at his name. "Dr. Graf." They pushed through the glass double doors and made a left, weaving through the normal lunchtime foot traffic. Lissa held up a hand to shade her eyes as they crossed between buildings. The sun shone down on them. A transit bus rolled by.

Stacy wrinkled her nose. "He didn't strike me as the disorganized type."

"He isn't. These files are left over from Peter's time. They're the microfinance in Africa files."

"That sucks for you. You want help?"

"No, just need to set up a system. Actually, scratch that. Yes, I can use your help." They rounded another corner and stopped beneath the red-and-white-checkered awning of Antonio's Italian Luncheon. Inside, the warm aroma of marinara sauce and buttered pasta clung to the air. Lissa breathed in happily and glanced around at the cozy fake-brick walls.

"What do you need?" Stacy asked as she perused a large yellow menu hanging above the cashier.

"I need time downstairs in the filing room. Preferably this afternoon, if you could just cover for me."

Stacy cast Lissa a curious glance. "You want to move those files downstairs to the filing room? Why?"

Lissa sighed. So much for hiding her discomfort with Jarren from anyone else. "Dr. Graf is a little high maintenance. I need time to work out a system. A little quiet time."

"He doesn't strike *me* as particularly high maintenance. He didn't call me once yesterday. Mark, on the other hand, called me at least twenty times."

Lissa blinked, startled. She'd been sure Jarren would have called Stacy to complete the setup of his workstation. "You didn't set up his computer and phone?"

"No. I assumed you finished it. I peeked in on him once. He was working. He didn't appear to have any problems."

Odd, Lissa thought. Well, if there was one thing Jarren seemed to be, it was resourceful. They got in line to place their orders.

"I don't get it. What is it about the new guy that has you riled?" Stacy asked as the line inched forward.

Lissa shrugged and pointedly looked at the menu above them again. Stacy wouldn't understand the extremity of the coffee incident. Truthfully, Lissa didn't understand her own emotional response. The spill had been an accident. But

Lissa still thought about it, still worried about it. Being that obsessive was unlike her.

And then there were his questions about her personal life this morning. It hadn't been the first time she'd been asked inappropriate questions. When he wasn't MIA, her father had often warned her that her beauty was bound to encourage rude and even downright illegal questions and propositions. He would know. Within the nonprofit field, most of the authority figures were still men. And how did she protect herself? *Be perfect, Lissa,* Ulises drummed into her. *Be perfect.* Her responses to Jarren had been anything but. The hierarchy of her office was extremely dated, but Lissa was used to conforming to male authoritarian norms.

Lissa practically blew up at Jarren. He'd been so forgiving about her dismissive behavior that she'd let down her defenses a little. Then he'd started digging into whether she was married, and he'd shown himself to be just another womanizing executive playboy. Lissa had been angry and disappointed.

Stacy interrupted her train of thought. "You think he's attractive. Don't shake your head at me. He's gorgeous. You have eyes!"

Lissa sighed. There was no use denying it. Her attraction to Jarren complicated their working relationship even if she didn't want to admit it. She felt like running again, but the urge to skip out on lunch made her empty stomach churn.

Stacy continued, oblivious to Lissa's discomfort. "Well, he's beyond gorgeous. He's astonishing. I'm inclined to think something isn't right with him. Men like him don't work at Earth Microfinance. Men like him are already married and living in the suburbs of New York with the buckets of money they made on Wall Street in their youth. And men like him must be real assholes because you can't be smart, beautiful, nice, and single in this world."

"Who said he was single?" Lissa quipped, raising a brow.

Stacy gave her a look as they got to the head of the line.

"Hello ladies. Can I take your order?" the male cashier asked as he took out a scratch pad, just in time to put their conversation on pause. Lissa released a relieved breath.

*   *   *   *   *

IT WAS THREE o'clock. Jarren picked up and then hung up the phone four times in the last hour. He still hadn't thought of a good reason to call Melissa. He tapped his fingers against the edge of his desk, an old Lyntan drum verse stuck in his head. His eyes fell on his now-empty office corner. The files. That was as good a reason as any to call her. She should be reporting her progress to him. Not that he expected much progress yet, given the mess he'd given her.

He'd found the files locked away in a closet in such disarray he was sure it would take her a week just to sift through them. It was amazing how Earth offices functioned, still using such archaic data storage as paper files. Lynta's sensory data jacks were much more efficient. Even Terrans' USB storage beat paper. But his mother had chosen this organization because they relied less on the most modern technology.

Jarren picked up his phone and dialed Melissa's extension. After the sixth ring, he was poised to hang up and go find her. Stacy answered.

"Good afternoon, Dr. Graf. Your call was forwarded to me. Melissa is downstairs in the filing room. She asked that I be on call to assist in case you need anything. Shall I stop by?"

"I'm sorry? She's where?"

"She's in the filing room. She needed the additional workspace. Large filing jobs are taken to the filing room so no documents get lost, and there's space to spread out and reorganize the materials."

Stacy's idle chatter seemed intentionally distracting. Was she trying to fill his head with clutter? "Where is the filing room, Stacy?"

"It's on the third floor, sir," Stacy replied. "It's really nothing more than an office with lots of table space and cabinets," she added. Jarren was willing to bet she'd been tasked with discouraging him from searching Melissa out.

"I'll find her there," Jarren replied as he moved to hang up.

"I'll come around. The third floor is locked for security reasons. Only a few people in the office have access, so I'll have to ride down with you." Jarren stilled. Melissa *was* hiding from him. He couldn't blame her. He'd been rude, overbearing, and unnecessarily nosy. She had every right to hide. And he had no right to abuse his authority and corner her. Again.

Smothering a sigh, Jarren reseated himself. "Never mind, Stacy. Please have her buzz me when she's back at her desk."

"Yes, sir." Stacy hesitated. He could hear the question in her tone. Just what was going on between him and the powerhouse who was Melissa Reyes?

CHAPTER 5

JARREN FINISHED READING the second of two World Bank reports on Indonesian microfinance and shook his head. Small business loans to micro-entrepreneurs in poor countries was certainly a useful way of promoting local market sustainability, but it was depressingly far from resolving the world's inequitable access to basic living necessities: food, water, shelter. At least in this stage of Terra's global development.

Jarren rubbed his eyes as his sight adjusted to the bright LED lights above. He looked out the window at the growing shadows of office buildings. Stretching, he pulled out a pair of dark sweatpants and a T-shirt from his desk drawer and got up. Jim had left a key to the executive weights room before departing. Now Jarren had excess energy to burn off before leaving for the night. He'd built up quite a bit of energy thinking about Lissa. A half-hour run on the treadmill and a half hour on resistance machines should divert his focused attentions to more useful endeavors.

He grabbed his tennis shoes out of another drawer and headed to the bathroom. He stopped as he turned the first corner. Her earthy aroma enveloped him. A moment passed before he actually caught sight of her. Jarren should have turned away to avoid her, but he didn't have that degree of control right then. Besides, he'd been pondering ways to see her all day. Forcing himself to relax, he waited as she appeared down the hall, her smooth gait disturbing the quiet with its rhythmic swishing. The sleeves of her white silk shirt were rolled up to just below her elbows, and she held papers in her hand at reading distance from her face. Her turquoise eyes flickered with surprise when she glanced up.

Jarren looked down at his watch. "You are working late, Ms. Reyes."

"Yes, sir. I've finished setting up the first of the files you gave me. They're locked up downstairs, but if you need them now, I can bring them to you before I leave." Her stride slowed, a little more hesitant, but at least she was still moving closer.

Jarren shook his head. "No need, Melissa." She blinked. "May I call you Melissa?" he asked. He was tired of the formality between them. Formality seemed ridiculous when he couldn't stop thinking about pulling her into his office and making love to her on his desk. How primitive he was. Shameful.

Her response was slow but affirmative. "Yes, sir. That's fine."

"Please, call me Jarren."

Her gait slowed to a stop before him. "Okay. Jarren."

The sound of his name on her tongue sent a throb of desire through him. He took in her scent. Her body was misted with a sheen of sweat, probably from lugging boxes of files around all day. She glowed with vitality. Jarren took a step forward, breathing in sweet papaya. Melissa did not take a step back but looked him straight in the eye. He could see the subtle challenge in her expression. *Come and get it.*

Jarren's arm rose instinctively. His hand trembled as it paused an inch away from the curve of her waist. He struggled to maintain the space between his fingers and her shirt. Jarren looked down into her eyes. His need for her plagued him until it hurt. But he was treading on dangerous ground. Clenching his teeth and fighting his instincts, he forced his arm to lower and relax at his side.

Goddess help him. He needed to get away from her, but he'd ruined any chance of keeping her away when he coerced Jim into reassigning Melissa. Now Jarren's control faltered with each heated breath.

"Dr. Graf—Jarren, I was just coming to see you to finalize your travel. I know you were hesitant to, uh, have me do this, but I think you'll be satisfied with your itinerary." She cleared her throat. He could hear her voice strain.

Satisfied? Travel? What in Creeds was she talking about? Jarren forced his mind to search for relevant information.

Melissa held out three sheets of paper. "If you want to take a look." Her tone fell flat as her normally challenging gaze hid behind thick dark lashes. Such controlled power as he recognized in many of the women working around him. They were burdened by many things, but a system that elevated some and restricted others based on their scent did not exist here. Here, there were no stations based on being

"Of," "Beside," or "Below the Family." Certainly in this city, none were classified as unviable.

Jarren automatically grasped the papers. Unbidden, his gaze fell to the soft curve of her neck. A fantasy of Melissa sprawled naked on his bed's black satin sheets popped into his head. Jarren's desire rekindled. How could she speak of travel right now? Breathing shallow to minimize her smell, Jarren handed the papers back and stepped away. "I'm on my way to the bathroom to change. May I take a look when I come out?"

Melissa cocked her head and glanced up, a question in her eyes, but nodded. "Of course. I wasn't aware you were going to the gym. Would you rather I speak with you tomorrow?"

Tomorrow? Creeds, no! She was slowly driving him mad. He needed to keep her at arm's length until Jim's return. "Just give me a couple minutes to change, and then I'll take a look at what you have." Jarren walked away.

In the men's room, Jarren twisted on the water faucet, splashed cold water onto his face, and looked in the mirror. Hazel eyes simmering with arousal shone over a confused scowl. His hand still shook with the urge to touch her. He grabbed a paper towel and wiped at the water droplets glistening on his dark hair. His grasp on his biological drive was fast slipping away. And the question of Melissa as a possible life-mate again forced itself into his thoughts.

"I *don't* want to know," Jarren muttered. He turned, shook his head, and entered a stall to change. But Jarren did want to know. He couldn't concentrate on anything else. The question would not go away.

Five minutes later, he emerged dressed in his sweats and T-shirt. His muscles tensed with frustrated energy, anxious to get upstairs. Pushing down his restlessness, he took a few short breaths and looked at himself in the mirror one more time. His sideways glance caught the unconscious movement of his hand rubbing the skin over his Subduer.

Maybe the Subduer was why Melissa seemed unaffected by him. She might be as obsessed as he if she inhaled his full essence. Bracing both hands on the edge of the marble sink, Jarren clenched his jaw and fought for control. Potent desire overwhelmed caution as he searched for an excuse. She seemed oblivious to him, his essence curbed by the mechanism that could grant them both ubiquitous pleasures.

"And why should I suffer alone?" He frowned. The question burned in his mind. A few moments with the Subduer off couldn't feasibly produce enough traceable hormones to endanger anyone. Jarren needed to know she wasn't a possible mate. Life-mate, true life-mate, no mate at all. It had to be the not knowing that was driving him insane. Jarren pressed his thumb over the Subduer, felt for the little metal catch, and pushed in. Then he stood still a moment. He didn't feel any different, but something had changed.

He needed to act quickly. Tracing such a small release of his scent from off-planet was impossible, but there was no telling when the mercs would locate Terra and send someone earthside.

Jarren walked out of the bathroom. Melissa stood waiting, itinerary in hand, her gaze expectant. Reaching out, he approached. "I'll take a look at those now." His voice shook with controlled tension.

"Yes, sir." Melissa stepped forward then stopped. The papers in her hand fell with a rustle to the floor as her eyes widened. Her mouth went slack.

Jarren frowned, worried. He hadn't expected such an abrupt response. "Melissa?"

As if entranced, Melissa walked toward him, her hands reaching until her fingers brushed across his heated skin then under his T-shirt. Jarren shuddered. His body stiffened in anticipation. Her hands blazed a trail up and over his shoulders as she leaned her body into him, coaxing a gasp of want from his suddenly parched mouth. Her breasts' warm firmness connected with his chest through the material of their clothes, heating the air around them.

Jarren groaned. She might not have been wearing anything at all. He couldn't resist. He was starving for her. His arms encircled her waist, pulling her closer as his body tingled with need. Jarren grew ready. One skirted leg brushed against him in invitation as all logical thought vanished.

He claimed her mouth, hungry, desperate. The earthy undertones of her natural fragrance, that Egyptian musk with such sweet papaya, swirled around him. His hand came up, weaving into the falling tendrils of her hair to hold her to him. His lips suckled hers, his tongue darting to taste her mouth's nectar, stroking the warm insides, lapping at her sweet moistness.

She moaned, her breathing erratic, her mouth searing his lips, tasting, teasing.

She pulled his head closer as her tongue danced with his. She caressed the warm walls of his mouth then drew away, letting the air cool the lingering impression of her lips against his. Her eyes blazed. She wanted him. He could smell her desire; potent, heady. It surrounded him. It taunted him.

A breath of Egyptian musk rose like an embracing cloud to envelop them both. His body vibrated with primitive need as realization struck. On a world light-years away from home, he'd discovered a possible life-mate. Jarren let go all control, reclaiming her mouth ardently. He pulled her against him, devouring her soft lips to dominate her. His nose filled with the fragrance of blooming papaya. His body craved to possess her, fill her, bind her to him forever.

She belonged to him and he to her. He wanted to thrust them both over the brink of desire. Pulling away, he placed demanding kisses along the curve of her jaw until he found the sensitive skin of her earlobe and drew the honey-sweet softness into his mouth. She moaned low and pressed closer, her warm breath caressing his skin. In a musk-induced daze, his eyes were drawn to the fullness of her breasts, the arching curve of her hips. He tightened in response, his need rocketing to the hard shaft between his legs.

Her mixture of scents intensified, calling to him, overwhelming him. He ached. His lips moved lower, tracing passion-heated kisses over the curve of her collarbone to her shoulder. Her fingers dug into his skin as her head fell back, the tresses of her hair clinging sensuously to his forearms. She gasped.

He buried his head in the slope of her neck as he was curtained behind the silky locks of her hair. Gods, how he loved her hair. Lifting her up, he inhaled her perfection, nuzzling his face against her full breasts. His blood pulsed as he absorbed the smell of her sweetness. She did belong to him. He belonged to her. His skin dewed with fever, and instinct took over. He would claim her now.

He'd just reached to push aside her blouse's collar when her body stiffened.

Fighting his instinct to mate, Jarren loosened his grip until her feet touched the floor; then he pulled away, his breathing jagged. He struggled to create a thought. Her aroma still tugged at him, drew him like the sweetest nectar. But he was endangering his world and her by revealing his scent. And he could sense she'd refused him. He would never force himself on a woman, not even in the primitive throes of their intermingling essences.

A new awareness crashed into him. The depth of his desire had forced his sanity to temporarily flee. Comprehension slowly re-emerged, and with it, his awareness that the ramifications of his actions could be catastrophic. He looked down at her horrified expression even as the last tendrils of her hair loosed themselves from the static charge between their bodies.

"Oh my God," she whispered. Her eyes widened as she lifted a hand, her fingers feathering across her kiss-swollen lips. Her breasts rose and fell in distressed shudders beneath the fabric covering them as she staggered backward, putting space between them. Her heels mangled Jarren's discarded itinerary on the floor. Shaking her head, she turned and bolted down the hall.

The likely repercussions for his actions finally dawned on Jarren. By the gods, what had he done? The possibility of revealing his location aside, he'd unintentionally forced Melissa into mating foreplay. She was a proud woman. She was Terran. She wouldn't understand she should not be ashamed of her behavior. Melissa would run.

Jarren froze with fear. She *was* running. Still taking deep breaths to slow the flow of heat through his veins, he grasped for ideas. Nothing this powerful had ever happened to him before either. But he needed her. And she would need him too. With a determined step, he followed her, only pausing as an afterthought to turn his Subduer back on.

Moving purposefully through the halls, he followed Melissa's scent. Her response hadn't been what he'd expected, but he wasn't intimidated by it. All Lyntans knew what happened when two mates found each other. Unfortunately, Melissa didn't know, and he had no way of gaining her trust without revealing his origin. Protecting her world and his meant he would have to court her without the knowledge or influence of his scent. Yet, all things sacred, he would give himself to Melissa Reyes. And he'd be damned if she didn't want him just as much.

CHAPTER 6

LISSA RAN. HER face burned with guilt. As she rounded a corner, she fought to gather her jumbled thoughts into coherent ideas. No good solution popped into her head for the situation she'd created. She stopped, breathless in the dim and silent reception area, and pushed the elevator button. Then she forced her scattered energy into a necessary pause.

The elevators never arrived quickly enough. Tears fogged her vision as she hugged herself and tried to forget how she'd touched Jarren. She'd opened the door to future harassment. Her lips still tingled. Goose bumps prickled in nervous clusters on her skin.

"Oh my God, what have I done?" Her thoughts returned to that moment when Jarren's mouth had covered hers. A distraught whimper escaped her. Drawn like a bee to a flower, she had moved toward him, her heart pounding. Her body had heated with desire. She breathed in his scent and reached for him, her hands coming up, running over him to slide through the thick ebony of his hair. She brought his lips to her, his mouth hesitant at first then desperately demanding. A fragrance unfamiliar to her yet so potent it made her eyes gloss, seemed to sponge into her pores. She had to taste him, claim him.

Every fiber of her had belonged to Jarren in that moment.

His name had reverberated in her head before settling into three coherent words. Dr. Jarren. Graf. She'd become intensely aware of her hands running over the corded muscles of his chest and arms. She stilled in shock but couldn't, then, bring herself to pull away.

Jarren seemed ignorant of her sudden awareness as he lifted her, nuzzling and kissing the sensitive skin on her neck, giving her the attention she had begged for. Then reality burst through her pleasure-induced immobility. It didn't matter that she'd been incapable of controlling her actions. Lissa had broken her two cardinal rules of relationships in the office: never give in to mutual attraction and always maintain control.

She'd lost control seven years ago. Another office. Another tall, dark, and handsome man. Derek James. Lissa stifled a groan as she leaned her head against the wall. Derek attracted her with his common ancestry and chivalrous manner. Half African American and half Haitian, Derek was fluent in Spanish and English and spoke passable French. Lissa connected with him instantly.

She remembered his sweet-soft words tickling her ear. He had requested she accompany him on business lunches with important contacts and treated her like a valued equal at the table. Then one evening he pulled her aside in the hall outside his office. The pads of his thumbs gently stroked her skin on that sensitive spot just below the roundness of her shoulders.

His nearness, the glint of restrained desire in his eyes...it was too much for Lissa. She pivoted and pulled him down to kiss her. Derek drew her into his arms without the slightest hesitation, turning her as he stepped into his dark office. She heard the door shut behind them.

She had wanted to believe he was falling in love with her, though that belief contradicted everything her father had ever said about white-collar men. Lissa certainly fell in love with him, and six months after that night, they were still seeing each other. Then he'd let the bomb drop that he was offered another position with the organization—in El Salvador. Lissa had been calm in her response. But he gave her the oddest look when she suggested they get married.

"Married? Why?" Derek tossed his jacket onto the white couch of his penthouse living room. He sat, facing her, their cups of tea rattling harshly on his glass coffee table. It would not be the only time that night. The late afternoon sunlight shone through tall windows facing the harbor.

"So we can move there together. If we're married, I'll move with you."

With a disbelieving glance, Derek shook his head. "No. You don't get to change the rules." He reached out and forced her back by her neck. Tears of pain and shame filled her eyes. She had to have been the most naïve woman on Earth. She tried to turn away and wipe at the blurriness in her eyes. Marriage had never been a conversation topic and for the first time, she was glad. He wasn't the marrying type. He was the wife beating type. How would she have known he was the type who controlled with a closed fist? And how would she have known one assault would leave her with so much trauma?

It only took one time for Lissa to get out, but she was never the same. She was still trying to forgive him for hurting her, and herself for not seeing what he was. She let him decide their future, and he had left that future in tatters. Well, he gave her Jasmine at least. Lissa had picked herself up and started over at the Microfinance Institute. She worked her way up until she was invaluable to Mr. Bigsby. She swore she would never have another relationship with someone in her office, no matter what. Doing so only threatened the future she was trying to build. Until tonight, she'd stuck to that resolution.

The elevator door opened with a ding. Without think-ing, Lissa stepped on and jabbed her thumb on the button for the lobby. In the recesses of her mind, she sensed Jarren approaching. A prayer accompanied Lissa's relieved sigh as the doors began to close. The elevator tapped shut, and Jarren's distinct sweetness was gone.

Lissa reached the lobby in less than a minute, and as usual, she exited out the back door, walking swiftly through the darkening alley. A gust of wind shifted chilly air about her, tangling through her hair and slowing her staggering pace. She breathed in the stench of dead rodents and spoiled food with a grimace. Too late she remembered she hadn't gone back to her office for her jacket. It was Jarren's fault. He was far too capable of provoking her with his mere presence.

Lissa reached the end of the alley and spied the bus stop. She hadn't bothered to bring her purse either. Sucking in an irritated sigh, she realized she'd have to go back. Maybe she could sneak in and pick up her stuff without Jarren knowing she returned.

With a hesitant step, Lissa reversed course back into the alley and stopped short. A stone's throw away, a figure towered over her, his six-and-a-half feet easily dwarfing Lissa's petite figure. Her breath caught. She couldn't see him clearly. His black-clothed form looked unnaturally distorted as if she were trying to spy him through translucent glass. Yet even without clearly seeing him, she sensed danger.

Lissa backed up and prepared to dash toward the street, but her feet suddenly wouldn't respond. Something held her frozen. The taste of copper, like she'd sucked on a penny, erupted in her mouth. A force gripped her, held her from the inside out. The person in the alley had sought her. And he closed in.

She tried to scream for help, but a thick hand covered her mouth. Another hand jerked on her arm, and she was twisted to face her assailant's expressionless gaze, the gaze of someone inhuman.

Lissa's eyes widened. Her heart raced. She wanted to fight, but she couldn't move. Without a sound, the thing holding her lifted his hand, slapped her across the cheek, and then began squeezing her throat closed, an excited grin breaking the monotonous bleariness of his expression. Heart slamming against her chest, air no longer reaching her lungs, Lissa panicked in her immobile state.

The assailant shifted his grip to pull her close as he sniffed her. Abruptly, he straightened. Placing both hands on the side of her head, he squeezed. A scream escaped Lissa's lips as the pressure of his palms increased. If she hadn't been frozen, she would have collapsed in agony. She was unable to make out any distinguishing features, murkiness covering her vision. Pain overwhelmed her. Futile tears slid from her eyes as she felt her skull being crushed.

Then he spoke, his voice a dry hiss of sound. "Celina's son."

In the distance, the pounding of running feet preceded an angry roar. The throbbing in Lissa's head eased as the hands that held her hesitated. In an instant, her attacker was cut down. His still-unclear shape lay prone, trembling beneath the onslaught of Jarren's fists, on the alley's grimy cement.

Merciless, Jarren beat her attacker. His outraged yell nearly shattered Lissa's eardrums. Her attacker fought to stand. Jarren's face contorted with rage as he roared again. He clutched at a thick neck and squeezed until a choking gasp echoed off the sides of the buildings.

When he let go, the body collapsed like a heavy sack, its oddly shaped head smacking against the stone. Jarren's haggard breathing registered in Lissa's ears as he looked at her. Her gaze centered on Jarren as he glanced down again at her assailant. Jarren's features reflected pure hatred. In the next instant, he bent and pushed the motionless body flat and reached into his side pocket.

A grunt escaped Jarren as he pulled out a silver, oblong, finger-sized object. For a moment, Lissa thought he held a bullet between his fingers. It was larger, though, and flattened. Pointing the object at the still shape, he squeezed the device, then waited. Her attacker's body jerked violently, and a piteous whine escaped him as he rolled onto his hands and knees.

As if a veil lifted, Lissa's view of him cleared, but then she wished it hadn't. His legs began to shorten. His body sprouted wiry hairs—the hairs of a dog—puncturing through his clothes, growing out of his hands, neck, through the foam that splattered from his mouth and dripped down his face. Punctuated by groveling whines, the structure of his face twisted and pulled painfully.

She resisted throwing up, her hand holding her heaving stomach, as she recognized a snout with whiskers jutting out of his jaw. What had been her attacker became the limping, disoriented body of a large black dog. Lissa watched it fall, regain its footing, then stumble away through the enveloping dark and disappear.

Jarren dropped the oblong object to the ground and stomped on it. He moved toward her. As if her incapacitation was connected to the object, Lissa's body relaxed. The metal taste in her mouth disappeared. But the attack had been too much for her. Unable to remain standing, she collapsed into Jarren's arms.

He picked her up, his eyes darting around, and made his way with her back into the building. "It's okay, my own. You're safe," he whispered in her ear.

Lissa barely processed his words. She was exhausted. It took too much to fight through her fatigue.

They were in the elevator going down. A heaviness slouched Lissa's shoulders, yet fear kept her wary. She started to speak, but Jarren shook his head in warning. "Don't talk until we are away from here," he whispered. Her throat burned anyway. Lissa nodded and closed her eyes, giving up control for the second time that night. She leaned her head against the solid protection of his body.

She was nearly asleep when Jarren's pace slowed. Snuggling into his shirt's softness, she rubbed her cheek against his chest and listened to his heart beat. In the quiet, she could hear Jarren's steady breathing. He didn't seem at all winded from carrying her or from fending off the earlier attack.

He stopped and lowered her, so her feet touched the pavement of the office garage. An unsettling quiet surrounded them, as if the world knew she'd seen something that would forever change her. He reached into his pants pocket. Fear tenderized her muscles, and she slumped as Jarren pulled the car door open. Onto a plush leather seat she went, and she sank into the normalcy of the feeling. Stopping, he turned his face into the air, but nothing stirred. Finally, he shut her door and rounded the car, and Lissa could only watch, too tired to put together a thought.

Without a word, he got into the driver's seat. The sound of his door shutting broke the enveloping silence. Lissa fought through her haze and studied his blank expression. He stared ahead, peering off into space, but he'd seen what she had, right? He'd saved her from something. She couldn't understand beyond that.

Jarren drove them out of the garage.

CHAPTER 7

LISSA FELT NUMB. Streetlights flew past the car window's tinted glass. The sky deepened into the indigo of late evening. She registered the soft buzz of the engine as Jarren shifted gears and accelerated forward. Her gaze fell to the bruises and cuts on his knuckles.

No thoughts penetrated the foggy coldness overwhelming her core. But the right side of her face throbbed from the hit she'd taken. Her body ached from the strain of trying to free herself. It was just that the pain couldn't break through the shock to her system. She turned away from Jarren as he drove, resting her head against the coolness of her seat.

"Where are we?" Lissa asked as the car slowed.

Jarren glanced at her, a concerned scowl on his face. "This is your home. You're home."

He reached over and gently turned her head to face him. "I am sorry for what happened." His hand slipped from her chin to squeeze her arm. Lissa stared at him, struggling to think, to process the situation. Looking out again, she recognized her mother's house. Not home. Her mother wouldn't be happy Lissa hadn't called.

"You saved me?" Hadn't he? She remembered the attack. She remembered his fists ramming into the man's face and body as if Jarren were possessed. Lissa only experienced that level of violence once before: so powerful and intentional. She gritted her teeth against the fear that slithered up her spine. What did she know of Jarren Graf? What could motivate a man to be so barbaric yet calculating? Why did she trust his violence more than she'd ever trusted Derek? Of course, with Derek there had been signs beforehand: mood swings, abrupt outbursts. But where Derek had seemed out of control, Jarren was anything but. Still, violence lived in them both. And then there was her dog attacker.

Wary, she looked at Jarren. He stared out the front windshield for a moment then faced her, sadness clearly flickering in his eyes, and possibly…regret?

With a sigh, he spoke. "Go in, Melissa. Rest. I want to see you in the office tomorrow…but not before eleven." He fumbled, reaching into his sweatpants pocket. Almost hesitantly, he handed Lissa a small wad of bills. "Take a cab in tomorrow. For your own safety, stay away from public places and mass transportation. We will talk when you get in."

Lissa would be happy to sleep. She bowed her head and turned to open the car door, but Jarren's hand on her arm halted her. Tenderly, as if she were as breakable as the finest china, he pulled her toward him then placed a kiss on the top of her head. Cupping her face in one hand, he looked at her. She could sense subdued angst in his posture.

"I am so very sorry," he said.

Lissa nodded, but she didn't know why. The evening's events had evaporated in her mind. He caressed her cheek once more before letting her go and staring ahead again. "Tomorrow. I will talk to you tomorrow."

Lissa got out, her heels splashing into a small puddle of rainwater. She didn't remember it raining, though. Closing the door behind her, she turned and angled toward her mother's house. She didn't look back. The pain in her face and the heat in her throat increased with each step, and she rubbed her hands over her arms to warm herself, but she didn't really feel the cold. Nothing could penetrate her numbness. She'd been attacked. She'd witnessed a violent side to Jarren Graf—a side she hadn't wanted to know existed. Those events alone were scary enough. But watching a man's metamorphosis into a dog made her question her sanity.

As she took the last steps up to the front door, she fought for comprehension. Warmth trickled through her, but so did the questions. How would she explain what happened tonight to her mother without sounding completely crazy? Her mother would think she was infatuated with Jarren if she didn't go to the police. She wasn't sure she wanted to report her attack, anyway. In the deep recesses of her mind, she knew her attacker had intended her death, but that didn't mean she should trust Jarren Graf. His violence terrified her, but it had also saved her. She had no wish to put him behind bars. And besides, how did one explain that the boss beat the crap out of a man who attacked you then transformed him into a dog? Better to tell her mother she took a very bad fall.

The door opened, and Lissa confronted her mother's chastising glare. Lissa turned in time to watch Jarren's car pull away. When she looked at her mother again, the older woman's frown was replaced by a look of concern. "The side of your face is red. What happened?"

Lissa sighed and plodded inside. Her mother wouldn't believe the lie Lissa was about to weave, but the truth wasn't any less incredible. "I'm fine, Mama. I fell and hurt myself."

"You hurt yourself on someone's fist! The side of your face is swollen and there are bruises on your throat. You *aren't* wearing your jacket. You *don't* have your bag. *Your clothes are torn*, and you are holding your side as if you cracked a rib." Her mother's eyes narrowed. "How did you get home? What is going on, Melissa Louisa Reyes?"

Lissa didn't know herself. Sighing, she lowered her head as she closed the front door behind her.

*　*　*　*　*

WHAT HAD HE done? Jarren watched Melissa walk into the house. Pulling the car away, he temporarily redirected his attention and scanned the block. Jarren studied the shadows for anyone lurking but saw no one. Leaning toward the window, he breathed in a cool zephyr. He sensed no hint of non-Terran entities nearby. Slowly rounding the corner, he pulled over and parked his car. He would be keeping watch on Melissa's house tonight. Unconsciously, he rubbed a crick in his neck then flexed his aching hand. His knuckles smarted, but he wouldn't go home tonight to patch himself up.

Bounty hunters. They had found him. He looked up at the stars. Somewhere up there, ships waited. And they probably now knew of at least one target. Balling his swelling hands into fists, Jarren cursed himself. Bounty hunters hunted in twos. It wasn't even remotely possible that the first bounty hunter refrained from reporting Jarren's scent on Melissa.

Another would be coming to find his partner and help make the capture. But hopefully Melissa's attacker hadn't had time to report her actual location before Jarren got to him and transed him into a dog. The hunter appeared to be trying to make the bag himself so he could claim the greater portion of the bounty. Still, the likelihood of him not communicating with his partner was slim. Safer to assume the other knew Melissa's location and would be arriving very soon. It was *safest* to assume her life was in great danger.

And he'd created that burden. Turning off his Subduer had covered her in his scent. His desire had put her in danger's way. He'd just realized too late. Even now, he could still distinguish his essence surrounding her despite the brick and stone walls of the houses separating them. His scent should not have been so potent. It shouldn't have clung so readily to her.

Buried beneath that, he now smelled the subtle inter-twining of fragrance created at the beginning of a bonding. They weren't bonded yet. Essence-bonding required many mutual exposures. But then he hadn't thought his scent would so overpower her behavior either. With Melissa, his essence had a life of its own. He just didn't know why.

Jarren got out and clicked his car door shut. He didn't fear attack for himself. His Subduer was on again, and he'd taken extra steps to simulate a slight masking smell over his own. Masking his essence wasn't something he liked to do, though. It was uncomfortable and disconcerting to be steeped in a scent not his. Eventually, he would become disoriented and unable to identify anyone else's smell. "Masking" essence so confused Lyntans, some had been known to suffer memory loss from overuse.

Lyntans lived by scent. They relied on their own fragrances like humans relied on mirrors. Fabricated essence distorted his face in the mirror. But Jarren had brought it on himself and the woman he burned to bond with. He'd endangered himself and Melissa for curiosity's sake, and he was paying for it. In contrast to what Melissa had gone through this evening, a few drops of masking fragrance was a small price to pay.

Jarren hissed out an angry breath and stamped down his ire. He could not protect her if he was too furious to concentrate. He paused to calm himself then strolled around the block in case he needed to get Melissa away fast. Returning to his car, he got in, leaned his seat all the way back, and closed his eyes. Sleep pulled at him as he realized guilt still had hours to feast on his conscience. His senses tracked Melissa's movements within the house. He would speak to her tomorrow, but by the gods, he wished tomorrow would never come. His stomach churned at having to face her and explain he was the cause of her danger.

CHAPTER 8

AT SIX O'CLOCK Jarren opened his eyes and stepped quietly out of the car. Minutes later, he managed to layer Melissa's home with the scent that protected his own smell. Jarren breathed in one final whiff from his car window then drove away. He couldn't identify his aroma anywhere.

Driving home, he only managed a quick shower, quick use of his recovery gel to heal his cut skin and swollen joint, and a change of clothes: tan slacks and a white dress shirt. Freshened up, he walked out the front door of his townhouse, raced down the steps surrounded by the early morning harbor chill, and got into his car. He'd yet to think through explaining to Melissa who and what he was.

Now Jarren glanced up at his office clock. It was 10:30. He'd told Melissa not to arrive before eleven. But with only a half an hour before she would get in, he still didn't know exactly how to explain the situation into which he'd dragged her.

His hand absently caressed his Subduer again, and he scowled as he recognized the motion. He fought the urge to shove back his chair in frustration and leave this employment. Just walk away from Melissa and the mess he'd caused. By tomorrow, his scent on her would probably be entirely gone. If he cared anything for her, he would leave now and take his scent trail with him so those who sought him would not stop at her.

Jarren thrust a hand through his hair and got up to pace. The thought of leaving made something in him ache. There had to be another solution, one that protected her but kept her with him. The truth seemed like the only answer. If she believed him, she would accept his protection until he could defunct his cousin's reign and end the onslaught of bounty hunters paid to find him.

Convincing her of his truthfulness would be the hard part. As species went, Lyntans and humans were essentially the same. There was nothing about him visually that would confirm his Lyntan birth. But Lyntan technology was vastly different, a thousand years ahead of Earth's. His Terran assimilation had been greatly eased by Lyntan technology's ability to duplicate the simplistic but necessary materials and currency that created social status and identity.

When Jarren arrived on Earth, he'd purchased all the appropriate accessories expected of his fabricated history and profession: Armani suits, Ralph Lauren and Hilfiger leisure wear, two Baume and Mercier watches, at $2,700 each, and all the necessary footwear to match, including his Testonis. He'd rented two immoderately priced houses: a completely furnished and refurbished townhouse in Baltimore's Federal Hill district and a large light-blue-and-white country house, only missing the picket fence Terrans obsessed over, in Barnesville, Maryland. His space jumper was cloaked in the field behind the house.

There was no way to prove his money had been fabricated by the jumper's replication chamber. However the jumper itself was both technologically advanced and Lyntan. The jumper could convince Melissa of the truth.

As small a movement energy signal as the jumper emitted, it was a non-Terran energy signal, and the bounty hunters would pinpoint his location within moments. He couldn't just fly it to Baltimore. He needed to bring her to his country house. He could tell Melissa any story he wished, but to convince her, they would have to take a trip.

A soft knock sounded on his door. Turning away from his window view, he called out. Melissa stepped in and leaned on the doorknob, dressed in a long-sleeved forest-green shirt and a matching ankle-length skirt. She walked forward with some hesitancy.

"Melissa," he muttered. He tried not to catch his breath. She looked so pale, so exhausted. He had done this to her. His guilt resurrected itself.

She nodded. "Sir."

"Please, sit. I thought I said you could sleep in this morning. It is not eleven o'clock yet," Jarren said as he gestured to a seat and waited for her to settle before reclaiming his own. The chair groaned under him.

"I know, sir, but I didn't feel okay coming in any later. I need to speak with you."

A warm tingle of anxiety spread through Jarren's chest. He needed to speak to her too. He just wasn't prepared. He hadn't come up with a viable excuse for the alley incident; he *hadn't* definitively decided to tell her the truth.

With his usual neutrality, Jarren replied, "Okay."

"Yesterday...well, I can't apologize enough for my behavior."

Jarren hesitated. "Yesterday?"

Melissa shifted uncomfortably in her chair. "Yes, sir. I behaved inappropriately. My actions were highly reprehensible, a violation of your person that in no way should be accepted in the workplace, much less anywhere else. I fully accept that my behavior will have to be reported to Mr. Bigsby. But I...I just wanted to say I'm sorry for accosting you. It will never happen again."

Did she believe she forced herself on him? Jarren concentrated on absorbing her words. She was talking about the kiss. Didn't she remember that he'd kissed her back? *Creeds,* didn't she remember him beating the bounty hunter who'd attacked her? By the gods, didn't she want to ask him about how he turned that man into a dog?

"You are speaking of the kiss in the hall last evening?" He had to be sure he wasn't misinterpreting the subject.

Melissa threw him a startled look. "Of course."

How would he tell her? Jarren leaned his chair back, crossed his fingers over his abdomen, and breathed. "I want to talk about the man who attacked you last night." He straightened as he spoke.

Melissa's glance darted to the window. "I don't understand."

Jarren tried again. "The man who attacked you last night in the alley. We need to talk about what happened," he said as he stared at her profile.

"I really don't see why we need to discuss that incident. It doesn't have any bearing on my ability to work for you."

"And discussing you kissing me does?" Jarren snapped. Melissa's narrowed gaze shot to him. He couldn't penetrate the façade of ignorance on her face, but he knew she remembered.

"I think my behavior toward you in the hall yesterday hinders our ability to work together. I have shown you no respect; therefore, it goes without saying I shall receive no respect in return. Respect is a necessary element for any good business relationship. As for the person who attacked me last night, he was nothing but a mugger."

Jarren stood and walked around the desk. He knelt next to Melissa and tilted her head with his hand. She looked up at him. "You are wrong about one thing. Your behavior yesterday only served to confirm my respect for you. A kiss between us is not indicative of a lack of respect. I am going to kiss you now unless you say no."

Jarren waited. Her simmering stare hit him. He kissed her. The desire Jarren had held in from the moment she walked through his door erupted. His mouth landed on her lips with a passion he now recognized originated in a primal urge to bond. He couldn't help himself. He half hauled her out of her chair, entangling his hands in her hair, his lips caressing hers, desperate to make her understand their kiss yesterday had been uncontrollable; they couldn't have stopped it.

Then he released her. Breathing deep, he let her slip down into her chair and reclaimed his own seat. Looking her straight in the eye, he repeated his earlier statement. "I want to talk about the man who attacked you last night."

It took her a bit to respond. He noticed, with satisfaction, her tongue dart out to taste her lips. Finally, she faced him. "I don't remember much of the attack. So I don't know what we could talk about. I only know a man attacked me and you saved me." Her gaze shifted down to her lap. "Everything else is a haze."

She was lying. He could practically smell the lie on her, though lie detection was not a Lyntan olfactory talent Jarren had inherited. Still, he knew she wasn't revealing all. He turned his attention to his computer screen. "We will have to talk about it at some point, Melissa. It seems now is not the right time for you."

She remained quiet.

Jarren continued. "You kissed me. Now I have kissed you. We are even, so let's move on to work. I spoke with Jim." From the corner of his eye, he noted Melissa reaching for her cell phone in her pocket. "He didn't call in. I called him. He got me the meeting with the Nicaraguan government official."

She nodded. "Yes, sir." She was back to the impartial sir again. Jarren impatiently rapped the tip of his fingers on the table and continued.

"He won't meet with me in the office. I suggested meeting at my Barnesville house. It's closer to DC." He paused and stared into her eyes. "I will need you to attend the meeting. My grasp of Spanish is not as good as it needs to be. Jim tells me you are a certified Spanish translator. This conversation needs to go smoothly." The lie slid like syrup off his tongue. She wasn't the only one who could lie without blinking.

Melissa frowned but nodded.

"Good. Please be ready to leave at three. I'm afraid I will have to keep you a little late this afternoon, but I will drive you home after the meeting, okay?"

Again she nodded. Jarren got up and walked over to the door. Pulling it open, he waited. Slowly Melissa rose and walked out. She seemed deep in thought, but she turned just outside the door and spoke. "Do we meet back here at three o'clock?"

"I'll meet you in the reception area. I can debrief you on the way if you have any questions."

"Yes, sir, I'll be ready. I haven't quite finished organizing the files you gave me. If we're leaving the office early today, I won't be done until next week."

Jarren raised a brow. "I did not think you would be done that soon. Your timetable is fine. We can discuss the projects you're working on for me tomorrow morning."

"I should finalize your travel. I don't know what happened to the copy I brought around yesterday, but I'll e-mail you the itinerary."

"That's fine. I'll take a look at it and let you know."

Melissa nodded and left. Jarren closed the door and stood still for a moment. He was digging himself into a deep hole. He'd just fabricated a meeting to get Melissa to his jumper. She only had to call Jim and accidentally mention the meeting for his cover to be blown. And then what? Would she report him to the local law enforcement? Would she tell Jim that Jarren had sexually harassed her in the workplace?

Would she just disappear? The last thought sent Jarren into a mild panic. He couldn't let that happen.

Pushing the small button in his transmitter, he forwarded instructions to the jumper. Within minutes he was able to monitor every call through Melissa's office and cell phone. The rest of the morning he spent listening to her conversations with the travel agent, Stacy, Jane, Jim's contacts, Melissa's mother, and "Miguel," whom Jarren guessed was her cousin. His humor reminded Jarren a lot of Marcus. Jim phoned Melissa once in the early afternoon, but Jarren disconnected the call. Dialing Jim to "check in," Jarren took a message for her. She would get the message after she heard Jarren out on the way to Barnesville. Jim would just have to do without his assistant for one day.

*   *   *   *   *

JARREN NAVIGATED HIS car west on Interstate 70. Melissa sat next to him, silent.

Here was the opportunity he'd lied and manipulated to get, and now he just drove, the strained quiet only interrupted by his car gears shifting. Jarren cleared his throat. "Melissa."

She looked over at him. He noticed her tense fingers grasp the purse in her lap. "I know the past few days have been stressful for you. It is unfortunate that I caused the stress and that you've been given the job of assisting me."

She shook her head. "Where is this going, Dr. Graf?"

"I still need to speak to you about what happened last night," Jarren replied slowly. He could see her shoulders tense and smell the tang of her nervousness.

"I don't understand why. I've already told you I don't remember what happened."

"Just listen then. It is necessary that we be on the same page, as they say, about what happened."

With an audible huff, Melissa looked forward again. Moments passed before her shoulders relaxed. "I'm listening."

Jarren nodded. He wished he could laugh at the challenge of the coming conversation. Time to convince Melissa that aliens were real and that she was caught up in an intergalactic political war. Discussing their powerful attraction to each other would have to come later. It would be a relief when he could finally explain the instinctive desire that he knew could bind them together, but what he was about to tell her would be unbelievable enough. He had, unfortunately, little time to persuade her of his honesty.

"Last night, after we kissed, you left the office and were attacked by a man in the alley. You remember this?"

She nodded.

"But you don't remember what the man looked like. You don't remember because whenever you looked at him, your eyes seemed to blur." Slowly, Melissa nodded. She glanced at him out of the corners of her eyes, and Jarren noticed the slightest sparkle of fear in her blue irises.

"And then I came and hurt him and did something to him. And he changed. Do you remember, Melissa?"

She turned to stare out of the window, her face an anxious reflection in the tinted glass. "I don't want to talk about this. Why aren't we talking about the meeting this afternoon? I don't even know who you're meeting with."

Jarren remained silent a few heartbeats. "We need to discuss what happened before we arrive. The man who attacked you last night…I changed him, and you saw it, didn't you?"

With a disgruntled breath, Melissa turned to him, tears in her eyes. "I saw something, okay? I don't know what happened last night, but I did see something. I've been scared ever since. Scared of him and scared of you. What did you… Why… why are we talking about this?" A tear slid down her face. She twisted away again and huddled closer to the car door.

Jarren wanted to pull over and comfort her, tell her that she had nothing to fear from him, that he would protect her from those who might hurt her. But she wouldn't believe anything he said without proof. "I'm not trying to frighten you, Melissa. I'm doing a horrible job explaining what is going on."

Her voice rose an octave. "What is going on? What do you mean 'what is going on'?"

Jarren glanced at his watch and took the exit for Barnesville. They were less than fifteen minutes away, heading down a dirt road in the middle of nowhere. There was no better place to tell her the truth. She had no place to go.

Jarren pulled over and turned off the car. "Melissa." He reached out to console her, but she jerked away.

"Don't touch me. I know something isn't right, here. Something isn't right with this entire situation. Who are you?"

"The correct question to ask, Melissa, is *what* am I? You know something isn't right because you saw me turn your attacker into a canine last night. You're lying about not remembering. I know you are scared, but I promise you have nothing to fear from me. I would never hurt you, and I would never let anyone else hurt you either."

Melissa trembled. Her hands fumbled unsuccessfully with her door lock. Instinctively, Jarren reached out again. "Please don't run. I won't hurt you." Her breathing became haggard. Jarren placed a calm palm on her chest. She was going to hyperventilate. Touching her only seemed to exacerbate her reaction.

With a jerk, Melissa let out a terrified yelp, balled up her fist, and punched him in the face. The force repelled him back into his seat. "Don't put your hands on me! You're crazy. I thought I was the insane one. With everything that happened last night, I thought I'd lost it, you know? It was the pressure of having to work with you and then my unconscionable behavior before I ran out that had gotten to me. I thought I had cracked." Her bravado seemed stronger as she forced out a breath. "But it isn't me, is it? I don't know what you've been giving me or how, but I know you're responsible for my behavior and for my hallucination in the alley."

There was no use answering. Sullen, Jarren rubbed the ache in his jaw then started the car and continued toward his house. She wouldn't believe what he was going to tell her. She would need proof, and she would need it before she heard him out. "I am not human, Melissa. I was born in another quadrant of galaxies, on the planet Lynta. I was forced to leave my planet.

"My father was Lynta's ruler until he died a Terran moon cycle ago. At my father's death, my cousin challenged me for the right to rule. As is Lyntan custom, it is his right to claim heirship to the throne. I invited him to stay at the palace until our Ceremony of Judgment. But he planned and executed a palace coup. I barely escaped with my life. I came to Earth to give myself time to come up with a viable plan for reclaiming my throne."

Melissa looked at him in awe. "You really are crazy. I would almost feel sorry for you except I am sitting in your car in the middle of nowhere, and as far as I know, no one knows where we are." Her lips curled humorously, but her voice trembled. He could tell she was only half joking about the danger she felt she was in.

"You've no reason to believe that I won't hurt you. That I am what I say I am. But you *must* believe me, Melissa. I can't protect you if you don't trust me."

"From what do I need to be protected?" Her gaze settled on the house as he drove down another dirt road, pulled into the circular driveway, and stopped.

Jarren rested his hands on the smooth steering wheel. "The man who attacked you last night was looking for me. And he wasn't here alone, either."

"So let me get this straight. You're an alien from another planet who goes around kissing innocent women while being intergalactically chased by beasts which can magically change into dogs. And I got in the middle of it. Does that about sum it up? Have I missed anything?" She whipped her head around, her hair framing her angry face like black fire. Her caustic tone was unmistakable.

"I know it seems ridiculous, but it's true, and I will show you proof."

"Whatever. Let's just get this meeting over with and get back to the office." She managed to unlock the door this time and stepped out of the car. Slamming the door behind her, she stood impatient. She crossed her arms and avoided his gaze.

Jarren got out and slowly walked around to face her. "There isn't any meeting, Melissa." His voice was a whisper on the breeze. "Please, let me show you the proof you need to believe." He needed to gain her trust, but he'd lied to her to get her there. Without an olfactory influence, he expected too much. Jarren pressed his Subduer clasp and allowed his body to produce a little of his essence. He stepped close. "Please," he said again.

She breathed in then nodded. Touching the Subduer again, he raised the masking scent a fraction to cover what might have been lost on the wind. "I won't go inside with you. You have to bring it out," she stated.

He clasped her arm lightly and guided her around to the back of the house. The low-cut grass padded their steps. The property wasn't enclosed by a fence. It sat three and a half acres off a one-lane dirt road that wound through the back roads. Open grassland ran the distance between dry road and house, only stopping to curve around a solitary tree growing in the vastness. Nearer the house, trees lined the dirt path that led up to a circular asphalt driveway. The smooth blacktop was oddly stately in an otherwise underdeveloped patch of farmland. In the distance, a cow mooed.

Jarren appreciated the quiet of the location. It was nothing like the southern region of Lynta, from which he'd escaped and where he'd spent most of his youth. The southern region was a mesh of small forests, deep woods overgrown with bramble and foliage, and underground waterways leading to small waterfalls and lakes. Among the vast green canvas lay booming urban cities.

His occasional trips to the northern territories had been geological wonders with causeways full of golden stalks of grain, lazy breezes whistling past the small scattering of trees, and that solitary domesticated animal grazing in the lazy afternoon heat.

Jarren's heart beat a little faster as he pushed down yearnings to go home. He looked at Melissa walking silently next to him, regret crinkling his brow. The Alliance had not come close to mobilizing enough to deal with Milovar, and Jarren was too close to being pinpointed to chance an off-world expedition. One day he would show her his world. For now, he just needed to convince her that what he told her was true.

"Over here," he murmured. He turned them into a shade of clustered trees thirty paces from the back of the house. Putting his hand to his ear, he accessed his transmitter and projected his voice so Melissa could hear him.

"Unit de-cloak." The air around them sweltered then shimmered like a mirage through the desert heat. Melissa put her arm up to cover her face, but Jarren brought it down again. She needed to see with her own eyes that the ship existed and had manifested out of thin air.

The area shaded by trees darkened, smothering the speckles of light that leaked through the overhanging leaves. Then the darkness took on a solid shape, like the ovular controller he'd used to trans Melissa's attacker, only thousands of times larger and black. When his jumper was completely visible again, resting under the cover of the trees, Jarren walked Melissa forward.

She reached out and touched the jumper's side. Finally, its surface beneath her fingers, she turned to him. Her mouth curved into an O, and Melissa promptly fainted. Jarren grabbed her before she fell and lifted her, speaking as he held her close.

"Unit cloak."

Without looking back, Jarren made his way across the lawn, up the back steps that set him on a wraparound porch, and then swiftly to the back door. Behind him he heard the hum of his ship re-cloaking. Reaching into his pocket, he pulled out the house keys and went in, his goal regrettably accomplished. Jarren kicked the door shut behind him, Melissa still unconscious in his arms.

CHAPTER 9

LISSA STRUGGLED THROUGH a haze of semi-awareness and opened her eyes. Afternoon light streamed through the windows on the other side of the room. She lay on an antique Victorian country chaise, the faded pink floral print not at all a comfort to her. Sitting up, she looked around.

The room was furnished as only her aunt Willy could have imagined it. Lace decorated every surface. A maple coffee table with lace coasters ran parallel to the couch. A Queen Victoria armchair with matching floral upholstery stood across from her.

Matching window shams and drapes with white lace tassels shifted lazily in an afternoon breeze that smelled of wildflowers. A smattering of small oriental rugs over glossed wood disrupted the dark floor beneath her. On top of a small credenza in one corner lay an old wooden-handled iron, an apothecary, and a small white cardboard box marked "sewing" on the side. Lissa could see through to the kitchen and a white door that she imagined led outside.

She heard a footstep to her right. At a darkened double door entryway leading into the room she lay in, she barely made out Jarren in the shadows. He leaned on the doorframe, his arms crossed. She didn't feel threatened, but a shiver went down her spine anyway. He straightened and walked out of the dark.

"You're feeling better?" His voice resonated as he approached.

Was she? "Yes. I...I just don't know what happened." Lissa shook her head and looked down at her hands. He walked around the coffee table to occupy the chair across from her.

"You fainted. Outside. Do you remember why?" Jarren's chocolate fragrance floated over to Lissa. It was oddly comforting. He leaned toward her, his hazel gaze penetrating.

Lissa rubbed her forehead and concentrated on the elusive memory. Fatigue still weighed on her. "I...I remember standing outside with you. You were holding my arm, and—" Lissa's throat closed around her words. The ship. Her pulse began to race as she leaned away from Jarren's impassive expression.

"Oh my God. What the hell's going on here?"

"I told you the truth, Melissa. I am not human. I needed to bring you here to prove that to you. And..." He paused and stared at her as reality and acceptance eased the pressure building in her head. "You believe me now, don't you? I can see you do."

Her head shook no, but questions escaped. "Why me? Did you search me out? What do you want from me?" His gaze traveled the length of her body, beginning from her head, pausing at the slope of her breasts, and lingering at the dip in her skirt where the fabric rested between her thighs. Lissa's body warmed in response even as her anger increased. How could she want him when the thought of him made her furious? It was like…like he controlled her somehow.

She stood and moved away until the couch lay between them. "You want sex, and whatever it is that makes you not human must be the reason I seem to hate and want you. I suppose your alien physiology, or whatever you call it, helps you hook the ladies?" Her limbs shook with fear. Her head ached with fury. For a moment, she couldn't decide which emotion was stronger. Then anger won out.

She pointed a quivering finger at Jarren. "My father once told me, 'They'll pretend they respect you, Melissa, but they won't. You have to be perfect, or the man who might have found you worthy of love will only know your imperfections and be tempted to exploit them. And when he is done, you'll be right back where you were before he got his hands on you—or worse, you'll have a child to care for.' He was right." Lissa ran a hand through her hair. "I promised myself never again."

Marching back and forth, deliberately keeping the couch as a barrier between them, she gulped in air. "I thought all men were users until I met Jim. He respected me, valued me, was there for me when I needed him. He would do all he could for me because that's the kind of person he is. And I'd do the same for him." Lissa's tirade ended. Her heart pounded in her chest, and she breathed slowly, trying to calm down. Her fingertips tingled where she'd been abrading them across the top of the chaise.

Blinking tears from her eyes, Lissa looked down to gather herself. Papa would have "tsked" his disapproval. She needed to scream, but momentary calm won out. "So, you want a good tumble."

Lissa remembered the kiss and the connection she thought they'd felt…but he wasn't human. Not human! What world was this? She didn't trust that her emotions, her desire for him, were her own. Maybe he had even affected her behavior. She'd certainly lost control when she kissed him in the office.

Jarren approached, his shirt unbuttoned at the top, his tan slacks rustling with each step, viscerally male. "I will not deny I want you. You have provoked my desire more than any other possible mate. I think about you at all times. I ache to touch you, to bring you close to me and kiss you so thoroughly you forget the world around us." He stepped around the coffee table.

Lissa backed up. Her heart slammed against her chest. "Don't you come near me, whoever or whatever you are!" Her fear lurched forward.

"Melissa, if you would please just listen. I do desire you, but I would never hurt you." He held up his hands tentatively.

"Right. You would never hurt me, but you kidnap me and cart me off to an empty house in the middle of nowhere. I *know* you did something to me. You put something in my food or my drink to make me want you. Were you going to do it again after you got me here?"

"I swear I did not intend to coerce you into making love. I brought you here to convince you of the danger we're in."

Lissa's hands trembled. In the recesses of her mind, she knew she was close to a breakdown. Lousy time for that to happen. "That's bullshit. Human or not, you're just like any other white-collar exec. You'll get what you want, even if you have to drug me or lie to me to do it."

In the blink of an eye, Jarren was next to her, his hand squeezing her arm.

His face contorted as he ground out words between clenched teeth and leaned close. "I did nothing to you. I lied about *what* I was, and I lied about the meeting this afternoon, but only to explain things. Nothing else. What overtook you when we stood in the hall was not a drug. It was my uninhibited scent, my essence. I will not and cannot accept full responsibility for the power of your response. You wanted me as much as I wanted you, and that truth is yours to own or deny." He pulled her close and pressed his grip on her, sending trembles down her spine. His eyes gleamed intensely.

Lissa shook her head and tried to pull away. Her hair tossed about her in a confused tangle. Then his hands cupped her face, stilling her movements, and she looked into his fierce gaze. "This is all I did, Melissa."

Lissa began to respond, but her nose, her throat, her lungs were suddenly assaulted with flavor. A powerful musk penetrated the pores of her skin and wafted close to embrace her. She might have taken a gulp of the freshest spring water. Every thought she'd nurtured disappeared, replaced by primitive need. Desire became an instinctive driving force.

Jarren's mouth came down on hers, and Lissa melted into his arms. She drew breath from him, pressed against him, pulled up his shirt to feel his warm, hard chest against her hands. His lips left hers to travel down her neck, dipping into the V of her blouse. His fingers undid the little pearl buttons.

Lissa groaned. Her hands skimmed over his torso again, and she pulled impatiently at his shirt. The buttons that did not slip loose popped. When the material hung open, she stared with yearning at the sun-kissed smoothness of his muscular chest.

"You will belong to me, and I to you," Jarren growled. He sank to his knees in front of her and began nipping at the skin on her stomach. Lissa put her head back and reached for him. Her fingers threaded through his thick hair as his scent's potent energy enveloped her.

With an anguished moan, he stood and pulled her around to the front of the chaise. He pressed her onto it and himself onto her, his body warming hers. His large hands clasped the sides of her face as he stared at her. Then his lips returned to hers, blazing a trail of hot need from her mouth to her shoulders. He reached one hand under her skirt and slid it up her inner thigh. The other moved beneath her back, working until her lace bra slipped off. He buried his face in the valley between her breasts. Lissa's back arched up, waves of pleasure washing over her, as his hands encircled her waist to bring her navel to his lips.

Pulling up her skirt and slipping a finger into the band of her panties, Jarren spoke gruffly. "You care for Jim so much. But why? He is unviable; he does not match your scent. You have not slept with him. I don't even smell him on you." His voice broke as he continued. "It was his mistake to love you but not claim you. I have wanted you from the moment you neared me in the coffee shop. Biology drives our desires. Not love. That is why our bond is special. Love can be controlled or overcome, but biology connects us; it can't be ignored, and it will never go away."

He leaned near, breathing her in. "Your essence entrances me, Melissa. I fought the urge to possess you and take what is so obviously mine. But no more. You will give yourself to me, and I will make you forget all others." He sounded at once both triumphant and frantic.

What was she doing? Lissa scrambled away from him. She was in Jarren's house, five seconds away from making love to him. He was speaking as if she were his possession. And Jim. Unviable? He thought she and Jim were lovers? Jim, her lover. Jarren, an alien. Lissa had no self-control.

Shoving at him and stumbling off the couch, Lissa stood and jerked her shirt together, fumbling to re-button it. She kept her gaze on him. Her skirt fell back in place. He lay where she'd abandoned him on the couch. "No," she said. "I won't do this."

He sat up and held out a hand to her. "Melissa."

Shaking her head again, she stepped back. She could smell him, his tantalizing sweetness; the smell was driving comprehension from her head. "No." She inched toward the kitchen exit, then swiveling, she made a dash for the door, turned the knob, and pulled. Surprise pushed her forward as the door opened with ease. Lissa ran out onto the porch and skidded down the steps. Her footfalls battered against the groaning wood then she paused in the afternoon sunshine. She heard Jarren at her back. The wide expanse of grassland spread out before her. She ran.

Lissa got thirty feet from the house before the ground next to her exploded. She jerked her hands up to protect herself as hard debris shot into the air and the booming sound of two objects impacting reverberated in her ears. Screaming, she ducked down. Her shoes skidded on grass and dirt. Someone was shooting at her, and she had no idea which way to run. Another boom and rumble landed near her left side. Her heart pounded in her chest. Chaos surrounded her, and Lissa waited for the next blast to hit her.

Sudden silence assaulted her ears as potently as a horn sounding in the night. Without looking back, she ran again, her legs pushing her up to the crest of a small hump in the land, and Lissa looked forward. The word "go" whispered in her head.

Lissa took two steps and then stopped horrified as she spied the familiar distorted image of a man angled her direction. Like the man the night before, he stalked toward Lissa, his thick, dark shape hazy to her eyes. Yet, he was obviously intent on reaching her. Lissa's body froze again, and she let out another scream as he pointed a familiar oblong object at her.

*   *   *   *   *

JARREN HEARD THE high-pitched laser fire blast from the porch before he saw the ground near Melissa explode. "Unit!" He jumped the steps and took off after her. Concentrating on her retreating figure, he pushed himself to run faster.

"Command," his earpiece prompted. Jarren couldn't respond yet. His chest burned as he bolted forward. He puffed and tensed his muscles to run faster.

Three more feet. Another explosion of dirt too close to her for his comfort. Lissa stood at the pinnacle of a hillslope, still as a statue. Then she screamed again. "Command?" Unit prompted again.

He still didn't answer. He had to have her in his arms before he could get them both away. Jarren reached into his pocket and pulled out his transer, a duplicate to the one he'd destroyed in the alley. There was no reason to try and hide his presence on Earth now. They knew he was there.

"Command?" Unit blipped in his ear once more. Jarren reached out, grabbed Lissa, and yanked her into his arms. The bounty hunter approached, its dark, shifting mass plodding toward them. Jarren forced Lissa behind him, aimed his transer at the hunter, and fired.

"Unit, emergency transport!" he yelled. Pressing Lissa to himself, he tucked her head into the crook of his shoulder. He covered her face with one hand and shut his eyes. A throbbing hum sounded in his ears, and he saw the bright flash of light even through his closed eyelids as they dematerialized then rematerialized within the small space. As the light dissipated, Jarren squinted at the dim interior of the jumper's front cabin. Lissa remained safely enclosed in his arms.

CHAPTER *10*

BLINKING TO CLEAR her blurry eyes, Lissa felt Jarren's grip on her elbow, leading her then lowering her into a soft cushioned seat. Jarren's hazy face came into view as he squatted near her. He squinted thoughtfully, then reached out and touched her leg.

"Rest a moment. The blurriness will go away. The first time transporting can be very hard on the body." He rubbed her arm and stood. "I've got to get us out of here. I'll be back in a moment, and then we can talk."

Lissa nodded and blinked again to sharpen her vision. In her mind, there was a burst of fear. Lissa tamped down the response as her street defense teacher taught her. To protect herself, she had to be thoughtful, not instinctive. She made out Jarren's features in the dim light, but her eyes still wouldn't focus quickly. With a stuttering sigh, she leaned back. She closed her eyes and waited for Jarren's return as the last jitters of adrenaline seeped from her body.

Anxiety ran through her as revolving thoughts surfaced in the quiet. Whether he'd intended it or not, Jarren controlled her now. He knew where they were, who was chasing them, and why. All Lissa understood was that something had tried to kill her. She rubbed the inexplicable coldness from her arms as her shivers increased, and she tried again to tamp the feeling down.

Lissa had never been good at helpless. She needed to see. *Deep breath. Think!* Leaning forward, she narrowed her eyes, concentrating her blurred vision on the wall. Slowly, the wall came into focus, and her surroundings gained clarity. Another couple of deep breaths and her heart rate slowed. Her gaze slid around the silent, low-lit cabin.

Turning, Lissa looked out through a porthole, searching for the man who'd tried to kill her. Outside, the sun still shone. The trees swayed with a lazy breeze. She could almost imagine she'd dreamed the attack. Almost. As her gaze wavered, a drug-like sleepiness overtook her. Her eyelids drooped, and she leaned back into the coziness of the chair.

"Melissa, don't sleep yet, alright?" Jarren's voice reverberated as he returned.

She looked up and frowned. She was exhausted. She only wanted to close her eyes a moment. "I'm only resting."

"You are tired from transport. You mustn't rest. We need to figure out what to do now."

Lissa sighed and looked out again. Her eyes caught a familiar shadow moving yards from the ship, and panic set in. With a gasp, she scrambled to rise. Those remnants of past memories dissolved. A warm hand came to rest on her shoulder.

"You are safe," said Jarren. "He can't see us, but we *have* to leave. We're running out of time, and we need to figure out where to go. Do you understand what's going on?"

Lissa pulled her gaze from the porthole to focus on him. It took a minute for his words to sink in. "Go? What do you mean, go?" She looked back through the small oval window. Outside, the dark shadow stood unnaturally still, only feet from their location.

"We can't stay here. I have to move the ship. He can't see or sense us, but he understands a jumper's transport capabilities are extremely limited. As soon as he reports, his orbiting ship will scan the vicinity. They'll locate us. My shields won't hold against any substantial attack. We have to leave."

Lissa dragged her focus away from their attacker again. Jarren sat across from her, his face reflecting concern. She gathered her thoughts. "You can stop looking at me with the expectation I'll faint again. I'm overwhelmed, scared shitless—excuse my bluntness—and couldn't offer you any conversation above a fourth-grade level, but I haven't completely lost it. We should go. Okay. What do you need me to do other than not sleep?"

"I don't think you understand the situation we're in. It's not that we can't stay here behind my house." He held up his hand as she opened her mouth to respond. "We cannot stay on this planet."

Her chest clinched as her heart began banging against her ribs. They couldn't stay on Earth? A nervous snort escaped as she shrugged with a nonchalance she didn't feel. "Okay. Well, just drop me off at the nearest Earth spaceport, and I will gladly pretend I've never heard of Dr. Jarren Graf. If that's even your name."

Jarren shook his head as he frowned. "Melissa, I cannot 'drop you off.' Your life is in danger now. They'll track you down and kill you."

Her head throbbed as she absorbed his words, her heart beating faster as time ticked by. "I don't understand. Why would they be trying to kill me? Before I met you, I dreamed of space travel, but I didn't believe in aliens."

He looked away. He knew something. Lissa reached out and grabbed his arm. "What did you do to me?" She fought to keep her voice even.

"They are following my scent. You are now wearing my scent. They will follow you to get to me."

"Fine. Then point me to the showers. I'll have a good wash then be out of your hair," she joked through her disgust. What could she tell Jim to make Jarren Graf disappear? Lissa struggled up and looked down at him. "Come on, Greater Being. Don't you even know where the showers are? Maybe they're behind door number one." She'd begun to babble. Turning, she walked toward what appeared to be a door as Jarren grabbed her hand.

Lissa snatched her hand away with a hard glare. Her anger boiled to the surface, urged on by the tense silence of impending doom. She hoped to hear him deny the implications of what he'd said. She waited to hear him say he would take her home. Reassurance was not forthcoming.

"I'm sorry, Melissa. I can't let you go. You can't wash off my scent, so letting you leave would be the same as killing you. I will protect you with my life, but I can't release you."

Her eyes narrowed in disbelief. "*Can't* let me go, or *won't?* How do I know you're telling the truth?"

He crossed his arms and stared down at her, stoic. "They attacked you twice before I even showed up. They're looking for me. They identify you as someone close to me. I am truly sorry for involving you. I would never have revealed my scent if I'd known they were *this* close to locating me." He seemed so sure, so matter-of-fact.

The jitters inside her stilled at the implications of his words. "You knew. You knew revealing your scent would mark me. When did you do it? Have I been walking around with your scent for two days? My friends. My coworkers. They've all been around you and me. What about my family, my mother, my—" A terrifying thought forced her breath to catch in her throat. "My daughter! She's in danger!" Lissa ran at him, arms flailing. "Let me out of here right now. I have to get to my daughter!" Her hands pounded against his chest. The air stuttered out of her lungs. Jarren didn't offer any resistance.

Halting and breathing hard, she stepped back and turned angry eyes at him. "Let me out."

Jarren shook his head. "I can't."

She slapped his face. A flare of pink appeared on his cheek. He didn't flinch.

"Let me out, damn it!"

"I can't, Melissa." He stepped close, but she shoved against him and strode toward a sealed entry. She'd raised her fist to bang on the door when Jarren grabbed her and pulled her around to face him.

"He's still out there. The minute he senses you, he'll kill you. Listen to me! I promise. You are the only one in danger of being killed. No one else is marked but you."

"I don't believe you." Lissa shook her head.

"I swear to you. Your daughter is safe, as are your mother and cousin."

"And how can I believe you? Apparently you thought I was safe as well…then those things tried to kill me twice. Did you know I was in danger last night when you left me at my mother's house?"

"I knew, but I watched over you all night and covered my scent there."

"You're a liar. If you can cover your scent or essence or whatever, then there's no reason for me to stay with you. Just cover your scent on me."

He shook his head and reached out hesitantly. "You've had too much exposure to me. I can't cover my scent on you again."

Lissa's world crumbled in on her. Her life, her job, everything that she'd worked for, was dissipating into a mist of freakish dreams. And at the source of her chaos and bitter anger stood Jarren. Lissa jerked away. "Bastard! You must love your hold over me. You could have left me alone. If you'd stayed away, I would be home with my daughter right now."

He took a moment to respond. "I'm sorry it turned out this way."

"I bet. You're sorry you dragged me out here? You're sorry you involved me? Right. You wanted to make sure I understood the situation we're in. Well, now I get it. We've got to leave, right?" Her voice oozed with disgust, and she tried to temper the violence she felt. He was the reason her life had been turned upside down. "I'm not leaving without my daughter. You can move this contraption to where my daughter is."

He shook his head. "I told you; your daughter is safe. But the bounty hunters have traced us to the vicinity. They could follow our trail from here. It could be hazardous to get your daughter now."

"If they know where we are, why aren't we dust particles?"

Jarren cast a distracted glance out the porthole. There was a hint of sour humor in his voice when he replied. "Yes. Bounty hunters aren't the most intelligent species of hunter there is, though even they must have the right to move among the galaxies."

She was too frustrated to understand that statement. "You will take me to get my daughter, or I *swear* I will try to break out of here every time your back is turned until she's with me."

Lissa whirled away, trying to force her thinking beyond her hatred of losing control.

"Melissa, please listen to me. She is safer apart from us."

She met his eyes, unwavering. "Can you guarantee her safety?"

He paused then shook his head again as he looked down.

"Then we will go and get my daughter, or so help me, I will make you pay," Lissa spat out. Blinking back irate tears, she turned away to reclaim her seat and stare silently out the window. She couldn't think straight. She was caught in a nightmare with no way to awaken.

"Okay. We will get your daughter. But you must follow every direction I give when we extract her. Your mother's life is threatened every second she's exposed to us. We must minimize our time there."

"Well, then we'll just have to bring her too."

"We cannot take your mother with us." Jarren's voice was strained.

"There's always an excuse. Let's hear it. What reason is there to leave my mother behind in harm's way?" Her voice broke.

"She simply will not survive the trip. Her heart isn't strong enough."

"So Miguel obviously wouldn't survive. His mind has always been the strongest part of his body."

He shook his head. "Not in my jumper."

Lissa glared at Jarren once more. "There's nothing wrong with her heart. You haven't even met her. How could you know what health problems she has?"

"I scanned her, you, and Jasmine when I took you home. Your medical technology hasn't advanced far enough to catch her complication so early. Nor would it need to. Her heart is only a problem regarding space flight. The g-force needed to escape Earth's gravitational pull would stop her heart." Jarren sighed. "She must stay, Melissa. If you love her, you won't endanger her without reason."

"But she's already in danger," Lissa snapped. Her chest tightened as tears filled her eyes.

"I adamantly swear your mother has not been exposed to my scent. And I adamantly swear as surely, she won't survive the journey."

Merciless, incomprehensible thoughts screamed in her head. Her breathing quickened as Lissa fought to think straight, to push down the feeling of drowning. Another step and Lissa would be out of the sane world. It was too much at once. She had to get control. She closed her eyes and thought of the dark. She thought of quiet until she had it.

Emotionless acceptance flowed over her. Her voice rang out, deceptively neutral. "So it's the lesser of two evils. Fine. We'll get my daughter, and you will make sure every precaution is taken to protect my mother here."

"I swear."

Lissa nodded without looking at him. She couldn't bring herself to say anything else.

"I am going to move the ship now. I'll let you know when it is time to get Jasmine. Everything will be fine."

His words rang hollow. Cold dread settled into her chest. Lissa felt nothing beyond the anger. She would get her daughter. She would go with him until she knew she was safe. And then she would escape. Lissa's temper boiled. His own sense of invincibility and his right to decide everything disgusted her! She prayed to God he would be hurt while protecting her and unable to follow. Pain went a long way to teaching humility. She had learned that personally.

*　*　*　*　*

JARREN GLANCED AT Melissa another moment, worried, then headed back to the pilot's deck. The vitality and fire to which he'd grown accustomed from her was gone, replaced by icy indifference. He deserved it. He should have known she would respond furiously to the danger he'd put her in. He would have responded just as vehemently. Jarren closed the door behind him, sat down, and jammed his finger on the recording button for a flash communication. Self-hate bored into his gut, but he would act. His encoded message to Marcus would have to be short and to the point. The longer the flash, the more likely his message would be intercepted.

Jarren pushed the record button on the module before him. "Marcus—Ter sector—five hours—crisis—head vector 282 and 537. Out." He looked down at his watch. Only five hours to get Jasmine, cover his scent traces around Melissa's mother's house, and get them to the coordinates he'd given Marcus. He only hoped Marcus would get the communication flash in time, if at all. There was no way to know how far to shoot the flash, and the farther it went, the more likely another could decode it. He'd send it out as far as he dared.

"Unit, maintain cloak," Jarren stated as he grasped the stick and eased the jumper off the ground. It wouldn't take him more than five minutes to get back to Baltimore normally, but Jarren ran the jumper at one-quarter speed. He needed time to figure out how to pacify Melissa. She was angry, but she needed him. She would have a great deal of adjusting to do. He was as responsible for her now as he was for the lives of every Lyntan citizen.

"Unit autopilot...vector 259 and 503. Shields at one hundred percent. Confirm," Jarren stated, easing his hand off of the pilot's stick as it adjusted its angle on its own.

"Confirmed, Captain."

Jarren rose and walked back to the forward cabin. It didn't look like Melissa had moved once while he prepared for takeoff. She still stared out the porthole, unblinking. The position he'd put her in was unforgivable—and he'd done it all for no reason other than his own desire.

Jarren scowled. He was no great leader for his people. He hadn't put the needs of the many above his own. Maybe Milovar had succeeded in taking the scepter because the gods judged Jarren unworthy of ruling. Not maybe—the truth struck him squarely in the stomach. His unsuitability had haunted the back of his mind since he'd bid his mother goodbye. Guilt floored him again.

Yet Jarren had no time to wallow. The need to protect Lissa overcame all other emotions. They had to plan in order to avoid immediate danger. Sitting opposite her, Jarren spoke. "We are on our way to your mother's house. When we get there, I won't be able to land. We will need to transport down and up. I'll make sure you get inside the house, then cover any traces I find of us outside. You should get Jasmine and say your goodbyes."

"And you covering our scents is how my mother will be protected?" She didn't look at him when she spoke, keeping her eyes on the blur of building tops and streets shifting by outside.

"Your mother carries no scent of me, Melissa. Lyntan scent does not work that way. My word to the gods, if I thought she was in danger, I'd find another way to protect her."

Finally she turned to him, her gaze dull. "So she will be alive. But will I ever see her again, or might she just as well be dead?" Her pained voice tore at his insides.

"I swear I will bring you back. I know I've turned your life upside down. I will repay that debt."

"The only thing I want is to be able to go back to my life and find it the way it was before you entered it." She stared out of the window again. "I really loved my job. That's gone now."

Jarren was dismissed. His heart hurt as he turned away. Back at the pilot's deck, Jarren watched as the jumper descended over Baltimore and slowed to a stop above the Reyes' townhouse. As much as he wanted to give Melissa more time to accept their situation, he knew even the jumper's slow speed probably had not hidden their energy trail from a ship scanning the surface.

She stood passively waiting for him when he reentered the cabin. "Time to go," he said. "It will not be nearly as hard recuperating from transport this time. Give yourself a minute to take a few deep breaths before you ring the doorbell."

"You're putting us at the front door?"

"The less your mother is aware of, the better off we'll be. As far as she knows, I require your assistance on a business trip. We'll need to come up with a story for your disappearance from work, but we can think of something later. Now, when we get back, I'll give Jasmine a sleeping agent to help her transport recuperation time. She is young, she'll be fine, but it will take a toll on her body. There's nothing for it but rest."

Jarren held out his arms, and Melissa stepped forward. He held her close. At least she hadn't hesitated. "Where do we go then? I can't imagine we'll stay hovering over my mother's house." Her monotone was so unlike her previous animated responses.

"No. I will pilot the jumper into the harbor. Water distorts our energy signal, and if I really need to, I can send the jumper under the waves and even under the seabed to hide. They can't track us below the sediment but withstanding that amount of pressure on the hull will drain my power reserves far too quickly. That's our last option."

Melissa nodded and leaned her head on his chest.

"Close your eyes," he said. "Do not open them until I say it's okay," Jarren stated as he covered her face again and hugged her pliant form to him. "Are you ready?"

She sighed. "Yes."

"Unit, transport. Lateral surface."

"Confirmed," Unit beeped in his ear as he closed his eyes. A moment later, they stood at Brenda Reyes's front door.

Jarren noted shadows beneath Melissa's closed eyes. He'd put them there.

"You can open your eyes." His breath bothered the tendril of hair curling around her ear as he leaned close.

She blinked a bit, but her vision appeared to clear quickly as she stepped away from his embrace. In front of the door, she looked back at him expectantly.

Her voice pitched sharply. "Do I explain you, or do you want me to wait until you're out of sight before I ring? It won't take either of them more than a minute to answer." She didn't want to have to discuss the particulars of her and Jarren's relationship.

"Give me a second, and I am off. I'll be back in about fifteen minutes, but please spend as little time as possible outside. The wind carries your essence. I will be covering our scents. It is useless to work against each other."

"Can we meet you at the end of the block? My mother will watch until she can't see us anymore."

Jarren nodded. His mother also tracked his scent whenever he left her until there was no trace left. "At the end of the block. Bring only the few small things that hold sentimental value. Everything you will need will be available where we're going. The more I have to transport, the more dangerous transportation becomes."

Melissa turned away and stepped up to the front door. "I understand."

Jarren took the steps down three at a time and was at the end of the block in less than a minute. When he looked back at the house, Melissa had already entered. With a wary scan of the area, he began dispersing a covering scent into the environment, his thoughts sober. He would make sure Melissa was safe again, even if it took his last breath.

CHAPTER 11

JARREN SAT ALONE in the dark, his mind numb. They'd been hovering in the shallow harbor waters for three hours. The five-hour wait time Jarren's communication burst had indicated was nearly up. They were all still alive. That was something. He looked over at a side monitor where he'd brought up a view of Melissa—his Lissa—and Jasmine asleep in the jumper's sleeper cabin.

Jarren's heart tightened at the sight of them in his bed, his metallic blanket covering them as they curled up together. He wanted them both now: a life-mate and a daughter. He'd met Jasmine and instantly fallen in love with the curious little sprite.

"Are you the reason why Mommy has to take me away?" she asked as he met them at the corner of their block. As straightforward as her mother. Lissa shrugged when he looked at her.

He cleared his throat. "Well, we *are* going away for a short period of time. You will be the first girl in your class to go exploring in the Mines of Mira," Jarren replied as he knelt down and held out his hand. Jasmine shook it with confidence. He grinned in response. "Doesn't that sound like fun?"

"Mommy says we are going to visit the stars, but that it has to be our secret. So since I can't tell any of my friends 'cause it's a secret, and since I can't tell my classmates 'cause I don't start school till the fall, and since I never heard of no Mira Mines, I can't say whether it sounds fun or not, Mister Doctor."

Jarren fought to keep the smile from his face. He stood up and reached out to take the solitary brown leather case from Lissa's hand. "Point well taken, Jasmine. You are very bright. We shall have to wait and see if you have fun."

"Mommy says that all the time, wait and see. I always forget to. I'm gonna try real hard to remember to wait and see when we get into space. I think getting into space will be fun. But I don't like mines as much as stars."

Lissa interrupted. "We have to go now, Jasmine. When we get to the ship, you may ask Dr. Graf more questions." Jasmine nodded, a thoughtful look crinkling her face.

Jarren stepped close as Jasmine put her arms around her mother's waist. "Is it time to put the blinders on, Mommy?"

Jarren quirked a brow. Lissa opened her hand. A black ball of padded satin unfurled into a crinkled sleeping mask.

"She's five. I couldn't think of any other way to make sure her eyes stayed closed. She's far too inquisitive."

He smiled. "That was a very good idea."

Jasmine pulled the facemask over her eyes. Jarren took them under one arm, held the travel bag in the other, and checking to make sure that they weren't being observed, transported them up.

Following Lissa's instruction, Jarren indulged fifteen of Jasmine's questions and then gave the little girl an inhaler of sleeping agent. Lissa intended on only putting Jasmine in the bed, but Jarren had watched the viewing screen as she tried unsuccessfully to slip out of her daughter's grasp. Finally, Lissa gave up and lowered herself into a comfortable slumber. Jarren smiled, grateful. She needed the rest.

Later, Jarren entered to change his clothes, stepping lightly so they wouldn't awaken. Pulling on a tight black captain's shirt and black slacks, he stopped briefly and stared down at them. Lissa opened her eyes, sleepiness softening her face. Then she turned to lay her head next to her daughter's on the pillow.

That was an hour ago. They were both still curled up, and Jarren wanted nothing more than to climb in and sleep with them. Well, he could play family from where he was as well. It was the responsibility of every mate to protect and cherish his or her loved ones. Jarren would get them off-planet and to the safety of his ship. He could serve no better function than that right now.

"Captain, rendezvous in two minutes. Proceed to vector 282 and 537 half sub-light speed," Unit chimed.

"Acknowledged. Unit, set in corresponding course and proceed with caution," Jarren replied. He prayed luck would be with him again tonight. Bounty hunters could be their fiercest when they sensed cornered prey getting away. Jarren knew full well he was nearly cornered.

If all went according to plan, in ten minutes they would leave Earth for an unknown period of time. The guilt Jarren had ignored returned to chew at his insides. At least he no longer felt isolated from Lissa. He now sensed a more subdued anger. He could only hope she'd come to understand he'd taken her from Earth to protect her.

But why would she believe him? She knew he was attracted to her, that he believed they should be mated. If she didn't already know how highly Lyntans held the instinct that drove them to their mates, she would soon learn. And there would be no way to persuade her that he had taken her from Terra for her own safety, not his own selfish needs.

A pang of unease ran up his spine as he slid a hand through his hair. The gods. His selfishness *was* the cause of her danger. Even if he hadn't been the cause, he remembered his desperation when considering leaving Lissa on Earth. The thought of being away from her had pained him, caused nausea to settle in his stomach. He couldn't leave her. He wouldn't. If only he understood why he needed her so much.

Again, his mother's voice recalling the Lyntan myth of true life-mates flowed into his thoughts. In the background of that memory, he heard the burble of water flowing from the atrium's fountain. "This story is about the pain of loss, Jarren. It is also how some of our people were cast down in our hierarchy. Intelligent, moral, kind people like my mother and father. This story has become a weapon. Listen so that you understand its use," Celina had said.

"You see," she'd told him, "the young woman's gold-sandaled feet slowed on the dirt path as the goddess watched.

Her shoulders hunched forward, weighted down by untraceable pain as her story poured out. 'I was pregnant,' the woman said. 'For many months, I searched for my mate until I was too full with child to search further. A family gave me shelter in a cabin near the forest. I was some weeks' journey from here. With the family matriarch's help, I brought my daughter into the world. She was a beauty and a miracle, and I kept her by my side. I grew strong enough to leave those that cared for us and continue on my way with her.

"'But the night before I was to find my home and my mate, my sleep was unusually deep. When I awoke, my daughter was gone. I searched everywhere I could think of but found no sign of her. Finally, the matriarch insisted I halt my search. "I'm old and cherish time. Time is slipping away from you. Go and find your mate. For surely, what took you from him in the night also took your child," she said. I knew she spoke true. I left and have followed this path and these fields to find my mate and love. It is his family that causes these lands to grow as fruitful and beautiful as that which you see before you.'

"The goddess was moved to tears by the woman's sad story. She gathered in close, a gust of warm wind on the woman's face, and breathed in her scent. Within her fragrance she drew the subtle aroma of the woman's true mate. 'I will bring you your mate, dear lady, for you and he have been together so long his scent intermingles with your own. Stay you here and await the south wind. At dusk tomorrow, shall I place your true mate at the rise of the next knob with the celadon sunset.'

"The goddess had begun to depart when the woman called out into the empty silence. 'Goddess, if you can smell my mate and bring him to me, can you not also bring my child?'

"The goddess surrounded the woman again, a strong swirling gust that stirred up the dirt at her feet. Then the particles abruptly settled. When the goddess spoke again, her voice was sad, soft. 'For your mate, I sense his essence. For your child, there is naught. Her scent has no connection to your own. I cannot trace her. Wait here, lady. I may at least deliver your mate to you.'"

All Lyntans citizens knew those considered "Of the Family" were descended from the lost woman. Below in the caste, "Beside the Family," were Lyntans descended from the forest matriarch's family. Most other Lyntans were "Below the Family." Few were even deemed unviable. This system of the powerful and those who served had ensured peace for millennia.

Jarren's gaze slid once more to Lissa and Jasmine's sleeping figures. A child. The urge to have a family with Lissa, to make children with her, burned painfully inside him. And Lissa and Jasmine would be deemed below the family at best just like Jarren's grandparents. Without royal dispensation, Jasmine would never be allowed to fly a ship and live on the mother planet. Perhaps, she would be gifted with a service position on a ship—restricted to cooking or cleaning but never anything academically challenging. It boiled his blood. And it had to end.

He looked away. Jarren was stuck within a hexagon prison. His world would strip Lissa of her internal fire; her dignity. This, as she discovered how much he desired her. Enough, she'd think, to enslave her within this caste system. He would have to stay away from her. She would believe his desire for her influenced his decision to take her. She would be right to believe that. It had.

He'd lied to her, but he *would* return her to Earth. If only she trusted him, and if only he were worthy of her trust. She'd assuredly not believe his promise to bring her back if he continued pursuing her, he realized. And in his gut, he knew he would never be able to let her go if they mated. It was for the greater good that he never uncover his scent near her again. At least not before his subterfuge allowed him to outlaw the olfactory caste system.

There was no way he could earn her trust while he seduced her with his essence anyway. Odd that she was so affected. Lyntan genetic males were much more susceptible to a mate's scent than genetic women, usually.

Unit chimed. "We are arriving at the rendezvous coordinates, Captain. Open communications?"

"Negative, Unit. Begin hover mode," Jarren responded. He looked out at the expanse of sea around the ship. The dark-blue waters shifted gently with the current, reflecting the moon's opalescent glow high in the sky. Not a cloud distorted Jarren's view above. No ship sailed nearby. If he hadn't known there were hunters searching for him, he would have found the scene peaceful.

His gaze landed on a red blinking light as an unusual external sound registered on the ship's sensors. "Captain, movement is detected forward right five secs of the ship's bow."

The ship's sub-light sonic lasers vibrated the waters. "Thank you, Unit. Please open communication. I believe our ride has arrived."

"Affirmative, Captain."

Jarren's com unit buzzed as he leaned forward. "Go ahead."

Relief flooded Jarren at the sound of Marcus's voice reverberating over the com. "Captain. Are you secure?"

"For right now I am, Marcus, but my position has been greatly compromised. I am functioning entirely on luck at the moment. Off-world rendezvous point?"

"Give me a moment to pinpoint the trajectory of all off-world threats." The com went silent. A minute later, Marcus was back. "Two ships were located scanning Terra. I think they may be closing in on your location. Probably this communication signal. Following protocols, we'll remain cloaked and prepare for off-world docking. Here are the coordinates. We will make every attempt to protect your ascent without a loss of life, but I can't promise anything."

Jarren had a family now. His "family." Regardless of whether he would be able to keep them, they were his, and their safety came first. Jarren's response was curt. "Accepted. Feed the coordinates into the jumper. I have to prepare our guests for flight."

"Guests?"

"My position was compromised. My presence endangered others."

"I do not understand. Your departure should ensure their safety."

Jarren stifled a groan. They didn't have time to argue. "I layered one of them unintentionally, Marcus. Feed the coordinates. We will take off in two minutes. Jarren out." He got up and moved through the cabin to his sleeper. Sitting on the bed, he leaned over and stirred Lissa with a steady hand.

"It is time to strap in. We'll be leaving the atmosphere in a minute, and the flight may be rough."

Lissa blinked and sat up. She looked at Jarren a moment, her face relaxed from sleep, then she turned hesitantly and shook Jasmine awake. "Come on, little butterfly. It's time to visit the stars."

Rubbing a hand across her eyes, Jasmine shot up. Her eyes twinkled as she jumped up in the bed then slid her feet across its smooth silver surface and landed on the floor. "We're going to the stars, Mister Doctor," Jasmine squealed as she ran over to Jarren and grabbed his hands.

Jarren smiled in spite of himself. "Yes, Jasmine. To the stars. You must go to the front cabin and find a good seat to look out from so you can identify all the mnemonics in the sky tonight."

Jasmine nodded energetically. "Yep, the constellations. I'm gonna find the constellations, and Abuela won't believe it!" She bounded through the door.

Jarren smiled and glanced at Lissa. She didn't smile in return. Her eyes simmered. "I hope she has the opportunity to tell her grandmother."

Without another word, she rose. Her bare feet padded across the carpet and through the door, behind her daughter. Lissa's words struck Jarren deep. He couldn't formulate a coherent response. Silently, he stood and followed them out.

*   *   *   *   *

LISSA HELPED JASMINE put her seat strap on and swivel to look out through the porthole, then slipped on her shoes and secured herself. Jarren disappeared through a door, shutting it behind him without a word. Lissa was still tired, but the view outside was awe-inspiring. The new moon seemed to grow bigger as Jarren lifted the ship away from the dark waters below. Looking down, she watched the moon's reflection leave a widening path of shimmering light as the water lapped.

Jasmine giggled and leaned forward in her chair to stare out. "They're coming closer, but they aren't getting any bigger, Mommy."

Lissa twisted to see where Jasmine pointed. "What?"

"The stars." For a minute, the ship seemed suspended in the air, then the jumper jerked up, giving a view of the darkness above. Jasmine let out a startled squeak and grabbed the armrests of her seat, but moments later she was giggling again.

The cabin rumbled, and everything outside the porthole became a dark blur. Lissa tried to wipe her eyes as they teared, but she couldn't move her hand, which felt heavy. She slowly turned to her daughter, who stared out, scowling. "I don't feel good," she said through tight lips.

Jarren's voice rumbled out of nowhere. "We are moving very fast, Jasmine. The feeling will go away once we've attained a certain speed. You should be able to move around again in a minute." Even as his words died, the pressure on Lissa's body lifted. Jasmine wiggled straight and shook her head.

"Was that fun?" Jasmine asked.

"I don't think so, but it shouldn't have hurt you," Jarren replied.

"My eyes got all watery." Jasmine wiped at the few tears on her face.

Jarren's voice responded again. "Your eyes were strained, little one. There was far too much information for your eyes to transmit to your brain. No need to worry. Look outside now."

Lissa and Jasmine glanced through the porthole again. At first it appeared as if they looked into blackness, but then the lights in the cabin dimmed, and Lissa's eyes adjusted to the dark. The murkiness evaporated into a collage of deep to midnight blues. Thousands of lights flickering pink, blue, and orange shattered the infinite depth of space.

"Look at the colors, Mommy. What are they?" Jasmine asked.

Lissa didn't have to wait for Jarren's response. "Those are stars, Butterfly." Her voice caught. The spectacle overwhelmed her.

"Stars? But stars are white."

Jarren's deep voice interceded. "Only from Earth, Jasmine. Up here, stars are all kinds of colors. The further away you are, the less you can see and the whiter they appear. And on Earth, the atmosphere keeps a lot of detail out. You're looking at suns and star clusters in nearby systems."

"Which ones?" Jasmine asked.

"One moment," Jarren stated. A soft droning sounded in the cabin, and Lissa felt lightheaded a moment before she realized they had regained gravity—and equilibrium. Jarren walked through a door at the end of the cabin. Lissa spied a cockpit—like on a plane—through the opening behind him. The cockpit door swung shut.

Jasmine unbuckled, jumped up, and ran to him. She grabbed his hand and drew him toward a porthole. "I see the stars now. That was really fun, Mister Doctor!"

Jarren grinned. "Yes, it was. Maybe one day you will be able to pilot your own ship to the stars. It's even more fun when you're driving."

Jasmine turned her biggest cow eyes to Lissa. Her mouth curved in a perfect O. A whirlwind of words flew from her lips. "Driving? I want to drive, Mister Doctor. Can I have my own spaceship when we get to the mines? I'll drive my own spaceship right through the mines." The words gushed out as Jasmine pulled Jarren to a stop. "Mommy, can I have my own spaceship? Mister Doctor says I can drive. Can I drive today? When can I have a spaceship?"

Jarren placed his hand on her shoulder as she began to bounce.

"There'll be no driving anytime soon, Jasmine. Dr. Graf was referring to when you grow up." Lissa glared at him. Why did he have to speak as if they would never be going home?

Almost as if he read her mind, Jarren spoke up. "Actually, Jasmine, your mother is right. I was speaking of when you are older. I was an adult before I learned to pilot such a large ship. But you could certainly attend one of Earth's space camps in a couple of years. As I understand it, you are very knowledgeable about the different solar systems and planets. Space camp would snatch you up the minute you applied." He flipped Lissa a look. "Your mother would love to see you take off and visit the moon."

So he wasn't speaking about them living on a far-off world where the kids were driving spaceships at sixteen instead of cars. Lissa's chest loosened.

Jasmine turned to look out the window again. "I would like to visit the moon, but I'd *really* like to visit one of the orange planets, Mister Doctor."

Jarren laughed and bent to look into Jasmine's eyes. "You may stop calling me Mister Doctor and call me Jarren if I may call you 'Butterfly' as your mother and grandmother do."

Lissa frowned. Why did he want to call Jasmine 'Butterfly'?

Jasmine pondered the trade. Her brow scrunched up in serious consideration until finally, a smile bloomed on her face. Jutting her head with her usual determined jaunt, Jasmine held out her hand. He shook Jasmine's hand as she spoke. "Okay, Mister Jarren."

He laughed, and Lissa was surprised the sound lightened her mood.

"Just Jarren, Butterfly. 'Mister' is not a word we use on my world. We show respect in different ways. Alright?" Jasmine's poofy pigtails bobbed in response.

Then Jasmine let out a gasp. She looked through the porthole at the gray craggy surface of the moon floating by. "That's beautiful."

Jarren stared out. "Yes."

Lissa looked out past her daughter as the moon seemed to slowly turn away from the ship. Jarren stood and nodded to Lissa as he abruptly began speaking into the air. "Go ahead Marcus, I'm listening." He turned to walk away. Someone was talking into his ear like a Secret Service detail.

She recalled that day in Jarren's office when he'd dismissed her so rudely. Not a mood swing or outburst—someone had been talking to him then as well. Lissa had assumed the worst—he'd exhibited behaviors like Derek. But that hadn't been it after all. Looking now at his retreating back, her face reddened. She didn't want to think of the words she'd considered spouting at his apparent brush off. Then, her identity had been tied to her work and her family. Now family still mattered, but how did one value life on Earth while floating above it? What even was value when the existence of aliens had finally been proven? Deep down, she'd known the universe was too complex for them to be the only life. There were so many things about the entire situation she hadn't understood. Her vexation with Jarren eased a little. They'd left the place she called home. But if what he said was true, Jarren didn't have a home anymore either.

"Okay. Jarren out." He looked at her. "We will be docking in a few minutes. When we de-board, we'll go straight to the medical unit. I don't want you to worry. This is the usual procedure for those returning after time on an unclassified world."

"Unclassified?" Lissa tilted her head.

"Earth is unclassified. You have limited space travel, low-grade medical facilities, and no exposure to non-Terran life forms. We will be quarantined for a few hours and given a medical checkup," he replied. Lissa nodded.

"Does quarantine hurt, Jarren?" Jasmine asked as she reached for his hand.

The gesture seemed to surprise him, but he clasped her little fingers without hesitation. "No, Butterfly. No one will hurt you. Go and get your shoes. I think they are still in the sleeper." Jasmine ran out of the cabin. Lissa looked out of a porthole as the ship steered away from the moon's mass. Of course it didn't glow in space, but it looked otherworldly and mysterious.

"Are you ready to go?" Jarren asked.

Lissa shrugged and looked down at her feet. "Well, I've got my shoes on, so I am readier than Jasmine. When will your ship arrive?"

Jarren smiled and gestured outside. The deep, dark, twinkling Christmas light stars and moon had been replaced with the large tan belly of a ship. Episodes of *Star Galactic* flooded Lissa's thoughts.

The jumper rumbled to a stop as she stared in awe. Tan and silver walls piled high with supplies and small ships in various stages of repair littered the bay. Even a card table was pushed into a corner. The only thing missing was people. From Lissa's vantage point, she couldn't see anyone.

Jasmine came bounding back into the cabin. "Ready for the next adventure?" Jarren asked as he clasped Jasmine's hand.

She nodded and turned to hold out her other hand to Lissa. Swallowing her nervousness, Lissa squeezed Jasmine's fingers. They walked through the secondary airlock and up to the outside hatch where Jarren pushed a series of buttons on the side paneling.

"I work with only my closest friends. Marcus Naas is my second-in-command. His father is a secondary duke and lord on a neighboring planet to Lynta. There's Navigation Officer

Faheel. He's the best there is. I am constantly fighting to keep him employed on my ship. Fortunately for me, he is Lyntan and gives me preferential treatment when deciding whom he will script with. I have him contracted for another four years but I'm sure I can convince him to sign on permanently next time round. I think you will like him, especially.

"Then there's Engineer Corsa. She is a mathematical genius. She built the engines for both my jumper and my ship, *Stardesire*. There is no other ship faster per capacity than either of my flying marvels. Corsa keeps mostly to herself. She's very shy, but shyness is a characteristic of her species. She is Terlian. I don't know much about them except that they live out of the sun, and I've not met one who wasn't a genius with numbers. I was blessed to have her script onto my crew. She is invaluable, as are all my other shipmates."

"How many crew members do you have?" Lissa asked.

"Forty-eight exactly. But for your protection and mine, until I've determined our best course of action, neither of us will be interacting with anyone not directly assigned to the ship's bridge."

"And that would be Second-in-Command Naas, Officer Faheel, and Engineer Cor?"

"Corsa. Yes, and a small number of others."

Lissa's insides rumbled nervously. Her life had slammed into a dead end, taken a ninety-degree turn, and shot up into the sky. She would be surrounded by aliens and hiding in science fiction (at least to humans) quarters, making sure none of Jarren's other crew knew she was aboard. As she glanced over, she found Jarren watching her.

"This is not an easy change for you, I realize," said Jarren. "I will do everything possible to make your stay here uneventful and abbreviated." He punched one more button on the panel.

The latch released with a hiss, and Jasmine took the lead, pulling both adults by each hand behind her. A dusting of cool air chilled Lissa's skin. She blinked as her eyes adjusted to the additional light. When she finally focused on her surroundings, she found herself staring into the face of a beautiful woman.

She was tall but didn't come close to Jarren's height. She had straight, white-blond hair that glistened down around her arms and ended at the curve of her hips. Her skin was caramel brown with an unblemished glow. Her face was decidedly balanced, lips not too full, high cheekbones, and gray eyes slightly slanted, reminding Lissa of a longtime Korean acquaintance. Jarren stepped forward with the most beguiled expression Lissa had ever seen on him. The woman's face cracked into pure delight as she leaned familiarly into Jarren's embrace.

Unexpected jealousy forced Lissa's mouth downward. She fought to maintain her cryptic smile as the two apparently reunited. What was all that crap about Lissa being his bonded mate? Maybe men on his world had more than one bonded partner.

Pulled away by Jasmine's little grasp, Jarren grinned. His already beautiful features dazzled Lissa. "Melissa, this is Healer Rila." Lissa's gaze came to rest on the woman's dress. Glittering green as if thousands of small sequins had been handsewn on, it clung to Rila's body, flowing out at mid-thigh, to leave a short trail behind her. Her feet were hidden underneath the soft material. She glided toward Lissa, her pace as smooth as running water.

Reaching out, she gave Lissa a hug. "It is lovely to meet you, my dear. I am the ship's Healer. I worked with Jarren's father for many years before this boy coerced me away and locked me in his ship. I've been wasting away here ever since."

Lissa pondered Rila's words, envy darkening her tone. "He must be in the habit of taking women prisoner. You worked with Jarren's father? Surely that couldn't have been all that long ago?"

"Actually, I worked for Jarren's father for about twenty years, and that was twelve years ago."

Thirty-two years ago? She barely looked thirty, much less old enough to be an adult that long ago. At Lissa's disbelieving gaze, Jarren laughed and kissed her hand. The action seemed such a natural gesture, she didn't think to stop him. "Rila isn't human. She isn't Lyntan either. She is Palmesian. Their life span is about thrice yours and mine. I should warn you, there are quite a few non-Lyntans on my crew and obviously no humans at all."

An excited "wow" from Jasmine made Lissa smile. "It is very nice to meet you, Rila," Lissa said, her jealousy easing. Rila squeezed her hand before gliding backward.

With another smile, she gestured for them to follow. "It is very nice meeting you as well. I hope your journey was not too taxing?"

"No. I suspect the brunt of the work getting us here lay on Jarren's shoulders. Jasmine and I slept most of the way."

At Jasmine's name, Rila stopped and turned questioningly to Jarren, then looked down at Jasmine huddled by

Lissa. With a scowl that evolved into a brief smile, she bent low to greet her. "Humblest of greetings, most blessed one," she said as she looked at Jarren once more then turned her gaze to Lissa. "Will you honor me with a hug?" Rila asked Jasmine as she continued to look up, concerned.

Lissa pushed down her befuddlement. Rila grasped Jasmine and patted her back but stared at Jarren. Her face scrunched as if she were trying to solve a difficult puzzle. Then her face relaxed, and she stood up.

"Jarren. You are bonded. And you've masked that girl. Why?"

Lissa looked from the confused scowl on Jarren's face to the neutral look on Rila's. "What?"

"You and him. It is obvious—" Rila stopped abruptly.

"I did not bond with her, nor did I mask the girl, Rila," came Jarren's clipped retort.

"Well, I couldn't see her," Rila replied now, looking down at Jasmine with a warm smile.

Jasmine pulled on Lissa's sleeve. "Mommy, am I wearing a mask?"

Lissa shook her head. "No, Butterfly. You aren't wearing a mask." Turning a suspicious gaze on them, she edged out a question. "Just what are you two talking about?"

No response was forthcoming. Jarren and Jasmine started walking. Rila glided ahead. As they approached a closed entry, Rila hit a combination on the keypad flush with the wall. The dull metal slid open. They stepped through into a long tan hall, seemingly made from the same material as the inside of Jarren's jumper. Lissa's cool skin warmed immediately, but her unanswered question left a chill in her veins.

CHAPTER *12*

THEY MADE THEIR way down a dimly lit hall. Lissa's eyes ached as they traveled past endless tan walls. She couldn't spot a change in the texture or a break in the wall to indicate a door—just one long tan hall. After several minutes of silent plodding, she began to hate the color.

"Mommy, this is a weird place," Jasmine whispered as her hand grasped Lissa's. "It doesn't *smell* like anything. I don't like it."

Lissa threw a startled look at Jasmine then sniffed the air. Nothing. Tilting her head forward again, she inhaled, searching out the now-comforting essence of Jarren or any aroma coming from Rila.

Not a thing. Hadn't Jarren said scent was important on his world? The question formed on Lissa's lips just as Jarren and Rila stopped and turned.

At first Lissa saw no reason for the abrupt pause. But with practiced ease, Rila leaned forward and placed her palm on the wall's surface. The nearest portion of wall disintegrated as they watched. Another "wow" emanated from Jasmine as Rila gestured them inside.

"Medical quarters. Please enter."

Jarren nodded with a reassuring glance. Lissa took a breath and stepped through the opening. Until then, she'd still managed to convince herself she was dreaming. But that step through the disintegrating entrance was a wake-up call. She was not in the safety of her home with Miguel down the hall. Her mother wasn't a phone call away. She had been taken from everything she knew: her life, her home, stability. Lissa stifled a gasp.

The light inside grew bright as she moved forward, Jasmine's little hand enclosed within Lissa's suddenly clammy one. Jasmine whimpered. Lissa tried to bend to reassure her, but something pungent stung her nose. Wafts of chocolate overran her olfactory lobe, almost knocking her down with its strength. What once had lured Lissa to Jarren like the flirtatious song of the Pied Piper now forced itself into her nostrils, drowning the air within, clogging her airways, choking her. Lissa stumbled back, one hand to her throat, the other pushing desperately at the air. The light glared, no longer passive but increasingly bright. Painful tears forced their way out from under her lids.

"Stop! Please." Lissa fell to her knees, one hand on her throat and the other covering her eyes.

Then the smell dissipated. The brightness within the room dissipated, and Jasmine grasped Lissa's hand. Lissa could hear her own struggling gasps bouncing off metallic walls.

"You *have* bonded with the girl!" Rila's angry voice snapped.

"I didn't know," Jarren's deep tone reverberated behind Lissa.

A sigh filled the room. "We have to release them. The little one is too young to endure this cleansing alone, and we may injure your mate."

The fluorescent-type brightness of the ship's medical ward lessened. Lissa blinked through the last of her tears, pulling herself to stand in the middle of a round domed room of rectangular metallic tiles. Jasmine shivered next to her.

At one curved corner of the room, Jarren and Rila stood looking at them, obvious concern written on their faces.

Lissa began to gyrate. At the deepest level of her consciousness, she wondered if the cold shivers were signs of a nervous breakdown. In the next instant, Jasmine's hand slipped away as Jarren's alluring sweetness surrounded her. Lissa's legs wobbled.

Jarren's iridescent orbs glistened as she fell. "Alright, my own. Alright. You are safe now. Just don't slip away yet." His arms surrounded her to hold her close. His warmth washed over her, pushing away the coldness creeping into her limbs.

He held her, his eyes piercing, worried. Then he lifted her up and placed her on a warm flat surface. Rila stared down from above, and a cool hand took Lissa's wrist. Heat spread through her body. Her heartbeat slowed. Lissa breathed easier as the cold receded, along with the stiffness in her limbs.

"I need to sit up," Lissa croaked. Her voice had lost its usual power. Rila nodded.

"You should be okay now, Lissa. Stripping your senses of your mate creates this adverse effect. I apologize for second-guessing your current condition. I sensed you were bonded, but I didn't act on that information."

Lissa tentatively sat up and glanced around. She was perched on a metal table that had materialized out of one sloped wall. Jarren stood to her side, his hand resting at the small of her back. He pointedly averted his gaze. Rila paused by her other side, one hand still on Lissa's wrist, the other placed maternally on Jasmine's head.

"Mommy?"

Lissa gave Jasmine a tremulous smile before turning back to Rila. "Tell me what's going on. I feel sick to my stomach." Rila's glance slid to Jarren. They remained silent. Lissa's hot irritation neared boiling as she repeated herself. "I said…I want to know what is going on here. Now."

Rila nodded. "You deserve answers. May I take Jasmine into the other medical unit? Jarren will want a moment alone with you."

Lissa's hand snaked out to grab her daughter's shoulder protectively. "Where?"

"We'll be next door. She will need inoculations, a Language Sensor, and a Subduer."

A large warm hand caressed Lissa's back. Jarren. "She will be fine, Lissa. I swear."

She'd heard that response one too many times. Still, she nodded. This, clearly, was a conversation only for Jarren and Lissa. Looking down, Lissa crooked a finger at her daughter. She looked into Jasmine's big eyes and sighed. "Okay, Butterfly. You go with Rila. She's going to give you a checkup. She's a space doctor. Same rules apply to all doctors, even space ones. I'll be there in a minute, alright?"

Jasmine scowled then turned to Jarren. "This lady doctor won't hurt me, will she? I don't want shots. I *hate* shots."

Jarren knelt and took both of Jasmine's hands in his own. "You are correct, Butterfly. She would never hurt you. Space doctors only heal. And your mother will be there in a moment. She must also have the doctor check her. Okay?"

Jasmine looked to Lissa again then nodded and took Rila's outstretched hand. The woman inclined her head at Lissa, glared a moment at Jarren, then turned and walked toward a doorway of disintegrated material. As soon as the two stepped through, the wall re-solidified.

With an expectant look, Lissa spat out, "Speak."

"I told you I accidentally marked you with my scent the night we kissed?"

"You mean the night you made me kiss you?"

Jarren's defeated sigh tightened a ribbon of guilt around Lissa's heart. She was angry but she wasn't vengeful. She didn't want to hurt him. "I'm sorry. I don't understand, but I need to. I'm aggravated."

"Lyntans' olfactory lobes directly stimulate the chemicals created when we are sexually aroused. As a human, you seem to be near enough to Lyntans' physiological makeup to be similarly stimulated. It's like eating ice cream or chocolate when you're depressed."

Lissa's gaze locked on Jarren at the word "chocolate." He smelled like the highest quality Belgian cocoa. Lissa spoke without thinking. "You smell like chocolate. Is that why?"

Jarren stilled at that question. As if by instinct, he moved closer, his eyes boring into hers. Then as quickly as he approached, he moved away. His hands clenched together.

He released a breath, and the anxious energy he exuded petered off.

"I don't smell like chocolate, Lissa. My essence causes your body to respond to me with the same chemical reactions as it would when you are emotionally pleased. Your olfaction associates those chemicals to a scent—in your case, chocolate. When I smell you, I smell a rare flower on my planet, the decypheny. Aside from creating an alluring scent, its petals are often used to enhance sexual arousal."

He paused, his muscles bulging with restraint under his tight black shirt. "I had no idea we were equally affected. If I had known you associated my scent with chocolate, I would never have sent you through the detox chamber. *Mutual* aromatic association is only indicative of those bonded."

Lissa frowned. "Detox chamber?"

"May I help you down?" Jarren asked instead of addressing her question. Lissa nodded. He caught her elbow and gently lowered her from the table. She found herself leaning into the comforting crook of his arm as her shoes touched the floor.

"I knew I covered you. I did not know we'd bonded," His voice was but a whisper above her head. "I never planned this. I only wanted to know if you were as attracted to me as I was to you. I apologize for opening that door."

He stepped away, but his eyes bored into hers. "I have no excuse except loneliness for turning off my Subduer. A Subduer quells the hormones that create my body's scent. It isn't the first time I've turned it off, but I guess I've not before been near any strong bonding candidate when I did so." He stared off, hesitant, before turning back. "I couldn't sense your scent after I kissed you at my house. It didn't occur to me we'd bonded scents then."

He hugged her, and Lissa felt his warm breath on her hair. His lips brushed the crown of her head. "We bonded so quickly. That moment should have been special. Just exposing my scent twice shouldn't have created a bonding. Creed's sake! I wish I'd thought of that possibility. You would be home with your mother right now, and I would still be safe on Earth."

"Rila knew I was bonded to you."

"She's Palmesian and a doctor. Her species is sensitive to Lyntan olfactory chemical interactions. Rila is also trained to know a couple's status."

"Status?"

"People aren't married on our planet, Lissa." He looked at her meaningfully, as if waiting for her to understand.

It took a minute for realization to hit her. "They're bonded, by scent. Wait. You're trying to tell me we're married?" Her voice squeaked. Tension squirreled up her spine. She couldn't be married. The mention of marriage had, last time, left her beaten physically and psychologically. Besides, her life was perfect the way it was. She had a great job, a loving family, a beautiful healthy daughter who adored her. She moved seamlessly through each day. She'd arranged her life so there were no situations she couldn't handle. Until that morning at Max's. That morning when Lissa's usually perfect acrobatic act didn't take her in and out of Max's without incident. That morning Jarren Graf had entered her life.

Jarren allowed her to step away. "It isn't marriage, per se. We are bonded, but there is no permanency. We could mate, but we don't have to. A bonding is just an indication we could compatibly mate and produce children. To continue our olfactory line. In normal circumstances, a couple must expose their scents numerous times to bond. For some reason, our essences bonded instinctively."

Lissa's gut clenched at the enormity of the situation. "No. I control my body, not the other way around. Just like my life. I know my life like the back of my hand. My world works like clockwork. I make sure it works that way. Now you want me to accept not only that I have been ripped from everything and everyone I know, but that I don't even really control the body I'm in?"

Jarren paused. He seemed to be at a loss. "You have not lost control of your body. I am not explaining this right. Usually people gauge their compatibility level by repeatedly uncovering and mixing their scents. It simply didn't occur to me we could bond without intentionally doing so."

"That's what you were talking about with Rila in the hall."

"Yes. There is a process involved with bonding. We bonded outside that process."

Lissa snorted. "Yet you want me to believe I haven't lost control of my body? Those bonded 'can't be detoxed.'"

"Detox removes the chemical wastes from the body, any chemical hormones the body induces or absorbs. It's the safest way to ensure you're not carrying any contagion. The detox composite tried removing my scent from you. If you are already bonded, removing your bonded scent by detox is a painful process not everyone survives. We use other ways to detoxify newly bonded couples."

Questions rolling around Lissa's head started tumbling out. "And Jasmine? Why couldn't Rila see her? Why did she say Jasmine couldn't be detoxed on her own?"

Jarren sighed before answering. He reached out to take a sliver of Lissa's hair, rolling the dark strand between his thumb and forefinger. The act drew an erotic tremble from her, and Lissa scowled. She really had no control.

Lissa's attraction to Derek had once blinded her to the reality that he didn't want a permanent relationship. She'd protected herself since by concentrating on her family and her work. She'd established a life of predictable harmony. But no longer.

"Jasmine is too young to be detoxed without a parent. You and she could have balanced the process, but…"

"But you and I are bonded. Right." She couldn't stifle her caustic tone, all apathy gone.

"I cannot be more apologetic. I came to Earth to protect my people. When you were endangered, I had to protect you as well. I have done nothing but present reasons you shouldn't trust or rely on me in spite of my good intentions, but I hope you believe I never wanted you to have to leave your home."

"No, Jarren. You've given me reasons to not trust, rely on, *or* care for you," she replied quietly. "You left your world only to endanger me on mine. I am on a ship in the middle of space with no way to return home. Your idea of protection seems ironically to equate with fleeing. Every decision you've made solely reflects what you think is most important. I've no doubt your people are your priority. I've no doubt you want what is best for them. But you have no clue what is best for me."

Anger twisted her insides. She didn't trust Jarren to tell her the truth, and she didn't trust him to make sure she and Jasmine got home safely. When it came down to it, his priorities decided his actions. If lying achieved his goals, Jarren would lie. The truth often means nothing to a person with a purpose.

Jarren remained quiet, but his jaw clenched.

Lissa gathered a breath. "You didn't answer my question about Jasmine. Why did Rila say she couldn't see her?"

"Rila does not see in the traditional sense of the word. Her retina creates different information for her brain to process. Her race works so closely and well with Lyntans because they rely entirely on smell to create images in their head. Smell *is* their way of seeing the world. When Rila looks at you, she sees patterns of essence and vibrations of movement, not color and texture. Our bonding masked Jasmine's scent. She is your daughter. Without consistent exposure to her father's essence, she adopts your bonded's scent."

Lissa absorbed his words. She couldn't begin to imagine what type of creature Rila must be. The urge to reunite with Jasmine and take stock of Rila's trustworthiness forced the air from Lissa's lungs. "I want my daughter, and I want to go home," she ground out. Anxious tears welled in her eyes.

"She is fine, Lissa. I will take you to her. You may see for yourself. But I can't return you to Earth now. Your life would be forfeited there."

"It's my life! I get to decide the manner in which I live or die."

Jarren's voice deepened, impassioned. "No. I am to blame for the threat to your life. You are Of the Family, but I did not know. I will correct that mistake. Once I rule Lynta, I will return you to Earth. I promise."

Lissa choked out a laugh. As if she were special in some way. Some useless way. "My regard for your promises, Jarren, is about as high as your regard for allowing me to make my own decisions. I hope you get whatever you need to let me go. I hate this place. I hate that you took me away from the only home I've ever known. You decided I would rather live in this cell you call a ship than die with my feet firmly planted on the planet where I was born." The planet where she was born? She could hardly handle the thought while stuck in an alien spaceship surrounded by creatures posing as human. Her home, her life on Earth, was slipping away. She stared at the wall, bursts of frustration flowing from the center of her chest to the tips of her fingers.

"It's never just our own lives we gamble with, Lissa. Just as I thought of my people when I left Lynta, you should think of Jasmine now. Her fate is interwoven with your own. Your life can't be sacrificed without impacting her."

Lissa turned on him, her eyes flashing even as guilt tickled her thoughts. She wasn't sure her anger was properly focused. "Don't lecture me! You have no idea what I would do for my daughter. No idea!" Shaking, Lissa took several breaths to calm her heart's panicked beating. She had escaped an abuser to protect her unborn child. That man had thought to control her too.

"I will play nice, Jarren. And you will take me home as soon as it is safe. Then I expect to never see you again."

Lissa's voice trembled as she pushed the words out. Holding back angry tears, she stared at Jarren until he nodded. He pivoted and strode stiffly away. Something in her response had hurt him. *Good. Misery loves company*, Lissa thought as she followed his dominating figure in search of her daughter.

CHAPTER *13*

JARREN MADE HIS way past "A" deck, an unforgiving frown on his face. He hadn't prevented his cousin's insurrection. He couldn't persuade his own mate to stay with him long enough to develop feelings for him. He was forever inadequate. Cool air hovered around him as he traversed the empty halls leading away from Lissa and Jasmine's guest quarters. He tapped a code into the soft wall panel and stepped through an opening hatch without breaking stride.

Damn it! This was his ship. Yet he felt like the alien here. Lissa had insisted he remove himself from her presence. Her stony expression was the last thing he saw as she punched in the final combination key to lock her suite. He'd stepped through the oval doorway just before it shut.

As he walked away, detachment settled on Jarren's shoulders. She had managed to alienate him from everything, even his own commission. The feeling was draining. Yet, even now, he leaned into the trace fragrance of tropical musk. Despite the Subduer she now wore, he sensed her essence in the air.

By the gods, he wanted her. Flexing his shoulders to relieve his stress, he advanced, determined, down another hall, slowing habitually in front of the entrance to his own quarters. The fantasy of Lissa, her black hair splayed and sweaty over the large white satiline pillows on his raised bed, danced before his eyes.

He could bring his desire for her to bear, draw the resistance out of her with one touch of his lips on her glistening skin, behind the shielded entry to his quarters. He need only turn down his Subduer and call to her. He hadn't mentioned it, but that they were bonded only made her more susceptible to his essence. Jarren placed a hand on his quarters' door longingly before moving on. She might be unable to resist the scent of him, but she couldn't stand the sight of him.

Finally, he paused in front of the hatch of the pilot's deck, exasperation burning a hole into his gut. This was not the way it was supposed to be. He'd made the necessary decisions. Lissa should have wanted to stay with him. She should have wanted to mate and bond with him, enjoy the passion he had for her as much as he would enjoy the flame he knew burned for him.

Jarren keyed the code to enter the bridge.

"Captain on deck," Unit announced. The crew stood to welcome him.

Jarren straightened the crisp shirt of his black captain's uniform as Marcus approached. His second's warm green eyes crinkled in welcome as he strode energetically forward.

Marcus reached out with both hands but grasped Jarren in a grateful hug when he neared. "You are breathing and well, Captain. The gods be praised. I've no idea how the hunters missed your escape. That was truly the worst piloting I've tracked in years." Marcus stepped back. "What kind of air were you breathing on Terra?" he added.

Jarren patted Marcus's back as he moved to the captain's chair and control panel on the bridge's dais. Faheel meandered forward to grasp one of Jarren's hands within his own. Jarren uttered a strained "hello" at Faheel's bent dark head. It should have been a happy homecoming. But his ship didn't feel like home any longer. Only that annoying Terran made him feel that way.

"Faheel," Jarren uttered as he squeezed Faheel's thin fingers one more time before Corsa took and pumped his hand between her jittering blue palms. She bowed her head, a foot and a half lower than his, her usual shy expression hidden behind a boyishly short curtain of straight red hair.

"High Caste," she whispered as she continued to stare at the floor of the bridge.

As quickly as Corsa grasped his hand, she let it go and teetered back to the engineer's station in the corner. Jarren smiled. None of them had changed. But somewhere inside, he had. And he knew it was Lissa who'd changed him. He just couldn't figure out how…yet.

"Damned lucky, Jarren. Damned lucky." Marcus's brusque voice interrupted Jarren's thoughts as he settled into the captain's chair and rested his palms against the pilot controls. On the large viewing screen in front of him, he studied the sparkling murkiness of space.

"Course, Captain?" Faheel shot out, taking his seat.

Jarren nodded. "Set temporary course for the Disper Cluster, Navigator. Accelerate to light speed five then maintain shadow proximity."

Faheel tapped his fingers on the smooth glass console before him. "Set," he stated after a pause.

"How does it feel to be back?" Marcus asked as he lounged against Jarren's chair. "We were sure you would be on that planet for a while. It hasn't even been a week."

"Yes. Some things happened. I wasn't safe there anymore."

Marcus turned to stare into Jarren's eyes. "And the 'somethings' would be our guests. Don't bother to find an excuse for them being here." Marcus leaned close to Jarren to speak confidentially. "Rila told me. I thought we agreed you wouldn't do anything stupid."

"I did not intend to, Marcus. Almost every decision I made was out of necessity."

Marcus narrowed his gaze. "Keyword 'almost.' This is not the place to discuss issues of a personal nature, but Jarren, I need to know what is going on. When do you want to debrief?"

"I'd like to introduce Lissa and Jasmine to the bridge crew first."

"Why didn't you bring her with you now?"

Jarren redirected his attention to the screen before him. "Let's just say she wasn't in a mood to socialize."

Out of the corner of his eye, Jarren saw Marcus's brows rise. "I think I am going to like your bonded. She obviously challenges you. The only other female who ever presented a challenge was Veena."

A soft "yes" escaped Jarren's mouth. He looked at Marcus another moment as an idea took shape. "Yes, Marcus. She is a challenge. And I think you will love her. I want you to care for her. There is a barrier between her and me. She won't trust me. But she needs someone to trust now, especially as she adjusts."

"Wouldn't she accept a woman more easily than a man?"

"On this ship, Marcus, you are the only person who comes close to thinking like a human. Humanity is what she's looking for. Not female companionship. Get to know her and her daughter a bit. Earn her trust. Protect her when I can't."

"And if I can't stand her?" Marcus asked with a low laugh.

"Toss me into space and take over my ship. That is more likely to happen. Will you do as I ask or do I need to think of someone else who might work?"

"I have not declined a request from you yet, Jarren. I only hope you're making a good decision. Her trust in someone else may not translate into trust for you."

Jarren shook his head to ease the tension again. "One can only hope, Marcus," he stated.

The ship's blaring alarm ended their conversation. Marcus bounded up to his post. Jarren turned to Faheel. "Report!"

Faheel's thin fingers keyed his panel as he perused the screen before him. "Captain, one ship approaching at sub-light speed, vector 257-9. I'm waiting for ship identification."

Jarren's muscles tensed as he registered the continued metallic blasting of the alarm. He clenched a fist, impatiently.

"I've got it," Faheel stated as he looked up. "We've got bounty hunters trying to scan the ship. Shields at maximum. Response, sir?"

Jarren shook his head. "Are their weapons powering?"

"Undetermined, sir," Faheel responded as he looked down at his pilot board again. A sudden jarring forced Jarren to press his hands into his chair's unit sensors. A bright light flashed before the front viewer as he looked on.

"They're attacking. Respond?" Marcus growled out at his back.

Another jarring sent the crew off kilter. Corsa spoke up. "They're attacking our gravity drive, Captain. They want to take the ship in one piece."

Jarren plotted *Desire*'s departure route in his head then manually fed the coordinates into the ship's artificial intelligence. Another blast jolted the ship.

"Damage, Unit," Marcus barked.

"'A' deck. Minor damage," Unit responded.

Jarren's breath caught in his throat. Lissa and Jasmine were feet away from "A" deck. Swiveling his chair, Jarren moved to get up, but Marcus gave him a warning look. "Captain—"

Jarren growled as he reclaimed his seat, frustrated. What was he thinking? He couldn't just leave now. Destroy the threat first, and then he could make sure Lissa and Jasmine were okay. He turned toward the viewer again, but every nerve inside him tensed with the urge to see to his mate. "Okay. Faheel, pilot up to vector 662. We'll do an underbelly sweep and take out its light-speed capabilities and weapons in one swoop. Plot the attack course, but I'll fly navigation once it's plotted."

Faheel nodded. His head bent, he tapped in the coordinates. As *Desire* altered course, a large spherical ship appeared on the screen.

Jarren called out to his second. "Return fire, Marcus. But don't let them know there's anyone with intelligence on board. They want the ship. We want them to think this ship is easy pickings."

"Yes, sir," Marcus replied. A laser blast erupted from *Desire's* lower cannons, streaking out across the blackness to hit the bounty hunters' right underbelly.

"What's their ship's damage, Corsa?" Jarren barked, his adrenaline now blocking out the loudness of the alarm.

"Minimal damage, sir. I expect they'll approach us on 'A' deck side. They know we've sustained damage there." His heart raced in his chest. Jarren's instinct to go to Lissa ate at him, but this time, his hate for those attacking stomped his instincts into dust.

"They're approaching on 'A' deck side, sir," Faheel stated, looking at his instruments.

Jarren nodded to himself. Bounty hunters were definitely not the smartest hunters around. "Let them get closer. When their proximity reaches three marks, give me manuals. Marcus, keep them on their toes without tipping them off that we aren't an easy board. As long as they want the ship, they'll be careful about damaging it."

"Sir." Marcus sent another beam across the hunters' bow. The hunters returned fire. *Desire's* shields deflected the shot.

"Any damage?" Jarren piped to Corsa.

"None, sir."

"Good, then let's make them think they've got us. At next weapon attack, put *Desire* into distress mode. We'll bring them in quickly."

She responded. "Yes, sir. *Desire* detects their weapons powering again. Attack is imminent."

Jarren nodded but didn't answer. The ship jarred, and Jarren's stomach clenched. Lissa would be terrified. Corsa's voice interrupted his thoughts. "We're in distress mode, sir."

Jarren looked to Marcus. "Have they tried to make contact?"

Marcus shook his head. "No."

"Well then, I can presume they won't be letting the crew go if they board."

"Indeed, Jarren. As Second, I support your observation that this attack is life-threatening. I advocate any and all necessary force."

"Okay. Corsa, are they responding to our ploy?"

"Yes."

"I concur, sir," Faheel added. "They are moving their ship into trajectory for boarding. They think we are incapacitated."

"Good. Estimated time for three-mark range?"

"Just approaching now, sir. It should be another minute and a half," Faheel stated.

"Give me audio to Lissa's quarters, Marcus. I need to make sure she's alright."

Marcus didn't hesitate. "You have audio."

Jarren listened a moment to the silence behind the blaring of the alert—no screaming or weeping female voices. Gods, he hoped she wasn't hurt or worse. Unfortunately, he couldn't think about that with the current threat. "Lissa, it's Jarren. The ship sustained damage near your quarters. Are you okay?" There was no response. Jarren spoke again, coaching his voice to sound neutral. It wouldn't help to express the fear gripping him. "Lissa, please respond. Are you okay?"

Jasmine's frightened voice ping-ponged through the bridge. "Mister Doctor? Jarren? Mommy is sick. Can you talk to her later?"

Jarren sat up, his heart beating faster. "Jasmine, what's wrong with her?"

"I don't know. She fell really fast. I think she's tired, 'cause then she went to lay down. I don't want to bother her, okay?" Her voice rose in distress, and it took everything Jarren had not to rush to Lissa's room.

"Did she get up and walk to the bed, Butterfly?"

"Yes," came Jasmine's high-pitched reply.

"Three mark, Captain. You have manuals," Faheel interrupted.

Jarren pushed his hand into the chair's navigation sensors. "Jasmine, I'll be there in a moment. If Mommy asks, tell her I'm coming."

"Okay."

"Marcus, cut audio. Faheel, take the coordinates as plotted. Corsa, make sure Engineering knows we're about to tax our shields. I've got to get us in close. There'll be some ricochet between our shields and theirs."

A unanimous "sir" met his orders.

Jarren moved his hand within the sensors, and *Stardesire* shot forward. They slid below their attacker's underbelly before the hunters' ship could get a blastoff. Rocking *Desire* up, Jarren gave the command for Marcus to blast out the hunters' engines. Cannons blasted; light erupted over the screen. A shattering of debris floated into view. The debilitated ship drifted away.

Marcus's voice broke into Jarren's concentration. "They have lost gravity shields and weapons. There are oxygen leaks on all decks."

"Corsa, get me a life sign count."

She stepped away from one screen to hit the console of another. "One moment. Estimated crew, twenty-nine. I'm reading twenty life signs on our sensors. Probably casualties for the rest."

"Life type?"

"It's a bounty hunter ship, sir."

Jarren paused meaningfully before responding. "I know, but I need to know whether we can rescue those on board."

Jarren heard her fingers hitting the console. "They look like Handler Keegan's bounties, sir."

"That's what I thought." The decision was made. Handler Keegan bred "Suicides." They'd track their prey down at all costs, attack without consideration, and kill their prey if they couldn't bring the capture in with ease. They were too dangerous to hold captive.

"Marcus, give them a clean shot up the middle with the light cannons. They'll kill and eat each other if any are left alive. Destroy the ship entirely."

"Yes, sir." A series of pulsing lights flashed before the screen. For a moment, no object could be seen around the blanket whiteness. Then the brightness dimmed, and the crew looked out at the blackness, pieces of jagged, twisted metal littering the screen. Jarren shook his head. He hated loss of life, even that kind of life.

Clearing his throat, Jarren sat up in the chair, his hands warm from connecting to the sensory manuals. Looking to Faheel, he asked, "Other possible threats?"

Faheel shook his head. "None detected. This ship most likely belonged to the hunters chasing you on Earth, sir."

"Good." Jarren got up and walked toward the door. "Take the bridge, Marcus. I'll be in Lissa's quarters. Have Rila meet me there." Jarren didn't bother waiting for an answer as the door slid open and he stepped through.

Jarren found Lissa's quarters locked. Sighing, Jarren spoke out. "Unit, unlock the door to Lissa's quarters."

"Lock released," Unit hummed. The entrance whooshed open. Scanning the room as he walked in, he sighed with relief. The Subduer couldn't cover the tart smell of vinegar emanating from Lissa's lagging fear, but the scent only lingered now. Lissa sat on her bed, Jasmine sitting next to her. They both looked up at his entrance.

"Jarren!" The little girl jumped up and ran to him, her hand catching his, her palms sweaty. "She didn't ask, but I told her anyway. I said you were coming. I don't think she feels good."

Jarren nodded, intending to evaluate Lissa himself. He walked over to the bed. "Are you alright?" he asked as he bent down and looked into her pain-filled irises. He wanted to pull her into his arms. Fear she might be hurt had played havoc with his heart.

She sat on the bed, one leg pulled up and cuddled beneath an arm. Her face contorted in a grimace. But she nodded. "I'm fine."

"Is Mommy okay?" Jasmine said as she stood at his side. Jarren turned to the little girl and took her clasped hands into his own.

"Yes. Go into the bathing room and have Unit tell you where the washcloths are. Then wet one with warm water. Do you know how to use the water accesses?"

Eagerly, she nodded.

"Good girl. Now go. Healer Rila will be here soon, and she will make your mommy all better."

Jasmine ran off.

Jarren turned back to Lissa. She glanced at him before looking down at her leg. "I might have broken it."

Jarren sat next to her and gently moved her hand so he could see both legs. An angry bruise traveled from below the inside of her knee to her mid-thigh. She flinched as he touched the swollen area. Frowning, he looked up again. "What happened?"

Lissa shook her head. "I don't know. One minute I was walking toward Jasmine's room, the next minute the room just went topsy-turvy. I fell, then my head hit something hard. I think I was out for a few minutes. Is something wrong with the ship?" Her voice trembled.

Jarren perused her injury again. The situation could have been much worse. He should have known bounty hunters would be able to follow the ship's energy trails. His lack of forethought could have cost Lissa her life. No matter where he was, he seemed to place her in danger. Avoiding her stare, he responded. "A minor altercation." His tone was purposefully mild.

"Jasmine said she heard a bomb. You checked on us." Lissa paused, waiting.

Running a hand through his hair, Jarren met her expectant expression. "As it turned out, we didn't escape unnoticed. I should have expected an attack given the variables. I didn't."

Lissa sucked in a breath. "They found us?" Her eyes widened.

"One ship, easily dealt with. If I'd been thinking intuitively, we wouldn't even have had to confront them. It's over now anyhow."

Concern crinkled her brow and mellowed her voice. "Was anyone hurt?" Jarren studied her. She seemed honestly concerned for his crew, people she had never met and had no reason to care for, at a time when she should have been concerned for herself.

He couldn't understand her. "Yes, Lissa. People were hurt. *You* were hurt. A leader should foresee the possible outcomes. I should have been prepared."

"You aren't perfect, Jarren. None of us are. Sometimes close, but not perfect. No matter how hard we try." The gentleness in her voice caught him off guard. He looked into her eyes and tensed. A strong emotion had touched her. She gazed at him intently, her irises sparkling with empathy.

Jarren reached out and stroked her cheek. Her soft skin slid against the roughness of his fingertips. The glow in her eyes intensified and her lips parted as if welcoming his mouth's plunder, and he wanted her then, hungered to recapture the perfection of her mouth. He leaned in just as Unit interrupted.

"Lissa, Healer Rila requests entry to your quarters."

Startled, Lissa sat up and pulled away from his caress. Her arm hit against the bruise on her leg, and she caught her breath in pain. Hissing through clenched teeth, Lissa responded, "Okay."

Jarren stood. Their connection had broken. Jasmine came running out of her room and bounded to the door, a dripping orange washcloth in hand. "I'll let her in, Mommy."

Jarren pushed back at the emotions flooding his body. He walked to the door just as Rila stepped through it. He glanced back again, re-evaluating Lissa's condition.

Rila glided by as Jarren spoke. "If it is more than a break, Rila, let me know." She nodded in turn. "I'll leave you to her." He stepped through the door hatch.

Lissa's unsure voice followed his departure. "Thank you, Jarren."

Jarren tilted his head but kept walking. Desire and something deeper, more powerful, warred within him. Lissa provoked an ache in him, and he couldn't get enough.

CHAPTER 14

"I'M SORRY, WHO?" Lissa asked as she stood in the doorway to her quarters. She could still hear Jasmine bouncing on the shiny multicolored bedsheets. Her squealing voice was almost hoarse from yelling. The man towered before her, his husky physique encased in a skintight tan shirt Lissa likened to the clothing of Tour-de-France cyclists. The shirt slid down a tapered waist to snug-fitting black slacks tucked into black boots. His crisp, no-nonsense look contrasted with the aura of calm and gentleness he emanated. Lissa breathed in. Ripe blueberries.

"I am Second-in-Command Marcus Naas, Melissa. I thought it might be helpful to introduce myself before you are barraged with formal greetings in the Salon later this evening. Please excuse my forwardness." He nodded his head, succinctly raising his brow. A warm tingle ran through her chest.

She pushed down a schoolgirl blush and concentrated on analyzing Jarren and Marcus, the only two alien men she'd ever met. Tall with sandy hair, Marcus had green eyes that reflected sensitivity and empathy. He stood as tall as Jarren, but where Jarren was lithe strength, Marcus was burly power. Lissa had seen Jarren in action. He moved like a tiger, agile, decisive, all his actions thought out to play on his physical strengths.

But she imagined Marcus didn't need great agility. Lissa glanced down his arms where his sleeves stopped midway on his sculpted biceps. She noted well-honed muscles and pumped veins. He had thick hands. He could easily strangle a man.

Yet her glance lifted to his, and she saw the twinkle of humor in his eyes, the same twinkle that made her heart turn when she sometimes met Jarren's gaze. His twinkle was so often hidden. Seeing that glint in Jarren's irises when his defenses were down was a gift. Lissa's breath would catch in her throat. Then the moment would be gone, and Lissa was again faced with that guarded look that textured Jarren's expressions.

Lissa looked into Marcus Naas's eyes. They still twinkled in welcome, and she smiled in response. "Please, come in. I was just entertaining my daughter on my wonderful bed. You know, it seems to catch us when we bounce. We haven't fallen off yet, and believe me, for Jasmine, that's a record."

Marcus entered and touched the privacy button that closed and locked the door behind him. His slightly multi-tonal voice rumbled out a laugh. "I would be surprised if she fell. The bed is made from an intuitive synthetic. Based on the pressure your body puts on it, the material interprets where the next pressure will land and adjusts slightly to accommodate that movement. If you wanted, you could walk the entire room, and the bed would shift with you."

Jasmine slid off the bed, her laughter reverberating on the lavender walls. "That sounds like fun. I want to do that." Stopping in front of Marcus, she held out her hand. "I'm Jasmine, Mister Sir. I'm going to drive a ship when I grow up. Jarren said so. Do you drive ships?"

Marcus bent on one knee and shook Jasmine's hand, nodding crisply. "It is very nice to meet you, esteemed daughter. I do fly ships. It is a good job, but you must study hard so that you too may fly one day." He looked up at Lissa as he continued. "With your mother's permission, I will continue your education while you're with us. That is a choice your mother must make, and she must make it without your interference. Will you let her think on it and speak with me about it later?"

Jasmine nodded quickly. "Oh yes, Mister Sir. Abuela tells me the same thing. I am very good at letting Mommy think, 'cause if I don't, the answer is usually no. And I don't like 'no' answers."

"Not 'Mister Sir.' If you really wish, you may call me 'Beside Family.' Now, how is Mommy feeling? I heard she fell and got bumped up?" he asked Jasmine with the straightest of faces.

"Oh, Mommy's fine. Rila came and put this little machine on her leg, and she felt all better. And it didn't even take no time at all. Not any!" Jasmine replied, her head bobbing with confidence.

"Very good." Marcus stood and smiled at Lissa. Lissa grinned. His pleasantness was catching. She had set out not to trust anyone on Jarren's crew. But if all his crew were as welcoming as Marcus, she would have a hard time keeping her distance.

"Mommy, did you hear me? I'm not going to interrupt you thinking about that, okay?"

Lissa looked down at Jasmine with a nod. "Thank you, Butterfly. Now let's find you something to do for a bit in your room. I want to talk big people talk with Mr. Naas. That would include deciding whether he can teach you."

Marcus interrupted with a hesitant hand on Lissa's shoulder. "Did Jarren show you the functions of the suite?"

Lissa turned. "No. I was only interested in sleeping. I could see the bed when we came in. I didn't ask about anything else."

Marcus nodded at that clipped response. "Well, let me show you what Jasmine may do. I believe she will discover a lot to capture her interest."

They walked through the doorway to Jasmine's room. Beyond lay an exact duplicate of the outer room, only everything was just slightly smaller. A child-sized intuitive bed with rainbow-striped sheets claimed half the room. A wood-like desk with three metal chairs flanking its three sides lay flush against a wall where an unknown light source illuminated the table's smooth surface below. On a far wall stood a door Lissa discovered led into a bathroom, the duplicate of Lissa's bathroom. An odd, oblong, midnight-blue object Lissa equated to a beanbag chair only softer, more malleable, sat in the middle of the floor.

Marcus led them over to the table and pulled out a seat for Jasmine. A screen appeared on the surface of the desk, and a female voice spoke. "Hello, Jasmine. Would you like to play a game?"

Jasmine's eyebrows shot up with surprise, and she turned to her mother. "Mommy, the table is talking to me." She let out a happy squeal and clapped her hands together.

Lissa grinned at her daughter. Satisfaction tickled her insides.

Marcus cleared his throat. "Unit."

The female voice responded immediately. "Yes, Second?"

"Please begin level one game, Colors and Stars."

Again, the female voice floated through the room. "Confirmed, Second."

A color appeared on the screen beneath Jasmine's hands. Marcus took a seat and pointed to the screen as he gave instructions. "This is a color game, Jasmine. I know you must be very good with colors. Here is the object of the game. The screen will show you a picture that you will need to draw. See the picture?"

Lissa glanced over Jasmine's head as she looked down at a picture of a clearing in the woods at night. "Okay. I see it." Jasmine looked at Marcus again.

"Good. Now look at the walls of your room." Marcus spoke, and Jasmine peered at the mauve of the walls as they began to lighten to white. Bold black lines ran along the walls clearly outlining the picture on the screen. "What you must do is call out a color. The screen will switch from the picture to the color you called out. Place your hand on the screen. Go to the portion of walls where you saw the color and put your hand on that area of the wall to change it to your color.

There are thirty colors used in this picture. Do you think you know the thirty colors?"

Jasmine nodded eagerly.

"Good. When you have finished the picture, the game will give you a prize. Nothing to hold, mind you, but I think you will like the reward, since I now know how much you want to fly ships when you grow up."

Jasmine studied the picture. "One other thing, young one," Marcus continued. "You must finish coloring your picture before you call us into the room. If you open the door before the picture is complete, the colors will fade, and your mother and I will not be able to see your work. Alright?"

Lissa smiled at her daughter's quick nod and frown of concentration. She'd already forgotten they were there. Marcus got up with surprising agility and gestured for Lissa to follow him back to her room. As they exited, Lissa keyed the door shut.

"Will she know the colors? Are they colors we have on Earth?" Lissa asked as Marcus gestured toward the larger table and chairs.

Marcus sat. "She will know all the colors. She is at the easiest level of comprehension. Identifying a color teaches her to use one side of her brain. Remembering where that color fits into an overall picture stimulates the other side. The synapses in her brain are also stimulated to enhance her ability to recall images. Finally, she is encouraged to finish a project before a reward is presented. Discouraging her from including you in the process stimulates her concentration on the job as well as her enjoyment of her own success. It is a good learning tool that can adapt to the needs of each child when an issue is identified by the game. I suspect she will be in there all night."

Lissa smothered a laugh. "Oh, if only. Is the game based on sequential or random patterning?"

"Sequential."

"Hmm. We probably have half an hour before she's figured out the pattern."

He raised a brow in disbelief. "This is a new game for her. I admire your confidence, but don't be disappointed if it takes her some time."

Lissa tapped her nose, playful. "Shall we make a little wager?" At his doubtful look, she went on. "Nothing ridiculous or anything. I won't ask for anything you wouldn't approve of. Live a little. You're the one in power here. Not me."

Both his eyebrows rose. "None of us have much power right now, Melissa, but you certainly have the least power. I'm sorry you were involved."

His words dampened her playfulness. Lissa had sat but now slouched in her chair. "We're all sorry I was involved. None of us more than me. But I think you're a nice person, Marcus. Place your bet. Distract me for a moment from the fact that I am on a ship racing eons of miles away from my home, from everything stable in my life, from everything I worked so hard to achieve."

With a resigned frown, Marcus nodded, and Lissa released a breath.

"If I am correct and it takes your little one all night to complete a picture, then you must allow me to teach her," Marcus stated.

Why would an important, busy man put aside time to teach her daughter? "Do you have any children?"

"I have a sister your daughter's age. Jasmine reminds me of her. My sister and I are very close, as our parents are true life-mated."

"They're what?"

Marcus waved off her question. "Never mind. I shall explain when we again have time on our hands."

Lissa let the dismissal slide. "Okay, so Jasmine receives her lessons from you if you're right. Well, if I'm right and she is done sooner, I want you to give me a personally guided tour of the ship…or at least the parts I am allowed access to," Lissa added when he opened his mouth to object. Jarren had been very clear she would not be allowed full access to his ship for both their safety. After a moment, Marcus nodded and held out a hand. She gripped his warm palm confidently then sat back.

Looking into his eyes, Lissa voiced the question in her head that no one else seemed willing to answer. "Why the hell am I here?"

He didn't hesitate to respond. "I will give you the most honest answer I have, if you answer a question for me first. Why do you call your daughter this word, bu-tter-fly?"

Lissa laughed. She was enamored of Marcus. He was as easygoing as Miguel. A picture of her cousin, knocking at her bedroom door to no avail, flashed across her mind's eye. Those thoughts caused her laugh to catch in her throat. She'd spoken to him only briefly from the ship. She'd had to explain her closeness to Miguel to Jarren. He hadn't understood how

Miguel's mother had been so willing to give her son to her sister when he'd been diagnosed with spina bifida. Jarren did understand why Lissa saw Miguel more as a brother than a cousin. Incredibly educated and intelligent, Miguel split his time living with either Lissa or her mother. It wasn't a breeze for him in his wheelchair. He did it as an excuse to financially support them both. Loss squeezed her heart as she thought of him.

Her cousin had wanted to know why she hadn't waited till he got home to say goodbye. Lissa mumbled some empty excuse, then quickly hung up. Now, light-years away, here was another man who reminded her so much of her cousin. She felt comfortable with him. Sadness entered her. Looking into Marcus's eyes, she replied, "My mother began calling her Butterfly—'mariposa' in her native language—when she was two. Jasmine had a little multicolored sweater with dozens of butterflies sewn onto it. Jasmine would run around my mother's house looking in drawers and climbing into windowsills. My mother said she looked like one big inquisitive butterfly, so she began calling her Butterfly. It stuck, as did Jasmine's curiosity."

"That's nice. I shall, of course, have to look up the species butterfly to understand the story to its fullest, but thank you for telling me."

Lissa laughed, but she wouldn't be distracted from her question. She gave Marcus a pointed look until he began to speak. "You are here because Jarren couldn't fight his natural instincts. Nor could you. And…because your life was in danger as a result of your unusual bonding."

"That sounds like a load of crap. You're talking in riddles."

He shook his head. "I'm sorry. I don't mean to confuse you. Let me try again. Jarren's instinct to bond with you, with your scent, caused him to release his essence. Your response to him was the result of your need to bond with him. Neither of you could resist your natural instincts. Bonding is biological. Your bonding marked you with Jarren's scent: the scent the bounty hunters were given to track and destroy."

"But I don't understand. Jarren's scent stimulated my natural instincts?"

"Didn't he explain this to you?"

"He tried. I didn't understand it. Maybe I didn't want to. He mentioned not having control over himself. But how could I believe that? I can't imagine him not controlling the stars themselves. And how can I believe I lost control of myself without the influence of some drug? My father raised me to take responsibility for all my decisions—even those I feel are out of my control. Blaming my hormones for a sexual attraction simply isn't an acceptable excuse."

"What you experienced is deeper than hormones, Melissa. Do not let your father's philosophy belittle your situation. And don't confuse acting on instinct with losing control. In your relationship with Jarren, he may seem to control you at times, but you should know you can control him as completely, should you wish. Especially considering how strong a bond you have with him."

What was he talking about? Lissa never considered herself intellectually challenged. Her inability to understand was beginning to grate on her. Her pitch climbed. "Control him? When have I ever exercised any control over him? He revealed his scent—as you said—and I was drawn to him; I couldn't resist him. It's our *biology*."

Lissa closed her eyes and prayed for calm. "He wanted to get me alone so he simply drove me away from everything I knew, from anything that might threaten his control over me. When he decided to leave Earth and take me with him, he did. He never questioned his decision, and I was helpless to stop him. He didn't even question whether he had a right to exercise that amount of authority over another person."

She paused, mid-tirade. She knew Jarren's self-confidence was a show. He'd fooled himself and even her for a while. But when she'd looked into his eyes after the attack, when he'd spoken of not foreseeing the threat, she'd seen through his brash behavior. He knew that he controlled the lives of so many. For some reason, it ate at him to have that responsibility, whether he admitted it or not. Lissa understood. Her mother had been perfect. She had worked herself to the bone, and Ulises had given Brenda Reyes his love in return. Lissa, too, strove to be perfect, to prove herself worthy of love. But there was no greater pain than self-disappointment.

"But what of the Sharing Ritual? Did you not feel some equilibrium in your relationship when you could control him?"

Lissa threw her hands up. "What the blazes are you speaking of? Sharing? I haven't sat down to do anything civilized with him."

Marcus sat back as if the wind had been knocked from him, then he got up and called out a question into the air.

"Unit, duty time."

"Remaining off-duty time is five hours ten minutes, Second."

Marcus nodded absently and headed for the door. As an afterthought, he turned back. "I'll talk to Jarren, Melissa. It is no wonder you don't comprehend what's going on. You've missed a piece of the puzzle."

Finally, someone had been willing to listen where Jarren had only demanded. The ever-present tension in her body eased. Marcus was trying to understand.

"It's 'Lissa,'" she said as he walked to the door.

He stepped through the entrance and out into the hall, glancing back. "What?"

"My friends call me 'Lissa.'"

A slow smile spread across Marcus's mouth. "Thank you for that consideration, Lissa. I have to go, but I will come back in a few hours to escort you to the Bridge Crew's Salon. In the meantime, if you need anything, just call out to Unit. I'll start putting together a work schedule for Jasmine."

Lissa threw a startled look at Jasmine's still-closed door. When she looked back at Marcus, he waved and walked away, but she spied a wide grin on his face. Obviously half an hour had already gone by. So much for a tour of the ship.

CHAPTER *15*

JARREN SAT IN appreciative quiet, the lights dimmed in his Ready room, looking over star maps as Marcus walked in. When Marcus strode toward him, Jarren tensed. Something wasn't right. His second seemed agitated. Sitting back in the plush chair, Jarren's fingers drummed on the oval meeting table.

"Second," Jarren stated.

Marcus didn't wait for further acknowledgement. "Why have you kept your mate in the dark? Especially considering she is an alien. She has no one to show her our ways."

Jarren quirked an eyebrow. *What by the purple Mocns of Lynta was Marcus talking about?* "Explain."

With a sigh, Marcus slid into a chair and leaned back, his head tilted to the clear dome ceiling that revealed the deep of space. Jarren waited.

Finally, Marcus's gaze shifted to Jarren. "You have not had a bonding ceremony with her. Your mate is terrified of losing control of herself. She thinks you control her biologically."

"That's absurd. As the female, she can exert more control over me than I her."

Marcus interrupted. "But how would she know that if you haven't taken sustenance with her, haven't entrusted her with the Sharing Ritual? How is it that you two have skipped so many layers in the process? I'm willing to bet she doesn't know we males are more sensitive to our bonded's scent than our gender opposites. You probably didn't explain why you *had* to turn down your Subduer to gauge her attraction. It isn't like you not to be considerate of your mate." Marcus paused before continuing. "I know you question many things right now, friend. But don't question this. You deserve your mate. The gods gave her to you."

"The gods did not give her to me, Marcus. My shortcomings as a ruler and my lack of self-control just happened to thrust me directly in her path. It's a great cosmic joke that my perfect mate as good as hates me."

Jarren got up to pace the quarter-moon shape of the room. Marcus remained silent. Jarren pushed down the guilt and pain in his heart. He had an obligation to the people on his ship, to the people of Lynta, and to the plan hatched at his birth to end a system of subjugation that would caste down Terrans as a sub-species. He might not be worthy of the responsibility, but it was his, nonetheless.

At least he could resolve Lissa's misconception. "You are right. She would be under the impression that she has no control. She's the one without the experience and knowledge."

"She is the one who lost her home and her life as well. From the way I see it, Jarren, you have been controlling her world from the minute you walked into it, the gods' interference aside."

Jarren thought back. "Actually, it was the minute she knocked me into it." A satisfied smile slid over his mouth. He could recall her smell in that memory, still.

"Excuse me?"

Jarren shook his head and leaned self-consciously over his star maps once more. The thought of Lissa had made him hard with desire. "Again, you're right, Marcus. I will complete the Sharing ceremony tonight. That is, if she is amenable. If memory serves, you were tasked with gaining her trust."

"Hmm. Well, I think I have her trust as much as one would expect. She has agreed to accompany me to the Salon for introductions later. She seemed interested in going, actually."

"Is it too much to hope that she be amenable to having me accompany her?"

Marcus laughed. "I've no idea. How did she act toward you last?"

Jarren rubbed his chin. "I thought I had put a small chink in her armor, but no need to push it. I'll meet you both there and will give her the space she needs. If you want me to commence the Sharing Ritual with her tonight, you will have to prepare her."

Marcus shot him an awed look. "You are not asking me to woo your mate for you, are you? I won't do that. The so-called trust I established with her, the trust you asked me to build, would be irreparably ruined. She barely knows me. And she is no gullible person who doesn't process the information given her. No mate of yours would be."

Jarren didn't want that type of mate anyway. Not any longer. Years ago, he would have let his essence decide his mate. Now she had to be a five-six, raven-haired, thoughtfully purposeful beauty. He would take no substitutions.

"I do not want you to woo her." He clenched a fist and cleared the emotion from his throat. "I belong to her. I just don't want her taken unawares. Explain the Sharing. Tell her I erred when I didn't offer her the ceremony. I will contact her before you arrive and ask her to decide what to do before the evening is out," Jarren mumbled.

Marcus nodded, then pushed away from the table and got up to pace. "That sounds right." Pausing at the door, he glanced over. "You know, you still didn't answer either question."

Jarren met Marcus's gaze. As the high prince of the royal line of Lynta, Jarren concealed his true feelings from those around him. He was a leader. Personal feelings were never expressed publicly.

But Marcus was a leader on his world in his own right. They spoke openly to each other when no one else could be considered a confidant. Jarren ran a hand through his hair as he let out a frustrated moan. "The woman overwhelms every inch of me, Marcus. I cannot plan or isolate the variables impacting my plans' outcomes, cannot make sense of the situation in which I find myself, can barely think straight when I am near her. I act on instinct alone. Protocol and tradition have been the last things on my mind. There's no way I would have thought about the Sharing Ritual. I should have gone through the ritual with her before we got to *Desire*. But when she is near, well…"

Marcus smiled sympathetically. "I daresay there are parts of you that focus on her whether she is near or not. She is your mate, Jarren. Maybe even something more," he mumbled.

The two men stared at each other a moment. But Jarren wouldn't ponder the idea that his bond with Lissa was deeper than that of a mate. He'd promised to return her to Earth when he reclaimed the throne, and he would keep that promise. The idea of having bonded with Lissa beyond normal mate status would devastate his life. Totally devastate it.

With a worried frown, Jarren shook his head then stared down at the star chart once more. Concentrating on a course that would keep *Desire* off the Alliance's radar as well as the bounty hunters', his eyes slowly plotted a course around the Andereas and Crynor star systems and through Hexion's asteroid belts. He picked up a map writer and leveraged its white tip against the dark-blue surface. As his hand moved slowly across the paper, the writer plotted a white line charting their final course.

Marcus turned to watch Jarren's progress on the viewing screen keyed to the map. When Jarren finished, he looked up to watch the unit plug in the coordinates for the remainder of their trip. Marcus nodded as the last coordinate locked. Faheel would follow up in a few minutes when he received the course.

Jarren wiped his hand across the map, and the white path disappeared. He pulled at the length of paper then folded it and placed it and the map writer in the small cubby built into a crevice of the table before retaking his seat.

Marcus continued to gaze at their course on the screen. "It's a good course. At the right speed, we should be at Deneb by tomorrow. It isn't the route we took to get you to Earth."

"No. I only thought, then, that the hunters might be in the vicinity. I was more cautious. They know where we are now, and speed is more important."

"Nasty things, hunters can be. What kind did Milovar send to Earth?"

Jarren's eyes narrowed. "Pure Bounty. I'm sure they originated from the ship that attacked us," he replied, clenching his fists in anger. Of often limited sentient comprehension, hunters were illegally bred on various planets throughout Jarren's galaxy then traded as "intelligent pets," servants, black-market bounty hunters, even purchased in bulk for dangerous jobs like mine labor. Hunters came in different breeds. Towering mutated biped creatures covered in a thin brushing of coarse dark hair follicles, they possessed unusual strength and stamina.

They were bred without a conscience by their Warlord Keepers from birth. The Pure Bounty hunters had a shield implanted which visually distorted their bodies, allowing them to blend into dark areas easily. The implant melded into its user's spinal cord, creating instinctive shielding. Modified to have a heightened sense of smell, they tracked and killed indiscriminately once their noses locked on a scent. And they hunted mercilessly until their keepers called them off.

Many years ago, Jarren's father had taken him to a newly located breeding planet on their way back from a diplomatic

Alliance meeting. His father wanted to impart the horrors of Pure Bounty breeding planets, firsthand. Abandoned by their keepers, the beasts had taken to killing and eating the weakest of their groups.

But they weren't starving. Their keepers had abandoned them mere hours before, and fresh food lay smashed in piles on the ground. Jarren and his father stood silently, staring out through the airlock of the jumper as it hovered over the desert that spanned below them. Bodies with blood pooling near detached limbs like large drops of black ink littered the orange ground. Brown furry faces stared up unseeing at the orange sun. The aftermath of a battle zone could not have been more horrendous. Jarren had rushed to the relief and retched.

Marcus's whistle brought Jarren back to his present predicament. "That bastard."

"You shouldn't be surprised. I'm sure he gave orders to bring me back alive, but using a Tracking hunter decreased the likelihood no innocent bystanders would be hurt or killed."

"Well, I cannot fathom hate that runs that deep."

Jarren thought about Lissa, and fire licked at his insides. If anything ever happened to her, he would easily kill those who were responsible without a moment of regret. "I am beginning to, friend."

Marcus plopped back into a chair. There were still other issues that had nothing to do with Lissa which they needed to discuss. Jarren had put it off, but now that their course was set, he needed to know the situation he'd be walking into. "Any news from Lynta or the Alliance since my departure?"

"No intelligence from Lynta, Jarren. I'm sorry. On the news vidcasts, the coup has been smoothed over. Milovar is using the footage of you and him together when he arrived at the palace, cutting and pasting a fictional situation. The story is you and he spoke and decided it was in Lynta's best interest for you to step down and allow your more 'experienced' cousin to rule while you mourn your father. That is, until such time as your experience makes you a fit leader."

Jarren subdued a growl as he leaned forward. "I already have the experience of a fit leader."

"Well, at least your mother is well protected with that tale."

Jarren turned his head up to look into space. "Then she is well?"

"Again, I don't have intelligence, but he has had to let her make several appearances in the popular reports to appease some growing unease both on and off-planet. There's footage of her in several video clips. She doesn't look happy, but she doesn't look abused either."

Jarren nodded. "And the Alliance?"

"There, I do have intel. Veena's person says she has a third of the Alliance openly calling for a meeting with Milovar about your sudden abdication. Another third of the Alliance will quietly support any move for you to retake the throne; money, weapons, anything you think you might need, you'll get."

"But not men?"

"Men can be traced to a political source. But resources can secure you men—"

"Who can also be re-purchased by the highest bidder. Any other good news?"

"My father has finally agreed to house you and host your strategy meetings, and he's willing to act toward an end to the system," Marcus stated with a lazy drawl. Jarren couldn't subdue a smile.

"Well, it's a good thing your negotiations were successful as we'll be arriving…when did you say again?"

Marcus laughed outright. "Tomorrow."

Jarren stood and stretched. "Yes. Lissa will not be separated from Jasmine just because Jasmine is considered 'Below the Family.' Which of your threats worked, anyway?"

"It was one of yours, actually. His face crumbled when I mentioned it. I think maybe he hoped I didn't know."

Jarren grunted. "Who would have known your father was superstitious?"

"You did, obviously."

A slow smile curled both their mouths in unison. "It's a good thing he is true life-mated. Threatening to curse his union at the temple of Janelle would not have worked otherwise."

Marcus's laugh rang out loudly as they walked out of Jarren's Ready room and toward the bridge. "Yes, Captain. It was a stroke of genius that your mother recounted the time she'd coerced my father. He helped her find your father the days he went missing on Deneb. And, of course, it was my mother who told her to say it."

"And it was your mother again who told you to repeat the threat this time around once you told her why," Jarren stated. Their laughter bounced down the hallway.

*　　*　　*　　*　　*

"LADY LISSA, HEALER Rila requests permission to enter," Unit's voice rang out. Lissa looked up toward the door from her perched position at the table.

"She can...uh, enter," Lissa said aloud.

She was still getting used to her unseen AI assistant doing everything for her. She'd gone into the bathroom and found a beautiful clamshell-shaped bathtub dominating the large space. It looked like marble, but as she ran her hands across the outlay of the tub, the smooth tan surface felt warm. What Lissa guessed were spigots, three conch shell knobs that stuck out at an odd angle from the tub, were somewhat rough to the touch like rounded coral. But as she pulled her hand away and glanced over at the wall-length dark-tint mirror, Unit spoke—from inside her right ear.

"Begin bathwater, Lady Lissa?" The artificial voice shocked her. She'd nearly forgotten Rila had inserted a microscopic Unit link-up at the tip of her spine. That Unit had asked the question shocked Lissa more. Were there cameras hidden where Unit could observe?

Lissa stepped away from the tub and out of the bathroom. Its mellow calming colors and relaxing earthy scent suddenly seemed like a pot of poisoned honey hung low to kill the curious bear. Something observing her was too creepy. "Are you watching me?"

"No, Lady Lissa." The metallic female voice grated on Lissa's nerves.

"Explain how you knew I was going to bathe, Unit." Lissa summoned all the crassness she could when speaking to the uncontained AI.

"Your hand touched the sensory knobs for the bath."

"Then you sensed my hand on the knob?"

"Yes. Your implanted Unit link-up identified a physical connection with the software that controls your bathroom functions. *Stardesire* does not have cameras installed in any bathrooms."

Lissa shuddered out a sigh of relief. "Thank you for the information, Unit." Then, Unit repeated the original question.

Lissa returned to the bathroom and took a long bath. The voice in her head would take some getting used to.

Now, hours later, Lissa looked up as her door slid open. Rila sailed in, her white hair flowing out behind her, her beautiful chartreuse eyes twinkling with merriment. Her face lit with a smile.

Rila wore another long, sequined dress—this time a burnt orange that offset the paleness of her hair and added a healthy glow to her skin. She reached out to squeeze Lissa's hands, then took a seat next to her.

"Hello again, Lissa. I thank you for your trust in me. I shall look after Jasmine well. I know this transition has been hardest on you, and you have had the least amount of support." Rila's words eased the stiffness in Lissa's posture.

Lissa gave a slight smile. "Well, I had instructions, didn't I?" Jarren had messaged earlier and pressed home that he would expect to see Lissa at the Salon gathering tonight. Then he'd continued, his voice somewhat placid, as he explained he wanted to conduct a traditional Lyntan ritual with her. Lissa said yes. What harm was there in attending a Lyntan ritual?

Rila's smile slipped a bit, but she responded, nevertheless. "Well, had you chosen not to attend because you wanted to stay with your daughter, he would not have forced you. It will be good for you to meet the bridge crew and to have another opportunity to speak to Jarren. If for no other reason than to, uh, discuss how you have hated it here: hate your chambers, hate the food—everything that has been on your mind."

Lissa stood up and straightened her dress. A plum-colored reception dress, it clung to Lissa's curves and flowed out to drape down over her ankles and back into a little train. Spaghetti straps held the layered scoop neck to her form, the alien material gathering her cleavage close and further curving in her figure.

"You look fine," Rila stated with a smile.

"This dress is appropriate? I guessed this event was a little more formal. There were several dresses in the wardrobe. I had no idea what to wear."

Rila moved over to the bed and sat. The edge molded into a makeshift seat. "It's fine, Lissa. Social rules for behavior and presentation are different on Lynta. Clothing to Lyntans relays so little information. Those social influences that Lyntans are concerned with are handled by the implants."

Lissa's hand went to her wrist to slide across the smooth flesh covering her Subduer. Rila tilted her head. "It isn't bothering you at all? You remember how to use it?"

Lissa nodded. "I remember, though I admit I'm still a bit confused as to why it's so important."

"Well, I imagine you will have a greater understanding of its use soon enough. And how is the translator working for you? You sound as if you've made a smooth transition."

"It seems to be working fine. I just have to get used to my mouth moving on its own when I think of responses to a different language. Not entirely a foreign concept, since I am bilingual. It was the right decision to have it put in. Jasmine seems to have made the transition without any issue."

The implanted translator chip changed any verbal communication into a language the user understood. Occasionally, the mechanism stimulated the user's oratories to reply in the language spoken, if Unit didn't sense a translator in use with the other speaker. It was a little discomfiting hearing foreign words come out of mouths then having to wait for the brain to create a definition for what was said. But Rila was clear Lissa would hear an uncountable number of dialects around her. She would have been at a disadvantage meeting someone who also didn't have a translator, and there were many planets in the Alliance where the technology wasn't used.

Rila nodded. "Children who are allowed always adapt to implants much easier than adults. All Lyntan children of the higher castes are implanted by Jasmine's age."

Lissa could not help but interrupt. "Higher castes?"

"Lower caste children are not often allowed off planet. Those who reach adulthood and show useful intelligence around interstellar activities are then given implants. Jasmine would not be considered a higher caste. Jarren has instructed she receive the same privileges as a child 'Of the Family.' We serve on this ship because he denies the Lyntan caste system. Our value is determined by our individual accomplishments and our commitment to changing this system, Here, we serve as equals, but on Lynta, we are subjugated by the system. He is the hope of many. Through his ascendency, many expect the caste system to change or end all together."

Lissa remained silent. Another dimension of Jarren and his world's politics she hadn't understood.

Done with explaining empire politics, Rila continued. "The brain synapses are still malleable. I have found that some Lyntan children could easily have their translators removed by adulthood because their brains have patterned all the languages they use. And they acquire new languages quickly. Quite extraordinary, actually. Jasmine's intelligence level easily rivals any Lyntan child. She may wish to have her translator removed once she is old enough. That is what Jarren decided when he came of age."

Lissa's smile faltered. Old enough? Of age? Rila's tone held a ring of finality. Lissa and Jasmine would be returning to Earth as soon as possible. Both their implants would have to be removed before they got home. If she ever got home, of course. Jarren seemed certain she couldn't go home soon, but his thinking was influenced by his biological need. He might delay her return for his baser instincts. She could use an ally to confront Jarren. Marcus wouldn't help her. Rila was as loyal as Marcus, but other crewmembers might not be so blinded by their personal loyalty.

Pushing the thought from her mind, Lissa walked over to the wall and pressed the button she'd found when she'd been looking for clothes she'd brought from Earth.

She had started pushing buttons and discovered a shelf that folded out where she could request food and drinks. Another wall panel flipped around to reveal a full-length mirror, and paneling slid away, revealing a large opening in the wall opposite the bathroom. Its recess was lined with all manner of clothing one found in the awards ceremony section of a movie star's well-sized walk-in closet. If she didn't know better, she wouldn't have thought she was a prisoner. Of course, prisoners couldn't leave when they decided.

Unit's voice chimed. "Lady Lissa, Second-in-Command requests permission to enter."

"Alright." She walked to the door. Rila's words about removing Jasmine's implants still bothered her.

Marcus stepped through the doorway and smiled at Lissa. He'd swapped his tan shirt for a maroon one. Returning his smile, Lissa placed her hand on his crooked arm.

"My lady."

Lissa smiled. "How chivalrous." She flipped her head back, her hair licking out at the air as Marcus escorted her to the door. "Thank you, Rila. Jasmine's asleep. She ate and bathed. I don't expect you to have to keep much of an eye on her."

Rila waved Lissa out. "She will be fine. I will call you if I need. Don't worry. Have a good time and enjoy yourself."

Lissa followed Marcus out.

"Unit could have watched Jasmine."

Lissa shrugged. "Call me old-fashioned."

"Are you ready for the Sharing?" Marcus asked as they proceeded down the hall.

"Jarren mentioned it would help me understand Lyntan olfactory stimulation better. I'm as ready as I can be. I need to get a grasp on my situation since I obviously can't change it." She knew Marcus watched her intently. "What?" Lissa asked as she met his thoughtful gaze. There was no way he could know she intended this event to recruit allies to help her get home.

Marcus studied her. "You are a very good match for Jarren."

"Am I?"

"You complement his behavior perfectly. He is not an easy one to match. I've only known one other to match him so closely." Lissa stumbled at that statement, her dress wrapping around her ankles. Was Jarren already matched to someone else? Reaching out as they paused, Marcus held her up while she pulled at and untangled her train.

Keeping her gaze pointedly on the ground, Lissa posited a question. "What other would that be?"

Marcus patted her hand as they resumed walking. "Princess Veena. She is Jarren's betrothed." He spoke so matter-of-factly.

Lissa nearly choked. How could Jarren long for Lissa as his mate when he already had a bride on the side? Thoughts of his reunion with Rila returned to her head. Did partners in this world have more than one bonded mate in relationships?

Well, she wasn't interested in Jarren anyway. Tonight she would find someone who could get her home, someone who wasn't blinded by lust or loyalty. And Jarren could go back to his original engagement. Lissa ignored the burn in her chest. "I didn't know Jarren was betrothed."

Marcus must have heard the confused anger in her voice. "She isn't his mate. Their essences were tested when they were teenagers. They are distantly related, as are much of those 'Of the Family.' It was just assumed that they would mate given their mutual status and compatibility. You are far more compatible. And it is obvious that Jarren wants you."

Lissa's pace slowed, and she tipped her head to look up at him. The illogical pattern of her emotions made no sense to her. She should have gleefully celebrated Jarren's other associations. After all, he didn't love her. They were simply bonded. His betrothal could only help put the distance between them that would ensure he returned her to Earth when she was safe again. That is, if she couldn't find her own way. But Lissa wasn't gleeful.

In her logical mind, guilt for considering ways to incite mutiny within Jarren's crew ate at her. She hated that he'd taken her, controlled her, yet she couldn't deny she found him annoyingly intelligent and responsible. He was born to lead. And somewhere in her depths, she knew she would never be lonely with him near. Well, he wasn't near now, and her loneliness reached out to encase her heart as guilt fought with homesickness—spurred by the hint of jealousy.

"We are nearly there, Lissa. You must wipe the look of unhappiness from your face, or Jarren will wonder what's going on. This is a happy occasion. It's best you present yourself with all the beauty I have seen within you," Marcus whispered, unwavering.

Lissa brushed at the tears in her eyes. There was no reason for her to feel so downtrodden. Shaking her head and taking in a breath, she turned up to Marcus with a slight smile. She was still Melissa Reyes. Survivor. Accepting that power took intention.

Marcus continued to stare at her, concern clearly written in his glance. He had no idea of the complex emotions battling within her. "A betrothal on Lynta has a different meaning than on Earth, Lissa. Believe me when I say your bonding with Jarren supersedes his match with Veena. Everyone will know the instant you and he are together. Your bonding is undeniable."

"Right, well, let's hope not. I want off this piece of metal as soon as possible. I'm fine. I was startled a moment, but I'm good now." Their footsteps slowed in front of a wide entryway. Lissa looked up, her composure reclaimed, and smiled her most entrancing smile. "Shall we?"

"Indeed, my new friend." He returned her smile, though concern still shone in his eyes. "By the way, I reviewed Jasmine's progress with her pictures. It seems I owe you a tour of the ship sometime. She finished three paintings in that half hour, then fell asleep."

"No surprise there. We'll do that tour soon, Marcus," she replied, generating false enthusiasm. His brows came together, his expression discordant. Lissa squeezed his arm reassuringly. She had buried the hurt deep, along with the guilt. He had nothing to worry about. Lissa Reyes would charm every person on this ship, if she had to, to ensure Jarren never became aware of the ache she'd felt. If she charmed every person in the room, maybe she would find the help she needed to get away from Jarren with his ready bride on the side. She would find someone willing to search for a way to mask Jarren's scent. Then Lissa would go home.

CHAPTER *16*

JARREN LEANED AGAINST a wall in the officers' social room, the Parlor, listening to Corsa's thoughts on improving the ship's hyperdrive. The woman's brilliant ideas, normally enthralling, simply bounced unheard, in one ear and out the other. A hesitant tug on his shirtsleeve drew Jarren's attention. "Sir. You haven't heard a word I said."

Jarren looked up. People mingled in the Salon. As usual, Jarren had sought Corsa out in a corner and engaged her in the only subject he knew she became animated about: engines. Faheel was present along with Wesla Taleek, also Lyntan and Faheel's life partner. Sitting at one round table among a scattering, were Security Chief Jamis Maradek, Second-class Navigation Officer Mina Kel, and Healer Janalese, Rila's apprentice.

The scent of warm papaya rushed into Jarren's nostrils. He was glad Rila altered his Subduer so he could sense Lissa again. Jarren straightened and glanced at the entrance; taking Corsa's arm, he walked toward the entryway. "You're right, Corsa. I'm not listening. Come and meet our guest."

Second Engineer Breena Solan towered over Karus Sim as they stood at a long bar that lined a wall of the Salon. Jarren's gaze returned briefly to Mina, Karus's mate, laughing at something Jamis said, as two wide, burly men blocked his path. Hairy faces appeared over uniforms that barely contained the untamed hair all over their bodies. Gimi and Girsch, like all species of hunters, were the well-muscled embodiment of the Terran Neanderthal.

The brothers were more recent additions to Jarren's inner circle, but they had proven themselves time and time again. They both smiled, almost unnoticeable tusks peeking out between their lips as Jarren slowed before them. Reaching out, he patted each on the brown tracts of hair that shot out from the splits at the shoulders of their vests.

Jarren eyed them, shaking his head. He hadn't told Lissa that there were hunters on board. He hoped she wouldn't be too surprised. The brothers, as part of the bridge's security and Jamis's lieutenants, were fully aware of Lissa's only experiences with others of their kind. They would be tolerant should she be frightened or taken aback.

Jarren winked as he spoke. "Greetings, men. It is good of you both to attend. I heard there was a wicked card game happening below decks. That's stiff competition for a stuffy officers' event."

Girsch laughed gruffly and shook his head. "Anyone can attend the card game. Only a few have clearance to be here."

"Besides, Girsch and I cleaned those boys out not a week before. All they've got left to bargain with is coins," Gimi grunted, then laughed the same laugh as his brother.

Jarren smiled. "Indeed, indeed. Well, I am glad you're here, whatever the reason." Corsa's head bobbed timidly in agreement. The hunters nodded a gentle acknowledgement at Corsa.

The waft of warm blossoming papaya grew until Jarren knew Lissa stood outside the doorway. Smiling at Girsch and Gimi, Jarren walked Corsa closer to the door and arrived just as Jamis approached, his brow crinkled. Jarren bit back a frown. He'd seen that look before. His attention was redirected as Marcus walked in, Lissa's hand resting on his arm.

A mixture of fragrances assaulted Jarren's nose. Lissa's warm essence disappeared beneath the musky scent of interest, then growing desire, which originated from Jamis beside him. Competition—enemy—Jamis's essence yelled compatibility and interest. Jealousy surged through Jarren. He itched to lower his Subduer, let his scent overwhelm Jamis's. Involuntarily, Jarren's body tensed as if he prepared for battle. A battle to keep his place at Lissa's side.

Jarren stepped forward and removed Lissa's hand from Marcus's crooked arm, then placed himself directly next to her. Out of the corner of his eye, he saw her cast a startled glance at him, but she didn't pull away.

"Lissa," Jarren said, his voice harsh.

She looked up at him, her soft blue stare approachable. "Jarren."

For a moment, Jarren forgot where they were. His eyes focused on her alone. His ears shut out all discussion and laughter. Only he and Lissa existed. Musky heat and welcome flowed out of her pores. Jarren breathed her in and leaned toward her.

Then the sour smell of another male's desire filtered into his nostrils. Jarren looked at Jamis again. The urge to beat him into the floor then snatch Lissa up and cover her until no scent of her own remained fought to break through his barely controlled passivity. Jarren's fists clenched as fury filled him. He'd just pushed Lissa behind him and faced his opponent when he heard Marcus clear his throat. Jarren jolted back to awareness, to his crew moving about the Salon, to eyes strayed uncomfortably toward him. What in Creeds was he doing? Jarren relaxed his stance. Jamis did the same.

With false neutrality, Jarren spoke. "Melissa, this is Security Chief Jamis Maradek. Jamis, my honored guest, Melissa Reyes." Jarren pushed down the need to claim their mated status. Publicly stating their association required Lissa's agreement, despite the scent everyone had to be aware of.

With the ease of royalty, Lissa stepped away from him and held out a hand. "I am pleased to meet you, Jamis. Excuse my innocence if Lyntans don't shake hands when introduced."

A soft tinkling of laughter erupted around Jarren. He hadn't realized they stood at the center of everyone's attention. "I am Lyntan, Melissa. We love to touch. It seems, as on your world, shaking hands is a form of welcome," the security chief responded.

As politely as he could manage, Jarren reclaimed Lissa's hand and turned her toward Corsa. The engineer's pale face was hidden behind her curtain of red hair. "Melissa, First Engineer Corsa. Corsa, my honored guest, Melissa Reyes."

Corsa skittered forward and bowed at the waist. Moving toward her, Lissa bent her knees until she and Corsa were at eye level, then reached out a hand. "Corsa, it's my honor to meet you. Jarren said you were the genius behind the power of this ship. I'm awed to be in your presence."

Corsa's head lifted a few inches, her hair falling a little away from her face where a curious smile appeared. A quaking hand appeared to grasp Lissa's, and Corsa's mousy voice rang out unusually strong when she responded. "It is a gift to meet you, Mated. I am truly glad you have come."

Lissa nodded and smiled before letting go of Corsa's palm and turning to the man that approached.

Lissa didn't wait to be introduced but spoke up holding out her hand. "May I presume you are Faheel?" She spoke with flirtatious conviction, her smile bright and welcoming. Jarren frowned. Where was his suspicious vixen?

The tall, lanky male stopped, startled. "Yes, lady." The words gusted out and he glanced first at Marcus then to Jarren with wide eyes.

The room rang with Lissa's laugh. "I was told I would like you, Faheel. Now I know why. You remind me of a friend. They work in my favorite coffee shop."

Lissa gifted Jarren with a whimsical smile, and Jarren's heart thumped. The oddity of her behavior be damned. He wouldn't taint this evening with accusations based on his own suspicious instincts. Jarren had noted Faheel's similarities to the young man at Max's in the shop that morning. Now pleasure filled him as he realized Lissa might also remember that day. She seemed pleased by the reminder of home. Her smile grew, and for a moment she seemed incapable of further speech.

Faheel's upbeat voice filled the pause. "Well, I've no idea what a 'coffee shop' is, but it sounds like a compliment. I shall take it as such."

Jarren patted Faheel on the back. "I believe it is a compliment, Faheel."

Jarren introduced Lissa to the rest of his crew in the Salon then gently urged her to a table in front of the view screen wall where she could watch the stars slide by. Aside from keeping an eye on Jamis, Jarren sat next to Lissa and answered her questions about his crew and ship. They sipped warm chulaa from mugs in the intervening silences. His openness seemed to nurture a companionable air between them.

Jarren noted Lissa's comfort around his crew and beat back a smile that had been lurking behind his countenance. She fit in as if she'd known his shipmates as long as he. She'd even adjusted to Gimi and Girsch after they greeted her with deliberate refinement. She'd smiled and cast Jarren a puzzled frown but five minutes later stifled her laughter behind a hand as the two hunters finished recounting their last card game with the engine room crew. She was made for Jarren's world, even if she wanted no part of it.

*   *   *   *   *

LISSA ADJUSTED HER bottom on the cushions of her chair. She didn't have a watch, but she knew the party would be winding down soon. She'd come to dazzle Jarren's crew, to make allies who might be able to get her home, and she was pretty sure she had succeeded. Lissa waited to feel some elation, but there was not so much as a zing. She cocked her head to find Jarren staring at her, his eyes glowing with intensity, unaware of her mutinous intent. Her insides heated, and she took in a shallow breath.

Jarren leaned toward her, his eyes intense in their perusal. His tongue peeked out to taste the air between them, and Lissa shivered. She could tell it was an unconscious act. With a jerk, Lissa stopped herself just as her mouth opened to respond. Chocolate wafted to her nose. The soft lighting and hum of surrounding conversation, like gentle waves lapping, relaxed her body. A fat cat, her belly full of tuna, would not have been more satisfied.

"I would like you to experience the Sharing Ritual with me, Lissa. I know you don't understand fully how the Lyntan relationship with scent works. You think you are powerless. But the truth is that it is the male in the Lyntan relationship that wields the least power. We are, in a sense, a slave to scent. A man expresses trust in the woman who matches his scent by participating in the Sharing Ritual. It is usually the first ceremony of a bonding couple," Jarren stated.

"We are already bonded." Lissa nervously tapped her fingers against the smooth surface of the table.

Jarren nodded slowly. "We are. This ritual isn't necessary, but it serves to help create and solidify the bond between two people. It is also a way of establishing roles within a relationship, such as the role of the female to exercise control over the male."

Lissa's breath caught in her throat. She needed to distract Jarren from his persuasive argument and break the building tension. "And do Lyntans not have bonded couples of the same sex?" There was a question to catch him up. Jarren leaned back a bit, thoughtful. The space between them cooled, and Lissa let out a breath.

"Yes. There are many same-sex bonded Lyntans, but for Lyntans who possess more female genetics than male, they have the dominant power—even if their partner is also female. It is tied to our genetics. There are many questions about Lyntan bonding that you have no answers to. Your questions will be more easily explained after you have experienced the Sharing Ritual. You have no reason to trust me, I know. But the Sharing Ritual does not require your trust. It requires mine. You will be controlling me." Jarren took Lissa's hand and caressed her knuckles with a finger. "You have earned my trust. I am trying to earn yours."

She'd earned his trust? He said this on the same night she decided to turn one or more of his crew against him? Guilt fought with desire. Jarren lifted her hand to kiss her fingers. His lips' warmth slowly crept up her arm and reached into her chest. Desire won. She shoved her mutinous plans to the back of her mind, her guilt receding as well. Technically, she'd done nothing yet.

The mellow lighting shielded his expression. He was offering her his trust. It was only for one night. Lissa nodded.

"Thank you," he replied. "Given that I will soon not be in any state to command my ship, I ask your permission to alert my crew that I will be indisposed," he said, and placed a last lingering kiss on her fingers.

"You're going to tell them you're indisposed?"

"No. I am going to tell them we are taking a Sharing Ritual—only somewhat more dramatically."

Lissa frowned. Everything to do with the Lyntan olfactory sensors seemed dramatic. "Explain."

"When you are ready to go, I'll ask for Nectar. This concoction is usually only used in particular ceremonies and rituals. Since we are already bonded, everyone will know why I ask. This is important to establish your place among my crew."

Lissa nodded. "What then?"

"I will drink. We'll leave. I will escort you to my cabin. As my comprehension diminishes, I will explain the process. You'll witness Lyntan scent association at its most primitive. It is when scent completely overwhelms me, Lissa, that you gain complete control."

His adamant statement startled a glance from Lissa. Automatically, she shook her head. "No. Absolutely not. I don't want any kind of control over you."

"I have tried to explain with words something that isn't understandable to any non-Lyntan without related experience. You lost yourself to me on Earth, Lissa. I want you to know I am as powerful and as powerless as you."

Power over Jarren? Wasn't that what she wanted? She wanted her life to return to normal. If she really had full control, there had to be some way to take advantage of the situation, to get home sooner rather than later. And she wouldn't need to coerce any of Jarren's crew into betraying him. Home, by his own hand, in days instead of weeks of persuading another behind his back.

Yet Lissa knew this ritual would change her, no matter who wielded the power. Earth wasn't calling to her like it had only hours ago. That was a worrisome thought. Still, his concern for her when the ship was attacked, his obvious guilt at the situation he'd put her in—this had already changed her feelings for him in some way. She wouldn't deny it. No matter when Lissa returned to Earth, she would never be the same. And she should better comprehend this social system she now occupied. Lissa couldn't protect Jasmine in a world she didn't understand.

Taking a deep breath, she looked into Jarren's patient gaze. "Okay. I'm ready."

CHAPTER 17

LISSA WATCHED, NERVOUS, as Jarren tilted the cup to his lips. The room stilled in silence. Glancing around, Lissa noted nods of approval and smiles directed at her. How could they so easily accept her? It occurred to her that they must know she encroached on another woman's territory. She turned to look over at Jarren as he finished the drink and placed the cup on the table next to where they stood. It was difficult for her to trust the situation for what it was. He had given her every reason not to place her trust in him. Yet he was placing his trust in her. She'd accepted the ritual, but what now?

"Is there anyone you'd like to say goodbye to before we leave?" he asked passively.

Lissa cast him a startled glance. "So soon?"

Reaching out, he clasped Lissa's wrist. "My time is limited, Lissa. Although I want to make clear that I am handing myself over to you, I don't particularly wish to share my mental reversion with those persons who place their lives in my hands every day." Jarren looked pointedly around again and repeated his question. "We must go. Is there anyone you wish to speak with before we leave?"

A little thrown off, Lissa descended from their perch and walked over to Corsa. The small woman turned a soft smile toward Lissa. Lissa reached out and clasped Corsa's hand within both of her own. "I will speak with you again soon, Corsa, if that's alright. I really would love to know more about the ship."

Eyes as wide as saucers, Corsa nodded. Her mouth clamped shut. Someone approached Lissa from behind. Turning, she faced Marcus and reached out to hug him, then sighed when he returned her affection. He must be used to emotional women.

Holding her at arm's length, he spoke for her ears only. "You have our support, Lissa. Never wonder if we accept you, and never doubt your importance to Jarren."

Lissa had kissed Marcus's cheek and pivoted toward Jarren when a hand touched her arm. Stopping, she came face to face with Jamis. "He does you great honor, but you are worthy of it," he said brusquely.

Lissa nodded, but her brows curled in confusion. She couldn't understand such a philosophical statement, and his words bothered her for some reason. Then her thoughts dissipated as her body responded to Jarren's scent in close proximity. Turning, she found him standing right behind her, his eyes a sparkling threat as he looked at Jamis. Jamis stepped away.

When he'd disappeared, Lissa met Jarren's gaze as he peered down at her. His voice was rough when he spoke.

"I'm running out of time, Lissa. I want to be able to explain this process to you, so we need to leave now."

Lissa smiled again at the faces looking back at them then headed out of the Salon. Jarren's warm fingers caressed the small of her back. The sweetness of his fragrance grew more potent as the room receded behind them. They walked down a silent hall toward Jarren's quarters, she assumed.

"Why did you single out Corsa to say goodbye?" His abrupt question caused her to misstep.

Lissa thought a moment as she fell back into step beside him. "She strikes me as somewhat childlike in her perceptions, searching for others' approval. I guess my maternal instinct to reassure kicked in. Did I do something inappropriate?"

Jarren shook his head. "No. I was pleasantly surprised." They looked at each other, and for a moment, Lissa almost felt the connection everyone else sensed. Then he cleared his throat, and Lissa remembered why she'd been determined to impress Jarren's crewmates. She looked away.

Almost studiously, Jarren spoke again. "I'm entering the third phrase of the ritual. You will notice that my eyes will start to dilate. My breathing will calm. My body will begin to relax. I may start to sound lethargic, but I am still with you and comprehend everything you say. Do you understand?"

Lissa nodded as she looked at him. He slowed their progress, taking her hands between his own, the warmth between their bodies growing. "While I am still coherent, I want to kiss you. It won't be the only time tonight that I will ask, but it will be the last time I can assure you that only my own desires are at play."

She looked into the deep depths of his eyes, his potent essence surrounding them both, and Lissa understood the urge to give in to whatever he demanded. But he wasn't demanding. He was asking. Slowly, Lissa inclined her head, pushing away first the guilt of desiring a man who might already be spoken for. Then ignoring the quieter feeling of foreboding. She had been accused of controlling another person before. Lissa packed away the guilt. She would deal with the existence of Jarren's betrothal later. The foreboding was harder to ignore but she'd lived with that feeling for seven years. Breathing deep, Lissa pushed the negative feelings out of her mind.

His head came down in hesitant juts until his lips pressed against hers with a gentleness that made her gasp. Her toes curled with pleasure. But it was over as soon as it started. With a start, she realized her eyes were closed, and she blinked at the sound of Jarren clearing his throat.

"We should continue," he whispered. Lissa stared up at him. He was so very beautiful. His hazel eyes had warmed to a molten amber. His mouth softened as her gaze rested on it, a sensuous curl appearing at its edges. His strong jaw tilted down as her head tilted up.

"If you continue to look at me that way, we won't make it to my quarters, and you'll learn nothing of this ritual," he muttered, his mouth suddenly inches away from her lips. Lissa wanted to groan with desire. She forced herself to take a step back.

Jarren straightened, a lock of black hair sliding back behind one ear. He gazed at her, heat emanating from his look.

"Alright," she conceded. "Tell me what happens next. We'll walk with plenty of space between us." Lissa tried to think beyond the loud pounding of blood in her ears and the pooling warmth at her center.

Jarren nodded, moving again. "Once my body enters into the next state of calm, my smell will change. You won't smell me any longer, Lissa. Any scent you will note will be your own, although you may not recognize it. Essentially, the Nectar temporarily alters my essence to reflect yours. For a Lyntan male, this means my own identity will be completely subsumed. The masking scent I used at your mother's house on Earth originates from experimentation with Nectar's effect on Lyntan physiology. Your scent, your desires, your emotions will become my own. I will have no will to act against you."

Lissa frowned. "This drug should be banned."

"You misunderstand. The effects of Nectar are only applicable for those who are mated or whose essences are as close a match as you and I. I could drink Nectar with Corsa and not undergo the physiological change. The necessary component for the change, Lissa, is you. I need your scent running through my system and surrounding me for the change to occur and be maintained. Five minutes after you leave me, I will revert without any side effect." Jarren's speech had slowed. He frowned as if confused. But he stopped in front of a door panel in the corridor.

His face in an ongoing befuddled scrunch, Jarren glanced at Lissa again, then began punching in a code. The door slid open without hesitation and Jarren stepped through, then held out a hand to escort her in. "My quarters," he murmured as he continued to look at her.

The captain's quarters were lush but not gaudy. Lissa squinted in the low light, but she could make out mauve-colored walls and three doors exiting off the main room. They stood in some kind of receiving room. A long onyx-colored table stretched before her, and as she walked forward and looked down, her gaze caught the flickering of little white lights under a clear glass surface. She looked closer, and the random blinking lights flickered into a recognizable picture. Star charts were embedded in the table.

Through one entry to another room, Lissa spied a large bed covered in black satin-type sheets raised on a dais. As far as she could see, every bedroom wall was layered from floor to ceiling in bookshelves stuffed full of books. To her right lay a small wood-like table, similar to the one in her quarters—chairs and all—and on the far side of the long black table, three of those bean bag chairs had been moved to the side. Between the open door to his bedroom and another closed entryway, a large-sized view screen stretched almost the entire wall length. She would have guessed this was Jarren's room even if she'd stumbled upon it alone. Every inch of the space embodied him.

Her gaze returned to Jarren's face. His eyes were impenetrable, his body still. Lissa couldn't smell his chocolate essence any longer. It was like he wasn't there. "Jarren? Are you still with me?"

Almost as if falling asleep, he replied. "With you, yes."

"Do you feel okay?"

He nodded, still staring at her. "I'm okay. I'm here. What…you have of me?"

The question shot desire through Lissa's center. Immediately, Jarren's eyes lighted, and he advanced. Lissa backed up, fear smothering her desire. Jarren halted.

"Not fear me," he said, laboriously slow. "What…have of me?"

This time, Lissa checked her response. Obviously, he would act on the power of her emotions. Or rather, her scent. Lissa paused in thought. She wanted to understand the power he'd given her. She wanted to understand him. And she wanted freedom from his smell to decide if her desire for him was her own or a construct of their mutual physiological need.

"Please stay where you are," Lissa ordered.

"I shall not move until you say," he replied, straining to complete his sentence, his eyes on her, still heated but passive. She looked at him unrestrained. Every detail of him had burned into her memory from that first moment in the coffee shop. She hadn't exaggerated his beauty in her memories. He was perfectly made. His body was fit, emitting a somber energy that told her he would respond with perfect physical efficiency to any need. His black captain's uniform clung to the well-toned muscles of his chest and arms, molding black material to honey skin. The crown of her head just came level with his chin. He continued to stare down at her with beautiful eyes as arresting as the face of a Roman god. He could hurt or protect so easily.

Her gaze lowered to the slimness of his waistline and ended at the tautness of the material where it came together between his legs. Lissa heard him take a ragged breath, but he didn't move. He clenched his hands at his side. She glanced up just enough to see his chest heaving with effort.

"Am I hurting you?" she asked as the bulge between his legs grow.

"I smell your desire. I want you. My pain is pleasurable."

Lissa could understand. The small heat between her legs had flourished into an uncomfortable throb. He wanted her, and she wanted him, but he wouldn't touch her without her permission. The power she had over him was dizzying, terrifying. Another had stolen that power from her years ago. She'd never fully recovered. Jarren now handed her that power freely. The heaviness she'd accustomed herself to eased. She had stopped him with one sentence, but who would stop her should she give in to the need warming her flesh?

Lissa closed her eyes. Her nerves felt raw, her body feverish. She ached to touch him, to let go of caution and let him make love to her, to take away the building ache. If she just got a small taste, she could concentrate on understanding their bond better. One kiss, one touch. But would he really stop at one touch?

He still stared at her, his breathing strained, his eyes glazed over with desire. But he hadn't moved. Lissa stepped close to him, and his heat beckoned her. She ran an unsteady hand over one quivering bicep. His head bobbed, his gaze following the advance of her palm on his arm, his shoulder, pressing against the hardness of his chest. His eyes closed, and he put his head back. He seemed to be in a battle of wills, but finally he let out a low groan and looked down at her again.

Lissa slid her hand down his chest and over the flatness of his stomach to rest at the front of his pants. The pads of her fingers tingled as she touched the tip of his manhood through the fabric, his shaft pushing at her hand. With deliberate purpose, she found his pants button and undid it. Lissa grasped then lowered his zipper. His body vibrated as she caressed him through the soft material of his underwear. The air around them grew hot. His sex struggled against the restraints of his clothing, shocking a gasp of desire from her.

But aside from the almost violent quivering of his body as he fought to remain still, Jarren hadn't moved. Lissa slipped her hand under the soft fabric and grasped his warm member. He lengthened in response. Lissa's heart beat faster as her center tightened. She wanted to taste him, to feel his body cover hers. God, she wanted to drown in the sweetness of his essence, but she couldn't smell him at all.

With one hand still caressing him under the confines of his clothing, she moved closer until her breasts touched the hardness of his chest through his shirt. He gasped, his body completely rigid. "Touch me," she whispered as she nudged her head against his torso.

His fingers wove into her hair. One heated palm lay against the roundness of her breast. His eyes bored into hers as she looked at him, her body on fire. "Make love?" he asked in guttural tones. Yes, God she wanted to make love to him. She couldn't, though she held the power here. She would be entirely to blame for the outcome of their union. A flash of memory invaded her mind. Home. Earth. If she made love to Jarren, what would the implications be for him letting her go home?

Besides, there was no Derek to blame for the repercussions of her action this night. As she pondered her situation, Jarren's body relaxed. He was responding to her mood change. Lissa sighed and stepped back. Even as her hunger cooled, he continued to struggle not to touch her. His eyes flashed as they met her own.

It was time to find out just how much control she wielded with him under the influence of the Nectar. Backing away, Lissa pointed toward his bedroom. His head followed her finger then turned back to her. Lissa took a breath. "I can't make love to you, but…lie on the bed." He turned and walked into his bedroom, his stride almost mechanical.

Cool air flowed over her heated skin, and she shivered. Lissa followed Jarren into his room and over to lie next to him on his bed. Following his gaze up to the ceiling above, she found herself staring, again, into a large twinkling star map. Her libido throbbed. She could have easily climbed into his bed and made love to him all night. Twinkling stars above, warm lights low for lovemaking. One perfect man who'd willingly handed over control of his body and mind to help her lose her fear of his strength. She could have climaxed among the stars, making love to Jarren, but that was not to be. The possible repercussions were too great.

Still, Lissa could not leave without ending the torture she'd put him through. It would be the ultimate test of power. Lissa sat up, lifted her dress, then straddled Jarren's hips. His rigid crotch caused sparks of pleasure to fly to her center. His member jutted back at her as his hands clutched the sheets in restraint. Leaning down, Lissa kissed him with all her pent-up desire, her lips suckling his, tasting, touching, nibbling at his masculine saltiness. She kissed his jaw, moved lower and kissed the angry vein in his neck, her mouth tasting the heat of his skin. He let out a strained breath.

Then she whispered in his ear. "Calm yourself. Slow your breath. I want you to sleep." Lissa waited as she rested her head against his shoulder, her mouth inches from his ear. As time slowly passed, his body relaxed, and Lissa raised her head to look at him. He still stared back, but the amber in his irises had dissipated.

"Sleep for me," she said again. Jarren closed his eyes. His hands let go of the sheet beneath him. In a minute, his member was soft. Lissa shook her head. So much power. If she had told him to kill someone, she had no doubt he would have committed the act. Her response to him in the office that evening he'd turned down his Subduer paled in comparison to what she'd just put his body through. Lissa climbed off the bed and stood staring at him, her heart caught in her throat. She'd wielded the power tonight, but he'd changed her forever.

She moved away from the bed. Returning to Earth was now a matter of necessity. She had always been happiest with her family, man in her life or not. And her family needed her—her mother and Miguel. Jasmine needed her grandmother. Lissa could not entertain the possibility of not returning. She was the strong one. She made sure everyone else's lives were full and happy, like her mother had done for her father. Lissa clung to that reality.

But she knew when she returned, nothing would be the same. Jarren had claimed a piece of her tonight. He'd given her a new desire that made her long *not* to return, to put herself ahead of everyone else. If it meant having him.

Advancing just to brush away a rebellious lock of hair from his head, Lissa spoke low. "Thank you, Jarren." She understood better, now, the purpose and importance of scent to Lyntans. But she wasn't sure that knowledge made her situation any easier. Instead, the Sharing had only complicated her feelings. She was still missing a small piece of the Lyntan scent puzzle. It seemed extreme to completely give up one's will to show trust in a mate.

Lissa turned and walked out of the bedroom, then out of Jarren's quarters. She refused to look back.

CHAPTER 18

EIGHT HOURS LATER, Jarren sat in his Ready room watching recent vidcasts of his mother's various state appearances. He idly fondled the blue butterfly hair clip he'd stolen from Lissa's bag on his jumper. He leaned back in his chair, relaxed. Jarren awoke refreshed, but he might have spent a very uncomfortable night turning and twisting in impassioned agony.

Lissa shocked him. She could have left him writhing in need, standing in the middle of his receiving room. The pain of being that aroused, of knowing she was right down the hall but being unable to satisfy his driving need, would have made him stir crazy. Even if he'd chosen to satisfy himself.

But she'd used her power over him to calm his body and send him to sleep. Remembering her kiss before she left provoked a burst of tenderness. He leaned back in his chair, a satisfied smile on his face.

The door behind him swished open. Jarren turned, expecting Marcus to report.

Instead, Jamis strode forward. Jealousy collected in Jarren's chest, and he pushed down the feeling. "Jamis."

He nodded. "Jarren. I know you're preparing to go surface-side."

"Yes. We are just orbiting Deneb. I expect we'll leave in a few hours. Rila is giving Lissa and Jasmine medical clearance for the planet."

Jamis's stride faltered. Hesitation was an unusual characteristic for the man. Jarren's brow rose. "What's the problem?" He got a whiff of nervous anxiety and sat forward, his fingers clasped on the table. "Speak, Jamis."

"Melissa. She is a bond match for me." Jamis met Jarren's eyes.

Even as the sudden need for violence stirred in his gut, Jarren stilled. "We are royal cousins. I expect she would be a bond match for you as she is a match for me."

"But the bounty hunters have your scent, Jarren. Her life is threatened by her bond with you. She would be safe with me."

A chill crept through him. His back straightened as he prepared to defend his claim. "She is my bonded, Jamis," he growled. Jamis stepped forward and lowered his eyes.

Jamis nodded but continued. "Her life is threatened as your mate. I can protect her."

Jarren fought the illogical urge for violence, his hands clasping and unclasping, clutching at the desk as he tried to open his heart to Jamis's argument. His nostrils flared as his veins beat the word *mine* repeatedly into his thoughts. He cared for her. How could he give her up? Jarren's glance caught on Lissa's hair clip lying on his desk, and his grip slowly relaxed. He could give her up because he cared for her. Biology be damned. Slowly, the encompassing red of anger receded to the edges of his vision and Jarren let go of the table edge. The situation Jamis offered was plausible, and for Lissa's sake, could not be ignored. "I can't give her to you, Jamis, even if I wanted. We both know she really doesn't belong to me. You smelled her reluctance last evening in the Salon. That's why you approached."

"Yes. But does she know she could go home if another covered your scent?" The question hung in the silence between them. Lissa didn't know, and Jarren hadn't considered it before that moment. Maybe he hadn't wanted to. It seemed his primal instincts had subdued his logic once more.

As he sat back in his chair, his shoulders relaxed. He'd taken Lissa away from her life. Here was an opportunity to give it back. He owed her the chance to choose. Jarren's heart sank. "Alright, Jamis. You may speak to her about it. The choice is hers to make. But that discussion will have to wait until after my meeting on Deneb. I won't be able to make any arrangements she might require until then."

The security chief turned to leave, then stopped and looked back. "I know you love her, Jarren. I don't love her, but I desire her, and I can protect her. I can help her go home. This is a hard situation for all of us." Jamis paused before departing, as if expecting a response, but Jarren couldn't speak. Love. He did love Lissa. His reliance on scent compatibility had blinded him to that knowledge. It was a painful discovery to make at a time when he had decided to let her go.

* * * * *

"EXACTLY WHOSE LIVING space is this, Rila?" Lissa asked as the two women sat with Jasmine in Lissa's quarters. They were waiting for Jarren and Marcus to escort them to Deneb's surface. Rila had just finished the last of Lissa and Jasmine's inoculations. Now they sat in comfortable silence, Rila's light-blue dress sparkling with each slight shift. Jasmine fiddled on the floor with a small multicolored puzzle game similar to a Rubik's Cube. Lissa had loved that game growing up.

"These are guest quarters. What you really want to ask is where the clothes came from, yes?" A blush burned Lissa's cheeks as she glanced down at her latest borrowed ensemble. She wore a long, flowing, white-and-pink-tinted dress with wide sleeves hanging down her arms and stopping at her fingertips. Peeking from beneath the light fabric was a matching pair of satin-like pumps. Lissa loved the outfit. The dress clung to her, gloriously soft. But who else had worn the dress before her? Veena?

"Okay, I'm fishing. You're right."

"Fishing? This word isn't translating," Rila stated with a bemused look.

"It means I'm trying to gets answers to a question I haven't asked." Lissa paused. "Has Jarren had many other women on board?"

Rila shook her head. "No."

"But the clothes?"

Rila rose and glided over to the door. "Jarren had the clothes fabricated when you came on board. He has a very good eye for what complements your beauty, doesn't he?"

Lissa shook her head in disbelief. "Rila, there are a lot of clothes here."

Rila began punching in the entry code. She turned and spoke as she hit another button. "Alien technology. You've no idea how easy it is to duplicate any material from food, to clothes, hats, shoes."

Shoes? Embarrassment spread pretty pink down Lissa's neck. *Jarren's shoes, the ones she'd spilled coffee on…*

Rila looked at her, a question on her face. "What's wrong?"

Lissa just shook her head. "I just had an embarrassing revelation. Nothing's wrong. Does Jarren's jumper have the same technology to replicate materials?"

"Yes," Rila replied, puzzled. She quirked her head in curiosity. "Why?"

"It's nothing…again. I was just curious."

"Good, because Jarren and Marcus are waiting for us outside. It's time to go."

"How do you know?"

"I can see them," she said, looking toward the sealed entry. She tapped her nose and winked as the door opened.

Lissa stood and held out a hand to Jasmine. The little girl got up, and together they walked out of Lissa's quarters and into the hall. Jarren and Marcus waited a ways down the hall, speaking in quiet tones. Lissa approached. Jarren looked up, obvious pleasure on his face.

Her gaze fell to where his shirt clung to his waist. Snug tan pants hugged the muscles of his thighs. Thighs she'd brushed her hands against last night. Thighs that stopped at the bulge between his legs. Lissa still remembered his warmth within her grasp as he grew under her deliberate ministrations. Her eyes shot up and met his simmering stare. They'd been thinking the same thing.

Jarren advanced just as Lissa found herself moving forward. He slowed as he came close, reached out, and slid a curl of hair off Lissa's face. Goose bumps danced over the surface of her arms.

"Are you ready to go?" he asked. His touch had driven speech from Lissa's mind. Maybe a relationship founded on biological compatibility had its perks. Love had always determined whom she committed to, but the thought of a physical relationship with Jarren warmed her in places she hadn't known she had. Clearing her throat, she nodded.

Jasmine's chatter returned Lissa to reality. They weren't alone. Jasmine started jumping. "We're ready, Jarren. Rila gave me all my shots, but none of them hurt, and I was a big girl. I didn't cry."

He looked down at Jasmine. Lissa focused on the dark waves of his hair as he spoke. "You are a fearless girl, Butterfly. I do not doubt that you weren't daunted by Healer Rila."

"Daunted. What's that, Mommy?" she asked as she turned to look up at Lissa.

Lissa nodded for Jasmine to begin walking. "We can figure it out later, Jasmine. It's time to go now."

Jasmine nodded. "Okay."

Jarren walked ahead, Jasmine a ball of energy at his side.

Rila glided behind Lissa, seemingly inattentive. Lissa turned to smile at Marcus as he idled up next to her.

"Hello," he greeted her. "You appear happier this morning." His gaze rested on Jarren then shifted back to her.

She placed a hand on his arm as they walked, her sight on Jarren's back. "I don't know about happier, Marcus, but I am more at peace. I think I'm looking forward to putting my feet on land again, even if it isn't my own land."

"And getting off this ship is the only reason for the change in your outlook?"

Lissa hesitated before answering. Exactly how much could Marcus guess, knowing Jarren had taken the Nectar? What did it matter what he could guess? "No, Marcus, that isn't the only reason, but you already knew that, didn't you?"

"I didn't know. I hoped when I met up with Jarren this morning, and then I suspected just now when I saw the two of you together." Marcus placed his hand over Lissa's on his arm. "I am happy you have some peace. You deserve it."

Marcus's words touched her, and at that moment, she did feel happy. A smile spread over her face just as Jarren turned to look back at her, and he returned her smile, his eyes warm. Marcus squeezed her hand once more as they turned a corner and continued down a long corridor.

Five minutes and one elevator later, they walked down another tan hall. As they stopped at a sealed door, it took Lissa a moment, but she finally recognized where they were. The dull metal entryway slid open. They stepped through and back into the ship's landing bay. Jarren's black jumper dominated the space.

"We're going to the surface in the jumper?" Lissa asked.

Jarren shook his head, but Marcus answered. "No. For security reasons, we'll use the jumper's transporter. *Desire* is cloaked at orbit distance from my father's envoy ship."

"Orbit distance? Why doesn't that sound terribly close?" Lissa replied, casting a glance Jarren's way.

Jarren waited until Marcus and Lissa stood beside him. "It's close enough for the jumper to get us over. Any closer, and we'd have to lower our shields to avoid dual-shield interference," Jarren stated.

"What?" Lissa raised her eyebrows in expectation. Surely, he hadn't expected her to understand what he just said.

Jasmine giggled and grasped her mother's hand. "It's like Hula-Hoop, right, Jarren? When I Hula-Hoop with my friends and we get too close, we bang hoops and then my hoop falls, and then I usually get angry but Mommy always says I shouldn't get mad 'cause it's partly my fault for not watching out for my friends."

Jarren nodded at Jasmine. "That's right, Butterfly."

Lissa ignored Marcus's snicker at her side. "Okay, I'm obviously the least smart person in this group. What happens after we transport over to the envoy ship?"

Marcus replied. "We'll take a ship-pod to the surface. My father had Corsa construct a vehicle designed specifically to transport people from their ships to Deneb's surface. He wants to maintain ecological equilibrium. Our planet has the cleanest air in this quadrant. Cleaner even than Lynta. No offense, Jarren," Marcus added.

"None taken. Besides, I take complete credit for the work. Corsa was scripted with me when I granted her request to work on your father's contraption. I should be collecting air tax from your people, Marcus."

"Can you do that?" Lissa interrupted.

Marcus urged Lissa forward as they gathered in a circle next to the jumper. Rila completed the sphere. Marcus spoke. "Actually, as ruler of Lynta, Jarren holds supremacy over all eleven planets in this system. There is no conflict there, however. Lynta is the home planet. The other ten are colonized and have been for the last nine hundred years. There are other systems in this quadrant that host sentient beings, but those aren't colonized by Lynta. Terlia, Corsa's home planet, and—"

Rila completed the sentence. "And Palmisi. My home planet. My solar system, along with the Antares system, are the only Alliance system members that are not dominantly humanoid. My species is in the minority of sentient life on my planet."

"Right." Confusion colored Lissa's response. One planet hosted more than one sentient species? Scientists suspected octopuses and dolphins were highly sentient, but most humans lived in happy bliss.

A breath on her neck sent a shiver up her spine. "Don't worry," Jarren stated. "I still do not know the makeup of all the systems of the Alliance, and I've studied the Alliance as part of my diplomatic training since I was four."

Jarren grasped Lissa's hand. "Marcus will transport with Jasmine. I will transport with you. Rila will come on her own. Okay?"

Lissa nodded, hesitantly. "As I now have access to Unit, couldn't I transport Jasmine over? For that matter, what prevents Jasmine from transporting herself out into space?"

Jarren laughed, his deep tone vibrating off the walls of the bay and caressing her body. "Jasmine has limited clearance. She can't transport anything. Unit will not respond to that command. You have clearance but no experience. I will set aside time to teach you how to use transport at some point.

Until then, I would restrict all your commands to the ship, the duke's palace, and the Mira Mines. But you do have total access, Lissa." He looked at her. He wasn't controlling her anymore. One step closer to home, at the expense of Jarren's trust. Too bad she felt no elation. Lissa laid her hand on the curve of his biceps, affirming their unspoken connection.

Marcus's throat clearing broke through the bubble of shifting emotions that surrounded them. Jarren glanced over then down again into Lissa's eyes. "Marcus, transport first. Give the all-clear once you've checked your quarters on the envoy. I'll follow with Lissa. Rila will proceed last. She's only going as far as the envoy, just to make sure you have no reaction to the Deneb environment. The envoy uses recycled Deneb air."

Marcus held Jasmine's little hands within his own massive ones. "Hear that, little one? You and I are to go over first. Your mother will come over after we make sure all of my father's guards are distracted. This is an important mission. Do you think you're ready for such responsibility?" Marcus winked over his shoulder at Lissa.

"I'm ready, sir," Jasmine replied with a salute. Lissa stifled a laugh. Jasmine's face was stern as she nodded to her mother and clung to Marcus's hands.

"Eyes closed, Jasmine," Lissa reminded her.

"I already know that, Mommy. Transporting is baby stuff," Jasmine replied, eyes shut.

Marcus chuckled. "Unit transport, Vertical surface. My headquarters."

"Close your eyes," Jarren whispered as he leaned in. Lissa closed her eyes just as bright light encompassed the room.

After a minute, Lissa blinked several times then looked up. Jarren's lips were an inch away from her own.

He looked down at her mouth. "I want to kiss you," he said. But as the words left his mouth, the sound of his voice seemed to wake him from whatever spell he had fallen under. Jarren stood straight, confusion evident on his face. "Sorry," he said as he stepped back.

Sorry? For what? Saying he wanted to kiss her? Damn it! She *wanted* him to kiss her. Wait. That couldn't be right. She didn't want a relationship with Jarren. She wanted to go home.

"It's fine, really," Lissa replied. They still held hands, prepared to transport over. An uncomfortable silence enveloped them. Lissa had just settled on a casual topic to help break the awkwardness when Marcus's voice rang in her ear.

"All set, you guys. Proceed. Unit has the correct coordinates. Transport when ready."

Rila's voice echoed in the bay. Lissa had forgotten all about her. "They'll be over promptly, Marcus. I suspect Jarren will need to shower before you all go to the surface. Cold water," Rila joked. She'd obviously noticed Lissa and Jarren's interaction.

Lissa looked up and noted an embarrassed grin on his face. She smiled back, stepped into his arms, and lay her head on his powerful chest. His gentleness enveloped her as they transported. Jarren wouldn't be the only one needing a cold shower.

*   *   *   *   *

JARREN WATCHED LISSA'S face light up in awe as they sat before Marcus and Jasmine surrounded by the clear walls of the ship-pod. The balloon-like vehicle drifted through the clear-celadon afternoon sky into Deneb's tropical atmosphere. On the far horizon, a greenish yellow sun lowered.

Jarren could understand Lissa's awe. Deneb was one of the most beautiful planets within the Lyntan planetary framework. Its abundant fauna, violet sand beaches, and mild climate attracted millions of Alliance member tourists each year. Unlike the harsher multi-seasonal Lyntan weather Jarren was used to, most locations on Deneb maintained a consistently warm temperature year-round. Its closer orbit to the sun kept most areas of the world warm. Many a bonding ceremony had ended with the couple making their way to beautiful locations on Deneb for a vacation.

In their rebellious youth, Jarren and Marcus had camped on one of the warm beaches for weeks, hiding out from Jarren's father. He'd been in one of his crazes. Camping under the open sky and watching Deneb's moon float across the dark night had been better fun than facing his dad, Drassel. The commander laid into him when Jarren forgot to attend his first meeting as the Lyntan representative at the Alliance conference on inter-system hunter smuggling. The meeting, and his standing as Heir Of the Family, had seemed so unimportant at the time. His mother had helped him understand.

That was then, Jarren noted silently. This was now. Lissa let out a gasp as the pod approached the royal grounds. It wasn't a coincidence that the pod provided its riders with a spectacular view of the Deneb waterfalls at Marcus's father's palace. Seventy-five feet in height, the waterfalls were best known for their fuchsia-colored water and naturally occurring mineral deposits found in the rocks of the waterfalls' cliffs. At the bottom of the falls lay a spirited pool that had a natural recycling system sending the waters up through old inlays in the rocks, back to the cascading pool at the top.

Swimming in the waters was like swimming in a rejuvenating spring. The same rock deposits that caused the water's color gave it restorative powers that left the swimmer feeling renewed and invigorated. If you drank the water, you would taste a natural sweetness that the Denebians had been bottling and selling for years. Denebian water wasn't for sale anywhere else. The replicators had yet to successfully recreate the taste. Add the lush, verdant moss greens of long-leafed foliage that enclosed the pool below, the sprinkling of large-blooming exotic flowers, and the natural rock formation with its smooth long surface, perfect for sunbathing in the middle of the large pond, and one had a veritable utopia.

Lissa's rapt stare hadn't lifted from the waterfalls. Jarren's gaze traced the pout of her lips to the soft curve of her chin, under and down to the delectable sensitive spot he'd kissed on her neck. Eyes drawn back to the waterfalls, he fantasized about Lissa within its waters, black hair plastered to her head, her breasts crowning the glassy surface. She smiled at him, calling silently for him to take her slick body within his grasp, lift her onto the sunning rock, and plunge himself inside her warm sheath.

Jarren sucked in a breath and glanced at his companions. They seemed oblivious to the erotic torture building inside his head. Lissa's gaze stayed on the waterfalls as the pod descended and the sparkling waters disappeared from view. Just as she turned to smile at him, her attention was recaptured by the palace's looming golden structure beyond the teal grass clearing that served as the pod's landing area. She let out a gasp.

Jarren smiled and sat back. Her awe stroked his ego. If she were impressed by Duke Naas's palace, Jarren looked forward to showing her his own fortress on Lynta. The duke's palace reached up, three small towers of violet and gold moldings. Similar to a picture of the Indian Taj Mahal Jarren remembered from an Earth magazine, its rounded domes with their jutted tips were molded out of violet and white smooth stone and inlaid with a gold element mined on Deneb.

The palace consisted of four pavilions surrounded by a tall stone wall, each with its own small minaret. The minarets squared off an open court whose primary construction was an eight-foot white-stone fountain sculpted into the goddess, Janelle, fed by a cold spring below the palace's foundation. The water served to cool the dry air within the courtyard.

Decorating the walls of the ducal palace were geometric motifs and etchings resembling all manner of life: beautiful swirls of flower petals, slithering likenesses of Deneb's snakes. The images and moldings had been commissioned in a variety of complementing colors—pinks and purples and blues from the lightest to darkest shades flowed seamlessly from one color to the next when entering and leaving a room. Lissa would be overcome by its beauty.

But the ducal palace of Deneb was miniscule in beauty and size compared to Jarren's summer palace on Lynta. He would show it to her one day.

The pod bumped down on the grass clearing outside the palace walls. Marcus got up and pushed on the clear door, unsealing the structure. A burst of calming Kush incense filtered through, and Lissa breathed in. He wanted to kiss her in that moment even more than when he'd gazed down at her sensuous lips. The fruity sweet fragrance of carnissus flowers assaulted his nose, pulling him into a reverie of home. If he kissed Lissa right now, he would taste the carnissus intermingling with her own honey sweetness. Jarren's body hummed to life.

Marcus's deep tone, entirely proper, pulled Jarren out of his reverie. "Your Highness, my father awaits you." Jarren had almost forgotten the part he was to play. He nodded and stepped out of the pod, willing his body to calm, and turned to help Lissa disembark.

As her hand touched and held his, she cast him an odd look. "Highness?"

Jarren turned, and holding Lissa's hand palm down at chest height, urged her forward. "Unfortunately, I am still on the run. We must play at being visiting royals from one of Lynta's neighboring planets. But don't be concerned. You and Jasmine will be escorted to Marcus's living quarters. You needn't say a word. You don't need to pretend to be anyone other than yourself."

"So we're undercover. It might have been nice to know, if for no other reason than my own awareness. Why is Marcus speaking so formally? Preparing for his role?" Her tone was caustic, but Jarren laughed. She was absolutely right.

"Yes. You are the smartest of us here, Lissa. Never think less of yourself," Jarren replied.

Lissa stared into his eyes as if searching for something, opened her mouth to respond, then shut it abruptly. Turning again to face the palace, she squeezed his hand and continued walking. Jarren glanced at Jasmine behind them; the girl held onto Marcus and jumped up and down in excitement.

Marcus's face remained impenetrable. Jarren turned away before his friend saw the humor in his eyes. Aware of Lissa's closeness, Jarren shifted his thoughts to the upcoming conversation with Duke Leor Naas. The ruler conceded to allow Jarren asylum on Deneb. But exactly how much would the man consent to help?

Marcus placed a hand on Jarren's shoulder to slow their progress. "My father is coming. I hope you've got a persuasive argument prepared. Mother tells me he's been in a bad mood all day. The Alliance is causing issues with your disappearance. They expect Deneb's full cooperation in tracking you down and bringing you before the Council to answer for your apparent abandonment of Lynta."

Jarren shook his head. "I am damned if I do, damned if I don't with the Alliance. Any way Aunt Geneera could sweeten your father's temper?"

"My mother is in the north right now. We had a conflict brewing between harvesters and manufacturers. She's in the middle of negotiations." Marcus was quiet a moment as he listened to his mother on his com. "She asks about Lissa. She wants to know if you purposefully bonded with her."

"What does it matter?" Jarren bit out. Lissa raised an eyebrow. Throwing her a grin, he halted and looked at Marcus.

"She says if you didn't intentionally bond with her, Lissa can soothe my father's temper as easily as she. You should introduce them." Marcus shrugged, his expression perplexed. "I'd do as she says, Jarren. She is never wrong where my father is concerned. We both know this."

Jarren sighed, nodded, and scooted Lissa forward again. Glancing at her, he cleared his throat, but Lissa interrupted. "I would be honored to meet him, but I have no idea what is going on."

"I don't expect you will need to, Lissa. Just meet him. I am asking, not telling, here. The duke has already promised us asylum. He would never go back on his word. We just need a bit more flexibility than he'd previously consented to."

Lissa studied him before answering. "Alright. I have nothing to lose at this point anyway." Jarren frowned but nodded to Marcus.

"I will let him know we'll use the east entrance," Marcus replied as he veered away slightly and connected to his father.

Jarren sighed. It might well be a very long afternoon.

CHAPTER 19

LISSA PUT ONE foot on the steps leading up to the palace entrance and paused. The building in front of her was daunting. Her pumps tapped on the swirling geometric design of stencils, lines of gold inlay traveling in perfect turns through a mosaic of blue tile and lilac stone.

Jarren walked ahead and stopped below the palace grounds' arched entrance. Hues of deep red, lavender, and gold etched around Lissa as she stopped next to him. Behind her, Jasmine gasped.

Marcus bent as Lissa held out a hand to her daughter. "I am glad you approve, young one."

"Are we here to see the king?" Jasmine asked as she walked toward Lissa but looked back at Marcus's paused figure. Jarren grinned.

Marcus responded. "No, young one. You are here to meet my father. You've already met the king."

"When?"

Lissa pulled Jasmine to stand in front of Jarren. Marcus's chuckle bounced off the pillars before them. "In essence, Jarren is the king, Jasmine."

"But he doesn't wear a crown. Shouldn't kings wear crowns and be old and give good girls pretty gifts?"

Jarren laughed. "I shall receive that as a compliment, Butterfly. And as a gift, I promise those within this palace will treat you like a princess. Would you like that?"

"Yes!" she replied. Lissa smiled as she looked up. Her smile slipped. An austere figure approached, wrapped in long cardinal-red robes. He was an older man, robust, with a gray beard that highlighted a piercing gaze. As he came closer, his stride created no sound on the stone floor. Lissa noted four figures walking behind him, two on either side.

Jarren stepped forward. "Your Grace," he said with a nod. Duke Leor ignored Jarren's gesture and passed him to stop before Lissa. His green eyes squinted thoughtfully before he turned to his son.

"Your mother told you to bring the lady, didn't she?" His voice slid out like thousands of raindrops plunking off metal gutters on a rainy day.

Marcus walked forward. He didn't appear put off by his father's brusqueness. As Jasmine shivered, looking up at the duke with fearful eyes, Lissa smiled down reassuringly. Seeming to notice Jasmine's discomfort, Marcus took her hand and gave a "don't worry" look at Lissa before he urged Jasmine forward. "You realize you're scaring her daughter. Stop posturing."

Leor looked down at Jasmine, and his eyes widened. Then he looked up again at Marcus, his expression suddenly shielded. "Does your mother know about the girl?"

Marcus shook his head. "No. Should she?"

"No. That would have been a rather nasty turn on her part, if she knew. I wouldn't have expected it of her."

Lissa looked at Jarren who turned a questioning gaze to Marcus. Marcus shrugged.

Taking them all in, the duke flicked a dismissive hand at their expressions. "It's obvious you all have no idea what I'm talking about. As your time here is limited and I must listen to your request, Jarren, I suggest we adjourn. Lissa, you have completed your task admirably. My mate will be delighted to meet you when next you are on Deneb. Jarren, I am now honor-bound to assist, to say nothing of the Alliance. You and your family will always be welcome in my house."

Lissa had no clue how to respond. Bowing her head, she spoke a gracious "thank you" and quirked an eyebrow at Jarren. He shrugged. A tall muscular man in flowing white robes came forward and bowed. "I am at your service, Highness." His long dark hair draped the sides of his head and shoulders, and he knelt, his eyes to the ground.

"Oh wait," Lissa said, shaking her head. "I'm not—" She caught the quick twist of Jarren's head and stopped speaking.

Leor began talking again, gracefully walking back beyond the pillars that held up a walkway above. "Tehrin. The lady is a foreigner," he stated as he tapped the man on the shoulder and urged him to rise. "You've embarrassed her. Please show Lady Lissa and her daughter to Marcus's quarters. They won't be staying long," he added.

He jogged away, red robes flowing behind him. Marcus stepped forward to follow and placed Jasmine's hand back in Lissa's grasp. Jarren turned to Lissa, concern forming a scowl on his face. "Before you ask, I swear I have no idea what that was about. I'll ask Marcus later. Will you be alright in Marcus's rooms while he and I meet with the duke?"

No, she wouldn't be alright. She was on an alien world. Everything around her appeared familiar, but nothing quite fit. The colors were just off, purples found in places like stonework, water the color of a violet; the waterfalls were the most beautiful natural anomaly Lissa had ever seen, but it just wasn't right. And the sun and sky. A deep-green sun shone through a pale green sky. Even the world smelled alien, the air filled with a touch of grape sweetness. Beautiful, but alien.

A longing to return to the cool neutrality of Jarren's ship gripped her. "I'll be fine," Lissa said.

Jarren nodded at Tehrin familiarly. "You have nothing more precious to me, my friend. They should not be bothered by anyone while we're here." Again, Tehrin nodded in obeisance. With a final glance, Jarren dashed forward to catch up with the duke's retreating party.

Lissa looked down at Jasmine. For Jasmine's sake, she couldn't show her apprehension. Lightening her tone, Lissa started walking. "Come on, Butterfly. I want to put my feet up before we're whisked away again."

Tehrin fell into step beside her. He led her across a blue-tiled entrance, through tall arched double doors, and under another pillar-lined walkway. Lissa looked out at a rectangular garden courtyard with stone pathways winding through to the surrounding pillars. The complexity of the colorful plants took her breath away. Lissa spied a fountain within the garden as Tehrin turned to push open a door. A woman sculpted from lilac marble reached for the sky. Water spouted out of her clasped hands.

Jasmine pulled away and ran forward, redirecting Lissa's interest.

This time the gasp of surprise came from mother not child. "You're kidding, right?"

Tehrin ticked an aqua-orbed glance at Lissa. "I'm sorry, Prin—Lady. I don't think I understood your translator."

"Whose rooms are these?"

"Marcus's rooms. At least whenever he decides to reside here. If you would rather stay somewhere else, I shall make arrangements."

Lissa looked up at the corner squinches supporting the pendant dome ceiling above. Gold designs of geometric shapes danced across the walls. Gold pillows lay all over the floor. A royal-blue chaise stood in the middle of the room, at the cross-section between two corner windows that stretched from floor to ceiling and were draped in translucent light-gold materials.

Decadence surrounded Lissa. Jasmine squealed as she ran over to a large bed on a dais and jumped into the piles of soft-looking blankets. "Jasmine!" Lissa snapped. "Usted le ha perdido mente? Éste no es su sitio. Consiga de la cama inmediatamente! Get off the bed at once!" Lissa repeated. Fear of breaking something almost paralyzed her.

Jasmine abruptly stopped bouncing. Sliding off the gold and burgundy covers, she walked toward her mother, her hands behind her back. "Lo siento, Mommy."

Tears formed in Jasmine's eyes. Lissa sighed. She'd been too hard on her. They were both under stress.

"Okay, Butterfly. It's okay." Lissa pulled her daughter to her. Behind them, Tehrin removed himself and pulled the doors shut.

"Was the bed comfortable?" Lissa asked as she leaned away. Jasmine nodded. "Well, it isn't okay to jump on Marcus's bed, but I'm sure we could lie down on it. I'm tired. Are you tired?"

"I'm a little tired. And I'm a little scared, Mommy."

"I know. Don't worry. I promise we'll go home as soon as possible. Okay?"

"Can I call Abuela?"

"There's no phone here that calls Grandma's house," Lissa replied as she edged Jasmine back up onto the dais.

A female voice rang out from the doorway. "Actually, Lady Lissa, I can help your little girl call home if she wants." One tall door creaked open, and a golden-haired woman stepped in. She wore a dress similar to Lissa's fashion, her own long-flowing gown shades of black and burgundy. Her hair was pulled up into a long ponytail that irritated Lissa as it swung in harmony with the sway of the woman's hips. She approached almost arrogantly, her posture straight, aristocratic. She held her head high even as she managed to look down at Lissa. Her golden eyes narrowed guardedly.

Without introducing herself, she knelt and took Jasmine's hands in her own. "Hello, little one. I can let you speak with your grandmother. Would you like that?"

Lissa began to see red. "And you are?" she asked as she stepped between Jasmine and the woman. Repositioning herself, Lissa forced the woman back a step. Lissa could have sworn she saw a scowl cross her thin face, but as she found her footing and looked up, a smile curved her petulant lips. Lissa shivered.

Bowing submissively, the woman spoke. "Apologies, lady. I was rude. I'm Jesalyn, Princess Veena's lady-in-wait. Jarren and I are cousins. He sent me to look after you. He said to relay that you should not get too comfortable. We'll be leaving soon."

Lissa didn't miss the slip. "We?"

Jesalyn bowed her head. "Yes, lady. I shall accompany you all to Mira."

It took Lissa another minute to register whom Jesalyn served. "You are lady-in-waiting to Veena? Jarren's bonded?"

Jesalyn was quick to correct her. "Intended bonded, lady. You are obviously Jarren's bonded. Any who meet you together can smell the bond. It is as strong as any I've sensed in years."

Lissa turned away. She'd never been good at hiding raw feelings, and raw feelings ran through her now. Was Jesalyn's connection to Veena what made Lissa uneasy? Maybe. Or maybe it was the unmistakable pitch of envy woven into every word.

Jesalyn's sap-like voice moved over Lissa's nerves, drippy and sweet. "Is it permissible to let the child speak with your mother? It is possible, I assure you."

Lissa faced the woman, her self-confidence only subdued temporarily. "I think we'll wait to speak with Jarren about making contact."

"I assure you, it's safe. You do not wish to bother the prince with such trivialities."

Lissa stifled a frown then stared at Jesalyn intently. "I tell you what. How about I decide what I will speak with Jarren about, and you decide to go find him for me while I wait?" Five years of correspondence with executive-level international bigheads had taught Lissa a thing or two.

Satisfaction hummed through her as Jesalyn lowered her eyes and made a slight bow before heading to the door. They both looked up, though, as the door creaked open further.

"Did I hear my name?" Jarren asked as he entered. Lissa's heart jumped, but she was reminded of her current predicament a moment later as Jesalyn idled near him.

"Highness, your will is my directive," she said and curtsied low. Jarren laughed and raised the woman with a hand on her shoulder.

"Really, Jesalyn. Your commitment is deeply appreciated, but we aren't at court. There is no need to stand on formality. Marcus will only laugh at me."

"I'm sorry, Your Highness," Jesalyn mumbled. Lissa's frown won out this time. Either the women of Jarren's world were subservient creatures within the aristocracy, or this woman was off. Jarren did not seem uncomfortable with Jessalyn's behavior, so the answer could be either or both.

Jarren walked up and held a hand out. "Are you ready to go?"

Lissa continued to stare at Jesalyn. "I understand Jasmine could speak with my mother?"

"If we had the time, yes, you could arrange a secure connection and satellite a call to Earth, but we have to leave. The duke is expecting a state-level diplomat from the Alliance, and I know the woman well. I can't risk her or any of her assistants recognizing me."

"Ready?" Marcus asked as he stuck his head into the room. A pained look scrunched up his face as he looked around. "The gods, I forgot how much I hate my rooms at the palace. I've no idea what possessed me to have Tehrin bring you here."

Jasmine ran toward the door. "I like it, Marcus! It's pretty."

Marcus scowled. "Yes, little one. Pretty. Exactly." Lissa had to grin.

Jarren cleared his throat. "You've met Jesalyn. We should be gone from here now."

"Okay. Point us to the exit," Lissa replied as she beamed him a smile, Jesalyn all but forgotten. She had no interest in catty politics.

"We'll be transporting to a jumper this time. There's a hangar nearby. The mines are only accessible by small vehicle." Jarren gestured to Marcus then called out to Jasmine. "Come along, young lady. You're to transport with us this time. Marcus will take Jesalyn. Okay?"

Jasmine reluctantly let go of Marcus's hand and nodded. Lissa had not seen such a forlorn look on Jasmine's face since her terrible twos. He prodded the girl forward then turned and held out his arm to Jesalyn. "It is lovely to see you again,

Jesalyn. Shall we depart?" Lissa's eyes narrowed. A wax smile froze on Jesalyn's face.

"Of course, sir. I would transport with you anytime." Turning back to Lissa as Jarren grasped Lissa's waist, Jesalyn cast her a smile of camaraderie. Lissa returned her most effective blank stare. "I will see you at the hangar, Lady Lissa. I am very happy we will continue our travels together."

"Indeed," Lissa said. "Jasmine, close your eyes."

A moment later the two were gone. "Interesting woman," Lissa muttered.

Jarren angled a concerned look her way, but his voice held no note of skepticism in it. "She is a child of court. She's a bit arrogant, but Veena trusts her above anyone else; Jesalyn has always supported my line to rulership."

"Right. Veena." Lissa pulled Jasmine close and kept her gaze on the ground. But those feelings she'd stifled last night returned. Like it or not, Lissa would talk to Jarren about his intended bonded. "Jasmine, close your eyes."

"What's wrong?" Jarren asked.

"I understand that Veena is your fiancée or betrothed or whatever." Tense, Lissa tapped her foot.

"We were expected to mate, Lissa. But it was an arranged match based entirely on our scent compatibilities. Veena and I have always viewed each other more as cousins then as mates."

Lissa still could not meet Jarren's gaze. "Why is that?"

"Probably because we *are* cousins." He paused. "Are you jealous?"

"No. I just don't like that woman. Does Jesalyn hate me for snagging you away from her princess? Sometimes it doesn't matter whether the relationship began intentionally. I've been accused of much more in my lifetime." Lissa started to wiggle within his grasp. She'd lied rather successfully about not feeling jealous.

"She won't be overly involved with you while we conduct our meetings. And once we've finalized our plan, she'll leave. She is necessary for what we need to do, but I'm sorry if her presence bothers you."

Lissa shook her head. Her unease had to be unwarranted. "It's nothing. Don't worry about it."

Jasmine tugged on Lissa's gown. "Mommy, we need to go. Marcus is waiting."

Lissa finally looked at Jarren again. His eyes bore into hers, searching for something as he spoke. "You are right, Butterfly. We're off. Eyes closed?" Following instructions, Jasmine piped a "yep." Lissa leaned her head into Jarren's chest and breathed in his scent. Even with their Subduers up, her body hummed in response. He hugged her to him, put a hand over her eyes, and spoke aloud.

"Unit transport, lateral surface pre-coded location." The darkness behind Lissa's eyelids disappeared.

CHAPTER 20

JARREN HELPED LISSA out of Marcus's jumper. The chrome side of the ship reflected the rock-brown surface of the mine's landing chamber. Lissa looked up, her eyes wide as she stared into the steep darkness above. The Mira Mines were a wonder of Deneb: natural catacombs of large and small stone chambers interconnected by rounded tunnels that ran through the belly of Mira Mountain. Throughout the mines were wall sconces with burning torches tacked high on the cave walls, splashing reflected light into the dark.

With the duke's grudging permission, Jarren had been granted access to use the mines' abandoned living quarters as temporary asylum. Jarren wouldn't normally have chosen the mines as a location for any activity. Mira's air particles were poisonous. Months of exposure could drive a person insane. The mines would not have worked for any extended period of time, but for Jarren, time had run out anyway. The debrief with Leor had rocketed home that reality.

As Lissa wandered away with a subdued Jasmine holding her hand, Marcus drew up next to Jarren. "Four days," Marcus mumbled.

"Well, Jasmine couldn't last longer than a week in here, regardless," Jarren replied. Their distorted voices carried in the massive chamber. "Did you reach Centuron Prime's Alliance advisor?" Jarren continued.

"Yes. We are to meet him and the other Alliance members tomorrow."

"What are their demands?"

"You mean aside from you possessing the scepter? I understand they want you to ratify the Hunters Breeding Convention."

"Marcus, I can't ratify it. I will be king, but the Council of Rule determines planetary law."

"Then I imagine you will need to give them some assurance the Council will ratify the convention when you return to power."

Jarren shook his head and gestured for Jesalyn to come over. "We aren't yet positioned to give them that assurance. My reign will only be as powerful as my father's. Besides, I must prioritize ending the caste system, not just improving the existence of one group of people. I will listen to their offer and go from there. Maybe we can come to some sort of consensus."

Jesalyn stopped before them and bowed. "Highness."

Jarren ignored Marcus's annoyed sigh. "Marcus and I will be meeting with Alliance members most of the day tomorrow. I need to burden you with seeing to Lissa's needs."

Jesalyn remained prostrate. "It is no burden, Highness. As your Rigelian second cousin, I am at your complete disposal."

"I know you're willing to help, Jesalyn, but Veena volunteered your assistance only for the immediate mission, not to care for another in your capacity as lady-in-wait."

"Well, as she is your bonded, Highness, it is my duty to perform such duties for her. She is my superior just as Veena is also my superior. I serve Veena faithfully. You have witnessed this yourself many times."

Marcus laughed. "Superior? Jesalyn. You are on a mission here. Jarren requests your help. Lissa is not your superior. She is simply one needing friendly assistance in a foreign land."

Jesalyn shook her head. "She may not have been born royal, but she is His Highness's bonded. She has become royalty. She shall be queen. I do not misunderstand my position." Her voice rose, distressed.

Jarren raised a hand to stop the impending argument. "Enough. I appreciate your willingness to assist Lissa. She and her daughter are alone, and they are my responsibility. Especially as I gave her no choice in leaving her world. Tonight, I will see to her comfort, but Marcus and I leave tomorrow morning. Jamis, Faheel, and Corsa will be around tomorrow to visit. If you could just be available should she need something, I would appreciate it."

Again, Jesalyn nodded.

"Good. Settled." Jarren called to Lissa. "Lissa, let's get you and Jasmine settled for the night." With a pat on Marcus's arm, he walked over to her.

Lissa raised her brows as he stopped at her side. "Are we roughing it?" she asked.

Jarren grinned. "No. The mines boast actual quarters. Before they discovered the gas source making the miners sick, the mountain was mined day and night. The miners had shifts and would go home, but the area foremen and their families had quarters here. They needed to be close in case of an emergency. We'll be in those quarters."

"Showers, toilets, everything?"

Jarren's grin widened. "It looks uninhabitable, I know. But for you at least, the rooms won't seem unusual. The showers are not connected to your unit, so you'll have to turn the water on and regulate it yourself. There are light switches, no rugs, and yes, even a draft. But there are thick covers if you get cold and slippers in Marcus's jumper. The rest you are familiar with."

As he spoke, he herded her and Jasmine out of the large chamber and through a lighted tunnel. They stopped at a wood door fitted into a rectangular stone recess. Opening the door, he motioned them in.

Jarren flicked the switch by the entrance. Light spilled down from a hanging ceiling fixture. "There is a living room, bedroom, and bathroom for these living quarters." He gestured to the round table and chairs in front of them, and a charcoal couch pressing into a corner of the room. An empty bookshelf sat against another wall. He walked over and pushed open one door. Lissa stood behind him as he reached in and tapped something. The room illuminated.

"Bed, chair, nightstand. Over there is a vanity. The bathroom is through another door off the living room." The rooms were pretty bare, but they'd been cleaned and prepared by the duke's staff earlier. A canopy bed with purple chiffon draping the poles dominated the left side of the room. The vanity at the back wall had been dusted and stocked with necessaries. But Lissa likely wouldn't touch the bottles. She couldn't read the labels and probably wouldn't trust the odd-colored mixtures anyway. The quarters would do for the next few days.

Lissa walked forward, holding Jasmine's hand. She glanced around until her gaze landed on Jarren. "Where will you be?" Her question washed over him.

His eyes strayed to the bed before he forced his gaze to the far wall. "We passed another door closer to the landing chamber. Marcus and I will be staying there. Jesalyn has offered to assist you in any way you need. She'll bring you and Jasmine your meals. The mines are secure, but I would prefer that you not journey out of these rooms unless it is to speak to myself or Marcus for some reason. This will limit your exposure to the cellular toxins in the air. No need to increase your exposure even if it is minimal now. Is that alright?"

Lissa nodded. Jasmine moved past them and jumped on the bed. Jarren returned to the living room and out into the darkness of the tunnels. He spoke to reassure her. "If you need me for anything at all, take a right back down the tunnels. I am in the very next room. Even if it's the middle of the night, I'm here, Lissa. I'm here," he repeated.

"I understand."

"Tomorrow, Marcus and I will be gone most of the day. Jesalyn will be in the living quarters past yours on the left.

Try not to go out to the large landing chamber. As I won't be here to protect you, I don't want to take any risks. Your essence is subdued for the most part. But it only takes one solitary wind to carry your scent to a cross draft."

"We'll stay in the tunnel, Jarren. I know why it's important."

"Thank you. Now, is there anything I can do for you? Do you need anything, or do you just want to go to bed?"

"I think we'll go to bed. When are you leaving tomorrow?"

"We will probably be gone by the time you get up. But I've arranged for a little surprise while we are away. I hope it makes you happy." Jarren stepped away from the door. He resisted the urge to beg her to ask him to stay. More than that, he resisted begging her to stay with him, even after Jamis would present the alternative, a way for her to go home. Her choice. Staying or leaving, what she did would be her choice.

A startled look crossed her face. "Well, thank you, I think."

Jasmine called out from the bedroom. Jarren could think of nothing else to keep Lissa at the door. "I'll let you get settled. I'm only steps away. Goodnight." Jarren retreated a step then turned back the way he'd come. He heard Lissa's soft goodnight hum behind him. It warmed his heart even as he worried this might be his last goodnight from her. Flexing his shoulders, he kept walking. Now if only he could find a way to ensure she didn't choose to leave with Jamis tomorrow.

* * * * *

LISSA WOKE WELL rested. She was sure the familiar level of technological comfort in her quarters made her feel less homesick. Still, she hadn't slept through the night, so feeling relaxed seemed an oddity.

Jarren and Marcus had already left. The air lacked sweetness, but it surprised her that Jarren's absence had an impact. She missed him. During the night she'd gotten up and paced in the near blackness of the bedroom, watching Jasmine's sleeping outline under the sheets and resisting the urge to seek Jarren out and finish what the Sharing Ritual had sparked between them. Desire, potent and uncomfortable. Lissa wanted to go back to hating him. Things had been less complicated then.

Lissa pushed away the memory of Jarren's taut, muscular body standing straight and unmoving before her. She still remembered the waves of energy and need that hit her when she realized he shook as he refrained from touching her. Lissa's heart jumped in her chest. What was happening to her?

A knock came on her outer door. She glanced back into the living room to catch a glimpse of Jasmine playing with a doll on the floor. "Come in."

Jesalyn walked in, carrying a tray of food. She bowed subserviently, but her posture was tense. Lissa smothered her frown and stood up. "Thank you, Jesalyn. I can take the tray. You know, you really don't have to bring us our food. If you tell me where the kitchens are or whatever they have here, I'll get our meals."

"Oh no, my lady. It would be improper for you to serve yourself. The food comes from the jumper anyway. Jarren specifically said I should be the only one going out there. Of course he did not restrict your movements, lady, so if you want to get your own meals, I shan't say another word." She kept her eyes lowered, but Lissa still felt looked down upon.

"No, Jesalyn. Jarren was quite right. I had no idea the food was on the ship."

"Yes, my lady. I've brought you breakfast. His Highness asked me to let you know you shall have visitors in a few hours." She backed out of the living room and into the hall.

"Visitors?"

"Yes, my lady. From *Stardesire*."

Lissa absorbed the information, let it settle for a minute, then nodded. She had no idea who would want to visit her from Jarren's ship. But with Jesalyn's subtle hostility as her and Jasmine's only company, Lissa wasn't about to question her luck.

Three hours later, she opened her door to find Faheel, Corsa, and Jamis waiting in the tunnel. The small woman stepped forward first, an act that touched Lissa. She knew it wasn't Corsa's nature to be assertive. Lissa grasped and squeezed her pale-blue hands. Behind Lissa, Jasmine gave a shout as her little feet pattered forward.

"Mommy, Mommy. We have visitors." Lissa looked down as Jasmine grabbed hold of her leg and smiled up at the three. They all smiled back.

Lissa pulled the door open wider. "Please come in. I'm glad to see you all. Have a seat."

As they sat, with Jasmine perched on Lissa's knee, Jamis spoke. "I want you to know that Jarren gave us leave to visit."

There was a meaningful tone in Jamis's voice that caused Lissa to tense.

Faheel spoke up. "Yes, we wanted you to see a few somewhat familiar and friendly faces."

Lissa smiled at them. "Jarren told me I would get a surprise today. He must have meant you. I appreciate you coming down. It isn't as if you really know me at all."

"We don't know your history, Lady Lissa, but we do know you. You are Jarren's bonded. That is great knowledge," Corsa murmured as she stared at the table.

"Besides, Rila told us much of you and Jasmine. Palmesians are a very chatty bunch," Faheel added.

"Well, I am grateful to see you. I think Jesalyn will be around in a bit with lunch. I would love to host you all unless you didn't plan on staying long."

"We would love to stay. That is what we intended. I think Faheel and Corsa brought food just for that purpose," Jamis replied. His eyes bore into hers intently. Lissa's heart pattered nervously. She didn't know what was going on, but Jamis, at least, had come with a purpose.

Almost as if they'd exchanged subliminal messages, Faheel and Corsa got up. "We'll find Jesalyn and help her with the food. Rila was a little too enthusiastic with the fabricator," Faheel said, laughing.

Corsa nodded. "Would you like to come with us?"

"Where is your jumper?"

Faheel shook his head at the question. "It's next to Marcus's. I'm sure Jarren doesn't want you out in the landing chamber."

Lissa just saw the bright pink of a blush on Corsa's pale-blue face as the engineer corrected herself. "No, he wouldn't. He would never want you to be anywhere where you could be in danger." If Lissa had asked for help, Corsa would have given it. She noted the knowing yet trusting gleam in Corsa's eyes. Somewhere in Corsa's past, someone had trapped her too.

Lissa stood and took Corsa's hand in unspoken gratitude. "Corsa, you're very considerate. Thank you for making the offer. I'll stay here. I have no interest in battling bounty hunters. I've seen them close up twice too many times. It was a learning experience I don't want to repeat." Corsa's red head bobbed.

Lissa frowned internally. How could she have considered turning any of Jarren's crew against him? Because she was Jarren's bonded, she'd gained Faheel's trust, and for some reason, she'd gained Corsa's understanding. But a relationship was not telling of a person's good intent. High-level aliens they both were, but they'd yet to experience the sting of human duality. Lissa wouldn't enlighten them. Hopefully, they would stay happily ignorant for the rest of their lives. She would get herself home or pray Jarren kept his promise. Maybe it was time to extend him a portion of the trust he'd shown her.

A moment later, Faheel and Corsa stood by the door, but Jamis remained seated. He flicked a hand to Faheel. "May they take Jasmine with them? I am sure she would love to get out, and I would like to speak with you a moment, alone."

Lissa paused. She would have been suspicious had it been any other three members of Jarren's crew. But Jamis was Jarren's security chief, no matter that they'd behaved less than civil to each other the last she'd seen them together. And Jarren referred to Corsa and Faheel with the highest level of respect and trust. It was Corsa's shy glance and determined nod that convinced Lissa to trust what she could not understand.

"Jasmine, you're going on a little outing, okay? Do you think you can go get lunch with Faheel and Corsa?"

Jasmine jumped up excitedly. "Yep, I can, Mommy. I'll be fine, and I'll listen. I will listen real good." Jasmine was at the door pulling it open before Lissa got a response out. The three disappeared through the doorway.

Jamis's voice interrupted her thoughts. "I want you to know that I am here because I want to help and because Jarren gave me permission to speak to you about this."

"About what?" Lissa closed the door. She did not really want to hear Jamis's answer.

Jamis's golden eyes glittered. "I know you and Jarren are bonded. The manner of your bonding, though, seems to have been a mystery to you both, so I am assuming that it was not planned. Is that correct?"

What a far-too-personal question. Lissa stared at him, unflinching, as she took a seat. If Jarren had known that Jamis was coming, he must have had some idea of what Jamis would tell her. "No, it wasn't planned. Why do you ask?"

"Jarren and I are rather distant cousins, but our scents are very similar. Lissa, I sensed our strong compatibility in the Salon. I could bond with you like Jarren has."

She directed a blank look at him.

"I could cover Jarren's scent, Lissa. You could bond with me instead and go home." Jamis paused to give her a moment to digest his words.

And Lissa needed the time to think. Go home? He wasn't joking. Lissa looked into his eyes and knew he wasn't. She was so far from home, on a world so very different—hiding, running. She had just given up the idea of using Jarren's crewmates to escape. Now home was being handed to her on a Jarren-approved silver platter. Her stomach dove as the once-comforting lamps that reminded her of Earth seemed to brighten to an aching glare. She barely contained her stomach's emotional roller coaster. Another way of returning home was nonchalantly recited to her now, and a burning question popped into her head.

"Did he know?" she asked. Her outrage began to gather.

"I'm sorry?" Jamis replied.

"Jarren. Did he know I just needed to 'bond' with someone else in order to go home?"

Jamis's eyes widened. "It isn't like that, Lissa. He may have known in the recesses of his mind, but this answer isn't an obvious one, and it requires a compatible mate. I just happen to be compatible. Jarren did not intend to hide this solution from you, I swear."

The angry blood rushing to her head eased; Lissa's chest loosened. "Okay."

"I want you to know I went to Jarren about this. I would not have offered this alternative without speaking to him first. He is your bonded. Attempting to sever a bonding without both partners' consent is illegal on Lynta. He knows I mean to make this offer to you."

Lissa sat back in her chair. How was she to process this information? She'd demanded Jarren let her go home as if her life depended on it. Maybe he was trying to give her that opportunity. But now the thought of not seeing him anymore, of not having him near her, of not talking to him, caused a throb in Lissa's heart that she couldn't ignore. "And Jarren was fine with this idea?"

The question seemed to take Jamis aback. "No, lady, he was not happy about my request. But he would not deny you the chance to go home when it was his to grant."

"And our bonding, yours and mine. What will that mean to us? Did I misunderstand that the meaning of bonding is equal to an Earth marriage? Marriage is a powerful commitment."

"Yes, lady, I understand Earth marriages. You're correct. We would essentially be married."

Lissa squirmed in her chair. A storm of feelings and doubts played in her head. "So you would let me go home to Earth and leave me there, and I would be married to you? Jamis, you are a great man. I couldn't make a sacrifice like that for someone."

He cleared his throat and stared off. "Actually, Lissa, should you return to Earth, I would go with you. Bonding will most likely keep you safe from trackers, but if Milovar has your picture from those incidents where you were attacked, he may still send others after you. Bounty hunters and scent may not be the only threats to your life."

Lissa threw her hands up and stood. Her chair bounced back on the wood floor. "I don't understand why this offer is any different than the situation I am now in. My life would still be in danger."

"We do not believe Milovar knows of you yet. You would be home. Jasmine would be home, and she would definitely be safe. She is only a child. He will not care about her, and I could cover Jarren's lighter scent on her as well."

"But I would still be a prisoner, just in a more familiar cell. And who knows what might happen if we were caught with my family present. Would they then also be taken?"

"I would not let that happen. I would protect you."

"But you can't control me or them. We could all converge, and you wouldn't be able to prevent the possibility of someone getting hurt or dying. Then there is the whole marriage thing. Maybe on your world, scent is all that's required to make a life with someone. Where I come from love, emotion, and attraction are also important."

His gaze slid over her. Jamis's voice roughened with arousal. "I know you do not love me now. But in time, I hope you will grow to care for me and I, you. You are my biological match more than any other I've encountered. It's intoxicating and will satisfy our relationship as only perfect bonding can. For emotion, I cannot say what you mean by this. I don't understand your reference. Attraction should be easy. I am strong. On Lynta I never lacked bed partners, even from those not attracted by my scent." He scowled with familiar male arrogance.

Lissa sat again and reached out to touch his clasped hands on the table. "I think you're very attractive. I like the tall burly types, truly. But…"

"But I am not Jarren, is that not correct?" Jamis finished for her. Lissa would not answer. They both knew it was true. She was falling in love with Jarren. She wanted to go home, but the thought of leaving Jarren caused her heart to constrict.

"It may be that I just need time to process all this. May I take a few days to think about this?"

"Lady, I don't know how much you know about Jarren's situation, but we all expect he'll be back on the throne before the end of the week."

"So soon?" Lissa's brows came to together. "Then why bother to make your offer when I could be home in two weeks?"

A boyish smile softened Jamis's expression. "I should think that was obvious. I find you very attractive and interesting. I could grow to love you quite easily. I want to bond with you."

After a pause, Lissa smiled. "Thank you for that. And thank you for your offer. I know you mean it. I understand what you were willing to sacrifice to stay with me. I, more than others, know what it feels like to leave everything behind." Lissa leaned over and kissed Jamis's cheek, then sat back. "When will you see Jarren?"

"I am to bring him and Marcus back from their meeting. I'll let him know your decision if you like."

"Yes, thank you. I don't know that I have it in me to speak to him about it."

Jamis got up and stretched. "Worry not, Lissa. I will tell him you declined without revealing your feelings. I've no doubt you will speak for yourself when the time is right."

Lissa nodded, then spied Jesalyn at the door. "You are a good friend, Jamis. Now, I think lunch has arrived. I hope you really intended to have lunch with me."

Jamis beamed a true Cheshire-cat smile, his self-confidence back in place. "Of course. The pleasure of relaxing hours in your company is of equal importance. Corsa seems quite innocent, but she'd have no problem putting a Deneb snake in my bed should I rob her of this time with you."

They both laughed.

CHAPTER 21

LISSA AND JASMINE sat on the bed singing their ABC's. Lissa hadn't seen the sky in a day, but her internal clock told her it had to be near bedtime. Jamis, Faheel, and Corsa had eaten lunch and shown Lissa pictures of their home planets to pass the time. Corsa brought vidcasts of the underground communities of her world; tunnels similar to the ones where Lissa and Jasmine were hiding, and large, domed cities where sunlight poured into holes bored in the fired-mud ceiling. The different colors found in the underground plant life on Terlia amazed Lissa.

"My family would be most honored to host you for a visit, lady," Corsa had offered with a shy glance. Lissa nodded eagerly and promised to try and visit at some point. She didn't know how, though. Jarren had agreed to return her to Earth as soon as he reclaimed the throne.

Lissa pushed thoughts of the future to the back of her head. She got up and propped Jasmine on her hip, then headed into the bedroom. "Come on, young lady, time for bed."

"I want to wait for Marcus and Jarren. I want goodnight kisses," Jasmine replied as Lissa placed her on the bed.

Lissa put a hand on her hip. "I don't think they are going to return before we go to sleep, Butterfly."

"Well, I want water, Mommy. Please?"

"You're stalling, little girl. Under the covers and scooch over, okay?"

Lissa heard a knock. Getting up, she walked back out into the living room and opened the door. Jesalyn waited, her head bowed. She held a tray in her hands. "I thought you might like some warm chulaa and dessert scones before bed."

Jesalyn's consideration touched Lissa. Taking the tray in one hand, she gestured Jesalyn in, but Jesalyn demurred. "Really, my lady, I should be getting ready for His Highness's return. I did not mean to intercede on your nighttime ritual."

Lissa placed the tray on the table then gestured Jesalyn in again. "I know that I haven't been very hospitable to you, Jesalyn, and I'm sorry. You've done nothing but try to find ways to make my adjustment as easy as possible. I really do appreciate it."

A hesitant smile formed on Jesalyn's lips as she took one step into the room. "I did feel you did not welcome my assistance, lady. I am glad that you appreciate the help I'm able to give, though it isn't much. I must prepare for His Highness's return, but if you are amenable, it would give me great pleasure to spend some time with you. Maybe we could get to know each other better."

Lissa nodded. There might be hope for Jesalyn's friendship after all. "Of course. Thank you. I'm not the easiest person to get along with, especially when I'm stressed and off my routine. I appreciate your tolerance. I'll speak to you tomorrow. We could sit down together for breakfast."

Jesalyn nodded amenably and stepped back through the entrance to turn down the hall. Lissa closed the door behind her. She'd had an overall positive day. Accepting that her attraction to Jarren was deeper than she'd first admitted gave her a lot of relief. And she had forged important friendships she wouldn't need to betray. Now she may have even gotten past her suspicions about Jesalyn. The only thing that could improve her day would be for Jarren to return, state his undying love, and drag her into his bedroom to make love to her all night.

Her daughter's high-pitched "Mommy" broke through Lissa's fantasy. She shook her head, picked up the tray, and then went back into the bedroom where she set the snacks on the bed. She leaned over to kiss Jasmine goodnight, but Jasmine's nose wiggled as a waft of heated chulaa filled the room. She sat up, her gaze on Lissa's cup.

"Mommy, I said I was thirsty. Can I have some chulaa?"

"That's mine, Jasmine," Lissa stated as she shifted to get up. Her daughter's doe eyes stopped her.

"But I'm thirsty. Please, Mommy, can I have some of your chulaa?" Lissa sighed. They'd been down this road before.

"You need to sleep. I'll give you the chulaa, but after that, right to bed. Deal?"

"Deal. I don't break my promises 'cause you won't believe me if I break my promises," Jasmine stated, rubbing her hands together.

"That's right. And tomorrow night, if you want chulaa, you have to tell me right after dinner, or there'll be no chulaa or any other drink for you before bedtime. Deal?" Lissa held out a hand. Jasmine shook it then reached for the warm drink. Creamy sweetness assailed Lissa's nostrils as she passed the cup along.

"Drink up. You need sleep." Lissa brokered no negotiation. Jasmine slurped then licked her lips in satisfaction. Lissa put her snack to the side as Jasmine slid under the covers. Her eyes drifted shut.

After placing a kiss on Jasmine's brow, Lissa took the next five minutes to throw on dark-blue flannel night pants and a T-shirt. She turned out the lights and climbed into the bed beside her daughter. Her eyes were just closing when a stifled groan from the living room revived her. Lissa's body tensed. Someone had gotten into her quarters, and they didn't want to be heard.

With a deliberately sluggish pace, Lissa turned in her bed so she could peer through her partially open door. Her eyes strained, making out the shadows of the living room furniture. Thank God for the line of light reaching under the tunnel door.

Lissa's hands became clammy. Sweat broke out on her exposed skin. She wanted to push Jasmine onto the floor and out of harm's way, but she knew someone watched her. An abrupt movement, and she would lose any advantage. The living room door swung wide and a figure in black, his body a shadow moving in and out of Lissa's line of sight, rushed forward, arm raised. Lissa had little time to react. Her heart mimicked the heavy pounding of footsteps as her attacker approached.

She couldn't let him near the bed. He might not be trying to hurt or kill Jasmine, but he might do so if he caught Lissa where she was. In one movement, Lissa pushed the covers away and rolled forward onto the floor, tripping her attacker as the raised arm lowered to stab down. Lissa caught the reflection of light off a jagged knife. She twisted her body away as her attacker fell with a grunt to the floor.

Lissa jumped up, trying to remember what she could use to defend herself. Fire pierced through her leg, and she looked down to see her attacker had stabbed her thigh. With a kick, Lissa yanked away and stumbled toward the living room door. Pain shot up her side. She heard her attacker get up and advance behind her. She couldn't move fast enough. Warm liquid seeped from the gash in her leg. In the foreboding silence, her mind screamed: *Jarren!*

* * * * *

"WELL, GENTLEMEN, IT seems we have a deal," Jarren stated as he rolled up his star map. He resisted the urge to rub the fatigue from his eyes. This meeting had taken entirely too long. He should have been back at the mines by now, and for some reason, his tardiness made him anxious.

The closest Alliance member stood with his light-blue hand held out. His heavy purple robes swept the ground as he moved forward. "Thank you for being so patient with us, Your Highness," he replied, his eyes downcast.

Jarren shook his head. "Not at all, Member. I share your concerns. If I had the authority of rule, this treaty would not be so plagued with political exceptions. Nevertheless, we will accomplish the most important goal for hunters: sentient rights."

Marcus stood as well and nodded to the six heads around the table. "You, of course, have my father's personal gratitude for your willingness to meet us today. And also for your willingness to come to a consensus."

The Alliance members represented at the table nodded their heads. An older, black-robed member spoke up. "Believe us, Marcus, it is not our wish to have Milovar ruling this side of the galaxy."

A towering humanoid stick rose as well, his long thin fingers gesturing about him expressively as he spoke. "Milovar attaining the throne would be a catastrophe for the Alliance. But we are unable to act against him. We must give the impression of aiding him in his search for you for fear that he will stop the food supplies to Alliance members. Lynta is an agricultural necessity. To have that food source cut off could destroy planet populations."

Jarren nodded. "I completely understand, Asserian. I know you are protecting those who rely on you. You need not—"

He stopped. The smell of fear—sweat, salt, tangy air—overwhelmed him. Jarren flipped around to look behind him. He was sure someone was going to stab him in the back at any moment. As he stilled and concentrated on the smell, he began to distinguish Lissa's scent. His eyes widened. It was her fear he sensed.

Jarren dashed from the room without looking back. He could hear Marcus's heavy footsteps behind him. In his mind's eye, he could almost see Lissa. A shape, a person stood over her. They were going to kill her. He darted down one hall, then another until he saw Marcus's mini jumper hovering next to a balcony. Jarren and Marcus were in the jumper seats, Marcus at the controls, within a minute.

"Jarren, what's going on?" Marcus asked in a huff.

Jarren sat in the copilot's chair. "Marcus, give me the controls," he demanded, instead of answering. His heart lodged itself in his throat.

"They're yours," Marcus replied as he punched in a code.

Jarren grabbed the stick, and the jumper shot forward. Marcus's question was forgotten. Jarren began to sweat. They were so far from home. How would he get to her in time? Who was attacking her? Creeds, he cursed not having his own faster jumper, right then.

Grim emotion tightened his face as he sped over mild deserts and lush tropical lands. By the gods, he would kill the person who dared attack his bonded. Drawn and quartered without mercy. A violent sneer curled his lips. His sanity slowly receded as he raced back. The anger in his eyes colored the screen before him red. Murder became his purpose.

*　*　*　*　*

LISSA HIT THE floor. The impact knocked her breath out. She turned to the side and stifled a groan. If Jasmine awoke, she would become another threat to eliminate, and that thought spurred her. Her attacker advanced slower this time, possibly because he had lost the element of surprise. She gathered her strength then jumped up and forward, catching her attacker off guard. That one moment of hesitation was all she needed to throw her full weight onto him. He stumbled back toward the bed. Together, they fell.

The air whipped past Lissa as their two bodies cut through the silence. In the next moment, her attacker's head banged against one heavy wooden canopy pole. Groaning, he slumped forward on top of her. Lissa pushed against him. His black-masked head angled painfully off the side of the bed. His body didn't budge as Lissa hauled herself up.

There was a sudden searing in her side as she breathed deep. It took another heave against the body for her to stand, her legs unsteady as blood rushed to the site of her new injury. Feeling her side through the wooziness, her hand touched the hilt of the knife lodged in the flesh. Lissa winced as her touch forced a cascade of pain through her body and pushed at her building nausea.

A shallow breath shuddered from her. "Don't faint," she told herself as she reached down to remove the mask from her attacker's face. Was he conscious at all? The mask slid off to reveal Jesalyn's rage-contorted grimace, but the woman's eyes were closed. She was out cold.

Lissa couldn't think through the increasing hurt. She stepped back then stumbled under waves of gut-wrenching nausea. Half aware, she noted Jasmine's sleeping form still snuggled in the bed. Lissa wasn't sure how she remained asleep, but she was glad for it. Inching around, Lissa tried to run for the living room. If Jesalyn had been sent to kill her, whom could she trust? Who could be waiting for Jesalyn's triumphant return?

Lissa barely made it through the bedroom door when her wooziness overcame her again. Her knees crumbled. She collapsed only to be caught and lifted before she hit the floor. She almost didn't register the strong arms holding her close. Tired, Lissa looked into Jarren's eyes. Marcus ran past them into the bedroom.

"Jesalyn," Lissa whimpered with what little strength she had left. Her side burned. It hurt to breathe.

"Okay, my own. Okay."

"Jasmine."

Jarren nodded as he walked over to the couch in the corner. "Marcus is checking on her right now. I have to put you down a moment, and then we're going to need to pull out that knife."

Lissa shook her head. "I want to sleep. Take care of Jasmine." Her eyes closed.

"No sleeping, Lissa. Just like before, right? You can't sleep now." Jarren's voice sounded far away, but a brisk shake of her shoulders startled her back to awareness. Jarren propped her up then turned away, calling out. "Jasmine?"

"She's been drugged. I'm not sure with what yet. I don't think she's in any danger, but I'd prefer to get her back to the palace." Marcus's voice droned. Lissa's eyes lowered.

"No, no, my own. I need you to stay awake. We're going to remove the knife then cauterize the wound, and then you should be able to walk."

Lissa choked out a response. "My leg is hurt too."

Jarren let her lay back. "What? Which one?" he asked as he moved to look at her legs. His hand gently slipped to her hip, just above where blood darkened the fabric covering her thigh. He would need to pull down her waistband to examine the stab wound.

"Marcus, tie Jesalyn up then help me with Lissa. She's badly injured." His voice lowered as his thumb wiped away a tear on her cheek. "We'll do the wound in your side first then move on to the other. It's going to hurt like the gods when I pull it out. But the cauterization should mangle the nerve endings and help with the pain. I'll do it quickly."

Jarren placed one hand on the skin around the knife then grasped the hilt with his other. Before she could consider what he was doing, he pulled. Nausea pummeled her stomach. She shook with its intensity. Lissa screamed then gasped, tears streaming from her eyes.

Another sudden burning sensation drew an anguished whimper. Dull throbbing jerked at her lungs and kept her gasping. She was barely coherent. The constant pounding of angry blood through her body drowned any rational thought.

Quiet voices floated into her ear. "Is she alright?"

"The wound in her side was the worst. The one in her leg just needs re-stitching to repair the damaged muscle. Your father's Healers will have no problem fixing her up."

"I've packed their things. We can leave as soon as you think we're able."

"And Jesalyn? Has she come around?"

"I don't think she's going to. She fell hard against something. She's alive, but we won't be able to question her anytime soon. I've tied her up."

"Have Jamis come get her. I want her looked after. I need to know where this attack originated."

"Milovar?"

"Then why go after Lissa? Why not wait until I return and get me? Something isn't right."

The massive throbbing in Lissa's head drowned out the words. Her temples had been positioned between compressing brick walls. As she was lifted again, restful oblivion encased her mind.

CHAPTER 22

LISSA'S WORLD LANGUISHED in a light blur before it solid-ified into an elegant golden room. Lethargy pulled at her limbs. With deliberate slowness, Lissa sat up in the soft bed, a large comforter falling down to her lap. Wind, full of the aroma of ripe vineyards, brushed over her bare arms and out through colorful silk-draped French windows. But Lissa wasn't in France. She wasn't even on Earth.

She pushed off the warm covers and looked down at her favorite pair of blue jeans and her purple spaghetti-strap shirt. Apparently someone had deigned to retrieve her clothes from Jarren's jumper. She wouldn't consider, for the moment, how her clothes made their way onto her body. Just fighting to remember what had last happened to her would be enough to think about.

A haze of memories stirred in Lissa's head. The dark tunnels, Jamis, hearing a sound in the room. That slit of light that revealed someone trying to kill her. And Jesalyn's crazed but frozen expression. Maybe Jesalyn hadn't been unconscious but would come after her again. Lissa's hand rose to smother an instinctive gasp.

"Lissa?" Jarren's voice sounded to her right. Turning, she spied him stretched out in a chair by the double doors of Marcus's apartments in the ducal palace. Her scrambled brain seemed to have settled into a coherent picture.

Lissa urged her legs over the bedside as she twisted to look at him. A small ache formed in her side, and she put her hands to where her wound should have been. No bandages covered her smooth skin. Lissa put the question to Jarren. "Rila fixed me?"

"No. It was one of the duke's Healers. Rila's healing gift is more prevalent, but your injury didn't require her level of healing and unnecessary time would have been lost bringing her down from the envoy. You should be all better now. How do you feel?"

Lissa gingerly pressed her fingers into her side until the ache returned. "It seems pretty much healed. How long have I been asleep? Where's Jasmine?"

"Jasmine's fine. She's with Marcus. You've only been out a day, but unfortunately, one day is all we have. Lissa," Jarren started gently, "Jesalyn's attack on you has caused some unforeseen complications, not the least of which is your safety. Whatever happened when she tried to kill you, she ended up bashing her head pretty badly. We can't revive her, so I don't know for sure why she attacked. Did she say anything to you?" he asked.

Lissa's mind drew a blank. "No. I don't remember hearing anything."

"Well, whether it had anything to do with Milovar or something else entirely, we have to leave."

Lissa listened to his words with dread. She closed her eyes briefly at the finality of Jarren's statement.

As she looked down at her lap, she heard him approach. Her hands shook at the thought of how closely her daughter had come to being harmed. "Jasmine could have been killed," Lissa said, looking up as he knelt in front of her. His eyes simmered.

"Yes, she could have been."

"My daughter's life is in danger just being near me. Near us."

"I know." The deep timbre of his voice sounded almost small beneath the high vaulted depths of the ceiling.

Lissa took a deep breath and blinked back the tears that threatened to escape. A pain deeper than the throbbing in her side surfaced as she realized what she would have to do. "I have to leave her. We have to find a place away from us, where she'll be safe," Lissa gasped. She choked, tears running down her cheeks. A warm hand rubbed her back. Jarren lowered himself onto the bed.

His reply came out in a sad whisper. "Yes."

"How can I leave her? How can I leave my baby?" Lissa ached; her heart clenched.

"Marcus will protect her. He feels a connection with Jasmine, and he can cover any scent I might have accidentally masked her with. He'll stay here with his father at the palace until we return from Lynta."

"And his father is okay with that idea? He's resisted involvement with your intrigues before now."

Jarren cleared his throat. "Actually, it was his idea. He said Jasmine was Marcus's responsibility now. You and I couldn't protect her any longer. Marcus adamantly requested that responsibility. He would not listen to anything I had to say about it. He swore only your wishes could overrule his in this instance." Jarren smirked as she glanced at his profile. "A first time for all things, I suppose." Jarren faced her, his expression now passive. "I have no idea why you were attacked, Lissa. I would feel better leaving Jasmine in Marcus's care until I've reclaimed the throne and can stop the payment of all bounties on my head."

"You don't think you can protect her."

"Honestly, I have no idea where this threat came from. Jesalyn was Veena's most trusted lady-in-wait. She knew the specifics about the plan to return me to power. She had a pivotal role in the plan. If she couldn't be trusted, I fear what my enemies may know right now."

The truth of Lissa's situation stung like the searching end of a whip. If she'd listened to Jarren, had trusted him, Jasmine would be home safe. "Where is Jasmine now?" she asked.

"She is with Marcus, taking her lessons in the courtyard. I will get her for you, but I need to know if you'll let Marcus protect her until we return."

Jasmine had never spent days away from Lissa with anyone but Lissa's mother. Now Lissa was being asked to entrust the most important thing in her life to a man she barely knew. An alien. Lissa closed her eyes and pushed down all her normal paranoia. Marcus's smiling face flashed before her eyes. He was so much like her cousin. And odds were Jasmine would be safer with Marcus than with Lissa at the moment. That realization had hit the hardest. Lissa wouldn't make the same mistake twice.

Lissa nodded as she dragged the words out of her mouth. "Okay, Jasmine will stay here until we are safe. The moment we can return without her life being threatened, you can retrieve her, and then…we'll go home." She couldn't look at Jarren as she choked out the statement. His hand fell from her back with the cold silence, and Lissa fought not to reach out to him. If only home were as easy to find as it had been when she'd left Earth. Her mother always believed home was where the heart was. Where was Lissa's heart now?

Jarren got up, his posture stiff. "I'll go and get Jasmine for you. There is very little time to say goodbye. I'm sorry we have only a small window of opportunity to restructure our plan and put it into place." As he walked away, his words rang hollow in the room.

Jarren stepped out then returned a minute later with Jasmine. Five-year-old bundled energy ran over to Lissa and kissed her cheek. "Mommy, you feel better!" Her happy voice soothed Lissa's apprehensions.

"Yes, Butterfly, I feel better. How are you? Are you okay?"

"Yep. I am working really hard on my learning with Marcus. He says I am very smart, and he promised one day I would get to fly my own ship on Earth 'cause I remember really well. Isn't that the bestest?" Jasmine bounced, her little poof-ball ponytails following suit as Lissa took her hands within her own.

"That's great. Marcus seems like a very smart man too. So if he says you will fly spaceships, I know you will. You'll be a NASA astronaut." She glanced up to see Marcus and

Jarren watching from the door. Jarren nodded. Lissa's time was running out.

"Listen, Butterfly, Mommy has to go do some chores with Jarren."

Jasmine frowned and stopped bouncing. "That means you are going away, and I can't come. I want to come too."

Lissa smiled and blinked to push back the tears from her eyes. If Jasmine saw her cry, she'd think something was wrong. "Not for these chores, Jasmine. I have to do some big people chores. But I've decided that you can stay here with Marcus if you are a very good girl. Do you think you can be a very good girl?"

"I don't want to stay here. I want to go with you."

Lissa pulled her close and kissed Jasmine's brow. "If you really want to fly ships when you're older, you must continue your studies. Don't you want to fly those ships?"

Jasmine nodded but looked unsure. "Yes."

"Then you need to stay here and work very hard and learn about space. Okay?"

"But how long will your chores take?"

Lissa looked at Jarren. As if prompted, he and Marcus walked forward. "She won't be gone longer than a week, Jasmine. And I think we can find a way for you to speak with both Mommy and Abuela. We certainly don't want you to miss Mommy too much," Jarren stated.

Lissa stood, clasping Jasmine's hand within her own. She turned to face Marcus as Jarren moved up behind her. "While I'm gone, Marcus will look after you. So you'll have to listen to him. I trust him very much, okay?" Lissa handed Jasmine over to Marcus. He picked the little girl up and stepped back.

Jasmine pushed against him until he put her down. Running over to Lissa, Jasmine hugged her legs. There were tears in her eyes as she looked up. "Okay, Mommy. I will stay and learn all my lessons, but you have to call me 'cause I'm scared a little."

Marcus stepped forward and put his hand on Jasmine's shoulder. "We will call your mommy. I know where she'll be, so you won't have to wait for her to call us. But…" He paused as he knelt to look Jasmine in the eye. "We can't call so many times that we keep her from finishing her chores. We want them to return soon so you can go home and show all your friends how much you know. Do we have a deal?"

Jasmine looked first at Marcus then up at her mother, then finally back at Marcus again. "I am making a lot of those. Deal. But I'm still going to miss my Mommy," she stated as she hugged Lissa's leg once more before grabbing onto Marcus.

Lissa reached out and scuffled Jasmine's head. "I'll miss you too, Butterfly. I love you very much. We'll be back soon. Now off to your lessons. Call me a little later."

"Okay, Mommy. See you later, alligator," Jasmine whispered as Marcus led her out of the room.

"After 'while, crocodile," Lissa replied as the door shut behind them. Her heart weighed her down.

Jarren's compelling voice whispered at her ear. "She'll be fine, I promise."

Lissa couldn't respond as she fought to keep her emotions from choking her. She nodded. Jarren stood behind her as she turned to look up at him. She hoped he saw the pain in her eyes. She hoped he understood what she'd just done.

He pulled her close and enfolded her in his arms. "I know. I promise I'll get you back to her as soon as possible." His chin settled on the crown of her head.

Shrugging, she rested her face against his chest. "Where are we going now?"

"We will transport to Marcus's jumper, then fly back up to the duke's envoy."

"Wouldn't it be easier to go up in the pod?"

"It seemed safe enough before, but now we need to avoid people seeing us. The pod worked fine when no one knew we were coming to Deneb. Now, I need to hide our movements. Actually, the duke has agreed to send off three jumpers to his envoy and two jumpers to his Alliance ambassador's ship when we are ready to depart. That will help cover our trails. We should go now. Ready?"

Lissa nodded and closed her eyes. Jarren's warm hand covered her face. It was just her and Jarren now.

*   *   *   *   *

JARREN SAT AT a blue-wood Terlian table staring at a wall. His VIP rooms on the envoy ship should have impressed even the high prince in its gaudy grandeur, but Jarren's mind was otherwise occupied. Exaltation and devastation fought for dominance in his mind as he found himself finally surrounded by the quiet.

True life-mates? How could that be? No one of Lyntan descent ever found their true life-mate off their home planet, much less out of their solar system. But that wasn't really the issue that pressed his heart. Lissa's words repeated in his head. *The moment we can return without her life being threatened, you'll retrieve her, and then we can go home.*

Hope had briefly emboldened Jarren. Jamis had let him know Lissa decided to stay. Now hope turned into a puff of noxious smoke, clogging his thoughts with regret. If only he'd had time to foster the care he thought he saw in her eyes; if only he'd had a chance to show her how he felt before Jesalyn's attack. Their relationship had become one massive missed opportunity.

Now Jarren knew Lissa was his true life-mate. Yes. Exhilaration and devastation. He could never bond with another. He would never love another. Her scent would haunt him for the rest of his days, constantly calling him, overwhelming his senses when he least expected it. It was some small consolation that he would know why he slowly retreated into insanity. There were those lost to mate-craze who never knew the reason.

Was it the influence of the gods or pure luck that revealed the truth of his and Lissa's connection? He had Milovar to thank in some way for finding her. Milovar chased him to Terra. He'd been forced into taking that first step. But Terra—Earth—was no small barren planet. Some greater force had directed him to Lissa on a world of some eight billion people.

Their meeting *had* been the intention of the gods. He was sure now he hadn't lost the scepter because he was unworthy to rule. And the gods had given him his true life-mate, who forever reminded him of her eagerness to leave his side. It hurt him to know he had to let her go even if the gods had manipulated their meeting. That painful certainty sat like an unmoving boulder in his mind.

Jarren breathed in, grasping some small liberation from knowing the gods hadn't condemned his leadership. Except his guilt at being judged unworthy of rulership, his insecurities, had allowed him to remain oblivious to the truth. Unintended bonding often happened with true life-mates. He should have guessed and made sure not to form additional connections like the Sharing ceremony.

Jesalyn's actions compelled Jarren to see the truth. Lissa's terror in the mines forced her to reach out to him. Their connection shook him some five hundred miles away. Her fear squeezed the air out of her lungs, and he would never forget the nerve-jarring shock of Lissa's emotions invading his body. That trauma would stay with him till death.

He thought back to his mother's folktale, rummaging through the memory in his mind. There must be a way out of their predicament, a way to break their bond. Lissa didn't want him. She wanted to go home, and he'd promised to return her when she was safe. But there had to be a way to avoid his descent into madness.

Not the least important, denying one's true life-mate was as much a curse for Lynta as Jarren. He owed his people every effort to prevent the craze, if possible. Balance flowed from the monarchy. The line of Graf had ruled for millennia. Thoughtful rulership had maintained intergalactic stability. Should he reclaim his throne, he would not be able to serve his purpose if he succumbed to the craze. Of course, if he managed to end the olfactory caste system before any knew of his descent, it might be okay. Or not.

The answer to mate-craze could be buried somewhere in the folk story. For the greater good, he had to find a way free, and the tale was the only clue to true life-mating's origin. The tale's end unfolded as he remembered the rhythm of his mother's voice.

"Then the goddess was away. She spread herself wide, blanketing Lynta with a cool breeze, following the fields of greatest prosperity to the long-lost home of the woman's true love. His body lay bruised, one leg bent and broken. Whatever had happened, his injuries had prevented his reunion.

"With a mother's embrace, she mended his broken tissues and bones then picked up the black-haired man out of his huntsman's bed in a small cottage at the edge of a forest. She blew gentle kisses at his face to keep him from waking. Through day and night she traveled back to the young woman, and as the sun set, she placed the man's slumbering frame at the pinnacle of the hill to awaken to his love.

"He awoke whole once more with his mate before him. The beautiful woman, who had waited as requested, was gifted with the joy of their reunion. Together, they two knelt and gave thanks to the goddess. Yet their reunion was overshadowed by the loss of their child.

"Again, the goddess came to them. So bereaved was she that she could not ease their pain, that she cast a binding spell upon them, which she leashed to the planet itself. Through their union, the world would prosper. And so it would be with every ruling couple—the empire would grow. Strong olfactory matches were essential to the health of the empire's expanse. As the sky darkened, the stars sparkled like teardrops on a black velvet cloak. She surrounded them, her great gusts pressing them together. And as they clung to each other, she melded their scents forever. They would never be lost to each other again. This bonding was the most sacred.

"Her hollow voice rang out as she swept around them, interweaving their fragrances. 'Children of this fruitful land, your loss is great. So great is it that I am moved to prevent it happening ever again. From this day on shall your scents ever mingle as one. What one feels, so must the other, so that you shall ever be connected and always find each other. And your children, born only of your true love and their true loves, shall forever be bound in their unique essence. And their mates, too, shall be bound with the mingling of their essences.

"'Your children and theirs shall never be lost again for you must always stay together. You and they are blessed.' With that, the embracing air ceased, and the mates' eyes followed the glint of a fast-falling metal object. At their feet, the royal Lyntan scepter landed heavily, its long, golden roundness carved with the images of the first true mates of Lynta in a lovers' embrace. Scent controlled the fate of the people, and the scepter held sway over Lyntan scent. Only the royal line could control the scepter."

Eight-year-old Jarren had interrupted as his hands swirled through the pool water. "But they were still sad, right, Mama?"

His mother smiled at him. "Yes, Jarren. They were sad. For although the children born after their reunion bore the unique scent of the two true lovers mated, they were never able to find their firstborn child. Her scent was unlike theirs. She would be forever lost to them."

"And that is the mystery of the lost child. And what of the Lyntans who've mated true since then?"

Celina looked up through the glass dome of the atrium into the twilight peeking through the foliage above. "Those lucky few who mate truly are seized by an obsession to possess their mate at all costs. The male is bound by the other's smell, can follow it undeterred, will never accept another once they bind themselves to their counterparts. Just as the goddess bound him up originally and brought him back to her. There have been instances when a ruler, when denied their true life-mates, fell into mate-craze. Once bound, resisting your mate is a heartbreaking process."

Jarren had looked up at his mother as she swept a raven lock of hair from his face with a finger. "Love makes people silly, Mama," he said finally.

"Not love. But biology, yes," his mother replied as she got up and pulled him to stand with her.

Eight-year-old Jarren had laughed happily at the time. Adult Jarren did not laugh now, as the truth settled in. Only one in a million had a true life-mate. That scent was so rare that a royal couple mated in such a way could change the trajectory of the Alliance. The tale, though, had not provided answers to his blessing—his curse. He searched for a way out where one did not exist. Jarren was true life-mated to a woman who would have nothing to do with him. Even worse: he loved her. He would not position her where she'd lose control of her life again—a prisoner held captive on an alien world to ensure the king's sanity.

After the caste system was abolished, the royal Graf line must step down to protect his people. This would save Lissa from a future he knew she would hate. She would accept her role without one misstep. Perfection and order meant so much to her. But she would hate her life and eventually him. He ground his teeth. No. He wouldn't tell Lissa or anyone else they were true life-mated. She would go home without guilt clouding her conscience. Jarren alone would pay.

Unit's voice brought him out of his reverie. "Lady Lissa requests entry to your quarters, Captain." He sighed as a last idea invaded his mind. As long as he never mated with Lissa, he had some years to beget a Lyntan heir before their separation drove him insane. With the Lyntan line secure, he could return to Earth and spend the rest of his limited time watching over her. He closed his thoughts to empty years of missing his child's laughter, of his child becoming a leader with his father absent. Jarren unclenched his fists.

Turning to the door, Jarren spoke. "Enter."

The door slid open, and Jarren studied Lissa guardedly as she came in. She didn't hesitate as she walked over to him, her scent more obvious to him now than in the past few days. She must have lowered her Subduer some. She reached out, and he caught her hand in his, bringing her soft fingers to his lips as he caressed a kiss across her knuckles. By the gods, how he loved her! He hardened. Her musky scent flowed around them, calling to him. His instincts fought for control.

She found him attractive—her anger seemed to have come and gone—but she wouldn't stay with him. He pushed down his desire. The stakes were too high now to take what he wanted. Under no circumstances could he make love to Lissa. Once they'd made love, only their offspring would be able to claim the scepter. The Graf line of leadership would truly end with him. That is the way it was on a world ruled by scent when true life-mates controlled the scepter.

He gestured to a seat. Lissa sat, her eyes glazed with arousal. If he'd seen that look on her face before he knew of their mate status, he'd have dragged her off to his quarters and made love to her for hours. He forced himself to look away from the subtle invitation in her eyes. "We will have company in a few minutes," he told her as he fought to resist her essence seeping into his pores.

"Who?"

"Princess Veena is arriving with Second-in Command Austent. We can expect them any moment." Lissa frowned at the mention of Veena's name. He'd forgotten her concern about his betrothal. He should have been happy that she expressed some jealousy, but he wasn't. He loved Lissa, would keep her with him forever if it were up to him, but he had to put space between them now. Having her would come with dire consequences.

"Does she know who I am? What should I expect from her?" Lissa asked as she leaned away from him slightly.

"She knows we are bonded. Be reassured, Lissa. She harbors no hatred for you."

"Doesn't it even occur to you that Jesalyn may have been acting on Veena's commands?"

Jarren laughed. "No. That would truly surprise me. Try to reserve judgment. Veena has never really seen me as a mate. We have always been cousins. You and she complement each other, so I fully expect that before the day is out, you will find many things to admire about her."

Lissa nodded, her silky tresses flowing like black waves over her shoulders. He resisted the urge to bring the locks to his nose and breathe in. He resisted the urge to pick her up and carry her into his bedroom. He could almost taste the scent of sex in the air as he thought of guiding her legs apart and plunging deep. He raised his gaze from where it had paused in her lap. She looked back at him, her gaze once more hot with arousal.

Jarren leaned toward her and reached out to cup her face. Just a taste of the forbidden. Only a taste. Unit's voice rang in his head. "Her Highness Princess Veena and escort Austent request entry to your quarters, Jarren." His gaze flickered toward Lissa. She pulled away. Obviously Unit had informed her of Veena's arrival as well.

Jarren sighed and sat back. It was for the best. He squeezed Lissa's hand in reassurance and called out, "Enter."

CHAPTER 23

LISSA SOUGHT A thought beyond the need that burned within her. The warm rumble of Jarren's voice slammed her thoughts home. Princess Veena would be walking through the doorway any moment, and anxiety dropped into the pit of Lissa's stomach. Jarren might be sure Veena hadn't ordered Lissa's death, but Lissa had no such trust yet. The door slid open, and in walked a small woman flanked by a tower of a man. His presence was palpable. He had to be taller than Jarren by at least a foot. His coal skin, encased in a marine-blue uniform similar to the one Marcus and Jarren wore, glowed with health. His bald head reflected the light from ceiling compartments.

Lissa took one look at him and hoped to God Veena meant her no harm. If this was Veena's bodyguard, Austent, no doubt he would do anything to protect the princess. Including get rid of any threat. Jarren stood to greet them both and enveloped Veena in a warm hug. The woman's knee-length bone-straight blond hair flicked about her.

Hair color aside, Lissa couldn't help noticing the similarities between Jarren and his would-be bonded. Veena's long, flowing multicolored dress was offset by a natural golden tan that seemed indicative of Lynta's royal line. Both their jaws had a familiar stubborn cut, and their hazel eyes flickered in welcome.

As Veena smiled at Jarren and turned away, the rainbow pattern of her ensemble swished about her whimsically. She could have been a sexy blond Mary Poppins having tea in a chalk drawing. She had the natural grace Lissa had noticed in Jarren when they first met, and she walked over to Lissa, one outstretched, blue-gloved hand accompanying a beautiful smile. Veena was the epitome of decorum.

Lissa couldn't subdue a scowl, and Veena's expectant smile faltered along with her pace. "What exactly did you tell her, cousin, to make her hate me at first sight? I was most relieved to know you had found a worthy mate," she said with a slight frown.

Lissa was taken aback. She hadn't intended to be so transparent.

Rising, she approached Veena, her hand outstretched in conciliation. "Your Highness, I apologize if I came off wrong. That certainly wasn't my intent."

Veena stared intensely at her a moment then approached once more. Without glancing at Jarren, she commented, "She's a natural diplomat. She will make a great queen one day, Jarren. Far better than I as your consort." Veena took Lissa's outstretched hand and shook it, smiling again.

"Don't be brash, Veena," Jarren stated as he stopped to stand at Lissa's side, his hand resting on her back. Lissa appreciated the support. The princess was abrasive, and she acted with the inherent expectation that others would do what she commanded.

Veena's mouth formed a mock O, and she stepped back dramatically, her hand coming to rest on Austent's broad chest. Austent shook his head and grabbed Veena's hand. "Veena, you know very well that Jesalyn came from your house. I'm surprised Jarren would even allow us in the same room with his bonded after the lady's near-death. Cut the theatrics and reassure Lady Lissa of your good intentions. Jarren's time is running out." Austent chastised Veena with a familiarity that drew a real smile from Lissa.

Veena snatched her hand away from his grip and pivoted to look at Lissa as she spoke. "Well, I really. The nerve of him saying I am the intimidating one. Him with his seven-foot-two, thick stature." Austent cleared his throat, and Veena sighed, her expression suddenly somber.

"Alright," she said, her voice lower, her tone more relaxed. "I apologize, Lady Lissa. I was—am—terribly nervous about meeting you. As if someone from your house had tried to kill me! By the gods, what a horrible first impression. I never suspected Jesalyn would attack you, despite her interest in Jarren. I swear I will take personal responsibility for your safety from here on out. I hope you can accept my apologies." She bowed her head, her words humming with embarrassed sincerity.

Jarren interrupted as Lissa started to speak. "*I* am responsible for her safety, Veena, which is why I also am owed an apology. Lissa had my assurance that Jesalyn could be trusted. You should have told me Jesalyn desired my mating."

"You have my deepest apologies too, cousin. I misjudged her level of obsession as no obsession at all. She once joked that we should share you, she and I. I did not see the seriousness behind her words."

Austent moved to the table and held out a chair for Veena. As Lissa reclaimed her own seat, her mind a maze of confused thoughts, she barely registered Jarren's second response. "Actually, Veena, my averages for protecting Lissa have been abhorrent thus far. You may fear not that you've marked an untarnished record."

Veena sat forward, an interested gleam in her eye. "Oh, really? Explain."

Lissa glanced over at Jarren as she fought to cool the blush on her face. He shook his head. "Another time. Austent is right. We have to figure out how to refashion our plan to work without Jesalyn's assistance. I'm at least relieved the likely reason for Jesalyn's attack was her unhinged jealousy."

"She was loyal to a fault, but I always knew something was not quite right with her. Your palace spies should know soon whether Milovar received word of the attack. Regardless—" Veena cut herself off.

She exchanged glances with Austent and Jarren sat up. "What?"

Veena spoke first. "We received intelligence that Milovar has moved up the day of his coronation to two days from now. Immediately following the coronation, the royal house is expected to move to the southern ice region and take up permanent residence in the winter palace."

Austent cut in. "Even at top speed, the duke's envoy ship will still take an entire day to get to Lynta."

Jarren's brow crinkled in thought. "Who could take Jesalyn's place between here and Lynta?"

"Jarren, one of the reasons I sent Jesalyn to you was because there wasn't going to be time to pick her up on the way. There is no one," Veena said.

They were talking in code, and Lissa grew irritated. "Just what are you all talking about?"

Veena glanced at Lissa in obvious confusion, then at Jarren. "You haven't told her the plan? Do you have a block for a head? No wonder you've been unable to protect her. You are keeping her in the dark about matters that affect her," Veena snapped. In that instant, Lissa recognized an ally. Whatever reason Jesalyn had to harm Lissa, Veena did not share her cause.

Jarren gave an uncomfortable laugh and held out his hands peaceably. "I am sorry, Lissa. Veena is correct. You not only have every right to know what we intend to do, you *need* to know. I won't go into the political specifics of my situation, but Milovar will not be granted full authority over Lynta and high authority over the surrounding Lyntan colonized planets until his coronation. It is Lyntan law that kingship is determined by the person who is capable of possessing the royal scepter and is legally coroneted by all the members of the Council of Rule."

Lissa frowned. "What do you mean 'capable of possessing the royal scepter'?"

"On Lynta, scent rules all things. Descendants of the royal line of Lynta have a particular scent that allows us to wield the scepter. If you do not possess that scent, the scepter becomes unmovable. It's simply too heavy to lift."

"And Milovar's scent is close enough to your own that he could seize the scepter?"

Veena nodded. "Jesalyn's scent was close enough to ours to allow her access to the royal palace, and which would also allow her to take the scepter and return it to Jarren."

"But obviously your scents are close, too. Can't you get the scepter?"

Veena shook her blond mass of hair. "Milovar won't let me anywhere near the royal palace. We were using Jesalyn because her scent was a close-enough match to those Of the Family to allow her access, but not so close a match that she would attract undue attention."

Lissa frowned. "Of the Family? I don't understand."

Veena nodded. "Lyntan society exists in a strict caste system. If you are 'Of the Family,' you are of the royal line. One may also be situated 'Beside the Family,' 'Below the Family,' or unviable."

Lissa sat back, struck. On Earth, historical and contemporary caste systems meant built-in subjugation.

Jarren leaned forward. "What about Neera on Celiun Seven? Can we get to her in time?"

Austent nodded thoughtfully. "You've a map?" he asked. Jarren reached under the table for his map and map writer. The four stood as Jarren spread the map out among them on the table.

Lissa struggled to focus. She had assumed Lyntan advanced technology boded a forward-aiming social scheme. Suddenly she understood the real importance of Jarren claiming the throne. He would not tolerate this caste system anymore. Somehow, he intended to end it.

"We're at Atarax now," Jarren stated as he pointed to their location on the map. "There's Celiun," he added, pointing to the map again.

Austent leaned down and studied the route. "It's out of circuit, Jarren."

"But the Alliance won't stop an envoy, and no handler would dare send hunters to board a diplomatic ship."

Lissa listened, trying to absorb the information thrown her way. This plan was essential. The conversation's volume increased in obvious desperation, and in her mind, the glimmer of an idea flickered.

Lissa looked at Veena as she too shook her head. "We don't even know that Neera would do it," Veena said. "She has been adamant about remaining neutral in the political intrigues."

"But that is why she would make a perfect candidate. No one would recognize her. She would assist if both you and I personally requested her help. And we could still make it to Lynta before the gates close tomorrow night."

Austent sighed. "We would be cutting it close, Jarren."

Lissa plowed through the thoughts in her head, concentrating on the elusive idea. Then that spark of thought lit a match and flared to life. Lissa spoke up. "Did you want a woman to infiltrate the royal palace?"

Jarren still studied the map as he responded. Austent and Veena watched her with dawning comprehension. "Yes, it is safer for a woman to go in. Rulership on Lynta is predominantly patrilineal. A man with a strong enough scent would be restricted from access to the scepter. A woman with the same essence would still have less claim to the scepter than

Milovar would, given the patrilineal tradition. He wouldn't restrict a woman. Generally, he pays no mind to females or those nonbinary," Jarren said.

Lissa cleared her throat. "Then I should be able to take Jesalyn's place. It was your scent on me, Jarren, that put my life in danger numerous times. It's nice to know that having something akin to your scent may finally be a help, not a hindrance."

With surprising speed, Jarren grabbed her arm. His fingers squeezed until it hurt. "Absolutely not! Never mention that idea again," he hissed, his eyes glittering. Startled, Lissa pushed her chair back. Her heart jumped inside her chest.

Veena's calm voice broke the tension. "Now wait a minute, Jarren. It's a good idea. We should have thought of this earlier. Even I could identify the compatibility of her scent to our line the moment we entered your quarters. And the bounty hunters aren't looking for your scent on a woman on Lynta. Last reports had them scouring Genesie near where your ship was attacked. Besides, who would consider you'd found a life-mate so quick? No one will expect your scent on any woman but me."

Jarren's eyes squinted, and his mouth ground out a ferocious growl as he redirected his anger. "She will not go. Don't speak of it again."

Veena put her hands up. "But—" She stopped as Jarren bounded around the table and advanced on her, his body poised to strike.

Deftly, Austent inserted himself between them, demeanor, placating. "Calm yourself, Prince. Calm yourself," he murmured.

Shaking his head, Jarren backed up and returned to the table. Lissa, her heart beating in her ears, observed the befuddled looks Veena and Austent exchanged. It was as if they'd never seen this side of Jarren before. But Lissa remembered that look. She'd seen it on his face when he'd attacked the first bounty hunter in the alley behind her office. The violence of his actions was something she had no wish to see again. She stood shaking from fear, wondering why he refused to let her help and why her suggestion had provoked so violent a response.

Jarren paused, then cleared his throat. His eyes focused on the map again. Only the clenching and unclenching of his jaw revealed his subdued anger. "Lissa is here under my protection. She is privy to the mission, but she *will not* take part in retrieving the scepter. Austent, let's plot out the fastest route to Celiun. Then Veena and I can prepare a blanket communication for Neera."

"Jarren," Veena tried, quietly this time. "May we speak about this in private?"

He didn't raise his head. "No."

Austent put a restraining hand on Veena's arm and shook his head. "We'll plot the course."

In a huff, Veena walked away from the table. She gestured to Lissa as she stopped at the door. "Since our ideas so obviously have no effect on your decisions, Jarren, I think I'll take Lissa for a walk around the ship. Has Jarren even bothered to show you around the envoy? It may be a slow vessel, but it is magnificent."

Jarren glanced up as Lissa neared Veena at the door, embarrassment and regret in his eyes. "Veena, I value your opinion highly. But just—"

"Obviously, cousin," Veena spat out, locking arms with Lissa. "Just not now. I'm sure you and Austent will figure out how to make time slow down so the mission is successful. Lissa, I am happy for your company." The door slid open before them.

"Of course," Lissa replied, feeling unusually demure. Veena whisked her out of the room and began a steady progression down the hall as the hatch slid shut behind them.

Stopping, Veena held Lissa's arm. "One moment," she said before speaking into the air. "Unit, this conversation has anonymity."

"Acknowledged, Princess Veena."

Turning back to Lissa, she continued down the hall. "Now this conversation will not be recorded, and Unit will obscure our words as we walk so we won't be overheard. It is a perk of being a royal diplomat. What happened with Jarren in there?"

Lissa could only mirror Veena's confused expression. "I don't know. I've only seen him react that violently once when a bounty hunter attacked me."

"I knew there was a story behind that earlier statement. You think he feels guilty about putting you in harm's way? It seems a rather extreme response to guilt. What is going on with you and him? Have you slept together?"

Lissa coughed in surprise, her hand going to her throat as she turned red with embarrassment. "I can only surmise he feels guilty about endangering my life again. We bonded unintentionally, and he hasn't forgiven himself for the danger that put me in."

Veena responded with the obvious question. "But you have forgiven him?"

A very personal question. "I forgave him some time ago, but he doesn't know that."

Veena regarded Lissa a moment. "You've bonded, but you haven't completed the Sharing Ritual? You haven't slept with him?"

"I don't know what you mean. We did complete the Sharing Ritual. I didn't know sex was a necessary component."

Veena snorted in an unladylike manner. "A man must have given you direction, Lissa." Lissa blushed again. She had only spoken with Jarren and Marcus about the ritual. "The ritual is a powerful tool for the woman because it puts the power of reproduction in the woman's hands when she may most need it. I'm sure it is the same way on your world, Lissa. A woman has only so many days in her cycle to get pregnant."

Lissa nodded. "True, but I can't say human men need to be provoked into having sex on those certain days. I've a beautiful daughter to prove it." Lissa let out a laugh then sobered, missing the sound of Jasmine's happy squeals.

"Lyntan men have the ability to withhold their offspring should they choose, and sometimes, even when they don't. The Nectar is manufactured to work only between bonded couples in order to protect men from being forced into impregnating women not their mates, and to ensure that bonded men don't inadvertently miss a woman's time to conceive. Lyntan women have a two-day window for conception. Maybe it is longer for you?"

Lissa nodded, again awed. Veena grunted as she continued. "Men never want to acknowledge that they cannot control their bodies. Often they speak of the ritual as if it were simply about trust. But *we* know differently."

They stopped in front of a sealed door. With a maternal gesture, Veena put her hand on Lissa's shoulder. "I think Jarren is self-sacrificing. He takes you from your planet and keeps you isolated from his world, his culture. He is guilty about his treatment of you. He feels guilt for having put the life of his bonded in danger. He isn't seeing the situation clearly, Lissa. We have to help him see clearly so that he makes the right decision."

Lissa shrugged her shoulders. "Alright. How?"

"The Sharing Ritual. There is nothing more clarifying than that moment when a man realizes they must give control to their bonded; it is more than trust. It is about understanding one should not always control the situation. You are his bonded. You care for him. Make him see clearly that your help is necessary."

Lissa sighed. No one seemed to be in control at the moment. "Why would he let me give him the Nectar? There's no reason for us to participate in the Sharing Ritual again."

Veena's expression sent shivers down Lissa's spine. "We won't tell him."

Shaking her head, Lissa stepped away. "I won't do that, Veena. I hated him before for doing to me just what you suggest doing to him. He took my power, and I despised him for it. I won't take away his power to decide for himself. Besides, I can't take the risk of getting pregnant again." Who knew if her birth control would work with Lyntan physiology?

"You needn't worry about conceiving. For you to conceive, even with the Sharing, you must tell him to impregnate you.

That is the way of it with life-mates. Our time has run out, Lissa. If Milovar is coroneted, he will be king until his death, and Jarren's honor will keep him from killing his cousin regardless of the consequences of Milovar staying in power. We won't reach Celiun in time. I'm sure when Jarren took you from your world, he only did it to save his own."

"No. He did it to save me," Lissa replied as she fought against the emotions threatening to flood her.

"Well, if Milovar's coronation can't be stopped then neither can the bounty hunters after Jarren. He took your life into his hands, now his life is in yours. Now, one last confession. You need to know Jarren's ascension has been planned since his birth. Our empire suffers from a caste system based on scent. We, the elite, enjoy every privilege but one. We may never marry or bond beneath our caste. My Austent is Below the Family. He is my life; we may never marry and never conceive children together. Jarren's mother is an anomaly. She is Of the Family by her scent, but her parents are unviable. She was taken from them and eventually bonded with our king. She taught Jarren to value each sentient regardless of their 'distance' from the Family. Jarren is the hope of not just those of us controlled by our caste system. Many sentients in the Alliance are also harmed by the system. They would see the system end."

Lissa leaned weakly against the wall. The idea of betraying Jarren's trust ate away at her insides. But she knew what she had to do. She could not deny people the right of self-determination and the right to love whom they wanted. She couldn't let Jarren run for the rest of his life. Not if she could help him. She loved him. Sapped of strength, Lissa moved away from Veena and toward her quarters.

"Lissa," the princess pleaded.

Lissa put up a hand to halt Veena's entreaty. "I'll do it tonight, Veena. If you get the drink into him, I'll make him accept my help. I'll make sure he understands why this is important to me." Veena sighed a restrained thank you, but inside, Lissa's heart hurt. The violence of his response to her suggestion replayed itself in her head. He would never forgive her for this betrayal.

CHAPTER 24

LISSA ARRIVED AT Jarren's quarters and spied Veena and Austent approaching. Veena gave her a nod as she grasped Austent's hand, possessively. He scowled at the princess but stopped in his tracks as his eyes lit on Lissa. His mouth dropped open. Lissa's gaze shifted back to Veena as they approached.

"You leave nothing up to chance, do you?" Veena's whimsical voice floated over to Lissa as she straightened her dress. She really hadn't left anything up to chance. Lyntans may not hold wardrobe choices in high esteem, but she spent two hours preparing for dinner anyway.

To seduce Jarren, she had to look the part. A skintight scarlet dress with spaghetti straps clung to Lissa's bust, then clutched at her small waist and hugged the curve of her hips before flowing below her knees. It was a good thing the material was alien. She'd have had to be poured into a dress like that if it were made from any material on Earth.

At the bottom of the large closet in her room, she'd located four-inch black stilettos. Now she waited for Veena and Austent to reach her side so they could put their plan into place.

"Are you ready, Lissa?" Veena asked.

Austent interrupted before Lissa could answer. "You must not do this, Veena. The Ritual should not be abused."

Veena tossed her hair away from her face and glared at him. Lissa could feel the tension between them. "We agreed about this, Aus. We can't get to Celiun in time to prevent Milovar's coronation. Lissa wants to help. We don't have a choice."

"Jarren has reasons for not allowing her to assist him. This is his battle. These are his people. Neither you nor Lissa has a right to question him on the decisions he makes as Lynta's ruler. He controls their fate."

A laugh bubbled out of Lissa. How ironic that she'd made the same argument to Jarren when he'd taken her from Earth. Squinting up at Austent, she spoke, surprised by the power in her voice. "You believe we have no right to intercede. To make decisions for Jarren when he decides things we know are wrong? I thought the same way not too long ago, Austent. Then a man came to my world. He put my life in danger. He removed me from all that I knew, all that made me who I was…all because *he* felt he had the right to intercede, to protect me from myself."

She couldn't disguise the caustic sound of her voice as the words faded away. Austent paused before he spoke. "But you are one person. Jarren makes decisions for an entire world, and he takes that responsibility seriously. He may well be the only person capable of ensuring peace on this side of the galaxy."

Lissa thought back. She had been so sure her anger was warranted. He'd taken her ordered existence and put her life, and the lives of those near her, in danger. She had hated him for a glimmer of time. But Jarren had seen what Lissa couldn't. Her life had to be protected. She had to live for her daughter and her family, and leaving was the only way to keep her alive. Jarren made the right decision when Lissa's anger would not allow her to see the truth. Now his guilt for taking her from her world blinded him.

"He doesn't weigh that responsibility in his head, Austent. His guilt won't let him. It's my turn to make the hard decision. If for no other reason than because I owe it to him."

Austent paused before responding. "You are his bonded. I firmly believe you are doing what you think is best for him. That's the only reason why I agreed to this ruse."

Veena sighed between them. "Good. Now that that's taken care of, shall we—"

Austent grabbed Veena's shoulder, his eyes narrowing. "Don't think I am happy about this, Veena. I know this was your plan, however necessary. For your part, I remain opposed. But I will not harbor anger for Lissa. She does what she must for the one she loves."

Lissa's heart slammed into her throat. How had Austent discovered the truth she'd tried so hard to hide? Were her feelings so obvious?

Veena leaned her body suggestively into Austent's side, her voice sultry. "I know how to gain your forgiveness, Aus.

You know I love a challenge." With a knowing look, Veena detached herself from Austent's grasp and patted Lissa's hand. "Austent is very perceptive. Do not think others see the truth as he does about your feelings. He's an honest person, and honest people perceive truths others cannot. Now." The hall stretched in silence as Veena spoke to the air. "Unit, permission to enter VIP quarters for High Prince Jarren Graf."

A moment of silence passed before Lissa heard the usual metallic sound of Unit in her ear. "You may enter."

The door slid open and Jarren stood before them, relaxed in a black long-sleeved shirt and sand-colored pants. Lissa peeked at Veena. The woman plastered her usual bright smile on her face as she swept forward. Her multicolored filmy dress ruffled around her from head to floor.

She reached out to grasp Jarren's hand in her own. "Jarren, Austent is angry with me again. Will you tell my lover I must be obeyed when I tell him to stop pouting?"

Lissa walked into Jarren's quarters, Veena's statement distracting her. She hadn't realized Veena and Austent actually slept together, though their physical relationship seemed obvious now. So, sex outside of one's caste was accepted? But commitment and children were forbidden. How heartbreaking and familiar. She didn't miss humanity's prejudices.

Lissa turned back to the large man, her brow raised in curiosity. He merely stared back, his gaze expectant. A warm hand familiarly touched the bare skin of Lissa's shoulder. Turning, she met Jarren's intense stare.

Bending his head to her ear, he whispered, "When I had the fabricator make that dress for you, I had no idea it would cause me such pain." Lissa shivered as his breath lingered on her neck. He stepped back, his attention again on Veena. "Veena, Austent always forgives you, given time."

Veena crossed to the table Jarren used for his star map. The smooth cobalt surface had already been set for four; two couples of chairs sat on either side of the large table. "Well, you shall help him forgive me by telling him he must."

Austent took the seat next to where Veena perched, his hand lingering possessively on the back of her chair. They could not marry but they seemed bonded. She'd been reminded often enough that a bonding was not marriage.

It didn't seem an appropriate question to ask when she'd known them for less than a day. Sure. And in less than one day she managed to conspire with an intergalactic princess against the man she loved. Lissa pushed down her guilt. Lowering her eyes instead, she took a seat. Her actions tonight weren't the products of Veena's intervention. In her heart, Lissa knew Jarren's future depended on her. She would have helped him regardless.

Again, Jarren's hand caressed her shoulder. He took a seat at her side, his gaze resting on her. If she intended to seduce him, she would have to overcome her sudden shyness. Lissa smiled at Jarren, appreciating his graceful power. A curious scowl flashed over his face, but he returned her smile nonetheless. Lissa fought not to become lost in the deep texture of his eyes.

Veena piped up. "I suppose your willingness to host dinner is your way of apologizing for your earlier behavior?"

Jarren continued to stare at Lissa as he replied. "I do owe you an apology. I know you both just intended to help.

I overreacted. I'm sorry I gave the impression I didn't appreciate your input." His gaze lowered to the crown of Lissa's breasts.

Heat permeated her.

Veena's voice interrupted Jarren's visual seduction. Dragging her gaze away from him, Lissa looked at the princess as Veena grunted. "So much chatter, Jarren. Enough. I forgive you, though I know your apology is really directed toward your bonded. I've never warranted your apologies in the past."

Jarren's brow rose as Lissa looked at him again. A small smile quirked at the side of his mouth. His hot gaze stayed on her.

"Dinner. Eat, Austent. Maybe food will soften your anger, my love," Veena teased.

As Lissa dragged her eyes away from Jarren, she caught sight of Veena's hand near Jarren's glass. Veena smiled innocently and glanced at her meaningfully. The Nectar was in the drink.

Veena reached for a pear-like fruit on her plate and bit into it, the juice dribbling down her chin. Offering the rest of the food to Austent, she giggled. "Drink, Jarren. Austent wishes to make a toast to nagging women."

Austent didn't smile, but Jarren relaxed back in his chair and sipped from his cup. "Veena, you are not a nag. You're a princess. It's just that Austent must protect you—even, sometimes, from yourself. Now, let us eat. We've an important day tomorrow. I want you well rested for our talk with Neera."

Austent stood, his towering frame casting a shadow over the table, and raised his glass with contrasting gentleness.

"A toast to…" He hazarded a glance at Lissa, his expression resolved. Acknowledging Veena, he shook his head. "A toast to nagging women." Jarren laughed. Lissa released a nervous breath. All was proceeding as planned.

An hour later, Lissa noticed Jarren's eyes dilating as he drank the last of the Nectar. Glancing over at Veena, Lissa played with her drink as the princess leaned toward Austent, revealing plump cleavage.

She pouted. "Aus, please don't ignore me. It hurts my feelings," she stated. She'd gotten into trouble again.

Jarren's voice drew their attention. He fought to keep his back straight. "I am sorry. I'm not well. We will have to end dinner early."

Lissa darted a look at him, now counting the time she had before he was totally enthralled. He'd steadily consumed the drink over the last fifteen minutes. It was likely she'd be rushed to coax his cooperation before he couldn't respond to her at all.

Getting up, she gestured to Veena and Austent. "I need to speak with you privately, Jarren."

Jarren rose as well, unsteady on his feet. Shaking his head, he repeated himself. "I am not well."

Veena stood, pulling Austent up with an authoritative huff. He glared down at her and then turned to Jarren, a final sympathetic look on his face. As he opened his mouth to speak, the princess interrupted. "We will go. Jarren, I'll talk to you tomorrow, okay?"

Jarren nodded, clearly confused. With a silent and grim Austent walking behind her, Veena departed.

Jarren turned to Lissa, shaking his head again. "Can—wait—Lissa? Something's wrong here."

The moment of truth had arrived. She learned the structure of their relationship well. She would use biology to achieve her goals, but a second thought dug in at the back of her mind. If love had driven his desire, she'd do more than help him reclaim his throne. She would stay with him forever. Lissa took a nervous breath then walked over to him and clasped his hand between her own. "There isn't anything wrong with you, Jarren. I gave you Nectar." She felt for her Subduer and turned it off. The change in him was immediate. He grabbed Lissa, and, pulling her into his heated embrace, claimed her mouth in a starving kiss.

The blast of desire that flowed between them almost made her forget her purpose, but Lissa resisted. They had one night of love, but as much as she desired him, loved him, her actions had a purpose. She pushed at him until her resistance registered, and he backed away. Jarren pierced a starving look at her but didn't approach.

"Why?" he groaned.

"I have to take Jesalyn's place on this mission."

He shook his head. "No."

Lissa came closer, and he reached out before her words stopped him. "Don't move. You will not touch me until you agree I will take Jesalyn's place."

Jarren shook his head again with apparent great effort, his speech stinted. "You not know what you ask, Lissa."

His breathing was heavy. His forehead glistened with sweat as he looked at her, his expression pleading. Lissa wanted to capitulate. But Jarren's world hung in the balance, and she cared too much for him to let him sacrifice his throne to protect her.

He wouldn't cave fast enough to agree to her terms before the Nectar quelled all his coherent thoughts. She had to make him uncomfortable, cause him pain, to accomplish her goal.

Bent on seduction and burning with desire, Lissa advanced, her hips swaying in the tight scarlet dress. She knew the picture of sensuality she presented as she walked toward him: dark hair flowing, skin aglow, body giving off sexual heat. Lissa reached out, her hand almost touching his lips. His hot breath landed on the sensitive tips of her fingers. With deliberate delicacy, she caressed him, her fingers tracing his sensual mouth, distracting his thoughts until he looked at her in surprise. She'd glided forward, her body now a breath away from him.

Jarren inhaled and closed his eyes. His fists clenched at his side. She could tell he struggled to maintain control. Placing a hand on his cheek, she angled his face down. "Don't fight your desires, Jarren. I want to give myself to you." Her hand reached down to fondle his hardened manhood, constricted within the material of his pants. "Let me help you in both ways: let me make love to you and help you save your world. Give me control. Trust me."

He struggled to speak again, comprehension fading, his eyes crinkling with frustration. "You know not what you ask, Lissa. Please, no."

Lissa pulled his head down and kissed him with all the pent-up desire she'd been containing since that night on Earth when her life had changed. The night when his scent had overtaken her. Her tongue caressed his with slow abandon. She slid her hand through his hair and pulled him closer. "Let me take her place, Jarren. One word, and we can relieve the ache inside both of us." Her voice escaped, part whisper, part moan.

A tear ran down the angle of his cheek. His beseeching stare gave her pause. "Please," he repeated.

For a moment, she stopped and stepped away, her breath expanding her chest painfully. She burned with desired, yet he resisted. Why did he need to protect her so fiercely? The question burst out of her mouth. "Why?"

He shook his head, refusing to answer, but she could tell his comprehension was almost gone. Lissa had to press on. The "why" didn't matter when she needed his promise now. "Promise that you will let me take Jesalyn's place. Promise, and I will give myself to you. I know you ache. I can see you want me. Promise, and I will stay with you all night." Her voice crescendoed. The comprehension in his eyes faded.

Reaching inside his pants, she wrapped her hands around his ready thickness. With precise expertise, she gave his shaft several heated jerks. Jarren tilted his head to the ceiling, then let out a capitulating groan. He was battling demons Lissa couldn't see. She wanted to comfort him; she needed his promise. Finally, eyes glistening with bestial need, he met her gaze straight on.

"Yes," he growled.

"Your word?" Lissa asked him again.

"Yes," he replied.

She barely understood him. Drawing close and leaning into him, breathing in the lingering scent of smooth chocolate, Lissa whispered into his ear. "I'm yours tonight, Jarren. Take me. Make love to me." She didn't have to say more. A rough hand pulled her into his arms as searing fingers fanned through her hair and held her hostage. His mouth came down on hers, hot and desperate, his powerful arms shifting to lift and carry her into his bedroom. Hot need caressed her from the top of her head to the tips of her toes.

He pushed the door shut and refused to release her. His hands roamed her body, heating her skin. She pressed into him, every inch of her aflame. As he carried her to his bed, his arms cradled her securely; her legs encircled his waist. Jarren laid her back against the soft sheets then straightened to unbuckle and unzip his pants. Pulling his shirt over his head, he cast the fabric away.

He was perfect, and for tonight, he was hers. Lissa's hungry gaze settled on his broad sun-kissed chest, then lowered to the ripped muscles of his abdomen. His pants now hung on tapered hips, the dark hair of his crotch peeking between the unzipped flaps.

Desire further darkened the amber of his eyes as he freed himself and straddled her. His thick shaft nudged the pulsing center between her legs. Lissa's sex throbbed. Need drove her as she reached up and captured his head between her hands to kiss him, unspoken words of love fighting for release. Stifling the confession, she quelled her worries to follow the instincts of her body. He suckled her neck then traveled achingly lower until one hand pushed aside the red material covering her breasts.

Air caressed her taut nipples as he shifted her dress out of the way. Then Lissa whimpered as his breath played a torturous game on the sensitive dark skin of her areolas. She ran her fingers through his hair and arched her body up in wanton offer. She yearned for him to take her into his mouth, and her own voice surprised her as she found herself haggardly begging.

"Please, Jarren." She wanted him, needed him to touch her so that, for that one moment, she could fool herself into believing he loved her.

Simmering eyes met hers as he pulled her hands from his head and raised her arms to imprison her wrists above her. He inched down, his eyes still watching her as he torturously licked one nipple. Possessively, he suckled her breasts, first one then the other, exchanging cool air for the warm cavern of his mouth. Her body shivered as he divided his attention, moving from one hardened nipple to the other in ecstatic abandon, the contrast of hot and cold forcing another gasp from Lissa's throat. Her reason for seducing him no longer held importance. Only love and desire remained.

Jarren lifted himself away, his hand grazing her stomach as Lissa arched closer. She missed his body's heat. Then he came close once more, and the primal ache between her legs flared as he teased the crevice of her thighs with his shaft.

"I'm yours," Lissa moaned. Her heart battled despair. She could only love him for one night. It had to last. She trembled with passion. In an instant, his roaming lips traveled the length of her neck and face, suckling until he tantalized her mouth with his tongue. His hands wrenched her dress up over her legs. He planted himself over her, staring down.

Eyes flickering with one final glimmer of comprehension, he clasped his wrist and turned off his Subduer. Chocolate musk filled the air. Lissa breathed in his essence before her own scent dominated. The aphrodisiac of his scent shot liquid arousal through her veins as he took her legs in his hands. Caressing the skin of her thighs, he reached under her. Lifting her up, he plunged into her with a groan of agonized pleasure.

The heat of him inside her eradicated every thought. The need to move against him overpowered all reason. Passion pounded through her body as he pulled out only to enter her again. Instinctively, she began to arch, her body easily finding his rhythm. Her breasts crushed against his chest as she pulled him close. Her pleasure built as they moved as one, a constant battle of retreating and advancing as his labored breathing filled the air.

"Oh, the gods," he cried as his rhythm began to increase. Her thighs tightened around him as she matched the thrust of his shaft. She wouldn't tell him she loved him, but she could show him. Her ache grew as fireworks of ecstasy erupted inside her. He claimed her lips, swallowing her groans of pleasure, his tongue darting in and out of her mouth. Her eyes closed as the growing tension of her desire tightened then broke. Blissful waves of pleasure swept over her as she cried out in release. She had reached the stars. Together they rocked, their bodies intertwined as they floated back to reality, sated.

*　*　*　*　*

LISSA WOKE TO the sound of running water. The place where Jarren had lain next to her was still warm. She would ignore that ache of loneliness as she sat alone in his bed. Glancing over at the open bathroom door, she spied Jarren's naked form stepping into the shower.

Climbing out of the bed, still wearing her dress, Lissa crossed the room. She blinked to adjust to the light. She took in the bathroom's brightness, a sharp contrast to the near darkness of the room behind her. The opaque shadow of Jarren's lithe body moved behind the smoky curving glass that ran from the top of the tub to the ceiling.

Jarren's silhouette bent over. One flexed arm rose to wipe at his face. But as her body began to hum, rekindling her desire, Lissa turned away. Guilt skewered her conscience. She'd accomplished what she set out to and had been gifted with one night with the man she loved. In return, she'd stolen his will. Lissa had done the right thing, but she had no right to ask any more of him.

"Lissa." The seductive deepness of his voice halted her steps.

Pivoting, she waited as the enclosure slid open and Jarren faced her. His golden skin glistened, water pelting off his muscles from the showerhead above. Her gaze followed the droplets' paths as they flickered down the angled lines of his body and into the thatch of dark hair surrounding his blatant erection. It seemed he was still enthralled.

His long shaft stood out gloriously between his legs, and Lissa's sex pulsed. She thought she'd been sated by their earlier lovemaking. Instead, that encounter only served to whet her raging sexual appetite. She wanted to back away, but she couldn't. Desire kept her feet planted where she stood.

"Lissa." He whispered her name this time, just loud enough to hear over the sound of falling water. He reached out. Without thinking, she walked forward as an arm invited her into the steamy enclosure. Taking his hand, she stepped close to the side. His other hand snaked out to push at the straps of her rumpled red dress, then a boyish grin appeared on his face as the red material pooled to the floor.

Wrapping his arms around her, he lifted her into the large tub. The enclosure sealed around them. Realization hit as his eyes gleamed with awareness. "You aren't controlled by the Nectar, are you?" Her voice wobbled.

"No."

Her inclination to run kicked in. Was he angry about what she'd done? "I had to do it, Jarren. This mission is more important than I am. I understand that now."

"You did what you had to. It is no less than I've done to you. I harbor no anger in spite of the price I paid." Lubricating his hands with soap, he massaged her body. His touch sent sparks of pleasure tingling over her skin. With deliberate sensuality, he soaped her arms, shoulders, and neck before sliding his fingers over the sensitized mounds of her breasts. Lissa let out a gasp.

"I harbor no anger, Lissa," he repeated as his hands slid across the flatness of her belly then skimmed lower to caress the mound at the crest of her thighs. His gaze pierced her as he manipulated his fingers within her warmth.

Lissa tried to back away, but his arm shot out and captured her waist. Pulling her unwillingly closer to the heat of his hand, he continued to caress her. Little waves of pleasure washed over Lissa as she finally capitulated. She leaned her head on his chest and warm droplets sprinkled her as water bounced off the honed muscles of his body. Ecstasy spread out from her center to the tips of her fingers.

She was so close to bliss. The tension in her stomach grew, and her nails dug into the skin covering his biceps as she let out a moan. She could feel the pressure of her climax just as Jarren removed his hand and turned her away, slanting her toward the shower wall. Water rained down on her as his hot shaft touched the cleft of her bottom. Grasping her shoulders, he pushed into her heated center with calculated intent. Lissa closed her eyes. He fit perfectly inside her. Filling her, he stilled and held her close.

*　*　*　*　*

JARREN FOUGHT FOR control as Lissa's warmth convulsed around him. He reveled in his ability to illicit such raw pleasure from her. It was enough to make him want to lose control. Mastering his desire, he began to move again. Placing passionate kisses on her neck, he guided Lissa's hands to brace the wall. He fought against the waves of pleasure as his hips collided with the softness of her bottom, and she let out a moan. Her body arched in wanton invitation as he drove in and out.

Flames of passion engulfed him as he cherished every touch of her petal-soft skin against his pistoning hips. Jarren starved for more. For the time left before reality invaded, he wanted all of Lissa, even that elusive part that longed for home. He wanted her heart.

He dominated their rhythm as passion colored his voice. "You forced my hand to achieve your purpose. For these remaining few hours at least, give me that part of you that you protect most. Ease my soul, Lissa." Jarren bit out the curt demand.

He didn't wait for an answer. His hand went around her waist and down to fondle her in concert with the fluid stroke of his hips. Jarren heard her let out a gasp. "Oh, Jarren. ¡Te quiero!"

He didn't understand her words. She must have switched languages mid-sentence and confused his translator. Her body tightened around him, and he lost the train of his thoughts. Unhindered, he drove into her. Heat hit him as she flushed with pleasure, convulsed then stiffened in release. It was a fight not to climax as her body throbbed in waves of liquid passion around his heated shaft, but Jarren waited. He wanted her to remember his love for years, and needed a memory that would last him a lifetime.

With gentle persuasion, his fingers manipulated her until she gyrated against him. Her hand clutched at his thigh, her body tightening around his straining member as he renewed the plunder of her body. "We are connected now, Lissa. Bound, whether you wish it or not," he ground out as all thought was overcome by instinct.

Entering and retreating in rapid succession, he abandoned all control as she clenched around him. With a shout, he rocked into her and loosed his seed into her heat. He had never experienced such extreme pleasure before. Papaya and musk pervaded his nose, and satisfaction blinded him. Sated, the sound of his own heaving breaths and the patter of water on slick skin filled his ears as time returned to normal.

Still holding her, he looked down at the glistening strands of her hair. She was exquisite. He wanted to worship her. Even as he withdrew, he turned her to face him, the warm water cleansing their bodies of the sweat of their exertions. She leaned against the wall as Jarren knelt between her legs and licked the honey at her core. Moaning, she tried to move away, but he grasped her bottom in both hands and inched her back toward him. His tongue lapped at her sweetness as he was gifted with her sighs of pleasure. Then her hands were in his hair holding his head as she moved with him, her rhythm persistent until she went taut and let out a cry of triumph.

By the gods, he loved her. Jarren rested his head against the flat of her stomach before rising and holding her pliant body. He looked down at her tired expression. Her eyes were half shut from exhaustion.

"Unit, end shower," Jarren called out as he picked her up and stepped out of the tub. Grabbing a towel from a counter, he carried her back into the bedroom and laid her on the bed. She fell asleep as he dried her. Jarren drew the sheets over them, then pulled Lissa into his arms.

In one night, Jarren had lost the ability to pass on the legacy of his reign. No child of his would ever rule Lynta. He wanted to hate her but couldn't. He would never love anyone as much as he loved her. His essence and Lissa's were forever intertwined; the Graf line would end with him. But he had gained the memory of the one night he would spend with the only woman he would ever love. The perfection of that night would have to last him a lifetime. The fates had spoken. Jarren closed his eyes and fell into a fitful sleep.

CHAPTER 25

A SOFT HUMMING in her ear woke Lissa from her deep slumber. Opening her eyes, she found the place beside her empty. Jarren had been gone a while, but she'd expected that. She only hoped he still forgave her.

She padded into the bathroom to relieve herself and get her clothes. Lissa picked up her discarded dress and pulled it on quickly, her eyes straying to the smoky-glass shower enclosure. A plethora of heated memories danced in her head. The memory of Jarren's touch warmed her body, but she knew the likelihood of ever being with him again was remote. She loved Jarren; he didn't love her. He desired her. He was bonded to her. But he didn't love her. She needed to go home. Lyntans didn't have to love their mates. Biology. Nothing but biology. Lissa sighed.

Just like Derek had loved the sex but not Lissa. Not enough. Not enough to get the therapy he needed to stop his violence. Not even because she was pregnant. She'd loved Derek. He'd loved the sex. Biology again. Lissa swatted at the wrinkles in the dress, smoothing it beneath her hands. Never again, she swore as she pulled her hair out of the way, patted her wild tresses into a semblance of order, and walked through the quarters and to the front entry. She shoved away the feeling of loneliness and hit the code to exit Jarren's room.

When the entrance opened, Austent stepped forward. Lissa's eyes widened in surprise. He bowed to her regally, his form graceful despite his extreme height. "Highness," he said.

Lissa frowned. Since when was she royalty? His expression looked so solemn as he straightened once more. Lissa let his greeting slide without comment. "Hello, Austent. If you're looking for Jarren, he isn't here."

An uncomfortable smile flitted onto his face. "I know. Jarren sent me to escort you to the Ready room and prepare you for the mission. Do you want to change first?"

Lissa looked down at her rumpled dress. "Yes, thank you. Something more comfortable." Bowing in acknowledgement, Austent turned and led her back to her quarters. She punched in her entry code.

"I'll only be a few minutes. When do I leave?"

"I will accompany you, Highness. The palace gates open a half hour after sunrise and close one hour after dusk. We are orbiting Lynta now. It's sunrise."

Lissa walked into her bedroom and left her door open enough to hear Austent. "Is Lynta's day on a twenty-four-hour rotation, like Earth?"

"No. Lynta has a slower rotation. Thirty hours. We will head for the surface in about five hours. We should have time to get in and out before the palace gates are slated to close."

Lissa pulled off her dress and threw it on the bed. Sighing, she tried to ignore her lingering loneliness. She rummaged in a closet, pulled out a soft pair of loose black pants and slipped them on. Next, she pulled on a floral print shirt with long tassels that tied around her middle.

Going back into her room, Lissa put her feet into her familiar pair of tennis shoes and bent to tie the laces. "How are we getting to the surface?"

"My jumper. It's been parked in the envoy for months, since the last dignitary I escorted to Lynta was here. Princess Veena often asks me to perform this type of duty."

They departed Lissa's room, and Austent led her down a hall. In the quiet, Lissa's insecurity about what she had done to Jarren reared its head. Her chest tightened with every thought. Did he hate her? He must be angry. He had made sure to depart before she awakened. "How is Jarren?" she finally asked.

Austent cast her a glance then continued staring ahead as they walked. They slowed to a stop in front of a large door and Lissa was sure she wouldn't get an answer. But as Austent reached out and punched in an entry code, he gave her a nod and spoke. "He fares well, Lissa. He wants you well protected for this mission. That is why I am going with you." He added a steady look to reaffirm his statement.

Lissa nodded. She wanted to know more, but her questions would be too personal, and she didn't think Austent would give her an answer even if he had one. They stepped into a large oval room where a table mimicking the room's shape dominated its middle.

A large viewer at one end, like the one on Jarren's ship, showed Lynta below them. Lissa moved forward, her attention on the planet. It seemed a more structured blending of colors than Earth presented from space. Large swathes of dark dense foliage swirled below them, and many smaller swirls of gold and red ringed around that, but Lissa saw very little water-blue anywhere.

"Where is the water?" she asked as Austent came up behind her.

Austent called out. "Unit, alter viewer to proto-geographical breakdown." Immediately the picture changed, and the world became a mass of large and small light-blue swirls.

Lissa looked closer in confusion. Austent's voice behind her drew her gaze away from the somewhat hypnotic movements of the water on the viewer. "Lynta's water source is subterranean. Water flows from the ice caps at the northern and southern tips, underground, to the planet's equators. There are several water sources all over the planet, small rivers that drain into massive ground holes, creeks that drizzle into nothing, waterfalls that replenish themselves from their own ponds. The waterfalls on Lynta are more amazing and beautiful than any you saw on Deneb."

"This sounds too incredible," she said as she sat in a chair at the large table, closest to the viewer.

"Maybe on Earth, but on Lynta, plant life is more active. The plants are the source of the water flow. Unit, alter viewer to surface geographical breakdown. Do you see the patterns now?"

She did. The flow of water beneath the surface followed almost exactly the type and density of the plant life on the surface. "Where are the cities?"

Austent sat to her right. "Most cities are within the dark areas. The foliage doesn't overwhelm Lyntan civilization, it's part of it. Lyntans use the plant life to harvest water. This is the Lyntan power to colonize."

The door to the Ready room slid open, and Veena glided in, her beautiful long fuchsia dress flowing out behind her. Her hands stretched out in greeting as she glided forward with a smile. Her vibrant voice called out. "Good morning, Lady, and well done."

As Lissa started to respond, Austent jumped up. His expression alarmed, he rushed toward Veena with his arm outstretched. With a frown of confusion, Lissa stood. The table between them, Veena abruptly stopped and inhaled a stuttering breath. Her eyes widened, and she froze in obvious distress as she looked at Lissa.

The door to the Ready room slid open again and Jarren ran in. Veena sputtered out Lissa's name. "Lissa, by the gods, I'm sorry. You mustn't—"

Dashing to Veena, Jarren slapped a hand over her mouth.

Jarren hauled the princess back toward the door and barked a command at Austent. "We need to push this forward. Get Lissa to the surface as soon as possible. Understand?"

Confused, Lissa watched Austent bow and respond with a clipped, "Sir."

Then Jarren pulled a flailing Veena back out through the entryway, and the door shut. He never once looked at

Lissa. "What the hell just happened?" Lissa finally demanded when she could find her voice. Her heart raced. She turned concerned eyes on her companion.

Austent shook his head and took his seat again. Looking down at the table, he let out a neutral reply. "I've no answer for you, Lissa. Only know that I am here to protect you with my life. I am asking a lot of you because I know you have so many questions you will get no answers to right now, but we are running out of time. I need to run through the plan with you at least twice and teach you some standard Lyntan royal mannerisms so that you and I can blend in and accomplish our mission. It's my hope that you will have all your answers when this is over."

Lissa fought to control the sudden fear dropping into the pit of her stomach. She trusted Jarren, so if Jarren trusted Austent, she would too. But they both knew something they didn't want her to know. Something that had created an alliance between the two men that not even Veena could break through. Lissa took a deep breath and nodded for Austent to proceed. The tickle of fear persisted.

Austent reached out to tap Lissa's hands clutched on the table. He offered her a sympathetic smile before speaking. "Good. Jarren asked me to inform you that the moment the scepter is safe, he will take you home. You need not worry that he won't fulfill his promise."

"Okay," Lissa said, her head bent toward the table. Her voice sounded normal, but the words tore at her heart. How sanitized. Biology could be understood, and its effects foreseen. Love was unpredictable and chaotic. She had no need to worry because Jarren merely desired her. If only she could turn his biology into love. She had tried so hard, all her life, to achieve success, balance, order—to be perfect. But Ms. Perfect barely understood the rules of Jarren's world, much less how to manipulate them.

"Let's take a look at the Palatial City," said Austent. The viewer hazed gray for a moment then an image of a forest tinted jade appeared. "Unit, Palatial City limits, southern entrance." The forest diminished until Lissa could see a tan street lined with tall cobalt trees. Ahead, the street widened, and small houses took the trees' places. Made from an odd beige-colored brick and topped with pointed arched domes of a copper-colored metallic substance, the city glimmered like an exotic Amazonian paradise.

"We will enter the city here on foot. There are LVs, Land Vehicles, that we will rent to get us to the palace gates, but outside the city only jumpers are used. LVs were once used between cities, but the fumes began diminishing the plant life at alarming rates. The ecosystem almost collapsed."

Lissa nodded her understanding. A planet dependent on plant life not only for food sustenance but also water would have to be cautious to maintain an ecological balance.

Austent went on. "See those houses? They are guard houses. They will identify you as royalty the moment we enter the city, but I will have to present identification. My scent bears almost no royal Lyntan essence as I am Below the Family. I am of one of the lowest castes. I don't want you to show any nervousness about this."

Again, Lissa nodded.

"Unit, slow and follow the streets through the south palisades." The viewer began to move forward, its central focus on the street. As they proceeded, Austent pointed out large warehouses that he explained were food processing plants.

He asked Unit to slow the viewer at one point as it entered an open area. Trees ringed a multi-tonal green and pink promenade. But in the middle of the beige stood a fountain statue of a woman, her beautiful figure wrapped in loose interconnecting cloths from shoulder to sandaled feet. She had one arm raised and within her palm lay a conch shell where water flowed out and splashed down on the cement below.

Lissa scowled. "Where does the water go? It looks like it's just disappearing into the stone."

"The streets may look and even feel like stone, but no city would survive built on a substance that cut them off from their water source. This material is also living plant life. It's hard to the touch and stone-like, but it behaves exactly like plant root."

"So I may assume that the industry of Lynta is agriculture?"

"Yes. When we attained space travel and branched out, we colonized many of the worlds in our solar system through the use of transplanted Lyntan vegetation. As our colonization efforts grew, the Galactic Alliance became aware of our existence and invited us to be a member. With our agriculture, additional non-Lyntan planets were colonized. Now we provide food and building materials to two thirds of the Alliance's members."

"And that's why the person who rules Lynta can maintain peace or create war throughout the Alliance. Provision of natural resources is necessary to planets not naturally self-sustaining. If planets must fight over limited natural resources, we have intergalactic war."

"Yes."

Lissa took a breath. "Well, now I know fully what rests on Jarren's shoulders."

"And what rests on yours. The scepter is the insignia of the king. The Alliance long ago agreed to recognize only the one who is coroneted with the scepter in his grasp. The scepter can only be wielded by one of the royal family or their bonded." Austent paused to look over at the screen where the statue continued to flow with water. "And only a royal, true life-mated, can have sole ownership of the scepter before his coronation."

Lissa listened, intently. When he turned to her again, she knew the weight now rested on her shoulders. "I understand, Austent."

"Good. Then let's continue. Here at Bronyn's Fountain, all royals traditionally wash their feet, so you should also. It is said to be for good luck. Bronyn is the goddess of water. Unit, proceed."

On the screen, the viewer wound its way through the beautiful city. Green sunlight reflected off the copper roofs, turning the copper into a golden orange. Her breath was taken away by the luxuriant beauty of the streets, the controlled growth of large-leafed plant life that hung on porches and spilled down from potteries lining the walks. The flora shaded most of the city, abundant large dark leaves twining down from filmy trees above. It was a good thing they intended to catch a land vehicle to the palace gates with only one stop at the fountain. There was no way Lissa could pretend to be unaffected by Lynta's beauty.

The viewer stopped before tall black gates overhung with an ivy-type plant. "The palace gates," Austent murmured. "By day, the gates are open, and the palace is accessible to any and all royals and their guests. See those rounded machines, with the clear glass domes? Those are the LVs. The king owns all LVs. He maintains them for each of the major cities.

"The vehicles are rented out by any who can pay the price. We'll have Unit secure a vehicle once we are in the jumper. We will leave the LV at the front gates. If all goes well, we won't need to leave the palace. If all doesn't go well, Jarren will have to transport us out. Getting caught isn't an option, Lissa. Lynta has courts, but Milovar won't hesitate to usurp that process if he feels directly threatened. Understand?"

Lissa paused, concern darting through her body. The image of Jarren smiling down at her, touching her, reinforced her resolve. She breathed. "I understand. What does the inside of the palace look like?"

"I don't have a clip of the palace or its grounds. Vidcasts have never been allowed into the palace for security reasons. The gate you see leads into the outer courtyard. It's about fifty paces to the entrance of the palace. I do have the palace schematics, though."

"Okay, let's take a look at it so I can at least feel somewhat familiar with where I need to go."

"Unit, Lyntan Central Palace schematics."

"Confirmed, Commander Austent." The viewer went dark, and a three-dimensional holographic schematic appeared on the table in front of them.

"Wow!"

Lissa leaned closer to the hologram as Austent laughed. "This isn't a public document. This comes from Jarren's personal records. So, this is where we are." Austent leaned over and pointed at the front of the structure. They spent the next hour identifying all the common areas of the palace, the throne room, the king's quarters, and the route they would take to get to the scepter.

Austent hammered their route into Lissa's head. They would be too close to Milovar's power center to make any mistakes that would give them away. If his personal guards captured her, it was all over. When Lissa knew the palace common areas with ease and could explain what rooms they needed to use to get to the scepter, Austent taught her Lyntan royal behaviors.

An hour and a half later, they were ready to go. They left the Ready room and walked, a silent pair, to the envoy's landing bay. Lissa stepped into Austent's jumper. She would practice Lyntan speech and behavior and get dressed on their way to the surface.

Lissa didn't ask why no one was around. She'd not really seen anyone except a Terlian engineer since she'd arrived. But Austent must have read her mind. "Envoy ships always carry minimal crew to avoid safety issues. Most diplomats travel with their own crew. That way, they can be assured of the loyalty of those around them."

"And Jarren?" Lissa wished she had been able to remove the wistful sound from her voice.

"He is preparing to arrive after we have reclaimed the scepter. He's fine, Lissa. Keep your thoughts on the mission, okay?"

Lissa bobbed her head. She wanted to focus on the mission. She had studied all the information Austent gave her. But her heart ached. He hadn't even come to say good-bye, to wish her luck. Lissa buckled herself in as Austent entered the pilot's deck. In for a penny, in for a pound, she thought. Jarren's fate rested in her hands: she had seduced it away from him last night. She hoped she could live up to her own expectations.

CHAPTER 26

"ARE YOU CRAZED?"

Jarren leaned back, waiting for the barrage to continue. Veena paced in front of him as he sat at the table in his quarters. Her long hair flipped around her as she shook her head irritably and looked at him once more. "What if she dies down there?"

"She won't die. Austent is with her, and I will be where I must be to ensure her safety," Jarren spoke evenly.

"Does she know? Does she even have the slightest clue that her life is now as important as your own?"

"No. And it will remain that way. I promised her she could leave me when this was done. I won't make her feel guilty by telling her I will fall into mate-craze once she's gone. As much as losing Lissa will cost me, her happiness means more than my own. It may be many years before I am totally incapacitated. I can find and train a suitable replacement before then."

"No offspring of yours will ever rule Lynta, Jarren. No Graf will ever rule again." Veena spoke with quiet resolve.

A stab of pain hit him in the chest. With a regretful murmur, he responded, "She is *not* to know I won't be able to pass the scepter on to any child I have outside of my union with her. The moment she touches the scepter, that fate is sealed."

"And of the present? You should tell her you and she are true life-bonded. If she dies today, you will go crazy today, not in years. It won't matter if you have the scepter. With your scent on it and you insane, Lynta will plummet into anarchy." Veena's voice rose in desperate distress.

A vision of Lissa asleep in his arms that morning tore at his insides. "She will not die, Veena. I won't allow it."

"But she and Austent are down there alone. You cannot control her from thousands of miles away. I swear to you, Jarren: she didn't tell you, but she loves you. If she must decide between her life and yours, she will sacrifice herself without realizing the uselessness of it."

Sitting up, Jarren demanded, "Did she tell you she loved me?"

Veena sighed and sat across from him, deflated. "No. But I am a woman. I can sense it as clearly as I can see the Moons of Lynta."

Jarren snorted. "You mistake life-mating with love. What you sense is that unique connection."

Veena stared at him as dawning widened her eyes. "You are in love with her. That's why you let her go. Because you love her and couldn't say no. She believes it is because of the Nectar."

Jarren returned her gaze and remained silent. He'd removed Lissa from Earth to save her life. She had hated him for that. This time, she asked to decide her own fate, even if it meant her death. Though both their lives rested in her hands, he couldn't deny her again. It didn't matter that she didn't know the power she wielded over him or the fate of a plan his mother hatched decades before.

Unviable parents gave birth to Celina, a child with the essence of royalty. Her parents had hidden her scent until her schooling, but there was no way to hide it in school. Lyntan's reclamation process removed Celina and placed her with a royal couple unable to bear children, but the kernel of truth was already planted in her head. She had been stolen from her parents because of this barbaric caste system. Then the gods blessed Celina with a son positioned to dismantle the system weaponized to hurt so many. It could not continue, and Celina cultivated the kernel of justice within Jarren. But it might all be for naught.

Veena got up and walked to the door. Her head jerked back in one final comment as the entry slid open. "She deserves to know that you love her, Jarren. If she may possibly give her life for you, she should at least understand the uselessness of the endeavor." Veena walked out. The door slid shut behind her.

Jarren returned his attention to the viewer again. The tracer he'd had Rila insert in Lissa's body, along with her translator, blipped on the map. At least the spies confirmed Milovar wasn't responsible for Jesalyn's attack. He'd be on Lynta in enough time to personally ensure Lissa's safety. But Veena's words had resonated in a way she hadn't foreseen.

Should he be captured by Milovar, Jarren hoped to the gods that Lissa knew he loved her more than life itself.

*   *   *   *   *

LISSA FINISHED DRYING her feet from her fountain dip and slipped on her soft white slippers as the LV pulled up in front of the open gates of the palace. Beside her, Austent nodded toward the palace then leaned over the front seats and thanked the driver before getting out. She gave a quick tug to her loose-fitting ivory colored dress. It flowed to her ankles, modest even as it clung to her small waist.

Lissa reached for Austent's hand and exited, her spine straight, as she'd been taught to present herself. Out of the vehicle, Lissa found her nose lifting to take in the clean floral scent of Lyntan air. The air was crisp like mornings on Earth after a rainstorm. It had to be the plants and subterranean waterways. According to Austent, rain almost never fell on Lynta, though they had no problem with maintaining moisture in the air.

Lissa was the alien on this world. Her stomach turned as they approached the checkpoint. Royals were allowed entry without showing identification, but the similarity of Lissa's scent on Lynta had yet to be tested. She stepped forward and started straight for the tall iron-like gates, her gaze ahead. She heard Austent fall into line three steps behind her.

"Halt!" a strong female voice shouted. Lissa immediately stilled. She had just passed the gates, one foot placed on the beige solid-plant walkway material. Turning imperiously toward the voice, Lissa waited as the guard approached. The woman, taller than Lissa by inches, wore a dark red and tan uniform that clung snugly to her body, much like Marcus's and Jarren's ship outfits. In her hand, she held a replica of the silver bullet-type weapon Jarren had used on the bounty hunter on Earth.

Lissa's heart beat wildly but she forced her face into a bored expression and put a hand on her hip. The guard moved closer, her long blond hair swinging at her back as she stared suspiciously at Lissa. "Identify yourself," she stated.

Lissa opened her mouth to speak. She and Austent had prepared a royal history for Lady Lissa of Adara in case her scent didn't pass easy muster to grant her entry. But the guard stopped five feet from her, and the woman's entire demeanor altered. She bowed in subservience before Lissa uttered a word.

"Lady, my apologies. I could not identify your royal status from my location."

Lissa blinked. She waited a moment to let her heart stop slamming against her chest before answering. Behind her Austent uttered a susurrus, "My Lady."

Lissa plastered a dazzling smile on her face. "Quite acceptable. My escort," she added, waving for Austent to come forward.

Smiling now, the guard nodded to Austent as he showed his credentials. "Austent. I think we've met before. I'm not sure when, though."

Austent smiled suggestively at the guard, and the woman blushed. "Undoubtedly we've met. I am often escort to Duke Naas's relatives. I've used the south gate several times. You, too, look familiar."

Lissa grew antsy. People were taking notice. After flashing the guard one more lopsided, promising grin, Austent bowed goodbye, and they continued up the wide path to the palace.

The path turned from beige to an asphalt-black in a matter of steps. On either side of the walkway lay freshly cut deep-green grass. It was the first grass Lissa had seen since their arrival, and it appeared picnic perfect. Austent cleared his throat behind her. "Don't stare. That behavior is unusual."

"Right, me staring at the only grass in an entire city will cause more notice than you holding up the entrance line while you and the guard woman make bedroom eyes at each other," Lissa snapped back as she reluctantly increased her pace. She couldn't see Austent behind her, but she heard his soft laugh, anyway.

"You wouldn't believe how more natural holding up the line is for those horny guards than a royal who stops to fawn over the cootcha off the path."

"Cootcha?"

"The green stuff growing off the path. Maybe your world refers to it as weeds or moss?"

"No, it's grass." Lissa almost turned to speak to him, but she remembered their differing stations at the last moment and kept her eyes ahead.

"Well, if you have much 'grass' on Terra, it must be a fast-paced world indeed."

Lissa stopped a moment in confusion. "I don't understand."

Austent was now one step behind her, and others did actually seem to be taking notice of Lissa's abnormal behavior. "Cootcha is a defensive plant. If you stepped on it for any extended period of time, it would sting you. This is well known on Lynta. Did you not notice that it only grows here defensively around the royal palace?"

At Austent's words, Lissa rushed forward, the nostalgic thoughts of picnics in the park on Sundays destroyed forever. She could not have been more painfully reminded of how she didn't fit in, of how she was the alien. She was about to hiss a very insincere thank you when the air caught in her throat. Even looking at pictures of the Royal Palace had not prepared her for the hidden grandeur of Jarren's home.

The Central Royal Palace was easily twice as tall and twice as wide as the ducal palace on Deneb. It was a towering, dark-blue cement-type structure, and a red-metal balcony chased violet windows around the fourth level of the massive palace. A tower of short deep-blue marble steps led up to an open courtyard overflowing with green flora and fauna. The pattern of blue, violet, and metallic red continued at the twice-man-sized double doors within the courtyard. The doors had been painted in swirling colors that matched the exterior color scheme. Lissa's eyes couldn't take in all its beauty all at once.

Something jabbed Lissa's back, and she turned angry eyes on Austent then stopped short. Visitors surrounded them. And they were looking at her curiously. One woman encircled by an entourage of servants stared at her with a great deal of suspicion. She could not keep up this charade if she wasn't more careful. Lissa turned and moved with fearful swiftness up the steps and through the courtyard to the large door the royal family used.

A quick spray of air hit her face, lifting her neat tresses up only to let the long lengths resettle again. The palace door opened, and Lissa stepped through with Austent behind her. The doors closed behind them with a rough snap, and Lissa found herself within a darkly lit empty hall. She and Austent had decided on expediency and fewer guards over subtlety in getting to the scepter.

They opted out of using the public entrance, instead taking the main entrance reserved for visiting elite royals. Restricted to diplomatic royals and their guests, the entrance was guarded by soldiers more familiar with the royal scent than those at the front gate. If Lissa's essence was verified at the royal entrance, they could proceed almost unchallenged to the throne room.

A soldier stepped forward as they approached. A man this time, but dressed similarly to the first guard, he presented the picture of civility. In a quiet voice, he asked for Austent's credentials then walked around Lissa. Prepared, she calmed her face into impassiveness. He moved away from them with a bow and a smile. "Welcome, Lady, to the Central Palace. Have you visited before?"

Lissa edged forward, her bearing as regal as she could muster. "I was here as a child. My mother died recently. It seemed fitting to return before accepting her title." Her fabricated history seemed to satisfy the guard's idle curiosity. Bowing once more, he faded into the dark.

Austent grasped Lissa's arm and led her along. "Well done. Remember, there's minimal security this route to the throne room," he whispered as they traversed the royal entrance and turned right. Lissa nodded.

They moved from one grand entrance to the next. Some rooms were well lit by hanging orbs giving off bright light to show intricate red, blue, and violet mosaic tiling. Other areas were left dark, the plastered red walls half hidden in shadow. Their route wound through the large palace, away from windowed areas that would let light shine in and away from people who would search their memories to identify the two of them.

Turning another corner, they ended at the bottom of a thin row of servants' stairs. Austent tapped her back once, then moved ahead of her and up the steps. Lissa followed after a moment. At the top, she found him lowering an unconscious soldier to the ground. They had expected to incapacitate a guard, and given how far along they were, Austent had already exceeded their expectations for how close he could get to the throne room without proper royal credentials. Non-royals required written approval from the king's advisors, or Alliance member immunity. But Austent had told her Jarren wanted him as close as possible in case of trouble.

Austent pocketed a small silver weapon and jerked his head for Lissa to peek out of the enclave where they stood. She straightened her clothes and stepped forward. She moved into the hall with one final glance his way, then proceeded ahead. On her right, just before where the wide throne room entrance cast light out, her eyes met with rows of portraits. She wanted to gasp at the similarities of the male subjects' hazel eyes and powerful chins to Jarren's. These long-dead ancestors were the source of Jarren's life. Her heart constricted.

To her left, hanging on beautiful red and violet wall paper, were portraits of the previous queens of Lynta. They appeared remarkably approachable, their beautiful alabaster faces smiling, their golden or midnight hair pulled up and piled at the tops of their heads or hanging in loose straight wisps about their faces. All regal, violet-eyed beauties. Lissa shook her head as she observed them. Veena had the same beauty, the same royal bearing. She seemed the obvious next partner to the king of Lynta, and Lissa pushed down her envy. This wasn't her home.

"Lady, may I help you?" A soft male voice brought Lissa out of her sad reverie. She focused on the tall, dark-haired man who'd stopped next to her. Gray hair sprinkled his temples. A frown line creased his weathered brow. He was dressed as most Lyntan royals, with an emerald-green robe that opened in the front and fell heavily to the floor. Her gaze settled on a gray shirt that clung to the soft lines of his torso and his well-tailored black pants emphasizing the slight bulge between his legs.

Lissa threw him a glorious smile. "No. I was just looking at the royal family portraits on the wall."

He flung an attractive smile at her in return, his golden eyes warming as his gaze slid over her body. "How charming. Have you not visited the Central Palace before?" To her disappointment, he reached out deftly and grasped her elbow. His hand held her at his side as he walked on.

Lissa calculated a shy grin. "I was a child when I last visited. My mother recently passed away. It seemed fitting to visit one of her childhood homes before I accepted her title."

"Your mother? I am sorry to hear of your loss. It's odd I hadn't heard of a royal dying. What sector are you from?" His question seemed innocent enough, but a warning tingle ran up her spine. Lissa began to feel a bit heady so close to him. She suspected he had lowered his Subduer to affect her, but she didn't know why.

Lissa shook her head slightly and looked up at the man. "I'm sorry. What was your question?"

He shot her a sympathetic look, then waved approaching bodies away. "Your family. Where are they from?"

Confused, Lissa looked around them. They'd walked directly into the throne room, full of women in multicolored gowns and men in dark robes. The soft whispering of voices accentuated by the occasional tinkle of laughter caressed her ears. Lissa's heartbeat slowed as she experienced some relief. She had gotten in without being stopped. "Uh, I am from Adara. The ninth moon base. I am Lissa Padna. My mother was Kensa Graf. Did you know her?"

He smiled as he halted, his tan skin crinkling into laugh lines around his eyes. "Yes, Lady. I knew Kensa Graf. I see the resemblance now. That side of the family was always exotic, as I remember. I am sorry to hear about your mother. I suppose given how distant Adara is from Lynta, it was decided not to give her a state burial."

"No. She wanted to be buried on Adara next to my father."

He guided her forward again. They moved through the room, toward the king and queen's throne, their gilded dark-wood chairs situated on a dais.

And there it was. In a standing glass casement before the chairs lay the scepter. A foot long vertically in the case, its thick round carved surface of gold inlays reflected light from the immense and brightly golden room.

Lissa glanced about at the beautiful tapestries hanging on the walls; some pieces exhibited exquisite needlework that captured mythical creatures fighting warriors of old. Other tapestries reflected the violets and reds found throughout the palace and mimicked the patterns of odd-shaped multi-colored waves that raced along many of the palace's walls. The room was domed from above by a substance that seemed to lighten to a glass transparency then darken into solidified stone at consistent intervals. Lissa fought not to allow her breathless wonder to become apparent to her new escort. Lissa threw him a sensuous smile, and his gaze darkened to a smolder. She hoped she wasn't pouring it on too much.

As they walked nearer the throne, she shivered in discomfort. Something wasn't right. People stared at them. Those before them moved aside to let them pass. Lissa looked back at the entrance to the throne room. There were guards there. Why hadn't she been stopped as expected? What about her had garnered the attention of an obviously powerful man? The blood beat through her veins, and Lissa tripped.

"Careful, dear one," he said beside her as he righted her.

Lissa struggled to cover her unease. "I am so clumsy. Thank you for the rescue. Now, if you would excuse me..." Her eyes rested on his hand still clasping her arm.

He merely smiled in return. "Are you trying to get rid of me?"

"No, of course not, but I do not even know who you are. Friend or foe, you know much of me, but I know nothing of you," Lissa replied, then wished she hadn't. His eyes narrowed with suspicion; his mouth set itself in a thin line.

"Adara is not that far away, my dear. Surely you've watched the vidcasts in the past few weeks. I am the king presumptive, Prince Milovar."

Lissa lowered her eyes. She could feel sweat sheen her face. Her dress clung to her body. Jarren's enemy stood before her holding her within his arms. Austent had warned her to stay as far away from Milovar as possible, and now he was a breath away. It hadn't occurred to Austent to show her what the man looked like. Every person in the Alliance had seen his face many times over the last month. Besides, that small detail didn't seem important to Lissa. Milovar had reportedly been visiting his holdings miles away for the day. Obviously, the report was wrong.

Grabbing at his hand, Lissa slid to the ground in a purposeful faint. Milovar clutched at her to keep her body from hitting the marble floor.

Around her, chaos erupted. A woman screamed. Feet pounded in all directions. Loud voices yelled for calm. A hand clasped Lissa's neck as someone lifted her.

Her stomach wrenched at the sour scent of the body cradling her. It took her a second to realize the pungency was Milovar's. He held her slumped body to him and walked swiftly away from the sounds of pandemonium. Several other footsteps chased after him, but where the king presumptive went, only quiet existed.

CHAPTER *27*

"DAMN IT, AUSTENT, report!" Jarren bellowed into his com unit.

Static met his frantic request. From Jarren's secure position within an LV at the palatial gates, he'd overheard accountings of a royal woman who'd fainted in the throne room. The similarity of the woman described and Lissa was too great for Jarren to ignore.

"Austent!" he yelled once more, his voice contained by the LV's soundproof glass. He would have to go in there, and he'd have to use a masking scent. Pulling out and operating the masker, he fought the beginnings of disorientation and pushed open the LV operator's door and stepped out. He tried not to breathe as he pulled out his false documentation declaring him a farmer from Celiun Two.

Jarren's eyes watered as he looked at his papers. He clipped a command for Unit to secure his LV. Pausing to gather his strength, he walked toward the gates. His head grew heavy. By the gods, he hoped he primed the masking scent high enough to cover any lingering royal essence. Certainly, the extremity of his use had impaired his thought functions. Jarren couldn't take any chances, though. Warning bells were sure to go off if they smelled Graf on him while he presented the documentation of an average off-world farmer.

Jarren followed the flow of traffic through the gates and stopped, holding his breath and scratching at the short beard he'd applied to obscure his identity. Hunching, he handed the young guard his papers and waited. The guard pulled out his scanner and ran the instrument along the documentation before nodding and handing the papers back. "Welcome, visitor. You will want to keep all your documentation out as they'll need to see it again when you enter the palace. Stay on the walkway and take the path leading to the left for the public entrance."

Jarren nodded and pushed ahead, then stopped as disorientation hit. Thousands of voices spoke around him. He couldn't remember who he was. Glancing about in total confusion, he jerked as a hand rested on his arm. The guard had returned. Jarren shook his head and searched for clear thoughts.

"Sir?" The guard's query sounded innocent enough at first, but as Jarren fought to maintain a semblance of normality, he caught the concerned sweep of the guard's hand as he called another to Jarren's side. Jarren shook his head, and for a minute, his purpose became clear. Lissa. She was in trouble.

"Sir, if you want to come with us…"

Like a dunce of a backward farmer, Jarren took off his wide brim farmer's hat and stuttered an answer at the guards. "I'm sure glad you are here. I feel a might like I need someone to get me to the entrance. So many people. I never seen so many people at Celiun's prime city," Jarren sputtered, with a slurred grunt.

The guards exchanged looks. Neither of them was interested in escorting around a small-time citizen. "No," the first guard began. He shook his blond head in denial. "We were under the impression you were ill. Our job is to guard the gate. Right now we aren't performing our duties."

The second guard chimed in, his eyes now shifting uncomfortably to the slowly growing line of those requesting entry to the grounds. "If you are well, you must make your own way up to the palace. There's only one walkway, citizen."

Jarren replaced his wide brimmed hat and cleared his throat. "Well, I'm fine. I just haven't been around so many people before. By the gods, I didn't mean to keep you from your work."

Both guards nodded, glad to be rid of the unnecessary burden of an off-worlder. They moved back down the path, the first guard uttering a warning to make up for his lack of assistance. "Stay on the path, sir. Cootcha's planted for the security of the palace."

Jarren's head throbbed, but he fought down a wave of nausea and kept his feet firmly planted on the ground. He mumbled a brusque thanks and pushed forward up the path, holding his breath. Desperation kept his legs strong. Should he appear disoriented again, his ruse would not work a second time.

People fell into line on the path around him. Feet stuttered forward. Jarren's strength waned. He struggled to maintain cognition and blend in with the other visitors. A pitiful laugh lodged in his throat. The high prince, relegated to donning a disguise for entry to his own palace? If he hadn't been so terrified for Lissa and so used to running, this embarrassment would have hit deep. But his embarrassment was just another pain for which he'd extract repayment from Milovar.

Those in front of Jarren slowed, and begrudgingly, he forced himself not to barrel to the front of the line to gain quick entry. Standing taller than most of the other visitors, he could see the entrance from where he was. The plain maroon double doors were blocked by a cavalcade of servants. The quality of their dress and bearing could only mean they worked in the palace. Finally, they began filing in, one servant at a time. The face of one woman turned profile to him, and Jarren saw a chance to get in: Milen. Pain shot through his head again as he exerted himself to push through others waiting before him and not breathe in too much of his odor.

"I've a message for the Head Soldier," he uttered as he stumbled forward. Their multicolored finery flipped around him as he struggled past another patch of people closer to the entrance. Almost there.

"Stop pushing, citizen!" The guard at the head of the line finally spotted him. Jarren altered his path, his head feeling heavier and pulling him off course. It might have been his proximity to the palace that now assaulted his senses. He could almost feel his essence willing itself forth through the masking scent. So close to home, his birthright struggled to dominate his body.

Jarren would have retreated if he hadn't heard that whisper about the woman in the throne room. His purpose.

Lissa. Jarren inched his way between two final people. As he took the head of the line, those behind him pushed forward.

Apparently the royal servants had all made their way into the palace. The regular citizenry could proceed. For a moment, Jarren didn't know what to do. His mind now couldn't complete a thought. He paused as confusion dominated him. A wave of people swelled around him. His balance teetered, but he righted himself. Sick people constituted a security risk. He'd never gain entrance if he fell over.

"Come forward, citizen. Others behind you are waiting for entry." Jarren glanced up at the voice. He needed time to think.

Like the overwhelmed visitor he pretended to be, Jarren dragged his feet getting to the palace doors. His hand shook with fatigue as he held out his papers. The man threw him a puzzled look, and Jarren's heart sank. The guard would be more diligent with Jarren because he sensed something wrong. Others moved away from him. With a heavy step, the guard walked around Jarren. His natural essence pushed forward again, and the man's eyes widened in recognition. As he opened his mouth, a deep female voice interrupted.

"Ah, there it is. Milen, you were right. I dropped my bracelet coming in." Jarren refused to look toward his mother's voice, but his heart ached. He was home.

"Yes. I knew I saw it drop. Crackus, bring that bracelet to me," Milen demanded, feet away from Jarren. Crackus stopped walking around Jarren and picked up the bracelet that had appeared at Jarren's feet.

"Lady," Crackus began, intoning his criticism with a quiet breath. "Please remind Her Majesty that her essence dominates. I could not get a clear read on this man for the scent she exuded."

Milen hummed an affirmative answer. "Her Majesty understands the importance of the work you do. Just as she understands why she is now being relegated to using the public entrance to enter her own home. But should you wish to make a personal complaint about the inconvenience you experience from this arrangement, I am sure she would gladly listen to your concerns."

Eyes still lowered in humility, Jarren spied his mother approaching. "What is the matter here?" she asked. Her brusque tone would brook no more delay. For a moment their gazes collided, and her eyes widened in recognition. Her mouth opened as if she were going to speak, but then her jaw clamped shut, and she turned away from him.

With a stiff bow, Crackus stepped forward. "Minor confusion with a visitor. All cleared up now, Majesty." Crackus handed Jarren his manufactured documents stiffly and waved the next person forward.

Now within the palace halls, mother, son, and lady-in-wait separated from the crowd and rejoined Celina's group, then melted into the darkness.

*   *   *   *   *

LISSA WAS PLACED on a soft surface. A bed, she thought. Still feigning unawareness, she listened to the intense dialogue that unfolded between the people in the room. "I've no idea who this woman is, Dracen, but it has become *your* life's work to find out." Milovar's words snapped out.

"Highness, I'm not sure I understand her importance. Why did you take her from the throne room? The Healers should be caring for her and contacting her family," an aged voice responded. This had to be Dracen.

"No family, Dracen. Find out where she came from, and then I will decide whether to tell her family where she is. Start with Adara. I want to know if Princess Padna recently passed away. I want to know what family she still has. Everything. And I want to know before my coronation tomorrow."

"I beg forgiveness, Highness, but what is the emergency?" asked another male voice.

A low female voice interceded. "His Highness has found a possible life-mate. Weren't any of you paying attention to her essence?"

Milovar laughed. "Of course the woman on my council would be the only one to notice. I knew it the moment I breathed her scent. There is something different about her essence that makes her scent blend perfectly with mine. I would add her to my current wives before tomorrow's coronation."

Dracen interrupted. "Highness, the Council of Rule demands that you have one wife upon your coronation. You want to add another to the four you already possess?"

"That is exactly why we must find out more about this beauty. The Council will approve of this one. They will not force me to discard any of them if I must discard the one of which they approve. No more discussion. I am the heir. We are conversing as if we are equals. Get out."

Lissa subdued a wince as the door shut and the room became quiet. The surface near her shifted as the man sat. A warm hand pressed against Lissa's forehead. She reacted without thinking and shrank away. She groaned to cover her blatant repulsion.

"Ah. The lady arises. Open your eyes, my beauty." Milovar's voice grated on Lissa's nerves as she blinked and looked up.

She lay on a large canopy bed. A thick ruby and gold comforter spread out beneath her. Looking up at the ruby, jade, and azure sheer draperies, she felt a soft breeze caress her face and whisper through her hair. There might be a window of escape.

The room was expansive with gold and azure rectangular patterns on the walls. To her right, her eyes followed a pattern of blue and gold until they landed on a large open bay window. Another gentle gust touched her face, carrying with it the smell of floral sweetness. How relaxing, like the calm before the storm.

Lissa tensed as a hand rested on her back. "Are you feeling any better?"

She resisted the urge to pull away again and sat up. "I am much better, Highness. Thank you for inquiring. Where am I?" Lissa asked, her mind running through the schematics she and Austent memorized earlier.

"You are in my chamber, sweet one. You fainted. Do you not remember?"

Lissa blinked in mock dismay. "I know we were walking, and I began to feel faint." Leaning into the heat of his body, she looked up at him, with as innocent an expression as she could muster.

"Yes, you fainted. I caught you." He moved to sit next to her on the bed, his gaze intent. "Now tell me, sweet one, why didn't you recognize me?"

"I am most embarrassed, Highness. I've seen many vidcasts of you over the past month, but when my mother died, I forgot everything else entirely. Even the purpose for this pilgrimage exists in my thoughts as my last farewell to her. And then, when I met you, there seemed something about you, something that drew me." Lissa paused and lowered her eyes, demurely. "You shall think me vain, but your essence blended so well with mine I became distracted. I would not have known had I been walking next to the goddess Janelle, herself. Please forgive my ignorance." Lissa could not have performed more convincingly if she were on stage playing Anna in the *King and I*. Her life, Jarren's life, depended on it.

Milovar reached out a hand and cupped Lissa's chin in his palm. His eyes bore into her as he leaned forward then kissed her eyelids. "Worry not, sweet one. I have always been somewhat overwhelming, but what *you* sensed is our life-mate compatibility. I felt our deep connection when I saw you in the Ruler's Hall. You distracted me; you drew me. Your arrival was fortuitous. I have been searching for a queen to walk beside me as I begin my reign."

His mouth lowered to kiss her lips, but Lissa jerked away. Her chest heaving from stress, Lissa stumbled away from the bed. "This is too much, Highness. How can you expect me to believe we are life-mate compatible? I am of no consequence."

A flash of anger shot across Milovar's eyes, and the seduction he'd begun a moment before melted away, revealing the man who'd sent bounty hunters to kill his cousin. His mouth curled as he advanced then grabbed her arm and squeezed painfully.

"Never speak against me, sweet one. You may not believe you're worthy, but the gods have deemed you otherwise." As abruptly as his anger arose, it petered back behind the arrogant glint in his eyes. "Now." His demeanor restored, he loosened his grip and led her back to the bed. "I know what will convince you of your worthiness. I ache to make you mine. Let me make love to you, show you how well we match. Turn off your Subduer and give yourself to me."

She needed time to formulate a plan. Staring at him, Lissa felt for her Subduer and turned it off. Milovar's eyes glazed over. He advanced, and Lissa blurted out the first excuse that came to mind. "My nerves are frayed, Highness. Will you call for hot chulaa?"

His face broke into a condescending smile. "Of course, my sweet. I had not expected to entertain so worthy a guest as you. I shall order your drink and give you a few minutes of peace while I take a shower. You are delectable. You smell of the ripest decypheny." With a graze of his hand against her cheek, he got up. "Unit, have the kitchens bring warm chulaa for myself and the Lady Lissa."

With a bow, he left through a door that blended into the wall, but he called back to her. "I am your servant. Back in minutes, sweet one. Make yourself comfortable." Then he was gone.

Her gaze trained on the door, Lissa exhaled. The strength left her legs as she sat on the bed. She had no idea what to do now, but the idea of Milovar touching her again turned her stomach. Could she sleep with Milovar to gain access to the scepter? Jarren's face, dark with hurt, manifested in front of her. He already hated being forced to let her go on this mission. If he ever found out she considered giving herself to Milovar to get the scepter, he would never forgive her.

"My Lady." Lissa turned toward the sound of a woman's voice and stared into familiar eyes. The suspicious royal she'd seen outside. Lissa waited. "His Highness called for sustenance. I'll put the tray here."

The older woman placed a tray on a table in a corner. Lissa could not discern either suspicion or welcome in the woman's movements. But as Lissa approached, the woman pivoted and grabbed her wrist to pull her close. Her voice came out harshly. "Your drinks as promised. His Highness has kept all his promises. You must keep yours as his mate. Understand? This is His Highness's cup. You must promise not to touch his cup. You understand?"

Promise? What a cryptic statement. With surprising gentleness, the woman let her go and bowed again. Her dark hair fell in long black and gray threads, hiding her face. Averting her eyes, she left just as Lissa heard another door open. Milovar ambled forward, wearing a blue robe that opened to reveal the tan of his chest.

Where is Jarren? she wondered. The smell of chocolate accompanied that thought, and Lissa looked up. He was near. Her eyes closed. The smell grew potent as she drew it in, and the mysterious woman's meaning solidified in her mind. *Poison in the drink. To knock him out?* As if she'd imagined Jarren's scent only until she understood the instructions, his fragrance faded, and another took its place. Milovar stood behind her. His nauseating essence seeped into her nose. Her stomach muscles tightened as she pressed down the urge to choke. *Concentrate on the job*, she thought as he enclosed her in his arms.

"I turned off my Subduer. I see you sensed me from far away. You are perfection; exquisite. Come and let me love you."

Opening her eyes and throwing him a hesitant smile, Lissa drew away but grasped his hand to pull him to the table. "I haven't had my drink, Highness. Will you drink with me?" Inside, her stomach turned, but her voice lowered, and she stared at him with every ounce of sex appeal she possessed.

He licked his lips and reached for his cup, his hand lifting the pretty, fragile porcelain. Lissa likewise picked up her drink, the woman's words ringing in her head, and took a deep sip. The sweetness wafted into her nose and drizzled deliciously down her throat, but she couldn't enjoy it. The word "escape" began pounding in her head. Play the part and get out! Her tongue dashed out to lick her lips. Milovar took another sip, his hand wobbling as she flirted. A third sip, and he put the cup down, his gaze hot.

"Enough," he demanded, grabbing her cup and clanking it onto the table. "I'm amorous. Let me solidify our mating." He swiftly lifted her and carried her back to his bed.

Laying her down, he kissed her neck, alternating his wet mouth on her trembling skin as he moved lower with words she barely understood. Lissa closed her eyes and prayed. His searching tongue made her want to retch.

He spoke. "I had not trusted the gods, Lissa, when you didn't seem to know who I was. But you have been vindicated. I left you to do more than just change. I left to check on your lineage. My advisors told me your mother did recently die. I apologize for not trusting a mate bonding. Tell me, sweet one, that you forgive me. It shall pain me if you do not," he demanded and pulled her hand above her head, preventing any escape. Lissa's gut went cold. She hoped she'd been right to trust something was in his drink. If she were wrong, there was no escape for her.

"I forgive—"

A sudden gasp from Milovar sent the man sitting straight up. He wavered drunkenly from side to side then tipped over onto the bed. His robe fell open at his sides.

Lissa jumped up, looked at his torso to study its slow rise and fall, and ran for the door. The palace floor plan played itself in her head as she wrenched the door open just enough to check that no guard had been posted outside. Another servants' hall. Inching through the opening, her feet making heart-wrenching small scratching sounds on the floor as she longed to be silent and invisible, she raced forward and made a right toward the throne room.

Lissa's Unit beeped, and she paused mid-step. She knew Austent put them on total radio silence, as communication could be traced from one source to the other. What could be so important that she was being hailed now? "Unit?" Lissa whispered.

"Urgent message from Princess Veena on Duke Naas's envoy ship. The princess asked to be contacted the moment you were alone. She asks to speak to you."

What else could go wrong? Lissa threw up her hands and backed into a dark corner. What was going on? Pausing the mission wasn't part of the plan. Maybe Jarren had been hurt. She thought Jarren had sent the mysterious woman to help her, but maybe someone else had been near, someone with a scent like Jarren's. Quieting her jittery nerves, Lissa whispered for Unit to connect Veena.

"Lissa?"

"Yes, it's me. What's wrong? We aren't supposed to use Unit communications."

"I know. If it were any other reason, I'd leave you to it, but you need to know something, Lissa. You deserve to know."

Lissa's body stilled. The memory of Jarren dragging Veena out of the Ready room, his hand over her mouth, resurrected itself in her mind. "You wanted to tell me something before we left."

"I tried. By the gods, Lissa, when I got close enough to breathe your essence, I knew you deserved to know the truth."

Lissa's body clenched. Something was wrong. "What are you talking about, Veena? Look, I'm not safe. I need to get the scepter, and I'm running out of time."

"Lissa, if you touch the scepter, you will never be able to go home. It is not just your life you're gambling with." Veena's words echoed in Lissa's ears. Lissa's heart clutched until she had to bend over from the pain. Jarren had once uttered those same words.

Shaking her head in denial, she slid to the floor. "No. Jarren promised to let me go home. Why would he punish me for helping him secure his rulership?"

"It isn't him, Lissa. It would be the Council of Rule and the Lyntan people. You are Jarren's life-mate. Touching the scepter will strengthen that bond. If you touch the scepter, no child but yours and his will ever rule Lynta. If you touch the scepter, Jarren's familial reign will end with him. The Council won't allow it."

Lissa couldn't breathe, could only choke on her reality. If he didn't rule, the caste system would continue.

"I am sorry, Lissa. I'm to blame. He knew you and he were life-mated before last night. I imagine he resisted you as long as he could, but with the Nectar…he had no chance. There is nothing you can do to change your bond, but you can still ensure Lynta may be ruled by Grafs.

"Don't try to take the scepter. His bond with you will never break, but he will have years to train another to take his place, understand how the caste system is a system of harm, and…he could still beget an heir with someone else. He could show those children the horrors that occur because of our caste system. And those children could challenge Milovar's offspring when the time came. Without you, change will take more time but would be possible. You can just go home."

Lissa bent her head to her knees as tears escaped her eyes. She loved Jarren more than her own life, but she needed to go home, back to where the world made sense and she made sense in it. Home, where she knew her mother loved her. Home, where she knew Jasmine would grow up happy outside this ridiculous Lyntan hierarchy of power.

And home. Home to a different caste system no less present and painful. Was that the home she longed to return to Jasmine? Wasn't that where her heart was? She loved Jarren, but she couldn't give up the life she'd struggled so hard to make for herself in the face of great challenge. She couldn't give all that up to stay with a man who didn't love her. He needed her physically, was drawn to her out of primitive instinct. But Lissa needed more. A life without love would slowly kill her from the inside.

"Lissa, can you hear me? I can get you out if you don't want to do it. Jarren will understand. He told me he would never control you again. That's why he let you go. Lissa!"

She could still leave and find Jamis. "If I leave, what will happen to Jarren?"

"Milovar will never find him. You have my word."

Time stood still as Lissa stared into the darkness before her. She loved Jarren. She wasn't perfect, but her love for him was. The jittering in her body slowed to emptiness. She wiped at her eyes. She let go of the dream of seeing her mother again. She let go of witnessing Jasmine grow up in the neighborhoods of Lissa's youth. She let go of the constant comfort that came with being totally in control. Love wasn't about being perfect. It was about making the right decision when the time came. Jarren was her heart. What he wanted to change, who he wanted to empower, was simply the right thing to do. She would not abandon him to a life of running and hiding for an empty dream, not just because he didn't love her.

"You said we were bonded forever, Veena. I can't abandon him. I love him. What he could do with his power, not in decades but in days, will change it all. Thank you for telling me. If anything happens to me, tell Jarren I knew what he was willing to give up. Tell him I love him. Unit, disconnect and maintain communication silence." The air stilled again. Lissa wiped the tears from her eyes then collected herself. Her path was set.

Pushing herself up, she ran to the end of the hall then paused to remember which way would lead back to the throne room. She was three halls away. She ran around a corner but immediately slowed to a walk as the elite pressed by her, their voices tinkling with frivolous happiness. Lissa nodded, glistening sweat coating her body, then walked on, hoping her violent heartbeat wouldn't give her away.

At the end of the hall, she saw a light. One more corner and she would be back in the Hall of Kings. She had to be optimistic that her association with Prince Milovar would get her past the guards and into the throne room with little effort. Lissa slowed to a deliberate stroll, her ears now tuned to listen for the sound of running feet behind her. She had no idea how much time she had. She wanted to hurry but resisted. No undue attention.

As she rounded the final corner, her chest eased a bit. Surely Milovar would be out for hours, and by the time he awoke, she would have given Jarren the scepter and be in the safety of the envoy ship. Her gaze fell on the guards at the door. She couldn't remember if they were the same guards who'd seen her enter with Milovar earlier, but she dared not chance any hesitation.

Holding her head high as all royals did, she stepped up to the entrance of the throne room and walked right between both guards. "Lady, His Highness has closed the throne room for the night," she heard behind her.

Lissa kept walking. The room was now completely empty and the lighting was low, but Lissa was halfway there. The scepter glittered gold from its case.

"Leave her, Tyler. She's the prince's mate," another voice coughed out. Lissa's heart began hammering in her chest. She was three steps away. Two steps. One step.

Pungent odor assaulted her nose as she reached out. "Why did you let her in? Get that woman right now!" Milovar's viper-like tone vibrated with rage. Running footfalls grew louder. Desperate, Lissa grabbed the scepter's case, her sweaty palms fumbling to find a catch to the glass container. Looking up, she shrieked as guards flooded into the room and headed straight for her.

Her fingers were slick upon the glass; she clutched in vain to keep the encasement from falling. One guard reached out to grab her as the scepter and glass crashed to the ground. Lissa didn't hesitate. A hand jerked at her arm. Her wrist skidded over the shattered glass on the floor, and her fingers grasped the scepter tightly.

Time stood still then sped forward to crack under Milovar's thunderous "No!"

Lissa's arm burned where she sustained cuts from the glass casing. She cradled the scepter and her arm to her chest and slumped to the floor. Something held her up. Out of the corner of her eye, she saw another person enter the room. The pain in her arm increased, and she looked down at a deep gash cutting beyond the skin into the meat of her forearm. Blood coated the sliced flesh, and Lissa became lightheaded as she turned away from the source of her pain. Despite the burning, she continued to grip the scepter. Her pressure on its smooth, molded gold made blood drip into small puddles on the floor. She was so tired. The flat surface called to her. She should lay down and rest.

"You may let her go, soldier." Jarren's voice flowed at the edges of her consciousness. Lissa was released from hands she hadn't known held her. As she looked up, Jarren walked into the throne room, his bearing regal, his eyes shining with concern. He put his hand out to her as he came closer. "It's alright, my own. It's alright."

A streak of red moved within her sight and then Milovar was two feet from her, a long, jagged knife raised to strike. Lissa screamed and backed away. As if in slow motion, she looked to Jarren as he ran straight for her. She caught another burst of unfamiliar color out of the corner of her eye, this time headed for Milovar. Milovar stopped a foot from her, his eyes blazing red, his expression contorted in rage. Lissa tried to retreat, but she knew it was too late. Jarren was too far away. She screamed.

CHAPTER *28*

LISSA HEFTED THE scepter to her chest and braced for his attack. Her heart slammed against her ribs, pumping adrenaline to her limbs. She wanted to move, but she had no more to give. A shadow appeared behind Milovar, and Lissa peered through scrunched eyes. Her heart pounded in her chest as the shadow took a man's shape. Two hands appeared on either side of Milovar's face, and the knife stopped in midair as his head jerked to one side, and a cracking sound rang out. Milovar's angry eyes clouded as his body slumped forward.

Austent stood behind him, now lowering Milovar's lifeless body to the floor. His chest rose and lowered in stressed heaves, but aside from that, he appeared unharmed. As soon as he'd caught his breath, he helped Lissa up. Jarren grabbed her seconds later and pulled her into a desperate embrace.

"Oh, thank the gods. I almost lost you. I'm so sorry, Lissa." His hoarse voice broke with emotion.

She couldn't respond. Too many thoughts ran through her head. The first comprehensive thought she had hit like lightning. Was she really alive? Gingerly, she ran her hand from her neck to her hips. No wounds except the cut on her arm. Lissa wheezed out a breath.

"Witness!" Jarren's voice thundered about the throne room as he faced the soldiers crowding around them. "Milovar tried to kill my mate. It is a crime punishable by death. Do any here not believe what they saw?"

Lissa stared out from the crook of Jarren's arm at the soldiers creating a small sea of maroon and tan bodies. No one responded. "Then this man must be held harmless from prosecution. He took a life to save a life. He took a prince's life to save *my* mate's life, and all present know her worth."

Heads nodded agreement. Lissa could feel herself losing track of the conversation. Fatigue returned to drag her down again. Her cuts burned. Austent straightened, his chest still heaving. Shaking Jarren's hand, he allowed Jarren to pull him into a bear hug as Lissa fought her body's fatigue. "Where were you, Austent?" Lissa whispered, but no accusation sharpened her voice. "I thought you'd been caught. I was sure you would have stopped Prince Milovar from taking me from the throne room."

Austent shook his head. "No, Your Highness. I had strict instructions only to interfere and make myself known if your life was in danger. Every person in the room could smell Milovar's attraction to you. His attraction was partially aroused because he sensed you were mated. Men know when a worthy rival claims something we covet, even if we don't comprehend this consciously. He knew you were mated, and to another royal, but he didn't care. Attempting to separate a mated couple is a horrible crime on Lynta. But far worse than his useless attempt to seduce you away from your mate was his attempt to kill the royal heir."

Royal heir?

Jarren held Lissa's uninjured arm to guide her toward the door. "Well, all is right again, Austent. We will leave the staff to repair this mess," he said quietly. He frowned at the other mangled mess of her arm. The soldiers parted before them.

Lissa warily eyed the soldiers. "Why aren't we under arrest?"

"Do those on your world arrest their leaders for occupying their own homes?" Jarren asked instead as he pulled out a tan cloth and efficiently wrapped her wound. The odd tingle where the cloth touched her skin almost distracted her. "This should help."

"Wait. I thought Milovar was the heir. They obeyed him without question the entire time Austent and I were here. We made every effort not to alert them to our intent. Now he's dead. Shouldn't they throw us in jail?"

"It is Lyntan law, Lissa. He or she who possesses the scepter is ruler if no other heir has a closer matching essence. Only he or she who possesses the royal essence may possess the scepter. While Milovar's scent covered the scepter, he commanded my guards. The moment you put our scent on the scepter, they followed me again."

"You don't fear another royal will come along and you will lose your throne again? Wait. I'm not the queen, am I?"

His muted laugh relayed his fatigue. "No, Lissa, you are my mate, although not of the royal house like me. Besides, the opportunity to usurp a throne can only be made before the high prince's coronation. Once I am king, the throne is mine until my end or until I choose to abdicate to another royal. It cannot be taken."

Lissa snorted. "So, I guess you will want to get the coronation over with quickly?"

Jarren looked ahead as he answered. "That is no longer necessary."

"Wait—"

Austent interrupted. "It grows late, Highness. Lissa has had quite a day, and you have royal obligations that have long been ignored."

"Were you near when I escaped Milovar's rooms?" Lissa asked Austent instead. The throbbing in her arm had eased. Jarren's first aid cloth was blessedly effective.

Austent gestured them both forward. Pacing Lissa, he looked at her curiously. "No, Highness. Another looked after you there. I did incapacitate the guard outside his quarters after Milovar received the false report of Kensa's death so you would not have to face his guards when you got out. By the way, Jarren, Kensa says you owe her a boon for her part in this. She apparently had vidcasts made of an official funeral and did herself up in a casket and all. Very disturbing, she said. You and Lissa must have her to dinner in the palace."

Jarren nodded, but Lissa stopped in her tracks. "I must?" The confusion in her voice was blatant.

A hush blanketed the crowd and the path in front of Lissa closed up as another path to their right opened. "Of course they must." The woman's soft voice cascaded over Lissa. Long familiar robes flowed behind her. Lissa looked into eyes she remembered looking at her from the palace entrance and again with their fierce intensity in Milovar's room.

"Lissa." Jarren hesitated as he spoke, his hand at her back. "This is my mother, Celina."

Lissa's heart fluttered nervously as Celina approached, but the older woman held out a hand to her and smiled. "I am sorry to meet you under such circumstances, Lissa. But I am so glad Jarren found you."

"Yes?"

Celina hugged Lissa once they were close. "You don't believe me. Our meetings were strained to say the least, but not from any doing of yours. I knew something was odd about you when I sensed you in the front courtyard. I could smell Jarren's scent all over you, but it had changed somehow. I could not understand the distinction. Probably because I thought you were nothing more than an agent of his, not his mate. I would not have thought he would find a mate on Terra. It is so far away with so many people."

She paused, thoughtful, then continued. "But Jarren found me, him smelling foul no less, and I told him where I thought you were. Your collapse was very dramatic, my dear. Had it not been so, you wouldn't have gotten past the guards when you returned to the throne room. Milovar offered you free access when he escorted you in. You probably would not have otherwise gained entry. With praise, the gods were watching."

"And you gave me the drink to drug him," Lissa added.

"Yes. Jarren worried Milovar would ignore your obvious mated status. He was right. If you hadn't yielded to Milovar, he would have taken your body without thinking twice. Even when he was a child, there was something in him that poisoned him. At some point, we'll identify what it was to prevent it dominating anyone ever again."

Celina embraced Jarren then stepped back. "But now," she took a deep breath, "all is as it should be. My son is home, and you are here to support him."

Lissa bowed her head, the last vestiges of regret trickling down her spine. Veena had been right. Jarren's people would not let her go home. But Lissa had made her decision anyway. She knew what she gave up when she entered the throne room to take the scepter.

The power in Jarren's tone interrupted Lissa's thoughts. "Lissa is to go back to Earth, Mother."

Celina swung her glance from Lissa to Jarren. "But that isn't possible, son."

Jarren pulled Lissa protectively to his side, but his words were distant. "She is to go back to Terra as soon as possible. I am king presumptive. My word is to be obeyed."

Celina looked at her son. Clear rebellion shimmered in her eyes, but after a moment, she bowed her head in acceptance. "Then we shall have to move quickly. Well, Lissa, I thank you for returning the scepter to my son and affording us an opportunity to change things." Her hand briefly reached out to touch Lissa's cheek. "I hope I will have time to show you the Hall of Kings. My mate's portrait is the last to grace the hall. My portrait is across from his."

As Lissa opened her mouth to speak, Jarren cut in. "I must take Lissa back to Deneb for her daughter and then return her to Terra. She won't be staying here for longer than it takes me to put things in order until my return."

Celina gawked at him. "Do not forget the great purpose. You must use this power. We have never been so close to ending this injustice." Jarren nodded once. "Yes. Prepare the Council for my return."

Celina shook her head. "But without the heir—"

"I know the importance. Prepare the Council."

The uncertain words of thanks she'd been about to utter to Jarren's mother caught in her throat. Perhaps Jarren still hated her for forcing his hand. But knowing he obligated himself to ruling without an heir cut Lissa deep. She retreated into herself, listening from the safety of an inner emotionless void, and spoke to Celina. "I thank you for the offer, Your Majesty. You are kind and very tolerant of me. Goodbye."

Jarren leaned forward to kiss his mother goodbye then took Lissa's hand and led her out of the throne room. Austent followed. With a gentleness that conflicted with Jarren's painful statement, Jarren took the scepter from Lissa's stiff arm.

Jarren's eyes locked with hers. "Austent, contact Veena and tell her to remote-land your jumper on the pad behind the palace. I will leave instructions with the Council for my mother to rule in my stead until I return." Jarren spoke to Austent, but his gaze stayed on Lissa.

"Highness. We are headed back to Deneb?"

Jarren nodded, his glance finally shifting to Austent. "Yes. Lissa and I must retrieve her daughter. And I prefer to make the voyage back to Terra in *Stardesire*. Up for a trip?"

Austent smirked, his handsome dark face crinkling in real amusement. "And since when do I make a move without Veena's permission? I am her willing servant, Jarren. You will have to ask her."

Jarren replied with a strained smile. "Of course." He turned Lissa in a new direction, and the three began trotting down a hall Lissa couldn't, at first, place. She thought through the schematics in her head. They were headed toward the jumper pad. They were leaving already.

"Aren't you at all afraid someone will try to take the scepter while you're away?" She was sure she asked this before.

The silence began to stretch before Austent responded. "The throne is Jarren's now. No other will ever claim it without his willing abdication. Milovar's death is proof of that."

"Oh, okay." But something wasn't okay. And the answer to Lissa's question lay in her own mind. She knew he couldn't pass the throne to any future offspring. She wouldn't be around to give him babies. But how did that prevent others from claiming the throne? He had a long life ahead of him. He should protect his birthright. She just couldn't put two and two together to make four. Jarren left Lissa and Austent in front of a beautiful large carved-wood door, slipped in, then exited a moment later without the scepter.

"Did you hide it?" Lissa asked.

Jarren gave her an odd look, tilting his head. Finally looking away he answered with a quiet, "No."

Lissa refused to ask anything else.

They arrived at the landing pad and Austent's jumper. Two guards waited with Lissa as Jarren and Austent moved within. Then they were off to the envoy. Lissa waved off every attempt to converse, ignoring the worried look Austent and Jarren cast in her direction. She had no more to give and did not wish to ask questions no one would directly answer.

On the envoy, Jarren escorted her to her quarters. She looked into his impassive expression. The urge to kiss him, beg him not to send her back to Earth, struggled against the pain in her heart. In the end, she could only muster a quick goodnight. Tears of regret swelled beneath her lids, but she managed to get into her rooms and shut the door before the pain overflowed. She cried out the hurt for the rest of the night.

CHAPTER 29

JARREN AND LISSA stopped in front of Marcus's Deneb palace chamber doors. Jarren's body ached with the need to touch Lissa, but he didn't. He'd spent a long sleepless night fighting the urge to go to her quarters and make love to her one last time. He would never have her again. But she'd been so reserved with him, had behaved as if it pained her to be near him. The heartache of her rejection fought with his need to sooth away that pain. Why would she be hurt that he did not reveal the truth of their relationship?

Jarren scowled at the air. Yes, Veena had made sure Lissa knew they were life-mated. Thankfully she had not revealed that their mated scent ensured he would slowly lose his sanity after she left. The princess confessed everything the previous evening when she stormed into Jarren's quarters. How could he let Lissa go, she'd asked.

"How can I not?" Jarren had bit back through gritted teeth.

"The shift of power to you when she touched the scepter revealed her likely pregnancy. I did not know you two were true life-mated, I would have tried to stop her. She would not have known she had to tell you *not* to impregnate her during the Sharing, that if the timing was right, she would get pregnant whether she demanded it or not. And the Council? Your mother? They just let her get back on the jumper with the likelihood the next Lyntan heir was nestled in her belly?"

Jarren hesitated. "I did not allow that conversation to take place."

Veena looked away and then Jarren knew. She had done something. Grabbing her arm, he demanded, "Tell me what you did."

His anger would have had anyone other than Lissa or Veena groveling at his feet, but Veena lifted her head and recounted her conversation with Lissa in the palace. "But I didn't tell her she might be pregnant because I did not know you two were true life-mated. I also did not tell her you would go insane." A spark of fear flecked in her eyes as his seething anger began to boil up again.

Jarren thrust her away with a disgusted growl. He knew his anger was misdirected. Veena had done nothing wrong. She cleared her conscience and offered Lissa another avenue of escape, fruitless as it would have been. Milovar would have found her, tortured her for not taking him into her bed, and then killed her when he could ensure Jarren would be in audience.

No. Jarren was angry because he knew Lissa had slipped through his hands the instant she'd realized he'd yet again refrained from telling her the entire truth, when she realized even not telling her had been a way of not allowing her to make her own decisions. That's why she'd withdrawn. He could give himself every excuse in the book, but what he'd done was continue controlling her. Freedom and free will existed when one possessed all the information and still made the same decision. He'd taken that from her—again.

Now Jarren watched as Lissa knocked on Marcus's rooms door. She was one step further away from Jarren, one step closer to Jasmine, closer to home. It was what she'd wanted from the moment they got into his car on Earth for a meeting that never existed.

"I'll give you some time alone with her and come back when we need to go. If you want anything, just let Unit know," he said as he started walking away. He glanced back just in time to catch a slow nod and a questioning look. Jarren turned a corner and barreled into the duke.

Jarren's brow rose when the duke bowed. "Why the formality, Leor?"

"You are king now, Jarren, coronation or not. And you are true life-mated. No one can take the scepter from you. My obeisance is a necessary formality upon first meeting with the new true life-mated king, and you know it."

Jarren grunted pessimistically. "Indeed. No one understands protocol like you, Your Grace. It is a wonder that you did not think to be king yourself."

"I'm not crazy, Jarren. Ruling Deneb has already carved years off my life. Why would I wish to start all over with the whole Lyntan empire?"

"Marcus would have been required to rule Deneb in your stead, thus robbing me of his lively personality. For that gift, I thank you. But I hear tell your daughter Rachel would have made a wonderful queen of Lynta, had your line taken power."

The duke snorted. "She certainly always knows how to get what she wants from me. She is as smart as a whip and always jumps to defend those with less power. I imagine that is the future of the realm," he noted with a deliberate glance. "But so does your little one, Jasmine. They two have been like peas in a pod this past week. Jasmine will make as great a queen as Rachel would."

"Jasmine isn't Of the Family, so that would never have happened, even as I move to eradicate the caste system. They are both special, though, aren't they? As we are speaking of your daughter, I wondered if I might mentor Rachel."

"We were speaking of Jasmine who *is* in succession for the throne, but we shall not argue that quite yet. This innocent conversation has a purpose, doesn't it? Well, I too have a purpose in speaking to you, Jarren." Leor's eyes darkened almost threateningly.

Jarren quirked a brow. "I thought you approved of eliminating the caste system. Is that not why you gave us asylum? Why you protect Jasmine, who would be considered unviable if this caste system remains intact?

Leor reached out a large hand and held Jarren's shoulder. "As an elder who is true life-mated, you should know the gods won't allow another to take the throne when there is a legitimate heir living somewhere in the universe. You must tell her you love her, Jarren."

Jarren's eyes focused on Deneb's far-off setting sun. "I'm sure I don't know what you mean."

"You are king of the Lyntan empire. You will not play the whimpering boy with me, Jarren," his Grace growled as he shook Jarren's form.

Jarren met his gaze.

"It is time that you understand the magnitude of your blessing," Leor tried again, calmer. "Do you not know who Lissa is?"

"She is my true life-mate; the woman I love and always will."

"But did she not provoke old memories in you? Did you not start recalling the old tale of the first true life-mates upon meeting her?"

"That was how I knew she and I were true life-mated before we were together."

The duke shook his head. "On Deneb we know more of the tale than what your parents told you, Jarren, and we know why. We know the true tragedy of the first true life-mates. You've asked yourself why would a god play such a filthy trick on two insignificant people, separate two mates?"

Jarren shrugged. "That is the way of gods, Leor. They behave outside of human understanding. They are petty and trivial deities. That is why a god took the woman from her lover."

"They are petty, but never believe that gods act without a purpose. No one knows which god took the woman from her lover—perhaps it was Akash—but on Deneb we suspect why. Lyntans paint their ancestors on a gilded canvas. She did love her partner as much as he loved her. And she relied on him as he relied on her. But he never told her he loved her, Jarren. He thought his actions were enough to prove it. The words never seemed to matter. Indeed, although she said she loved him regularly, he did not see the importance in the act.

"One god mistook his actions and foresaw some version of the future. *This* god believed her lover had not returned those words of love because her line should be greater than all others. *Of* the Family. Because this god was petty and foresaw a future, the god set the Family higher than all others and prescribed the Family the requirement to rule alone. Purity even above love. That is the pettiness of a jealous god. For after all, what is worship but receiving praise without having to reciprocate?"

Jarren's body grew cold as he realized where the conversation was headed.

The duke continued. "The god took her from her love and would have been done with her, except that she had a child. And although she loved that child, she never told the child so because she was too preoccupied with finding her lover again. So, that same interfering god took the baby far away, away from the other gods' interference, until we Lyntans were capable of loving all sentient life equally. Not to worship, but to love."

The duke's stare penetrated Jarren as he continued. "In a way, the god's fears were justified. Words are magic. Because the woman spoke her love—and he to her upon returning— her connection to her lover was made. The goddess Janelle reunited them and bound them together for the good of the people. But a baby cannot talk, so one remained lost as the god intended."

Jarren paced the smooth marble hall like a trapped animal. "Why are you telling me this?"

"All true life-mates have suspected where the child was taken. We can sense her descendants' restless and broken link. You are true life-mated, Jarren. Can't you sense where they are?"

Jarren's feet stilled as he was hit with a sudden, quiet dread. He shook his head in denial. "You're telling me Lissa is descended from Lyntans?"

"Not just Lyntans, Jarren. From the royal line, the first child of the first true life-mates. That is why Jasmine is the Prime Heir, though she is not your only. She has your scent and Lissa's scent, but she is also a direct descendant of the royal line. They are alike, Jasmine and your unborn child, don't you think?"

Leor stepped back, a patient gleam in his eyes. "Now you're faced with the same decision as our ancestor when she lost her child. Will you obsess over the things you cannot control, or will you cherish your gift and tell Lissa you love her?"

Jarren ran a haggard hand through his hair. "I can't. I made a promise I've yet to keep—to let her go. I made a promise to myself to never try to manipulate her again."

"These promises have become your obsession to the detriment of your love for her. Don't repeat the mistakes of the past. You are being tested, Jarren. The similarities of your story and your ancestors is clear."

"I know she's pregnant."

"Yes."

"If I let her go, I'll never see her again."

"If you don't tell her you love her, she will never want to see you again, and if you don't honor your connection to Lissa as the lost Lyntan descendant, we will all be punished in ways we cannot perceive. The gods do not reward squander. Make the final sacrifice, Jarren. Tell her you love her and open yourself to the connection…or lose Lissa and your only child, and allow Lynta to lose its only heirs."

Jarren's eyes widened as the duke's words beat against him. The soft tropical smell of the Deneb air thickened until the scent swathed his lungs. His body knew what his mind would not admit. He was being selfish. No one would win because of it. With a swift turn as he exhaled the air grown stale in his lungs, he strode back to Marcus's door and walked in without knocking. His heart was lodged in his throat. Lissa looked up from her position playing with Jasmine on the bed. Taking one glance at Jarren's demeanor, Marcus nodded from where he relaxed in a chair then got up and called for Jasmine to follow. The girl scooted off the bed without a word.

"But—" Lissa's head followed their movements with perplexity.

"I need to speak to you," Jarren said, moving forward as the door clicked closed behind him. He strode toward the bed but stopped shy of the dais.

"I will take you home," he began, and Lissa's eyes lowered. Jarren continued. "But my soul will be lost if I don't tell you I love you." He heard her suck in her breath. "I love you, Lissa. I had to tell you. I couldn't make that mistake twice."

He prayed some sort of physical response would tell him he had hope. Her stillness fizzled his dreams. Jarren turned away but paused as she spoke.

"How did you make this mistake before?" she asked.

Lissa's question wrapped around the threatening coldness collecting in his heart. Facing her again, he breathed deep to steady his pulse. "I let you go down to Lynta without telling you I loved you. I was scared to cross that bridge, to accept we were connected beyond just true life-mates, but by love, also. I had to tell you now."

Lissa looked up, tears flashing like stars in her eyes. "I thought you didn't want me, that you hadn't forgiven me for forcing your cooperation in retrieving the scepter. And then, Veena told me only your children could inherit the throne, that me touching the scepter would only strengthen our bond. I thought you hated me like I hated you when you took me from Earth. After all, even true life-mating is nothing more than biology."

"I could never hate you, Lissa. You are my true life-mate. The most powerful gift of the gods is that of a bonding. I thought the gods judged me unworthy to rule when Milovar succeeded in driving me from Lynta. Now I know we were both born for something greater. They sent me from my world to yours not to escape, but to gain the power to end the Lyntan caste system and to be saved from a life without your love. Only a king true life-mated can change that law. Because of you, I can."

He pulled her to him and looked into her eyes with demanding intensity. "What I feel is more than biology. I love you, Lissa, whether you are here or leave me to return to Earth. I will love you every minute I breathe." He claimed her lips in a kiss, his mouth caressing hers in abandon as he bared his soul.

When he pulled away, Lissa put her hand up to his face. "Alright. My time to confess. I love you, Jarren. I'm yours. Every part of me. I thought I needed my life on Earth. I thought that life gave me the purpose I needed to be happy. But I don't think I could feel happy again if I wasn't with you. The thought of leaving you hurt me more than I could say. My home is with you now."

Jarren's heart jumped. He reached down to place a hand on Lissa's abdomen as he showered kisses over her face. "I will always be your home. Your home to you and our child."

"Child?"

The surprise in her voice drew the sides of his mouth up. "I suspected you didn't know. That night we were together, you gave me a command to make love to you. In a true life-mating, that command as much as demands I impregnate you. It is that way with any who are true life-mated, though I wasn't sure until you left for Lynta. There's more potency in the Sharing with our bond. If you had not wanted to get pregnant, you would have had to command me not to."

"Would I have gotten pregnant that first time we 'Shared'?"

Jarren shook his head and kissed her nose, one hand stroking the beautiful waves of her hair. "I do not know. The impact of a true-life mating is a bit murky. Some believe no spoken request is needed if both partners unconsciously desire a child with each other. If I'd made love to you without you asking, I think I could have controlled the process and prevented your pregnancy. But I'm not sure."

"And I'm pregnant now?" she asked as he captured her hand under his on her abdomen.

"Yes."

Understanding flickered in her eyes. "The heir. I carry the heir. It was our child Austent referred to. Could everyone sense it but me?"

He nodded. "All near the scepter as you grasped it could sense it, yes. It took you touching the scepter to reveal both our bond and your pregnancy. No one else knew, however, and I only suspected. Even Milovar, until your hand touched the scepter, had no idea the child was mine. Had he been able to cover my scent with his, he would have bastardized your first child. That he tried to kill you after you claimed the scepter sealed his fate. You carried the heir, so his death was guaranteed."

A small smile quivered on her lips. "Well, I guess I really did ask to get pregnant this time. My father hadn't approved of my first pregnancy, but a child created by love? He would have been happy Jasmine had a sibling from someone who loved us both." Her voice lilted, lightening the conversation's somber mood.

"It will be a boy, Lissa," Jarren replied. Warmth settled in his chest. Gone was the hidden emptiness that had lodged itself in him when he'd stared at her and Jasmine asleep in his jumper. That memory felt like a lifetime ago. Jarren kissed her nose.

"How do you know?" Lissa asked as she kissed his jaw in return.

"Because I put him there and because I can smell your body changing to accommodate him. And because I already have a daughter. She is my heir, too, and she is waiting with Marcus."

Lissa flung her arms around him joyously, and she leaned her tired body into his warm side. "I'll stay with you, but can I visit my mother and cousin? I should be able to go back every once and again, shouldn't I?"

Jarren kissed her hard and hugged her close. The scent of papaya and decypheny now intermingled with warm choco-late. Two scents as one. He hadn't smelled both their scents as one before. The power truly had to be in the words. "We'll leave right after I convene the Council, if you like. It is time to end Lynta's caste system. I am the happiest man in the galaxy, Lissa. I could not deny you the whole of Lynta if you asked it of me, right now."

Shy eyes met his bright ones. "But I only want your heart, Jarren. Just your heart."

"You have it," he answered, lowering her onto the bed. She clung to him as he pulled her shirt above her head, his eyes boring into her. He'd become her home and given her his heart, but she had filled the emptiness inside him with love. The gods could have given him no greater gift.

EPILOGUE

MARCUS GROWLED WITH impatience. That little sprite had run off again.

"Unit, open communications to Jarren and Lissa," Marcus said aloud. He stood in the middle of the dark-blue-leafed Poacher's Forest, in the small takeoff area. Tonight, darkness equaled freedom for the heir to the Lyntan throne, and Marcus had arrived two minutes too late to stop her.

"What's up, Marcus?" Jarren spoke into Marcus's earpiece.

"She just left."

Marcus heard a sigh on the other end of his com unit. "Well, Lissa warned me she was too young to learn jumper technology. I thought she meant she wasn't knowledgeably advanced enough. I realize now, Lissa meant Jasmine wasn't mature enough."

"I said that too, Jarren," Marcus told the king. "She is more advanced than most Lyntan children. You could have taught her to drive when she was fourteen and she would have understood the technology. But you should have waited until she was thirty. She's a brat."

"Now now," Jarren soothed over the com. "That is no way to speak about your pupil, Marcus. She has been under your tutelage for eleven years now. She is a reflection of you as much as her mother and I."

"That doesn't make me feel any better. Now I have to go find her again when I should be home attending to planetary business. There is no reason for her to keep running off!"

"Of course. Don't worry yourself, Marcus. I will find her. You go home. You've supported us enough for one day."

Marcus guffawed at that statement. "I have barely assisted. No, I'll find her. It's the least I can do. Take care of Lissa and kiss my newest godson for me. You and Lissa did very well. I'm out." Marcus hung up and marched back into the encroaching foliage, his black pilot boots crunching on the dry pre-winter season as he breathed in the moist air.

Jarren sat back and relaxed in the blue satin-covered bed beside Lissa. "So he is off to get Jasmine?"

Jarren let a small smile appear on his face. "Yes. He needs to get away. He isn't like his father. He can't sit behind a desk and feel any sense of accomplishment. And he isn't life-mated like his parents."

Lissa laughed and snuggled closer, fatigue from giving birth to their third son hours ago finally overwhelming the adrenaline in her body. "This is the fourth time you've managed to cajole him away from his duties as duke of Deneb, Jarren. Eventually he will catch on that your excuses for asking him to personally find Jasmine are nothing but just that."

Jarren nudged his nose against Lissa's neck and pecked a sweet kiss on her cheek. "Not if we continue to create reasons not to find her ourselves."

"You want to have more kids so we can tell Marcus to go find Jasmine? Aren't four children enough? And I have my duties with the Hunters Rehabilitation project." Jarren ran a finger lightly up Lissa's arm, coaxing a giggle from her. "Stop that, would you? I'm trying to be serious."

"Well I'm trying not to be. Marcus needs to get off of Deneb every once and again to retain his sanity, and the only reason he has ever left that planet was to chase after Jasmine. He needs children of his own. I've no idea why he hasn't settled down yet. Besides, Jasmine is getting too old to play the part of his adopted daughter. We'll have to come up with something better. I particularly like the idea of having more children. By far it's been the most pleasurable excuse we've discovered."

He nipped another kiss on her neck as Lissa laughed. Looking into his eyes, she became serious and kissed him back. "We'll figure something out, my love. Maybe we can enlist Jasmine the next time, instead of just letting her run off. Maybe she needs purpose to keep her preoccupied. I'll talk to her."

A droll grin landed on his face. "Sounds good. This is my fault. I showed her how to drive a jumper."

"Well, I gave her the jumper for her birthday. I should have known she couldn't stay away from space. Has anyone ever desired the stars more than Jasmine?"

Jarren shook his sable head and leaned down to whisper, his eyes twinkling. "Only you, my love. Only you."

Lissa shook her head as she pulled him close.

THE END

AUTHOR'S NOTE

I have been blessed to never truly have experienced partner abuse. I lived on the periphery of that trauma as a child. My mother, previously harmed by the man who fathered me, dedicated her younger adult years to protecting and supporting primarily women escaping abusive relationships. I spent my adolescence between a battered women's shelter and a rape crisis center. As a tween, I watched my mother run the National Coalition Against Domestic Violence with an eye for protection, healing, and empowerment. Domestic violence is as ugly as it sounds, whether emotional, physical, or both. And the impact hits every person who loves the victim. If you are in an abusive relationship, there is help. You deserve help. You deserve to control your own destiny and to be free of the pain and fear. Reach out to the National Coalition Against Domestic Violence today at <u>www.thehotline.org</u>. There is a path to freedom.

ABOUT THE AUTHOR

VENUS CAMPBELL is the Principal of the Book of Venus publishing and the Winner of the Kroger Award for Excellence in Creative Writing. She has finaled in various writing contests such as the Central Ohio Ignite the Flame and the New England Chapter- RWA First Kiss. Campbell is a member of the Romance Writers of America (RWA) and the Authors Guild. *To Desire the Stars* is her second publication. Campbell focuses on interweaving paranormal elements into romance stories, creating unique worlds which challenge people's perceptions of self and preconceived notions of human love and relationships.